CHRISTMAS IN STORIES

CHRISTMAS IN STORIES

M. Wayne Clark

Copyright © 2018 M. Wayne Clark

ISBN 978-1-938796-39-5
Library of Congress Control Number: 2017917052

Published by Fruitbearer Publishing, LLC
P.O. Box 777 • Georgetown, DE 19947
302.856.6649 • FAX 302.856.7742
www.fruitbearer.com • info@fruitbearer.com
Edited by Jeannette DiLouie

All Scriptures are taken from the Thompson Chain-Reference Study Bible (NJV) or The New Interpreter's Study Bible (NRSV)

The characters in these stories are all fictional and created by the author. With the exception of the names of some family members, any resemblance to individuals living or deceased is purely coincidental.

While "A Child With No Name" uses names from Navaho history and draws from their spiritual beliefs, all incidents in the story are fictional.

Printed in the United States of America

For my mother
who loves all her children unconditionally.

For my wife, Susan,
who loves me every day.
You always send a smile, sometimes a tear,
sometimes a look of confusion,
but always encouragement.

For our children, Nathan and Nicole,
and our son-in-law, Andrew,
who are the love of our lives.

For children everywhere
I've had the privilege of reading my stories to on Christmas Eve.
You are the reason I continue to write them.

For dear family and friends
who enrich my life every day.

ACKNOWLEDGMENTS

In memory of my Junior High English teacher, Elaine Travis, who gave me my first creative writing assignment and then gave me a smile and a nudge to continue.

I would like to personally thank my dear friend David Wendel for his patience with me, his excellent computer skills that have moved these stories forward, and his generosity of time, emotional support, and companionship as this book came together.

I would also like to thank my publisher, Candy Abbott, for her guidance and skill, enduring presence, and the confidence she has in me to bring this book to fruition. In a short time, you have become a special friend! God bless.

CONTENTS

Foreword

I couldn't tell you the exact date when this storyteller from the midwest first contacted me, and I don't remember how he found out about my publishing company in Delaware. But, I do know that his writing pulled me in at first glance, and I vividly remember the immediate quickening in my spirit to commit to helping him get his collection of Christmas stories into print.

Since he referred to himself simply as Wayne, it wasn't until months later when I began picking up clues that led me to learn he is a pastor. And what a pastor!

Because of his gentle and compassionate manner, I began opening up to him about my challenges of full-time caregiving for my husband who has Alzheimer's. It turns out that, in addition to his steady prayers and encouragement through email and phone calls, Wayne often speaks on the topic of dementia and has written articles and poems which he freely shares with me. When he found out I had written a book about our personal journey, *I've Never Loved Him More*, he not only purchased a copy, and then more copies, but became the number one advocate of my book. I tell you this not for self-promotion, but to illustrate that Wayne possesses the very heart of God to help people.

It is that same tender heart that shines through his creative tales and fables. Christmas has become so commercialized that, other than church nativity plays and a few movies like *It's a Wonderful Life*, it's difficult to find engaging stories of faith that offer a fresh perspective of the true value of Christmas.

Through a variety of settings, Wayne's fictional stories, from mythical to legendary; poems; plays; and stories within stories, include humor, warm dialogue, and character growth. Some stories will captivate you and have you on the edge of your seat. Your heart will be touched as families are torn apart, reunited, and new families are formed.

Step off the hustle-bustle, merry-go-round and "musts" of your holiday trappings, and carve out some quality time to gather your family around for storytime. You may want to curl up with a blanket and a cup of hot chocolate to read some of these stories silently, but the most benefit will come from reading them aloud to your loved ones and then talking about how they enhanced your holiday spirit. These stories will keep you and your family captivated for hours causing you to pause and reflect on your own experiences. It may even encourage you to start a new Christmas tradition.

Merry Christmas to all, and to all a good read!

Candy Abbott
Fruitbearer Publishing, LLC
Georgetown, Delaware

INTRODUCTION

Years ago, I wrote an original story for my friends, family, and parishioners. The next year, I wrote another one. And another the year after that. Soon, I had a much-anticipated tradition which has developed into this anthology, a collection of some of my favorites:

- A grandfather tells his grandson how the first Word Speaker came to their people [chapter 3].

- Two orphan children from the east travel to a small Midwest town fearing what might be ahead of them [chapter 4].

- Patsy and Betsy share their feed trough with an unlikely visitor as winter's cold wraps around their stable [chapter 5].

- What helps a young boy stay focused on a task his father gives him but believes his enthusiasm for the work will quickly fade away? What Christmas surprise is waiting for both father and son if the task is completed [chapter 6]?

- Where does a young midwest farm boy find hope rise out of the grief of letting go all that held his world together? The resilience of the human spirit is discovered in the answer assisted by the greatest gift humankind will ever receive in this season [chapter 8].

What do these stories and the many others found within these pages have in common? The simple answer is, of course, *Christmas*. It is my desire to have captured in these stories the best humanity has to offer. You alone will know if I have accomplished that task for you.

The power between these covers comes when children experience and understand the true message while adults discover stories within stories for their minds, imagination, and hearts to ponder and savor.

Pull up a chair and snuggle in. It's story time.

Chapter 1

CHRISTMAS,
NO STRINGS ATTACHED

"**A**ren't you bidding a little high for that calf?" Sam asked, chiding his neighbor Joseph Barnes, or as his friends called him, J. B. Sam watched amusingly as Joseph gave another discreet nod to the auctioneer.

"It's for my granddaughter, Chrissy," Joseph responded quietly as his eyes scanned the wooden bleachers across the way for the opposing bidder. As he sat among his friends and neighbors, Joseph's eyes soon fell upon his competition, a well-known livestock buyer for a large cattle company.

"I have one hundred dollars," barked the auctioneer. "Who will give me one-ten? Do I hear one-ten?"

His two helpers cautiously prodded the calf with their stock canes so it would move around, giving everyone a chance to see it. At the same time, they also searched the crowd for potential and serious bidders. While one of them moved his eyes quickly between Joseph and the

1

crowd, the other helper continued to prod and search, always keeping the livestock buyer in sight.

This afternoon's sale had an exceptionally large crop of freshly weaned calves, a commodity that always drew a large mixture of farmers, buyers from large feed lots, and cattlemen. Every one of them had their own way of bidding while holding or leaning into their livestock canes or setting them aside if they decided not to bid at all. Even so, it didn't take long for the auctioneer and his helpers to realize there were only two serious bidders.

On the auctioneer's third appeal, one of the ring helpers saw the cattle buyer slightly raise his middle finger on the hand holding onto his livestock cane, indicating his bid.

"Yup!" the helper yelled out enthusiastically. Then, with a fixed smile, he also turned his attention to Joseph.

"I've got one-ten," the auctioneer confirmed. "Now, who'll give me one-twenty? Do I hear one-twenty? How 'bout it folks? Who'll give me one-twenty for this healthy Black Angus bull calf? He'll make someone a fine bull someday."

The crowd smiled when they heard the auctioneer describe the calf. Besides being a bit scrawny, the calf appeared to have been recently weaned from its mother and still seemed a bit wobbly on his feet, details that didn't stop the auctioneer from continuing.

"One-twenty . . . do I hear one-twenty? Now, folks, they all start out this way. Do I hear one-twenty . . . one-twenty?" With a quick turn of his head, he looked toward his old friend and said, "It's show time, J. B."

"It's more like show-and-tell time, J. B.," Sam said, amused. And then, as he looked once again to see if J. B. was still interested in the calf, he added, "He looks a little bony to me."

Joseph looked like he was deep in thought when the auctioneer once again called out: "One-twenty for this fine calf." Even though he ignored the ribbing and smiles, his attention was still divided between watching the calf move about and keeping an eye on his opposing bidder. Less enthusiastic though the gesture was, Joseph gave another nod to the auctioneer, who looked somewhat surprised even while his helper yelled out, "Yup!" to acknowledge the bid.

Knowing Joseph to be an excellent judge of cattle, auctioneer Mike Watkins took a quick drink of water as he thought, *Joe must see something in this animal none of us sees. Maybe I should be bidding on this scrawny-looking calf myself.* Yet he got right back to it as soon as he swallowed.

"Folks, I now have one-twenty. Who will give me one-thirty? How 'bout it, Ed?" He leveraged the comment right at well-known area cattleman Ed Barker, Joseph's only remaining opposing bidder. "Show-and-tell time."

Ed looked across the way toward Joseph and then, with a wry smile, shook his head. "No."

"Folks, I now have one-twenty. Who will give me one-thirty?" It seemed the auctioneer was almost playing with the crowd. But while scanning the bleachers, he could see that the only biting being done was by a few guys chewing on candy bars. And so, he gave in. "Okay, folks. One-twenty going once. Going twice. Sold for one hundred and twenty dollars to card number one hundred and fifteen!"

He nodded toward J. B., who already had his sale number up above his shoulder so the sales clerk could record it.

"Do you know where the calf came from?" Sam asked, thinking about how it probably hadn't come from a local herd. They both knew no one local would be selling a calf this early.

"Yup," Joe answered.

"Okay, tell me." His tone reflected somewhat of a doubting request.

"I checked earlier when I walked through the barn," Joe said as he lowered his paddle. "Mike told me it was born in a swamp pasture down in the Carolinas. Wasn't expected to live, so they just threw him in with the lot."

Sam knew Mike was the auctioneer and owner of the sale barn. He also knew he would sometimes bring up swamp cattle and fatten them up before they were sold, or he'd sell them just as they were when the barn's tally was low for the week's sale.

"Kind of a risk, isn't it?" he pushed.

Like everyone else who knew him, Sam recognized Joe as a very good judge of cattle, so he would often even ask Joe to go to sales with him and advise him on which animals to buy. So, buying the young calf seemed unusual, to say the least.

If he was looking for some revealing information from his friend, though, he was probably disappointed because all Joe would say was, "Yup."

Sam shrugged. "You must think quite a lot of your granddaughter. But that calf will be lucky to make it home."

Joe softly replied, "Yup," again before adding, "It is going to be her 4-H calf. He'll need some fattening up before I give it to her."

"Oh, I didn't know Chrissy was in 4-H," Sam said, surprised.

"She doesn't know it either," Joe told his friend. "She'll know later this afternoon when I ask her to come over. I'll show her the calf then."

"Good luck," Sam said.

He could remember back to the time when Molly, Joseph's only child, was in 4-H during her early teens. But interest in other activities had eventually encroached on that time until she no longer participated in the club at all. Since Joe had often talked to Sam about Martin and his family's method of farming, Sam knew from Joe's perspective, Molly and her husband, Martin, were more interested in crops than animals. Despite being raised on a farm, Martin had never been in 4-H. His father farmed quite a few acres, putting almost all of it into crops that stretched from fence row to fence row.

Sam also knew that Joe thought Martin was definitely following in his father's footsteps today except for one detail. He and his family lived in town while their hired man and his family lived on the Franklin's home place. Like many people in their small community, Martin was a commuter. It was just that, instead of heading to the city for a better-paying job, he commuted out to the farm. "That's just not the way good, really good farming is done," Joe would often tell Sam.

The late October wind was crisp, whipping Joseph in the face as he stepped out of the sale barn carrying the small calf to his pickup. "You're going to need some special attention before you're fit to be a show animal," he said to the listless creature, who showed no signs of understanding the noise Joseph was making. Even so, it only took a few minutes before the calf was settled in the back of the pickup and the duo was on their way home.

Joseph and his wife, Stella, lived on the Barnes's family farm seven miles north of town. Both his grandfather and dad had been farmers, so it had seemed natural for him to go back to the farm when his dad became ill. That meant Molly was raised on the farm until she left for college and then returned to raise her own family. Stella was now teaching their granddaughter's fourth-grade class: the circle of life.

Stella was standing out on the porch already when he arrived, one hand instinctively ringing the bell that had summoned the Barnes family to meals and emergencies for at least two generations.

Yet she didn't ask about his experience at the sale barn until after they had sat down and the food was passed. "So, did you buy something?"

"Yup," he answered without further explanation.

"Well?" she prodded, clearly curious.

"'Well what?" Joe smiled, knowing full well what she meant.

"Why do you do that?" she asked in an exasperated tone. "You know you're going to tell me. So why don't you just tell me what you bought?"

"Why didn't you just ask me, 'What did you buy today?'" Joe's smile was mischievous despite her frustration. "Oh, all right. I bought a calf."

"You what?" That was not the answer she was expecting.

"A calf," he repeated. "I bought a calf. For Chrissy. It will be her 4-H project." Even as he said it, he knew what her reaction would be.

"Joe, Chrissy hasn't shown any interest in 4-H. And I'm sure neither Molly nor Martin has talked to her about joining." Between her words and tone, it was obvious she thought his action would not be well received by any of the Martin clan.

"They don't have to talk to her about joining 4-H," he replied, remaining confident. "We will. I'm sure once she sees the calf and we support her in joining, she'll be excited."

"'We?'" Stella questioned. "You know all too well that most of your 'we' ends up with me being the one doing the talking. And I'm not sure I want to have that talk."

"Okay, okay." He couldn't disagree there. "I'll do it when she comes over. I'll talk to her at lunchtime. That way we'll both be here."

Joe thought, *Neither Chrissy nor Molly would say 'no' to the calf or 4-H if they saw that Stella also supported the idea.* He was hoping that if he ran out of words or didn't quite know what to say, Stella would pitch in and help him out.

They apparently weren't on the same page with that. "You're going to have to tell her yourself. Don't come looking to me if your tongue gets tied or Chrissy decides to argue with you. Are 'we' clear about this?" Despite her insistence, her voice softened just a little at the end, and she let a fond smile slide across her face.

"Yup," Joe said as he swallowed the last of his coffee, putting away the possibility of Stella coming to his rescue. For the time being, anyway.

That might have been the reason why he ended up putting the conversation itself off for a bit as well.

The second Saturday of November dawned with a surprising dusting of snow across the pasture grass, but by mid-morning, the sun was shining brightly enough to dry the fields. That meant the farmers were back in the fields with their big machines, eager to combine the last of their beans and corn.

At the Barnes's farm, Martin had finished doing that the week before. So all that was left for Joe to do was clean up the corn around the bins before heading into town to pick up Chrissy.

Joe always enjoyed his Saturday-morning drives to get her. He took delight in seeing the way nature slowly painted the landscape different colors as each season passed.

Spring brought light shades of green and fading browns along with fresh smells. Summer introduced darker shades of green, along with the smells of freshly cut hay mixed with the perfumed aroma of flowers. There were also the different stages of growing beans and corn to take in, of course. Then fall, for its part, was usually the drying-out time, with the leaves drooping down on the corn stalks, soybean plants becoming brittle, and vegetable gardens offering their last round of tomatoes, onions, and other offerings. In addition, beyond what the visible eye could observe, potato plants were supplying the last of their nutrients before being plowed or dug up to provide families with garden potatoes throughout the winter months.

It wasn't too long after Halloween when winter might play a little trick-or-treat itself, making its presence known early. Regardless, the season came full of its own surprises, sometimes including icy drops of wind-driven rain or intense storms that blanketed the fields and roads deeply enough to keep farm families shut in for hours, if not a day or two.

There was something to like about every season of the year, but Joe liked November most of all. Harvest was on its shoestring. Winter was sprinting forward but hadn't quite reached full speed. And there was also the grateful feeling that came with Thanksgiving. It always left its mark of thankfulness, which sprang Joe forward into the Christmas season.

That was his normal line of thinking during these drives. This Saturday, however, the young calf was taking center stage.

The critter just wasn't gaining weight the way he should. Doc Johnson had given him shots and done what he could, but the calf didn't have the appetite it should. Joe was giving him mash made of creep feed, which should have been easy enough for it to handle. But it didn't seem to be the case, though, and he wasn't sure what was happening.

Admittedly, it had been a while since he had raised calves. And this one was in definite need of some special care. For these reasons put together, Joe figured he should wait to see how things went with the fella before he introduced him to Chrissy.

Placing the decision aside, he did know he would hold off introducing Chrissy to the young calf for weeks. It was hard not to notice how she was showing less and less interest in any type of conversation about the farm—or pretty much anything else concerning her grandparents. Joe did have hope the ride back would be different this week, but he knew that possibility was up in the air.

Like his pickup, Joe's thoughts shifted gears as he drove into the Franklin's drive and honked his horn. Molly came right out, sending him a warm smile with her wave.

"Hi, Dad. Chrissy is putting on her coat." She brushed back a strand of hair. "Thanks for coming to get her this morning. I'll be out to pick her up when I return about four, okay?"

"Yup," Joe said through the open window. "Four o'clock. See you then."

"Hey, Grandpa," Chrissy said with a slight smile as she climbed into the pickup cab and scooted over toward him while holding onto her cell phone and tablet.

Joe always had a flush of good feelings when she smiled, even though that didn't distract him from delivering his familiar warning: "Buckle up or Old Red just won't shift pass neutral."

"Oh, Grandpa." Yet she still complied right away.

"How's your week been?" he asked as they drove away.

But she already seemed to be deaf to her grandfather's words because the earbuds for her MP3 player were already attached to her head and her fingers were tweeting away on her smartphone.

"Chrissy, Santa Claus ran out of reindeer this year, so he's going to use bunny rabbits to pull his sleigh instead."

Chrissy didn't look up. "Oh, that's nice."

Disappointed, Joe returned his full attention to the road, his driving, and the calf. *I guess this weekend isn't going to be a good one for you and Chrissy to get together, little fella. In fact, you might not be the brightest idea I've had all around. We'll see.*

Further confirmation for that thought came as soon as Joe parked beside the house and Chrissy popped open the door with one hand, expertly picking away at her phone with the other.

After watching her find her way to the back porch, he sighed, reached over to shut her door, and then drove the pickup into the garage. Picking up the tablet she had left behind, he also headed toward the house as a cold brush stroke of northern wind came out of nowhere across his path. Up above him, a flock of geese was heading southward even while sudden dark clouds chased across the sky after them.

How did I not notice those clouds before? Joe thought as he reached for the back porch door.

"The weatherman said we might have a measurable snow this afternoon," Stella greeted him as he walked into the kitchen.

Her voice and the smell of her freshly baked cinnamon rolls complemented one another, as if they were always meant to be.

"I figured as much," he said. "A good snow will make your rolls taste even better."

That made her beam.

"I have some things to do out in the barn." While he spoke, he moved toward the cinnamon treats, his long arm already reaching toward the counter to grab one out of the pan. "I'll be out there if you need me."

He avoided looking at her as he headed out the door with his confiscated doughy goodness.

Watching him walk away, Stella shook her head. "After all these years, he still thinks he's being stealthy. Don't know why that man doesn't just sit down and take a few minutes to eat what he has and then be off."

10

She also knew full well he wasn't really going out to the barn to putter. He was going to check on the calf, a subject she didn't want to ask about in Chrissy's hearing. It probably wouldn't have mattered anyway, but Stella wanted to be cautious all the same.

Following her grandfather's lead, Chrissy came over—still entirely engrossed in her technology—and reached over for a cinnamon roll to go with the glass of milk her grandmother had already poured her. "Thanks, Grandma," she managed to say as she settled back into her chair.

Stella shook her head with fond amusement. It had taken her a bit, but she now realized Chrissy's behavior was the norm for children her age today. She and her book-study friends often talked about how much harder it had become to interact with their grandchildren unless they also were connected to the newest and greatest gadgets. The ladies even agreed their own sons and daughters were too reliant on technology, wearing their smartphones as often as their wedding rings.

At their last gathering, one of her friends had summed it up with, "I've just come to realize that 'friending,' 'tweeting,' and 'sending to all' is just an updated version of listening in on a good old-fashioned crank telephone party line." The conversation had devolved from there, straying far from books and the Christmas dinner and exchange they were supposed to be planning.

In somewhat similar fashion, the sound of the back door opening disrupted her current line of thought.

"Stella, you'd better give Doc Johnson a ring," Joe called out.

He was about to say more when he realized Chrissy was sitting at the table with her tablet opened to something, probably that "Game with Friends" thing Stella had told him about. She wasn't paying any attention to him whatsoever, so he softly stepped inside onto the kitchen rug.

Joe lowered his voice while Stella moved toward him. "Please call Doc Johnson. I think he needs to come out and look at the calf. He didn't touch any of the mash." He shook his head in concern. "None of it."

"Okay." The look on her face was just as worried. "I'll do it right away."

Joe was going to go right back to the barn, but it would have been nice to have a moment of happier distraction. That's the thought prompting him to call over to his granddaughter, "Chrissy, it looks like a blizzard is brewing outside. You ought to come take a look."

"Oh, that's nice, Grandpa," she said, with fingers flying but her head stuck in park.

Joe's responding grin was more out of habit than any actual humor. If anything, it just made him sadder.

Arriving back at the barn, he found the small black calf curled up in what seemed to be a comfortable position. After unlatching the pen's gate and walking over to sit down beside him, he couldn't help but notice his listless eyes. The critter showed no signs of recognizing someone had entered his pen, nor did he indicate any response to Joe's voice when he stood up and sprinkled a little more fresh straw around the calf.

"Come on now, boy. There's a fine mash for you just waiting to fill your stomach."

It didn't move.

Joe continued to coax it. "You have a big world standing by, wanting to greet you with a big 'Hello! You'll make a fine 4-H project."

Still nothing from the calf.

"There's a young girl I know who will truly love you when the two of you become acquainted. What do you say? You want to be well, don't you?"

When it did not respond to that either, he knelt back down. He couldn't hold the calf, so he did the next best thing by making sure he was warm while gently stroking him. Taking the little animal's head in his lap, Joe reached for the milk he had brought earlier. Every one of his movements was careful as he turned his patient's head slightly to one side and used a syringe to try dropping liquid into its mouth.

Sadly, he watched as the milk drizzled right back out.

"Oh my." Joe made sure to whisper the two words softly just to make sure the calf wouldn't hear him.

Two more attempts yielded no better response, so he placed the syringe on the ledge and sat down on the nearby milk stool, leaning his back up against the wall while he waited for the vet.

Despite the obvious problem in front of him, the barn seemed very peaceful. Joe found it usually was like that during this time of the day. There was the sound of the wind pushing the winter skies farther across the countryside, along with the occasional banging of a hog feeder. One of the barn cats, meanwhile, slipped through the bottom slat of the pen's gate and found a corner in the pen to nestle down. As the cat watched the calf right along with him, it felt like she was offering support. The only audible factor that seemed out of place was an irritating dripping noise somewhere around him.

Time seemed to contradict itself, passing ever so slowly but quickly for the next hour until Joe's steady gaze on the calf and the barn's quiet atmosphere was interrupted when the barn door opened.

"Hi there." Doc Johnson's voice already carried a note of concern as he climbed over the railing with bag in hand. "No change, I take it?"

"No change," Joe agreed. "Well, not exactly. I think the little fella might be a bit worse."

"Hmm . . . Hmm . . ." was the most Doc Johnson would say until he thoroughly examined the calf. Fumbling through his bag, he took out a syringe. "I'm going to give him another dose of penicillin, but other than that, keep trying to feed him something—the mash, warm milk." He frowned. "At this point, he's probably more likely to take the milk."

Joe watched him administer the shot and waited for any further instructions.

"Here," the doctor said. "Let's help him try to stand up."

With the gentleness of a nurse handing a newborn baby to his mother, Doc and Joe helped the calf stand. He was able to hold that position for a few seconds on his own, but then, with the awkwardness of a newborn, fell face-first back to the floor.

The fresh straw Joe had previously laid out didn't seem to cushion the calf's fall, and he let out a whimper of pain.

Doc sighed. "Well then, it would be a good thing if he was a little warmer. Not too much so—we don't want him to get too hot. But a little warmer wouldn't be a bad thing."

He put his instruments back into his bag and started toward the barn door. Just before stepping out into the cold, Doc turned back toward Joe. "Call me if there's any change. And if I don't hear from you, I'll call in the morning."

"Will do," Joe agreed.

Doc lingered nonetheless. "I hope he gets better, Joe. He seems to be a fine calf." His confusion was almost tangible. "I don't know. There just seems to be something special about him. Maybe it's because he's so weak and vulnerable. From what you told me over the phone, the little guy should already be dead, but he isn't. That's a good thing. Maybe he's just stubborn, and that isn't always a bad thing."

Running out of things to say, he turned away with the odd air of someone hiding something. Joe didn't ask, though, watching his friend walk to his van and then waiting for the sound of a horn honking. It was Doc's way of saying, "'Bye for now."

Joe left the barn, as well, making his way to the kitchen and Stella in particular.

She greeted him as soon as he was inside. "How's the calf?"

"'Bout the same." Joe paused. "Doc thinks it would help if he was just a little warmer. Maybe we could put him somewhere, like the mudroom." He purposely looked straight at Stella while he spoke. "I don't trust putting a space heater in his pen. Would be too dangerous and probably become too hot for the fella."

"Oh no, Joe." Her face was largely blank at first. But then she shook her head with a much more emphatic no.

"What?" Joe did his best to look surprised. "I didn't ask for anything."

"Yeah," she said. "You didn't ask for anything, just like a little boy who wants a horse for Christmas but doesn't dare ask because he knows he'll hear the word no. So, he just drops hint after hint instead."

"What?" Joe ramped up his air of confusion. "Stella, I think you would have been a good school counselor. You know, one of those people always second-guessing what kids are thinking or feeling."

"Don't be so silly." She waved her hand in the air, but the movement was distracted. "Hmm," she mused. "Well, I guess."

He waited hopefully.

"We've had baby chicks in their hatchery boxes back there for a whole week before." She wasn't talking to him anymore. "And how many smelly, stinky, cute little runt pigs have we kept and bottle-fed in that room 'til they could fend for themselves?"

Her musings seemed to be in his favor so far.

She turned to him now, her eyes lost in the memories. "I remember that lamb you brought home for Molly, and she cried and cried until you let it stay in that room for a while. I bet you never knew the times she sneaked it upstairs and let it sleep with her."

He thought he had her, but he couldn't be sure until her next line, which was filled with irritation.

"Joe, you are twisting my arm here."

"I haven't said a word for the last five minutes," he protested. "You—" Rethinking that line of logic, he rephrased it. "With that said, I think you might have the right idea. How 'bout, after Chrissy leaves, we move the calf up here. I'll help you clear the room out," he offered, nice- as-you-please.

Stella scowled. "Now Joseph, don't think for one minute you've pulled the wool over my eyes. You are deliberately taking advantage of the fact that I'm a softie."

He tried his very best not to smile, but perhaps he didn't succeed as much as he intended.

"Oh, and you can clear and clean out the room yourself."

It was, she realized, a win-win. She had intended to clean it out before the holidays anyway. *It will be easier to clean up and air out the room after the calf has been in there than to clean out all the clutter in there now*, Stella thought.

As for Joe, he decided the trade-off was worth it, too. So, with that agreement in place, they walked into the kitchen for a quick lunch of sandwiches and cookies with their attention-distracted but physically present granddaughter.

Joe had enough outside work—or, as Stella would say, "puttering"—to keep him busy for the afternoon. Periodically, he would look in on the calf, which seemed to be nestled comfortably in the corner of the pen. When Joe was looking at him that way, it wasn't at all apparent the critter was struggling to survive.

How can you look so peaceful and yet be barely hanging on? There must be something more I can do. He just couldn't understand, no matter how hard he tried. It was still troubling him when he got around to sharpening some tools in the machine shed, which was right when Molly poked her head inside.

"Hey, Dad." Her normally pleasant voice sounded concerned. "Mom just told me about the calf. How's he doing?"

"'Bout the same, I guess." Joe turned toward her. "We'll know more in a day or two. Your mom said it would be all right if I made a place for him in the mudroom where the washer is. We'll move him after you and Chrissy leave."

"Yeah, that's what Mom said. We've already cleared a space and put some things out into the old wash house. Mom said it was your job to do, but when I offered to help . . . well, you know Mom, but she did leave some heavy lifting for you." She switched gears. "She also said that you wanted to talk to me about something."

Despite that question, Molly didn't give any indication she wanted to visit much longer. Chrissy, no doubt, was already in the car and ready to leave.

"Yes," Joe said. "But I can see you're on the way out. It can wait. I'll talk to you next weekend."

He couldn't help but notice the brief look of relief on her face.

"No, not next weekend," she said. "Remember? We're leaving Wednesday for Kansas City. It's Marty's sister's turn to have

Thanksgiving, so we'll be there for the weekend." She was hurrying away already, talking to him over her shoulder. "Oh, and Marty has finished maintenance on the combine, so that's put away. He thinks we've had another very good year."

She was at the car now. "We'll be having Christmas here, though. And I'll come visit when I bring Chrissy out after Thanksgiving." There might have been a twinge of guilt as she continued rambling. "I'll bring coffee cake. You know, the kind you like with all the nuts in it. We can have a good visit."

Joe could see she wasn't going to stop talking long enough to let him slip in his concern about a possible storm they might run into before reaching the Missouri state line, so all he said was, "Be careful. Snow might be coming. Goodbye, you two. Have a nice Thanksgiving. Tell Marty's family 'hello' for us."

Then they were off, leaving him alone to turn back to the shed and his puttering.

When Molly and Marty were away at school, and especially after their wedding, Joe and Stella had come to accept the reality of sharing their child with Marty's family during the holidays. That also had to be true regarding sharing their one and only grandchild. They understood, as did the Martin family, the give and take of sharing family members. Besides, the times when they could all come together made the holidays much more meaningful and delightful.

Joe and Stella had also known they could pretty much make their own happiness. Whenever it was just the two of them for Thanksgiving, they participated in their church's holiday meal and worship service. So that's precisely what they did this time around. After Joe finished all the outside chores, including what Stella would usually do since she was baking, they drove into town. At church, they immediately went to work filling the car with Thanksgiving dinners, which they delivered to shut-ins. They even knew a few couples and individuals who just seemed a little too proud to say they would like a meal. In those cases, they took special effort to deliver their meals, along with a visit. And, of course, Joe would drink a cup of coffee when it was offered.

When the car was finally empty, the two of them returned to church, where everyone, the men included, prepared their own fellowship dinner, which was followed by a celebration of worship and song.

After that came football. It just wouldn't seem right to have Thanksgiving without it, even in church. So, someone always seemed to not only bring a widescreen TV but also have it set up in time for kickoff. At halftime, there were pies, cookies, apple cider, and "sacramental" coffee—an all-around good time. Once the clock struck five, though, football took a backseat to other traditions. Whether the game was over or not, Joe and Stella, like so many of their fellow participants, had to say goodbye and head home to do their chores.

By the time Joe had changed clothes and walked into the barnyard, the milk cows were already at the gate waiting to come in for the evening milking along with their ground corn and hay. It was amusing to once again see how routine could grow into habit, even for the animals. When he didn't go out to the field to bring them home, or if they didn't hear the familiar "Come, boss" from the barn door by a certain time, they usually found their way up the lane anyway.

Amused, he found himself speculating about which cow might decide how long the herd should wait for him until they realized there would be no hay for them tonight and start walking back to the field.

I guess I'll never know, he concluded. *At least not in this lifetime.*

His final chore for the evening would be checking on the calf, which was still in the mudroom. Knowing that Stella would have already tried to feed him, he hoped the fella had felt like eating.

19

"He's looking pretty good," Joe said, coming in to the kitchen from the mudroom with a quart jar of per-separated milk and a pint of fresh cream. "Did he eat anything?"

"Yes, he is looking a little better," she nodded. "He drank his milk straight from the pail and ate all his mash. I think he's strong enough to go back to the barn."

"Why, Stella, I thought you'd just want him to hang around here. You know, help you decorate. Maybe taste your soon-to-be-done Christmas cookies and help put up the tree." He grinned. "You know how clumsy I am with that sort of stuff."

"Oh, just stop all that nonsense now." She didn't even look at him. "You know he's strong enough to head back to the barn, and down to the barn he's going."

He chuckled.

She wasn't done yet. "And by the way, as much as I love that little guy, you're the one who's going to be scrubbing down the porch linoleum with ammonia." Now she did turn to him, all trace of teasing gone from her voice. "You also need to decide what you're going to do with him."

"I thought all the room would need was a little airing out. Is scrubbing down with ammonia airing out?" he asked, avoiding her last comment.

Joe knew he wouldn't receive any further explanation from Stella, so he moved on to answer her question. "What I'm going to do with him?" Now he felt a little puzzled, even though he thought there was no need for an explanation. "You know what I want to do with him. I want us to give him to Chrissy for a Christmas gift so that, just maybe, she'll decide to keep him for a 4-H project."

Stella gave a deep sigh of obvious disappointment because Joseph had not given up on his idea. "Joe, I've already asked Molly what Chrissy might like to have for Christmas. She and I are going shopping when they return from Kansas City."

That hurt a little to hear, he couldn't deny it.

"Didn't Molly tell you?" Stella said, not waiting for an answer. "Besides, while you and I might like the idea of giving Chrissy the calf and you getting to work with her because of that, there's still no guarantee she'll like it, much less want to join 4-H. All of this is more your dream than anyone else's." Her voice was gentle but firm. "I'm willing to work with you to make the little critter stronger, but I don't understand why you're hanging on to this idea so tightly."

That last point was a fair one. Joe had never really shared with Stella why this dream of his was so important to him.

"I guess," he started slowly, "I wanted to belong to FFA or 4-H so badly when I was growing up. Remember how I told you I was given runt pigs but nothing else? And they died an hour or two after birth."

Stella nodded.

"My friends all had calves or pigs, and a few had horses. And I thought a calf would make a good project—that, just maybe, Dad would teach me how to work with it. But he said we couldn't afford for me to have one." He let out a breath through his nose. "I finally did get one as a Christmas present. Didn't have a halter or anything for it, but I didn't care. I made one out of bailing twine."

Smiling at that, Stella let him continue.

"It was finally my mom who helped me learn how to lead it and teach it how to stand. I think Dad just saw it as a nuisance since we often didn't have enough feed for the cows, much less the calf. But I placed third at the fair, and my neighbor brought us home." He shrugged. "Turns out it was really the neighbor's calf all along. What I really received as a present was permission to raise a calf. So, after that, the neighbor paid me for the care and took his property home."

"Oh, Joe," Stella said, looking like she wanted to give him a hug.

He gave her a small but reassuring smile. "Maybe Dad saw how much it meant to me after all because he took me to the sale barn where we bid on a calf much like the one we have now. But I still had to take out a loan to pay for it."

"I remember you telling me that," she said.

Joe nodded. "When the fair was over and I sold the second calf and paid the bank back, I had eight dollars left. And since eight dollars wasn't enough to buy another one, that was the last year I was in 4-H." He paused, searching for the right words to go on.

"So that's why you want this so much," she gently prodded.

Another nod. "I'd really like to help Chrissy work with the little guy out there—to lead him, to help him stand right, and take care of him so he'll gain weight the right way. That's why all of this matters to me." He squared his shoulders. "You'll see, Stella. It will eventually work out. You'll see."

The problem was that he saw, too. In his mind, he knew she was right, but he wanted to make this Chrissy's dream so badly. He was fully aware it was not an unconditional gift. But he just couldn't seem to let it go.

He did let the calf go back to the barn, though. Doc Johnson came out to examine him, and, while stating that his breathing still seemed a little labored, he thought everything else was looking fairly good.

Doc's lips pursed in amusement. "This calf's had good care. Do you think Stella would let me use her back porch for a few more critters?"

Joe snorted. "You ever want another piece of her pie or a cinnamon roll, Doc?"

That elicited a full-out laugh. "I'll take that for a yes."

"Pretty much," he agreed.

Doc turned to the calf. "I guess your cousins will just have to weather their own barns, little fella. Sorry." Then, speaking to Joe again, he added, "I'll check in a week or two unless I hear otherwise."

Then they both headed for the house to enjoy a piece of apple pie.

The daylight hours were shortening, and winter had picked up its pace to roam across the fields and farms like it owned them. Sometimes, it seemed like a force of invisible wind warriors would thrash through the countryside, rattling old farmhouse windows with their goal of getting in everywhere. Its howling energy drove dry snow through cracks in the old barns' outer walls. Snow arrows were quick to sting anyone's face who dared to walk against the wind while doing outside chores. Other times when there was little or no wind, the quiet snows gently fell, glistening across meadows and fields, inviting dreamy winter music and early Christmas carols.

Thanksgiving was now solidly tucked away for another year, and Christmas was coming. Whether precluded by peaceful snowfalls or stormy snow-warrior assaults, it made no difference.

Another storm hit with a vengeance in the early morning hours of Saturday, December first. It was, therefore, no surprise to Stella when Molly called her to say Chrissy wouldn't be out for the day. Also, she had forgotten to tell them that the birthday of one of Chrissy's best friends was coming up, which meant she couldn't come the next weekend either. The girl's mother had planned an all-nighter for the girls at a motel in the city, followed by a day of shopping that Molly had agreed to help chaperone.

"I couldn't say no, Mom. Please tell Dad I'm sorry. We both wanted to come out . . . but, well . . . you know . . . I just couldn't say no," she tried to explain.

"No, I don't think you could have or should have. Chrissy needs to spend time with her friends, and it's good that you can go along," Stella said.

"Yeah, but I promised Dad I'd make a coffee cake and bring it out." Molly sighed. "He had some things he wanted to talk to me about. Do you know what they were?"

"I have a notion," Stella answered truthfully and without enthusiasm. "But you'd better wait and talk to him, Molly."

"All right." She didn't push it any further than that. "I promise we'll be out on the seventeenth. Remind Dad that I'll bring coffee cake with extra nuts like he enjoys, okay?"

"Don't worry, Molly. Your dad isn't deprived of his share of nuts," Stella reassured her. "But I will tell him. You and Chrissy just enjoy yourselves, and we'll see you on the seventeenth."

Still, she knew that Joe would be disappointed.

Since Chrissy was old enough to hold a crayon in her hand, she and her grandpa had kept a particular tradition. Starting with the Saturday after Thanksgiving, they would cross out each calendar day that passed since her last visit. They would also redo their Christmas lists, with both of them known to change their minds on what they really wanted, what they hoped to receive, and what they wanted to give other people, including each other. So, her absence two weekends in a row was going to be felt.

Sure enough, Joe was outwardly disappointed when he heard the news. After a pep talk from Stella about how grandparents were apt to be—or at least should be—more forgiving than a young girl's best friends, he let out a sigh. "I guess we'll just have more X's to place on the calendar when she does come."

24

Stella was quick to affirm that. "Yes, you will. Now why don't you make some coffee, and I'll warm up those scones I made last night."

The week went by slowly when it came to doing chores. While the rhythm of the routine—milking, feeding the livestock, gathering eggs, shoveling snow, tending to the calf, and milking again—seemed to have a certain harmony to it, the winter weather gave it a slower tempo. It was a pace that demanded a certain respect and appreciation, as farmers well knew. Despite the entirely different temperatures, the winter cold was as much of an intrusion on machinery, beasts, and humans as the hammering heat of an August day.

Even so, most farmers could easily measure the time from one milking to the next, and Joe was no exception. Despite the bother of year-round daylight savings time, an invention he disagreed with, he did his best to help both the cows and himself maintain normal hours and a routine schedule throughout the year. Sometimes, however, that routine schedule just wasn't possible.

Early Saturday morning, the day Chrissy was supposed to come out to the farm again and just seven days before Christmas Eve, Joe came in from milking later than normal. The sun hadn't quite yet yawned its way out of its eastern bed when he walked into the kitchen with his boots off, carrying a quart jar of fresh milk.

In the process of pouring pancake batter into the hot griddle, Stella had her back to him. "I was almost ready to come looking for you, Joseph."

Joe's next words were more than sufficient to explain the delay. "I called Doc from the machine shed. It's the calf. He's down again."

His tone was one of utter bewilderment. And when Stella turned around, she could see his expression matched his state of confusion.

"I can't explain it," he said. "We did everything right the first time, but Doc says it just happens sometimes. Says it might be another strain of pneumonia, or it might be something else."

Joe's voice was getting gruff. "He still isn't ruling out a swamp bug. But whatever it is, I'm afraid it's hit him with a vengeance, and I don't want to do any second-guessing."

"Oh, Joe," Stella said, unsure how else to respond in the moment.

"We need to wait until Doc gets here," he added, laboring over his words. "But the little guy just doesn't seem to have the strength or will to see this through a second time around. I guess we just need to give him some of ours."

Joe sank into a silence that caused his gaze to fall to the floor. Not that he was ashamed to cry in front of Stella, but now just wasn't the time. Now was the time to do everything he could for the ailing animal he had developed such a strange attachment to from the very first moment in the ring, maybe before that when he was first inspecting the livestock offerings.

Even now, with everything pointing to a negative outcome, it wasn't enough for Joe to lose his belief that his little friend could win. He was determined not to give up hope, which was about the only thing left to hold onto—that, and the strength in knowing he had Stella's support. She might have doubted the wisdom of his purchase from day one, but never his devotion, and he knew she cared about this newest undersized member of the Barnes family just as much as he did now.

Proving as much, Stella moved to put her arms around him. "I'll make more coffee and put away the hotcake batter. I'm sure Doc will be hungry when he comes over, so I'll just make some rolls and bring them down to the barn when they're done."

"I knew you would." Joe, touched more than he could say, did try to move his lips upward while searching for a smile. He had to clear his voice before he could speak again. "I just don't understand it. He was drinking and eating more."

Stella let him talk it out as much as he could.

"I wonder—I mean, the weather got worse on Thursday, and last night was the coldest Friday we've had for this year. I wonder if—" He cleared his throat again. "Maybe we should have left him in the mudroom a little longer."

She wanted to reassure him, but he was already contradicting the thought.

"No, we did the right thing," he reasoned. "It wouldn't have mattered where he was. His pen was plenty warm. It's just that—" He had to stop again for a deep breath. "When I went in to care for him this morning, I guess I wasn't prepared to see him the way he was. I just don't know."

Stella cut him off then for his own sake. "I'll pray, Joe. Okay?" After another thought, she started to add, "You might—"

"I already have and already am," he said, instinctively knowing what she was going to tell him and already agreeing with it.

Understanding each other completely in that moment, they embraced tightly before Joe gave her a kiss on the cheek and headed back toward the quiet stillness of the barn.

The walk there was illuminated by the steady glow of the angel on top of their tall decorated Christmas tree, which stood next to the living-room window. Yet Joe didn't pay special notice to it, taking it for granted while he carried a horse blanket to wrap around the shivering calf that was once again struggling for every breath he took.

When he went to cover him, the little critter made no effort to move, prompting Joe to talk to an audience of two: himself and the calf. "Seven more days. Only seven more days before Christmas Eve. And then, after that, it's Christmas."

His voice became calm as he addressed his audience up above. "Dear God, are there any miracles left for a small corner of this gigantic world that You already have Your hands full taking care of? I know there are so many, many people asking—crying out to You. If there are miracles left, may we have just one, just one miracle before Christmas? I won't ask for anything else." He had to catch himself there, though. "Well, maybe I'll also ask for Chrissy to love and want this little critter. He's one of Your very own, I might add."

Realizing he actually had a long Christmas wish list, he kept going. "Maybe I'd also ask, if You have time to listen, that she'd want to show him at the fair. I know he needs to put on a lot more weight, but that's our responsibility. We would help him do it."

Another tear fell. Another swipe banished its physical presence from his face. "Oh, I know she might not want to join 4-H or any type of club. We can deal with that when the time comes. But all the rest—how 'bout it, God? Will You help? Please?" He let the next tear go. "That's all, just one, small—"

It might have been a mere cruel trick of his imagination, but it sounded like the calf's struggle to breathe got worse for a second. So he quietly covered it with the blanket, addressing it like a sick child.

"Don't want you to become too hot, little fella. But this might warm you until the doc arrives."

No sooner had he spoken the words than he heard Doc's pickup coming up the driveway.

Joe remained at the calf's side while the engine shut off right in front of the barn.

Doc was talking to him before he even climbed over the fence. "Sorry about how long it took. I was on my way but slid off the road."

Joe made some appropriate response even though his attention was really on his struggling little friend.

"Fortunately, Harry was coming from town with a load of pig feed," Doc continued, unaware. "So, he had traction enough to help me out. And, of course, we had to visit a bit. You know how it is. Still, it's a good thing your neighbors rise in the morning as early as you do."

"Yeah," Joe agreed, and then switched the conversation right away, his eyes moving back and forth between the calf and the vet. "I wish this little guy could do better visiting with us than he is right now."

"I agree, but let's have a look." He stooped down to do so, listening to his lungs first. "Yeah, I hear labored breathing. Very shallow." His eyes squinted as he uttered a soft, "Hmm." Examining the calf once more, Doc slowly rubbed his chin and repeated, "Hmm . . . hmm."

Joe finally couldn't wait any longer, expressing himself with an attempt at humor. "You sound just like my heart doctor, except she does her 'hmms' in harmony."

This little joke was his best effort at creating a mood of optimism. His hope was believing the calf would make it through, leading to positive results. And his spur-of-the-moment humor was his best guess at doing that.

"Well," Doc said, "I could try to 'hmm' it all together, but they didn't teach that part in vet school. Somehow, I doubt your heart doctor had an official course in 'hmm' either."

He stood up, pausing long enough for a respectful quiet to come over the three of them. This time, Joe didn't speed him along.

"I think we should try to put him back into a warmer climate," Doc finally expressed. "But it's the same thing as before—we can't let him get too hot."

Joe crossed his arms over his chest as something to do.

"I'm going to try this other medicine, along with another shot of penicillin." He was rummaging through his bag again. "The next forty-eight hours should make a difference one way or the other, although the barn's draft might just be too cold for him." His brow furrowed in thought. "Maybe you can nail some slabs of plywood on—"

"He'll do no such thing." The sound of Stella's voice surprised both of them as she came through the door.

In her hands was a picnic basket filled with a thermos of hot coffee and two pans of cinnamon rolls, all of which she handed to Joe. Unsure of what to say to that opening, he simply took the whole kit and caboodle and found a place for it. When neither Stella nor Doc made another comment, he went so far as to pour three cups of coffee.

Not until the two men started to drink their coffee did Stella speak again. "You'll bring 'im back up to the mudroom. I just rearranged it, and he'll get more attention being up there. Truth be told, he probably should have stayed there a while longer the first time." She looked intensely chagrined. "Maybe I was a bit too hasty in wanting the room back to the way it was before the holidays came."

"No such thing, Stella." Doc managed to interrupt her around the bite of the warm, delightful cinnamon roll he was still enjoying. With his mouth half open, he went on, "Now, if you were to feed this little critter a pan of these delights"—he lifted up his almost-finished treat—"he'd probably be up kicking his heels in no time."

"Oh, come on now." But her eyes shone a little brighter. "This other pan is for you to take home, though. Sue called to tell us you were on your way out, and I told her I'd send a pan home with you."

Doc gave no indication of objecting.

"She said your daughter was coming home later today from college," Stella added. "So I wanted to send a little welcome-home present for her."

She brought herself back to the moment. "Now, the two of you just bring the little one up when you're ready. Like I said, the room is waiting for him, and this calf is going to get better. I know he is."

Listening to her, Joe found he couldn't help but feel encouraged by her confidence.

"Oh," she slightly switched topics, "Reverend Geoffrey wants to know if the little fellow could be part of our live nativity play." She pressed her lips together in amusement. "He asked Chrissy yesterday if she would be a shepherd, but she's not sure since she can't use her smartphone while coming through the field or standing at the manger."

That made both men snort in amusement.

"Actually," she said, "the reverend is asking all the kids to leave their gadgets at home. And wouldn't it be a real Christmas miracle if he could get the parents to do the same thing?"

"Stella—" Joe did feel obligated to switch the topic. "Maybe you shouldn't be too quick to volunteer the mudroom again."

"Nonsense." She made sure he couldn't finish his rationale by turning to the calf. "Don't you listen to him, fella. You'll be bouncing around by Christmas Eve. You'll show everyone what you're made of."

With that, Stella walked out of the barn, focusing her attention on the bright angel's light peering out the living room window directly at her.

By afternoon, the calf was settled back in the mudroom with his nose nestled in the horse blanket. Just like before, the two of them were trading shifts to feed it a syringe full of milk mixed with the medicine Doc had prescribed. It was Joe who first heard the sound of voices outside, and he shouted out to Stella.

"They're here. Better put the kettle on for tea."

"Yes!" Molly said gleefully as she pushed open the door. "We're here, Dad."

Chrissy trailed behind with her earbuds set in their seemingly permanent place.

"Hi, Grandpa." She gave him a glance and a quick smile, speaking over the music only she could hear.

"Hi to you both." Joe stood and moved away from the calf.

At the same moment, Stella opened the door to the kitchen just in time to catch a deep hug from her daughter and a side embrace from her granddaughter, who was already reaching out for a cinnamon roll sitting in the pan on the counter.

"Come in out of the cold, both of you," Stella instructed while she scooted them both toward the kitchen table and Joe closed the door. The warm, fresh smell of baking bread added to the delightful atmosphere, and the tea kettle started whistling right as the other pot of coffee finished brewing, showing that all really was ready for company.

Joe took out coffee cups from the cupboard while Stella filled Molly in about Doc Johnson's earlier visit.

"He wants to try a new medicine on the calf, so your father and I've been giving it to him." Breathlessly, she went right on without a pause. "And you would have never guessed it, but Reverend Geoffrey called, asking if the calf could be in the live nativity. Of course, I said he could."

Molly finished taking off her coat, a look of surprise covering her face.

Stella called her out for it right away. "Now, Molly, you stop that. You and your father! I swear you have his expressions."

"But, Mom—" Molly tried her best to edge into her mother's one-sided conversation.

"No 'buts,' young lady. Reverend Geoffrey has no way of knowing the little fella has been slightly ill."

"Slightly?" This time it was Joe's turn to interrupt. "I want the calf to be well. I want it more than anyone can imagine. But, I also don't want to promise something to someone." He had every intention of saying more, but Molly's facial expression revealed an unspoken message that she wanted the conversation to go in another direction.

"Slightly ill," Stella maintained. "That's all."

"Chrissy!" Molly made sure to speak loudly and directly at her daughter, turning her shoulder toward the living room while she did. "Why don't you go into the living room for a minute?"

Chrissy complied without any argument, but as she turned, she saw the worried look on her mother's face—the same kind of worry she was used to seeing whenever she was asking for something Molly perceived as worrisome. For that matter, she had seen the same expression lately when her mom and dad talked about borrowing money for more large machinery. It was a concept she really didn't understand. Why would they want to buy more when it seemed to her there was a lot of machinery on their farm already?

As soon as Chrissy disappeared from view, Molly turned to her mother. "Okay. What's changed? Only yesterday, when we talked on the phone, you told me how concerned you were about the calf's survival and how you believed Dad had set his hopes too high."

She cast a quick apologetic glance at her father before continuing. "You're also the one who told me Dad wanted to give the calf to Chrissy for a Christmas present, hoping—no, planning—on her wanting to join 4-H. And you—"

"Yes, yes," Stella cut in with every display of confidence that she wasn't contradicting herself one bit. "I did say all those words, but if you were really, really, really listening, you would have heard what I was trying to say."

Molly did not have to weigh in again before Stella realized where she had been going with her line of chastisement, though.

"Oh," she said. "I understand now, Molly. You think Dad and I take on lost causes too often. I know that's what you think, but most of the time, with love and care, it all seems to work out."

She waved away her daughter's attempt at any further explanation. "But that's not what I was upset about. What I was upset about, and what I've been disagreeing with your father on—and probably still do— is his stubborn hope that Chrissy will want this little fella for her own and will be eager to join a group like 4-H."

She sent her husband a glance that was two-parts love to one-part unwavering certainty. "He wants to help her learn how to make this a show calf and raise it properly, something he missed doing with you and what his father never did with him."

"Oh," Molly said.

Joe just looked at the floor.

"When you were growing up," Stella went back to addressing her daughter, "it didn't take you long to find other interests outside of living on a farm or raising farm animals. And Chrissy seems to be heading in the same direction. It's not wrong for her, just like it wasn't wrong for you. Your father and I celebrated the fact that you were involved in music and other activities." Her eyes softened with memories. "I don't think he ever missed one of your concerts, except for the time the cows were out and one got stuck in the creek."

"What?" Molly asked. "I don't remember that at all."

"I don't suppose you do, sweetheart," her mother acknowledged. "I don't think your dad ever made a big deal of it. I think he just told you he had some problems finishing chores."

Joe remembered the day, and yes, that was precisely what he had said.

Stella went back to her original line of thought. "Bottom line is, I just don't want your father to be hurt. When I think hard on it, I'm not afraid of your reaction or Chrissy's lack of interest. It's how your father might feel that worries me."

That was a good thing, considering how Molly's expression was one of defensiveness.

As before, that didn't faze Stella. "What happens between you and your father and Chrissy will be something all of you have to work out. But I'm going to keep on believing it will all work itself out because, beneath all this confusion, we still do and will love each other. I just know it."

"I don't know, Mom," Molly stated. "I think you're afraid. Like most of us, you just let things be, try to avoid the consequences, and want the problem to go away on its own. And . . ." She hesitated with an unhappy frown. "I don't know if I can do that. I don't think we should put Chrissy in the position to have to say *yes* to please her grandpa. Marty and I have never wavered about expecting Chrissy to accept consequences for not following the rules we set. But Dad doesn't want to just set a rule for Chrissy. I think he wants her to fulfill his own dream instead. That just isn't fair to Chrissy."

But the opposition only seemed to open a door for Stella to be honest with her daughter in a way she never would have been before. "Molly, if we do not face our fears, they can become a corral fencing us in and limiting who and what we are, along with what we can be. To go beyond such fear takes courage to believe that faith, hope, and love are on our side."

Joe noticed Molly's frown hadn't gone away.

Stella, however, wasn't intimidated. "It's that kind of courage and belief the least of us need as God's creatures—people and animals. And Molly, as long as we have more than they do, God expects us to give all we can. No. All that is *needed. This* being nearly Christmas and all, what do you think God's act of reaching down so very far to give us His Son, Jesus, actually means?"

Molly really didn't seem to be in a thinking mood about anything related to Christmas for the time being, calf or no calf. "Mom, you're sounding a lot like Reverend Geoffrey. You're just too preachy for me at the moment."

Personally, Joe was amazed Stella had expressed herself so openly. He also had to admit he was both surprised and hurt by Molly's response. A silence filled the room from there—an almost peaceful stillness that left Joe unprepared for what his daughter said next.

"Dad, it isn't going to work. You can't put your dreams I didn't fulfill into your granddaughter's life. *I won't let you.*" Her last words were adamant and framed within a voice of strong determination. Her facial expression was not lacking for confidence. After taking another breath, she seemed to speak more thoughtfully. "Chrissy doesn't share this vision. In fact, she probably doesn't even have a clue about the hopes Marty and I have for her, either."

Nobody interrupted her while she continued. "Can't you just give her something without any strings attached? Didn't what you, Mom, and I went through before this cause enough problems? I think it would be worse now."

As soon as she said those last few words, she regretted them. But they couldn't be taken back. "I'm sorry, Dad. I'm just afraid you want to give her something that is going to die, and even if it does live, it might mean more to you than it does to her. I'm sorry. I—"

And then silence descended again.

At first, Joe just sat there looking at the table. Overwhelmed with sadness, Stella didn't move either.

Finally, Joe arose and went over to the coffee pot and poured another cup of coffee. Then quietly and slowly, he said, "I'm sorry too, Molly. I never realized I gave you or Chrissy anything with conditions tied to it."

Molly opened her mouth to say something, but no sound came out.

"I'd better go sit with the calf," Joe stated. "It might be the last time we have together."

Then he walked out to the mudroom and pulled his stool up close enough to hear his little friend's shallow breathing. His thoughts went nowhere, and so he washed them down with a swallow of coffee. There didn't seem much else to do about it. Any of it.

The kitchen, meanwhile, remained quiet. A tear had found its way to Stella's cheek and got stuck there, unable to move. Molly's tears, however, were flowing freely.

Neither of them had any idea Chrissy, with earbuds detached, was standing at the kitchen door. She had been hoping to come in and ask for another cinnamon roll when her mother's elevated volume stopped her from entering but not from hearing most of the conversation.

She'd heard her mother and then her grandfather. She'd heard the words about the calf, dreams, and 4-H. But most of all, she'd heard the tears. Those were all too evident in her mother's words. In the quiet. In her grandfather's exit. And, for the first time, from a distance, real or imagined, she heard the tears in the shallow breathing of the calf trying so desperately to truly live.

"Chrissy," her mom called out after some time had passed, "we have to leave now!"

Chrissy retreated to the sofa and placed the buds back in her ears, turning the volume up so loudly that her mom didn't bother calling her again. Molly just shook her head and stood in front of her, lifting her arm while using her index finger to point at the door.

Quietly obeying, Chrissy turned her music off entirely as she passed from the den through the kitchen to the car without saying her usual goodbyes. The ride back to town was a quiet one, as both were detached from each other and deep in their own thoughts. It was a very long ride.

For the next several days, no news came from the farm as far as Chrissy knew. Classes and homework kept her busy until the third afternoon, when her mother picked her up from school. She just couldn't keep her thoughts and feelings to herself anymore.

"I want to go see Grandma and Grandpa," she said. "Please, Mom."

"You'll be going tomorrow," Molly said. "I have—"

"Mom, please," Chrissy interrupted, practically pleading. "I need to see Grandma and Grandpa. Really. It's important I see them now."

Molly relented. "I don't really see the hurry, but I guess we can swing by there for just a few minutes. Just a few minutes, though, okay? We can't stay long."

She couldn't ignore her daughter's tone, even if she had no idea why she wanted to go so badly. Plus, she knew very well she had unfinished business left at her parents'. Her regret and disappointment about what she'd said and how she'd said it had hardly disappeared over the last few days.

The ride to the farm passed without any more words spoken. As soon as the car stopped near the farmhouse's garage, Chrissy ran out of the car and went toward the front of the house instead of going her usual way through the back porch. She entered the front hallway and went straight to the kitchen, where her grandmother was fixing supper.

"Grandma!" Chrissy shouted, hurrying over and giving her grandmother a big hug. "I missed you. Where's Grandpa? How's the calf?"

She didn't wait to hear the answer, almost running out the door to the mudroom, where she found the duo she was searching for. Joe was sitting on the stool, observing the calf after giving him his feeding and medicine.

"Hi, Grandpa." This time her greeting was much softer, even though the hug she offered was just as fierce.

This unexpected show of affection threw him off balance, and he tumbled onto the floor with Chrissy landing beside him. Sitting on the floor like that, they both began to laugh, and Joe reached out to give his granddaughter a loving squeeze of his own.

That simple action threw Chrissy for an emotional loop, preventing her from saying more than a single syllable. "Grand—." Then her sobs were uncontrollably clogging her words, loudly and indiscriminately, with unashamed tears falling freely to the floor, onto her grandpa, her school coat, and the calf that was almost in both of their laps.

Tears that felt like they'd waited a young lifetime to fall kept pouring down, interspersed with words that were filled with grief and apology. "Oh, Grandpa, I heard . . . I heard you and Mom. Don't be mad at her. Please? Be mad at me . . . . I mean, I love you . . . ."

Her breath was coming in gasps, as was her intended message. "I do want the calf . . . . I know I will love the calf, too. Grandpa . . . I just couldn't take it . . . because . . . I'm not sure I want to be in . . ." Still crying, she shook her head. "Oh, whatever. I don't care now. I . . . I want the calf to get well. If you still want to give it to me for Christmas, I'll be so happy. Even if it's just for a day or a few days . . ."

Joe did try to get a word in edgewise at that point, but there was no use. Chrissy seemed to be calming down now, but that didn't mean her words weren't still rushing out.

"I just hope it will be for a while. I already named him. After you, actually. I named him Stubborn. Well, actually I'm naming him after you and Grandma and Mom. And me, too. I guess we're all stubborn, aren't we?" she sniffled. "But most of all, I think Stubborn is a good name because he doesn't give up. Neither do you and Grandma, and I won't either. And I bet when Mom sees us all working together, she won't give up either."

Chrissy finally came to a stop, taking in deep breaths and waiting. She knew in her head and heart there were no more words to express. She'd said it all.

Hearing all of that had thrown Joe for so many loops. He was confused, then surprised, and now, most of all, dizzy with happiness and joy.

"Chrissy, Doc says the calf—I mean, Stubborn—is going to live. He's going to live! In fact, he'll be going back to the barn tomorrow. With Christmas coming, Grandma says she wants her mudroom back. She says she doesn't want the house smelling like a cow."

His granddaughter let out a teary laugh.

"I'm sorry, too," he went on. "Your mom was partly right. Part of my wanting you to have the calf was so we could turn him into a grand champion. I never had the chance to really have my own. My father saw it as a luxury, not something important to hang onto."

Chrissy swiped a hand across her eyes.

"Your mom was also partly wrong," Joe added. "Grandma and I always wanted her to have her own dreams. I have to say, though, at first I was disappointed your mom didn't want to be in 4-H or want to work with the livestock like I did. Unfortunately, that led to some early misunderstandings mostly on my part, but I was always so impressed and proud of all she accomplished. No matter what, I always told her I loved her. Your grandma and I wanted her to know we were and are always there for her. Just like we are and always will be there for you and your dad."

Chrissy sniffled again, but other than that, she let him talk the same way he had let her when it was her turn.

"Then again, your mom was also one hundred percent correct regarding giving something with conditions. But I've learned. Stubborn here, comes to you as a Christmas gift from Grandma and me with no strings attached. Guess he wouldn't really be a gift otherwise, huh?" With those words, Joe handed her the rope buckled to the small halter he had bought for Stubborn to wear.

She threw her arms around him again for another big hug. The two of them had been so fixated on one another and stubborn, they didn't realize Molly was standing in the doorway.

"Oh, Dad, you're the best!" She stepped over and reached her arms out to hug them both. While her arms were still holding the two of them tightly, she continued, "I had mixed emotions about coming out so soon, but I do have to say I was relieved when Chrissy made the urgent effort for us to come. You let me say what I said. You didn't ignore me. I guess, truth be told, you and Mom have always let me speak my mind. Mom says I inherited that from you more than from her. I know we were both right and not quite right; but more importantly, even on the way to town that day, after all was said (mostly by me), I never doubted your love." As Molly finished speaking, she freed the two of them from her embrace.

Now it was Joe's turn as he wrapped his arms around his daughter, kissed her lightly on the cheek, and said, "It can hurt a little to hear you speak with such determination, but you are mostly right. I love you." With those final words, they retreated to the house, where Stella was waiting.

In the remaining days before Christmas, with all the attention Stubborn received, he not only recovered but exceeded the weight gain Doc Johnson expected. That earned him a green light to be in the live nativity.

So when that evening came around, the only girl shepherd— minus earbuds and smartphone—arrived on the scene with a young calf named Stubborn. It was said that when the angels, wise men, and shepherds sang "Silent Night," Stubborn swung his tail in agreement.

Grandpa said the little fella went so far as to keep time, but you know how those grandpas can be sometimes. Or maybe we should say, all the time.

There's only one more thing to say before this story ends, and that's, "Merry Christmas, Chrissy! Merry Christmas, Stubborn! And Merry Christmas to all—unconditionally!"

Chapter 2

THE CHRISTMAS LEGEND OF ONE SHOOTING STAR

With the approval of Grandpa Roger, who was sitting inches away in his favorite recliner, Jacob and Joshua put the last of their homemade Christmas decorations on the brightly colored Christmas tree. And then, as brothers sometimes do, they wrestled with each other in an attempt to land in their favorite spot on Grandpa Roger's lap.

While they were wrestling, their only sister, Annie, who was named after her grandmother, came into the room from the kitchen. Not wanting to be left out, she managed to wiggle her way onto the coveted seat while simultaneously holding a large bowl of popcorn.

Once she accomplished this amazing feat, she announced, "Grandma said you would tell us a story, Grandpa."

"Grandma did, did she?" Grandpa Roger asked as he reached out to catch the tipping bowl of popcorn with one hand and corral his two grandsons with the other arm so they wouldn't fall.

"Yes, she did." Annie replied. "She said you know a lot of Christmas stories."

"We want a good Christmas story," young Jacob said, speaking directly into his grandfather's ear.

"Our Sunday school teacher said Jesus was born in a manager," Annie declared confidently.

"He wasn't born in a 'manager.'" Her oldest brother, Joshua, slapped his hand to his forehead. "Jesus was born in a *manger*."

"Wasn't." Annie retorted loudly.

"Was too." Joshua insisted.

Jacob's attention, however, didn't seem to be on his brother and sister but on something going on outside in the darkness of the December night. When they paused to take a breath, he pointed toward the picture window with some excitement. "What's Jacob?"

But by the time Grandpa Roger could take a look, it was gone. "What's what?" Grandpa Roger asked his littlest rascal.

"Uh . . . uh." A puzzled look began to draw itself across Jacob's forehead, but only seconds passed before he eagerly pointed toward the dark sky again and yelled, "Jacob!" Swinging his pointer finger straight forward, he barely missed hitting the popcorn bowl in the process of indicating the starry sky.

"Those are stars, silly," Joshua answered his younger brother who was still staring out the window.

"I know stars! They twinkle." Jacob dug his stockinged feet tightly between Grandpa Roger and the recliner. "Geez . . . Maybe one of those stars was carrying a flashlight." And then he got excited all over again. "There it is again!"

He pointed out the window once more, hoping someone else would notice what he was seeing, only to directly hit the popcorn bowl this time. It capsized right into Grandpa Roger's lap, spilling popcorn on his grandfather, the recliner, and the floor.

"Uh-oh," Annie said. "You're in trouble."

"Oops." The apology was real but just distracted by the strange happenings outside. "Grandpa, look!"

Instead of pointing this time, Jacob took both his hands and turned his grandfather's face toward the direction where he had, only seconds before, been watching the unknown objects.

Now it was Joshua's turn to sound surprised and excited. "I see it too! I see it! Jacob, you were right!"

"It's falling out of the sky," Jacob said in concern, turning toward his grandfather. "Will it hit us?"

"No," Grandpa Roger answered calmly.

Jacob wasn't totally convinced, though. "Will it hit your car? Or Debbie's house? Oh no! Will it hit our house? Will—"

"Jacob," Grandpa Roger interrupted with the same calm tone. "Hush, now. It won't hit your house or Debbie's house. It's probably a hundred miles, maybe even a thousand miles from earth. It would run out of gas before it even came near here."

"I think it's a shooting star, Grandpa," Joshua spoke up.

"Why, I suppose it is, Joshua," he replied, hoping the phrase wouldn't be so disturbing. "We'll call it a shooting star."

Annie, who was more concerned about the spilled popcorn, was grabbing fistfuls from her grandfather's lap, alternatively stuffing them into her mouth and dumping them back in the bowl.

"It looks to me like the light is running across the sky," Joshua, always the thinker, explained after once again seriously gazing at the streaks of light.

After his grandfather's comment about running out of gas, Jacob was dancing around the room. And now, with his feet crunching on the popcorn laying on the floor, he started to giggle.

"Grandpa, the Christmas story." Annie had grown tired of just looking out the window and wasn't afraid to say as much.

"Okay. A story you shall have," he said, smiling. "Jacob, dear, come on back up here and I'll tell you all a story."

After a few more crunches, Jacob climbed onto his grandfather's already crowded lap.

"So, you're interested in stars, hmm? I think I'll tell you the story called, 'The Legend of One Shooting Star.'" And so, Grandpa Roger began. "A long time ago—I mean a very long time ago—"

"Before you were born?" Annie asked.

"Were there dinosaurs?" Jacob wanted to know.

"Be quiet, you two." Joshua scolded.

"Yes, before I was born. No dinosaurs, though," Grandpa Rogers said. "Now, let me see. Where was I? Oh yes. A long time ago, God was having a talk with Gabriel, His head angel, while they were drinking tea and eating delicious scones. 'Gabriel,' he said, 'I think it's time to tell Mary she's going to have a baby. She'll name Him Jesus, and He'll be the Savior of the world.'

"God told Gabriel a lot more, but later, when Jesus' friend Luke wrote all of this down, I think this is what he remembered the most."

Annie took another fistful of popcorn, this time out of the bowl.

"Gabriel was really excited that it was time for Jesus to come down to earth," Grandpa Rogers continued. "He called all the other angels together, and they sang praises to God and danced around the heavenly throne."

"I bet just like Jacob dances," Annie suggested.

46

"Yes, Annie," Grandpa Rogers agreed. "I think you're right. Just like Jacob dances."

"Dancing on top of popcorn?" Annie questioned, wanting a clear picture of what was happening around the heavenly throne in the story.

"They don't have popcorn in heaven, silly." Joshua's comment was as matter-of-fact as could be.

"Oh," said Annie, thinking hard about it for all of one second. "Maybe we could send some to God for Christmas."

Slipping back off his grandfather's lap, Jacob started to dance all over again. Moving, stomping, and wiggling as he turned around and around, he shouted out, "Is this how angels dance in heaven?"

"Something like that, I think," Grandpa Roger answered with a mischievous smile on his face. "Maybe you can ask Pastor Chris next Sunday during the children's message."

"So, what about the story?" Now it was Joshua's turn to prompt the story back into existence.

"Come back up here, Jacob." Grandpa Roger motioned toward his lap, and the little one quickly did as he was told.

While they were trying to settle in and get comfortable, there was the general ruckus one would expect from three excitable grandchildren, including several squirms and comments.

"Ouch! You're crowding me, Jacob."

"You're sitting on my leg, Annie."

"Am not."

"Move over, Joshua." And without taking another breath, Annie turned directly to her grandpa and continued, "Grandma is going to come in and tell us to be quiet. You better 'hush' us up, Grandpa."

Grandpa Roger, seeing they were hushing on their own without his intervention, restarted his story. "The angels danced for a long time, and God was pleased with all of them. In fact, He was so pleased, He had Michael—another very important angel—go to the kitchen and bring back tea and scones for everyone. Then He turned to Gabriel and said, 'Well, Gabriel, are you ready to go tell Mary the good news?'

"'I am! I am!' Gabriel replied, bowing before God. 'I will leave right away.'

"'Good.' God said. 'I know her cousin, Elizabeth, will be happy to know we finally told Mary. They'll probably want to get together and visit. Maybe they'll have a baby shower for each other.'

"'I'm sure they will.' Gabriel smiled as he remembered Elizabeth's initial shock, and then her surprise and excitement, when he visited to tell her she would have a baby and so would Mary.

"Now, Gabriel checked his wings to make sure they were in good working order for his long flight and then made a quick list of chores for the cherubs to have done before he returned. After all was completed, he went to tell God goodbye. But on his way, he remembered something.

"'Oh no! I can't go see Mary just yet. I promised the choir master, Raphael, I would sing the solo for the cherubs' graduation service tomorrow. I won't be back in time.' He shook his head in concern. 'I'd better go ask God what He wants me to do.'

"So, Gabriel rushed to God's workroom where He was busy tending to earthly matters. When the secretary came into God's office to tell Him that Gabriel had returned and had something very important to talk about, God dismissed his helper and called for Gabriel to come right in.

"When Gabriel came in, he immediately told God about his problem. 'I am so sorry, but I forgot about the cherubs' graduation concert. Raphael is really counting on me to sing the tenor solo. And I can't send Michael to tell Mary, because he has to sing bass.'

"'Yes, yes,' God said, rubbing His chin. 'I was wondering when you would remember the concert. I do see your dilemma.'"

"Grandpa," Jacob interrupted. "What's a 'da lemma'?"

"Quiet!" Annie scolded. "Grandpa, keep going with the story. I want to know what happened."

Refusing to be ignored, Jacob started to wiggle with swinging feet so his body began to slip out of his grandfather's lap.

"Hold on, Jacob," Grandpa Roger insisted, pulling him back up.

"But what's a 'da lemma'?" Jacob asked again.

"It's a baby llama." Joshua looked puzzled even while he said it. "But I don't know why God would be looking at a baby llama. Do you, Grandpa?"

"Well, kids," Grandpa Roger explained, "a dilemma is not a baby llama. It's what you might say when you're stuck right in between two identical problems."

"Oh, I get it." Joshua was right back to sounding sure of himself. "It's like when you're told you have to eat one of two things on your plate or you won't get any pudding, but you don't like either one of the things."

"Ah, yes," Grandpa Roger agreed.

Annie jumped in next, cute and impatient as ever. "I still don't understand, but will you please go on with the story anyway?"

"Okay. Let's try once again." Grandpa Roger nodded. "God said, 'Yes, I see the dilemma. Gabriel, why don't you send another angel to give Mary the news? You've already gone to see Elizabeth. I guess it wouldn't hurt if someone else went to see Mary.'

"'Say, that's a great idea, God! It gives us a way out of this mess,' Gabriel replied. 'I know what I'll do. I'll send Chamuel. Chamuel is good with people. I've had him help a lot of people before, and he does a fantastic job.'

"'Yes, yes, he can do a good job,' God agreed. 'Chamuel it will be. Go and tell him quickly. He mustn't delay.'

"'I'll do it right now. See You later, Boss. Oops! I mean, see you later, God.' Gabriel's wings were already fluttering, ready for flight, as he finished speaking. And then off he went.

"In no time at all, he found Chamuel and didn't waste any time telling him he was being sent on a mission. 'Now, Chamuel, I just talked to God, and He's giving you permission to deliver this very important message to Mary, one of God's servant girls. She is very faithful, and you are to go directly to her. Do you understand?'

"'I understand.' Chamuel had listened to every word of the directions, so he was confident he had them down. 'Go directly to Mary, a servant girl.'

"'Yes, ahem. Where was I? Oh, yes. Go directly to Mary and say to her, "Mary, you are going to have a baby. You are to name Him Jesus. He is God's Son, and He will be the Savior of the world." Gabriel made sure to use his most serious voice. 'That is the exact message you're to tell her. Don't tell any funny jokes or give her any more information. She will have a lot of questions, but you don't need to go into detail. That will all come later.'

"You see," Grandpa clarified, "Chamuel, like some grandchildren I know, had a bad habit of trying to interrupt Gabriel."

"You mean like Jacob, don't you?" Annie was quick to volunteer.

"Does not," Jacob said with all of his might.

"Well," Grandpa Roger cut in with the wisdom of a grandparent, "why don't I just continue the story?" Then, as the children all settled back down, he continued.

"So Gabriel told Chamuel, 'Don't go into detail. Don't waste time talking about the weather.' And then he added, 'Just tell her nothing is impossible with God. Do you understand, Chamuel?'

"Gabriel's look told the other angel he wanted a reply.

"'Ah, sure. I understand—I think. When do I leave?' Actually, Chamuel could no longer recite all the details, but he did know that any direct word coming from God had to be delivered just as it was told.

"'Right now!' Gabriel reply.

"Chamuel definitely understood that part. 'Right now' meant exactly right now! So, he looked directly at Gabriel and said, 'I'll leave immediately, boss.'

"'I'm not your boss,' Gabriel corrected, but it was no use. Chamuel was already flying away.

"Just as Chamuel was ready to take off for earth, a cherub named Sarah pulled on his wing. 'Where are you going?' she asked. 'Never mind. Remember, you said you would help me find my harp? You told me, "Right after I go and see what Gabriel wants, I will help you."'

"'Oh yes,' Chamuel replied. 'But I . . .'

"'You promised!' Sarah's voice carried the word *promised* with a much stronger tone this time.

"'Well, I guess a few more minutes won't hurt,' Chamuel reasoned. He took a hold of Sarah's hand, and off they flew looking for her lost harp."

Grandpa Rogers thought it might be a good detail to explain, so he stopped the story for a moment. "Now, angels don't really have watches, and heaven doesn't run on our time."

Joshua looked surprised. "Oh, I didn't know that."

"Me neither," Annie agreed.

"I wish I had a watch," commented Jacob. "Maybe you and Grandma can buy me one for Christmas, Grandpa."

"Maybe," he said. "We'll see. But for now, let's go on with our story."

"Yes!" all three children shouted.

Grandpa Roger obliged them. "Chamuel was good at helping people and angels find lost objects, but finding Sarah's harp was really hard. She had no clue where she might have last left it, and he lost track of angel time. He was just about ready to tell Sarah he had failed when he ran across Gabriel coming into the angel music room.

"'Chamuel! Are you back already?' Gabriel asked, surprised to see his friend.

"'Back from?' But then it dawned on him. 'Oh no! Gabriel, you will never guess what happened. Sarah stopped me—'

"Sarah would not let him continue. 'He's right. I did stop him.'

"Poor Sarah. She hadn't known about Chamuel's assignment, and now she was afraid she had gotten him into trouble."

Unconvinced, Annie broke in. "Angels don't really get in trouble."

"My Sunday school teacher, Miss Debbie, said they can," Joshua declared. "So there!"

"It's okay, Annie," Grandpa Rogers assured her. "There were a bunch of angels that found themselves in a peck of trouble one time, though, so I guess it's possible."

"If you say so." Annie wasn't completely convinced, but grandpas did tend to know these things, so she figured she should accept what hers had said.

"Grandpa, the story," Jacob demanded, digging his feet into his grandfather's leg.

He picked it back up as requested. "Gabriel was surprised to see Chamuel. 'Chamuel,' he said, 'I gave you the most important message you probably will ever deliver in all your angel years, and you forgot? You are supposed to help people, and—'

"'I was helping Sarah,' Chamuel said as he tried to somewhat defend and redeem himself. Hanging his head almost to the cloud below him, he muttered, 'I am sorry. I am really sorry.'

"'I will discuss this matter further with you later, young angel.' Gabriel tried to make his words sound truly firm, but it was hard to be genuinely upset when Chamuel was so repentant. At the same time, the message to be delivered was so important. 'I'll just have to go myself. Sarah, please go tell the choir master he'll just have to wing it at the concert.'

"When Gabriel heard his choice of words, he started to laugh, which gave Sarah and Chamuel permission to laugh also. As Sarah began to flap her wings for takeoff, Gabriel added, 'By the way, Sarah, your harp is hanging in the choir room where it is supposed to be.'

"'Oh yes! Now, I remember.'

"Sarah flapped her wings even more excitedly, causing her to take off so fast she did a double somersault and almost hit Gabriel before she corrected herself. Then, with an angelic smile on her face, she went on her way. Without any further words, Gabriel started his own journey just to earth.

"Chamuel was so worried about how things might be between them that he forcefully thrust forward, chasing after Gabriel to apologize again. 'I'm sorry I failed you, Gabriel. I'm worried you won't trust me for future assignments now, but I'll do anything I can for your forgiveness. May I go and sing to Mary while you deliver the message?'

"'No,' Gabriel said most definitively before picking up more speed. But then he slowed down a bit until Chamuel was at his side again. 'Chamuel, it's too late. You can't go with me this time. However, I have to be in Bethlehem when Jesus is born. I'll let you come along, and you can go out to the countryside and tell all the shepherds their new King and Savior is born.'

"That made Chamuel very happy.

"'In the meantime,' Gabriel said, 'I want you to go home and practice your speed of flight. Remember, when we go to Bethlehem, there will be no slow-poking or becoming sidetracked. Now, go practice.'

"With those words, he was out of sight in a flash."

Seeing the looks on their faces, Grandpa Rogers explained, "Chamuel took Gabriel's words very seriously, just like you kiddies do when Grandma gives you instructions on how to do something."

"We don't do that when you tell us something, though," Annie declared with utmost honesty. "Do we?"

"Not always," he agreed. "I wonder why that is?"

"'Cause you don't give us biscuits," Jacob offered.

"Shhh," Joshua said to his brother. "Grandma said we aren't supposed to give away her secrets."

"That's not the entire story, is it, Grandpa?" Annie asked.

"Good point," Grandpa Roger acknowledged.

"So, Chamuel practiced and practiced. He flew to the right, and he flew to the left. He flew upside down and straight up to the highest sky. He flew by—rolling and spinning, zigzagging, crisscrossing, and straight-lining from north to south and east to west. He flew around Mars and Jupiter, then the sun and the moon. And then, just so his wings would stay in shape, he got permission to fly to the top of the Rockies and the top of the Alps. He even flew across Mount Everest, although he had to fly super fast when flying to the top of the mountains because he didn't want his wings to freeze.

"He also flew in earth time. He flew in the daytime and the nighttime, at dawn and dusk. He flew on standard time, central time, and all the time zones across the world. Whew, that Chamuel flew!

"Finally, the time came. About nine earth months after Gabriel had visited Mary, Mary and Joseph went to Bethlehem and found an economy motel."

"You mean a stable, don't you, Grandpa?" Joshua questioned. He had never heard Miss Debbie tell the story quite like his grandfather did, but she always said Mary and Joseph stayed in a stable.

"I guess so," Grandpa Roger said with a sigh. "But remember, this is my story."

"Okay," he agreed. "What's next?"

Grandpa Roger continued, "Mary and Joseph found a stable to stay in because there was no room for them at the motel. So, the baby Jesus was born there. At the same time, shepherds were tending their flocks at night on a hillside just a little way from Bethlehem, when who should appear streaking across the sky but Chamuel!

"Slowing down, he stopped right in front of them so he didn't scare the sheep. 'Hi, guys! Hi, sheep!' he said. 'Hey, don't be afraid. I have great news for you! Listen closely: This very night is born to you and for everyone else in the whole wide world, in the city of David—that's another name for Bethlehem, by the way—a Savior—that means "Christ the Lord,"—and his parents are calling him "Jesus."'

"Chamuel's smile was radiant as he continued. 'If you need help finding Him—because there are a lot of stables in Bethlehem—He's lying in a cow's manger behind the Inn on Bethlehem Boulevard on the north side of town. You can't miss it!' He had made sure to say the last part very slowly so the shepherds didn't miss a thing. 'You got it?'

"'Got it,' said the boss shepherd. 'Inn. Stable, Bethlehem. North side of town. Savior. Yup. I think WE have it.'

"'Yep, you have it,' responded Chamuel. Then he did exactly as Gabriel had told him to do before they came to earth. He flapped his wings twice, and a lot of angels appeared, singing songs to honor the baby Jesus' birth."

That was smiling. "He sure did a good job, huh, Grandpa?"

"He sure did," Grandpa Roger answered. "In fact, he did such a good job that God and Gabriel used him many more times to deliver messages. To this day, there are people who will tell you that, on a clear night, if you look outside, you'll see a streak of light every so often that travels across the sky. Some will call it a shooting star, but we know—"

He was just about ready to deliver a big finish to his story when that shouted out with glee, "It's Chamuel! It's Chamuel! Isn't it, Grandpa?"

"Yes, yes, you rascal!" he said, giving that a tight squeeze and then doing the same to Annie and Joshua. Then he added a slightly modified ending. "And so, if you look carefully in the night sky and see a streak of light whizzing by, it just might be Chamuel delivering another message that could be coming directly to you from God or Gabriel. The end."

"I liked your story," Joshua said. "I'll tell Miss Debbie. Maybe she'll ask you to come tell it to our Sunday school class."

"How about my class?" Annie squealed. "My class. My class!"

"We'll see. Now let's go ask Grandma for some biscuits," Grandpa Roger suggested.

"Yeah!" they all shouted and marched into the kitchen with crunching sounds beneath their feet.

As they did, just beyond their picture window, a streak of light paused for a second or two in front of the house. And then it was off again like a flash, its message delivered.

Chapter 3

A Child with No Name

Glossary of Terms and References

Navajo names for boys and girls in this story have also been used for their adult names. Their meanings include the following:

Abalone Shell: One of the four sacred mountains in Navajo belief

Ahiga: Name meaning He fights

Arroyo: Canyon

Athabascan: Ancestors (They were believed to have formed the language of the Navajo and the Apache who, at one time, were the same people.)

Atsá: Name meaning Eagle

Bisahalani: Name meaning Orator

Churro: Lamb or sheep

Clan: A word often used to mean "family"

Dibé: A proper name meaning Lamb

Diné: Referring to the people

Doli: Name meaning Bluebird

Ever-changing Woman: Represents nature

Glittering World: The world where humans live

Hózhó: Perfect order (A person's good deeds can help maintain order, while thoughtlessness destroys it. Fortunately, thoughtfulness helps restore it.)

Liná: Name meaning Life

Mesas: Flat-topped hill with steep sides

Nakai: Mexican people

Niyol: Name meaning Wind

Ooljee: Name meaning Moon

Pueblo: an American Indian settlement of the southwestern US

Shaman: Holy Man

Shicheii: Grandfather

Shilah: Brother

Shiye: Son

The Evil Way: A chant to ward off evil

The Right Way: Living life the right way (This pleases the Creator and the Son, also known as the Talking God.)

Tibah: Name meaning Gray Travois: Framed structure used to pull heavy loads (sled)

Tsé: Grandfather, the narrator, whose name means Rock

Yiska: Grandson of the narrator whose name means The Night has Passed

Yei: Holy people (like angels)

While a cool breeze from the cottonwoods swept around them, Yiska looked up at his grandfather and asked him, "Grandfather, where did the sheep come from?" He said this thoughtfully as he sat beside his grandfather near the warmth of the evening fire, hoping for a story.

Tsé waited in silence until the winds passed through the arms of the cottonwoods, bringing a quiet space for the story to be told. "That is a good question, Yiska," Tsé answered, pausing to see just how curious his grandson might be.

"Tell me, please?" Yiska asked again, speaking slowly to not show disrespect or reveal any impatience. "Where did the sheep come from?"

"Our sheep came from the Havasupai village." Tsé smiled, knowing only too well his grandson's real question was burrowed deep into the canyon wall. "The herder, Hawk, sold them to me and your grandmother."

"Please tell me the story of how our people first came to have sheep." Yiska was not sure if his grandfather was testing him or if he wasn't really interested in telling the story again, so he added, "I wish to know more: How the sheep came. How the horse came. How your great-grandfather and great-grandmother first heard the Messenger, and how the Messenger changed the lives of our people even to this day."

"You have many questions, grandson," Tsé said. "There is no one answer to any question. There are only stories."

Yiska hoped he would continue.

He did. "This story, I will tell you. As certain as the earth and sky bless the sheep we raise, the corn we grow, and the horses we ride, our stories will be bundled together into our beliefs. The answers to your questions, like kernels of corn held tightly together, are not bound by time because they are just as important to us today as they were: first to the Athabascan, then to the Holy Earth People, followed by the Diné—the children of the Holy People—and finally, grandson, they came to our time and our people."

Yiska gave an inward sigh of relief since it was obvious he was going to get the story he wanted to hear after all.

"Time is not important in our story," his grandfather said. "The songs we sing are prayers to the Yei and the Creator. The 'Blessing' song is special because it is a prayer for a long and happy life. The story cannot be heard until it *sees* we are ready. My son, are your ears opened so your heart might take you into the story?"

Yiska opened his ears wider for hearing, his mind for understanding, and his heart to go into the story with his grandfather. Finally, with a smile, he replied, 'Yes, Grandfather. I am ready."

Tsé waited until the winds passed through the arms of the cottonwoods, bringing a quiet space to tell the story. When the story was ready, he began.

"When the Nakai came, many thought they were brought here by the Trickster to punish our people. But meanwhile, some of our elders saw their great power as gifts from the Creator.

"We know these thoughts are like stories tossed in the winds and then trapped in the cottonwoods of the arroyos. And so, they linger, calling out to some who pass by, hoping to lure them into their presence so they can breathe again. But they are without roots, so they will not last.

"The Nakai came and brought us suffering, disease, and their shamans, who used sacred words. Some of these Word Speakers were thieves of our people's souls and were crueler than their warriors. Others were as wise as our own holy ones, but they came later.

"In the early days of our story, the Nakai Word Speakers did not care very much for our stories or beliefs. They cared nothing for our people except to enslave us or tell us we were wrong and had to be taught. They treated us like children in order to be obedient to their gods. They called us heathens. They carved their gods and symbols on pieces of cottonwood and paraded them through our villages. They shamed us by forcing us to sing the songs they brought with them, but their ears were closed to our own songs of praising the Creator for creation and our prayers for hózhó. They laughed at our prayer sticks and broke them and then threw them into the fire. Our beliefs and words for the four sacred mountains were called foolish, and they whipped or beat us if we mentioned them.

"One day, the Trickster brought some Word Speakers without the Nakai warriors to our village on the mesa of Canyon de Chelly, and they asked about our stories. At first, our shaman did not speak for fear of the people being punished, but after a while, they sat with the Word Speakers and told them how our ancestors came from the fourth world, or Glittering World. They spoke of the Creator, also known as the Talking God, and how hózhó, or perfect harmony, is strengthened by good deeds. They also said that every part of the day is recognized with song and prayer.

"Then, with looks of sadness, they spoke of how hózhó had almost been destroyed by the first Word Speakers (who came with the Nakai) because of their cruelty and refusal to respect our holy ones or elders.

"It is said that the Word Speakers cried and asked our people to forgive them for their brothers' misdeeds. Then they asked if your great-grandfather, the storyteller, would give them a blessing and offer a prayer for their journey.

"Because they had respected our grandmothers and grandfathers, who now live without time, our storyteller said that he and his people would listen to the Word Speaker's stories. The Word Speakers told how the Talking God, whom they call Jesus, came from the Creator to the fourth world to restore and give a way for hózhó to never be lost in our world. The Word Speakers said that Jesus was the first Word, who has always been in Life with the Creator.

"Our grandfathers and grandmothers heard these stories about the Creator and the Talking God, and they believed them to be true because the stories honored their own beliefs. The hearts of the Diné opened wide for this hearing and believing, and to this day, we believe as well."

"But, Grandfather," Yiska wanted to know, "what about the Trickster? How can he bring the Nikai and bad Word Speakers one time, but then bring the good Word Speakers another time with words and beliefs we cherish now?"

"I'm not sure," Tsé said sincerely. "I'm not sure that the Trickster always brings just the good or the bad. I believe how we see and experience what happens to us influences what power we give the Trickster for the good or bad happenings in our lives. We all have the power to either upset the hózhó around us or cherish the balance. All creatures have a responsibility to maintain the Glittering World our Creator has given us."

"Oh," Yiska said quietly. Then, he blurted out, "But Grandfather, the Nikai . . . they are—"

Since Tsé knew what his grandson was going to say, his interruption was only meant to remind the young one. "Remember, Yiska, the Nikai choose how they will act. The Word Speakers who honored our people with respect were also Nikai, and it was the Nikai who brought the churro and the return of the horse to our land. Until then, the Diné were earth walkers and hunters. They moved about with their travois pulled by dogs. Yet after they came, our grandfathers saw it as a sacred mission to take back their horses, and our grandmothers and the children became herders of the churro.

"Our women soon learned that the wool of the long-legged churro was good for clothes and blankets. They learned to weave from the Pueblos. Our people soon acquired a good many churro and horses, so we started to build hogans and then stayed. Soon, we planted corn, beans, and squash, and the trees in the arroyos and on the mesas gave us fruit to eat.

"Before long, our ancestors were great sheepherders and horse owners. But the Nakai kept coming, and after them, others came from across a great body of water. That's when the hózhó became out of balance once again."

Tsé did not speak his last words directly to Yiska. He was already turning toward Abalone Shell, one of the sacred mountains to the west, to which he softly sang a healing prayer.

When he was done, he gave his grandson a small sad smile. "Do not worry. I have not forgotten. You have asked for a story, and so we will both listen. This story is about a young warrior, Atsá (your great-great-grandfather), and his young bride, Liná."

Yiska gave a very slight but very real sigh of relief.

"For some reason unknown to Atsá," his grandfather, once again back into the story, continued, "the deer appeared scarce, even though he had spent most of the day hunting. It was not until the sun began to slip behind the Abalone Shell in the west that he brought down a buck.

"Atsá gave the blessing song, thanking the Creator and Holy People for hózhó, which had guided him. Then, laying the deer across his back, he started back toward the village. He knew Liná would be waiting for him. She would smile and quietly speak of his skill as a hunter and warrior to be able to bring back such a feast—more than enough for them. They would have meat to share and a fine skin from which to make his boots for the winter, which was even now winding its way through the small arroyo the outsiders called Canyon de Chilly.

"The trail he followed led up to the mesa where their village rested. It was a familiar walk, yet something was out of place. He was not hearing sounds from the sheep or horses that by now should be in the stockade outside the group of houses.

"Although the day's hunt had tired him, Atsá was steady on his feet as he began the steep ascent that opened onto the mesa while the winds broke overhead. When he happened to look up, he saw a raven, which started talking to him while circling overhead. Atsá wondered what it might be saying, but his sometime friend known as the Trickster did not repeat himself. Instead, it circled once more and then flew back in the direction he came.

"This alarmed Atsá, and he quickened his pace.

"At first, the sound came across faintly, like a churro crying when stuck on a ledge or caught in a thicket. But it wasn't a churro. Just before his path could disappear into the canyon wall, Atsá turned sharply to the right, where the way opened wider. It was there he found his very pregnant Liná standing in the shadow of the canyon wall with only a few of the young and old. To his ears their crying, as tears dropping to the ground, sounded like the mourning song mixed with fear. A few female churro and two dogs stood silently at their side.

"'Liná! Liná! What has happened?' Atsá called out as he dropped his kill to the side and ran toward her.

"'The Nakai—'she sobbed. 'Atsá, the Nakai came. Our men tried to fight them off, but they are now so few and the Nakai so many. They killed the old ones, young women—'

"Liná paused, and tears of pain and disbelief swelled inside a deep moan that came out of her heart to Atsá's ears.

"'They killed almost all of the children,' she managed to get out. 'The little ones tried to run and hide, but the Nakai caught them. They took all of our horses and all but the three female churro you now see. So many came.' Her voice broke. 'Iron men.' It broke again. 'There was no warning. They took our warriors, our young men, away in chains to be used as slaves. They took all of the young women to be sold or to keep for themselves. We know that is why they took so many. What will we do, Atsá?'

"Liná's voiced faded altogether as she buried her face into her husband's chest. He held her tight, afraid to let go until she was ready. They both knew from the stories of the elders that the Nakai were never satisfied until they took everything and left no one behind. So, they realized they must hurry because the enemy would be back to chase after the few survivors left, regardless of how few there were.

"That's why Liná did not cry on him for long. Yet before she left his embrace, they both felt the kick from inside her. Atsá allowed a look of determination to cross his face as he whispered to Liná, 'Our child will be safe. I promise.'

"'I know. I know,' Liná whispered back, hoping he did not see the fear that still gripped her attention.

"Ahiga, the only boy child to survive, had been slowly approaching them, and he now wrapped his small arms around Atsá's leg before he started to cry. As he cried, his slender body began to shiver.

"'Hey, little one,' Atsá said as he bent down to lift him into his arms. 'You are cold. I have a warm coat for you.' Atsá held Ahiga tightly with one arm and, with the other, threw off his buckskin jacket to wrap around the child. He did not have to ask where his parents were because he already knew they were no more.

"Then he turned to Liná. 'We must be quick. We need to find a new home. I know the arroyos as the old ones do. I know now the Trickster was warning me of danger. Maybe he has been sent by the Creator and the Yei to help us. Maybe he will lead us to a safe place.'

"'Atsá, how can he?' she wailed, her voice filled with sorrow. Liná made it clear she was not as strong a believer in the Trickster's potential helpfulness. 'He did not save us from the Nakai. Where was he when they came? Where was he when the Nakai killed—?'

"Liná fell quiet as she looked beyond Atsá to the three other children.

"'We will see,' Atsá said. Then, as an afterthought, he added, 'I want to believe the Trickster is sent by our Creator and Yei. But now—'

"For the first time, he allowed his eyes to survey the small band who was with Liná. Along with Ahiga who stood at his side, there were two young girls, Dibé and her sister Doli, who were tightly clinging to an elder, Tibah. Both Tibah and Ooljee, the only other apparent surviving grandmothers, were known to be skilled weavers and sheepherders.

"Meanwhile, the only surviving grandfather was Niyol, who was a shaman (holy man). Miraculously, these six individuals and Liná had escaped the massacre. But as Niyol now warned them, the Nikai saw them flee and would come in pursuit. They would not want anyone left behind to tell the story of their awful deed.

"Apart from the two dogs, three female churros were all that remained of their entire herd, coming along on instinct as Tibah and Ooljee fled the terror. Other than that, everyone had managed to carry a little something out of the village—items they now held ever so tightly like priceless treasure. Their assorted collection included a small basket of corn, bread baked for the morning, a shearing knife, and the kind of hooks needed to cut and weave churro wool. Niyol also had his colors for the paintings that, when used with prayer and song, brought the Yei and opened the Creator's ears. That was it, though.

"'Dibé and Doli, come with me,' Atsá said. 'We must gather some branches to make travois for Dog and Wolf.'

"Fortunately, the little girls giggled when they heard him name the dogs, who'd had no names before. As fear loosened its grip on them, their fingers also slipped from Tibah's hand so they could follow Atsá, who carefully stood Ahiga back on the ground.

"'Ahiga, stay and help Niyol make ready for our move,' he instructed. 'Watch and listen closely, shiye. I know you will protect them.'

"While they were working, Atsá kept Dibé and Doli's ears full of stories about his aunts and uncles and the elders of their village. He told them of the Tewa, who lived in stone houses along the cliffs, and how the Diné were first called the Nabahu, which means 'planted fields' by the Tewa.

"Dibé and Doli listened as they worked with Atsá, and in a short time, the branches were gathered. Atsá continued to hold their interest by showing them how to make the travois. When they were finished, he let Dibé and Doli harness Wolf and Dog to their travois. Their smiles brought a sense of comfort to Atsá . He marveled at how something so simple as what they'd just done could offer a sliver of light amidst the darkness and fear the children had so recently experienced.

"Dog and Wolf stood obediently still as Atsá and the small clan carefully but quickly loaded the two travois. When they were finished, Niyol took a few crumbs of bread and held them gently in his hand while facing the east. After he let go of the crumbs, the wind picked them up and carried them away.

"'Creator, accept this gift. Protect us now. Take us to a safe place here our enemies cannot discover us.' Niyol ended his prayer with a chant telling the Creator, 'Now that we have shared our bread and Your stomach is full, we know You will most certainly want to walk with us.' He bowed his head before turning to the remnants of their clan. 'It is time.'

"'It is time,' Atsá agreed, and then whistled to make Dog and Wolf move forward at a quick pace. Overhead, he heard the cry of a raven—the Trickster—flying past.

"'He smelled the crumbs,' Liná mused aloud.

"'I am sure the Talking God has found our gift by now,' Niyol reassured them all, using his name for the Creator when the two of them converse during his visions.

"As a hunter and leader for his clan, unlike Niyol and Liná, Astá had both good and bad experiences with the Trickster. So, as he said, 'It's time to go,' his eyes also carefully traced the Trickster's trail ahead of them. 'We must move quickly!' Both Niyol and Liná nodded in agreement. Then he looked directly at Niyol with an unspoken question: *What does his appearing mean?*

"Instead of hope, he only found the shaman's face filled with apprehension, along with his words, 'Atsá has spoken correctly! We must hurry.'

"They traveled a steady pace for several hours, with Atsá leading his new family through interconnecting arroyos. If the Nakai were following, he had to make the trail harder for them. That meant familiar sights like the Little Colorado River seemed so far away now. Yet somehow, Atsá knew he was moving in the right direction.

"He followed almost invisible trails of the shilah—the deer and other animals of the arroyos and mesas. As they walked, he once again felt the wind door opening enough that he could catch a glimpse of the Trickster circling them, spiraling upward on the side of the arroyo.

"Atsá traced the raven's journey until his eyes fell upon a broken trail he knew they must follow. By then, he had long since stopped wondering if the Trickster was pointing the way either to safety or harm. All he knew was he must find a safe place. So, after ascending the trail for a short distance, he turned back to Liná and the others.

"'I think I have found another trail we can follow.' He made sure to keep his words soft yet deliberate. 'Hopefully, it will lead us to a safe place.'

"'Did you see the Trickster?' Liná sounded mistrustful.

"'I did,' Atsá said, offering no further explanation.

"'Was he hungry?' Doli asked innocently, even while her stomach growled some more.

"'I'm not sure.' Atsá smiled easily as he touched Doli's face. Then, with words that were becoming so familiar, he said, 'We must go,' while he bent down for Ahiga to climb upon his back.

"Dibé grasped Ooljee's outstretched hand, while Tibah reached for Doli's. At the same time, both women carefully balanced the bundles on their backs. With Atsá's help, Liná was up on her feet, gripping the cottonwood staff that Niyol had found for her to help steady her walk.

"Now, understanding the unspoken message in Atsá's words, without asking he tied another braided strap to each of the travois, securing their loads even more tightly for the journey ahead.

"Wolf and Dog must have sensed the change coming, too. They were up from their short rest and ready even before Atsá whistled for them. The sound of Niyol's prayer song for safety accompanied them as he led the group around the next sharp bend and onto an ascent that gave no promise of leveling.

"After the prayer song ended, there were no more sounds from either adult or child. It was as if the small group's entire collective strength was needed to concentrate on sure footing for the trail. Even when Ooljee stepped on a jagged rock and the pain ran up her leg, she caught the scream before it could escape her mouth by biting down hard on her lips.

"Nonetheless, Niyol, seeing the pain dance across her forehead, quickly took hold of Dibé's hand so Ooljee could steady herself again. The older woman could feel the blood on the bottom of her foot from the rock's gash through both her moccasin and flesh.

"'I will be all right,' she said with a smile while Niyol extended his empty hand to her for the three of them to continue the climb.

"'Will we be safe, Grandfather?' Dibé inquired, looking up toward Niyol.

"At first, hearing the young girl speak sounded very strange to Niyol, and he could not answer. He wanted the words to come out—his hesitation came from his desire to be sure he said the right words to bring comfort without false promises.

"'We are on The Right Way, Granddaughter,' he finally answered.

"'The Right Way?' Dibé asked in a very hushed voice. 'What does that mean?'

"They continued their steady pace even while Niyol responded. 'The Right Way has been given to us by the Word Speaker, the Son of our Creator, who is the Talking God. It is the way He taught us to live our lives through the teachings of the Talking God.'

"Even in the midst of their flight and the possible dangers surrounding them, Dibé's mind seemed to become more unsettled by Niyol's words. 'What about Ooljee and Tibah? What about Doli and the baby Liná carries? Will the Nakai take The Right Way from us?' She sniffled. 'I am afraid, Grandfather. Where is the Word Speaker now?'

"That was a question even Niyol had asked himself already. *Where are You, Word Speaker? Is our danger from our own doing, or does it come from the thoughtlessness of those who rob the hózhó of its gifts for their own selfish use?* Yet each time he asked that question, he always came back to trusting that the Word Speaker had never betrayed nor abandon the Diné, nor any who sought hózhó. He knew the Word Speaker walked with them.

"Niyol also believed there was something sacred about the Trickster, even though now he was aware of Atsá's uneasiness whenever the Trickster appeared. In his own vision quest, during his transition from childhood to manhood, Niyol understood he would become a holy man for his people. He had viewed the Trickster as the Creator's messenger. Niyol believed it carried the Talking God and Word Speaker's word to the hearts of the Diné. Of that, he was very confident, yet he realized his pause must have seemed very long to Dibé.

"'Dibé, The Right Way is in your mind's heart, and with The Right Way comes the Word Speaker. The Creator breathed life into the first Glittering World-walkers. The Creator's breath also gave all people the way to know right from wrong. Choosing The Right Way pleases the Creator. Since that time, The Right Way has been born in each of us, like the presence of the Word Speaker, although it can grow stronger or weaker through choices we make.'

"This didn't seem to assure Dibé, whose young voice shivered in apprehension at the very thought of following the wrong path. 'How do I know to make the right choices? The Nakai took my mother and father. Who will now teach me to grow The Right Way you say lives in my heart?'

"Niyol gently smiled down at the child. 'You will know, granddaughter. Your grandmothers and grandfathers—the Yei—your elders, and all of us have a responsibility to guide you.'

"Ooljee, who had been listening carefully to Dibé and Niyol, took the opportunity to affirm his words to the child. 'We are your family now,' she said. 'Atsá and Liná are your parents. Doli, Ahiga, and you are their children, just as they have spoken and given their word to the clan.'

"Dibé looked as if she would ask another question, but Niyol knew they needed to be alert to what was around them. He held onto her hand more firmly to steady her pace. 'Come now. We must not trail behind.'

"'Yes, Grandfather,' Dibé answered, sounding more confident now that her fears could be met with not only her own courage, but also the love and courage of her new clan and elders. 'We are not alone. Thank you, Word Speaker,' she sang, seemingly to herself.

"Niyol smiled deeply.

"Time was passing quickly, but at the pace Atsá was traveling, his small family could not keep up. Only the three long-legged churro were able to manage the climb, much better than Dog and Wolf who were now laboring beneath the weight of the travois. Breathing heavily, with their tongues flapping out of the sides of their mouths, they still were obedient to their master's intermittent call to stay the course.

"After watching Liná struggle for a while, and glancing at Ooljee, who was bearing heavily on her uninjured leg, Tibah called out respectfully, 'Atsá?'

"Atsá understood her concern without having to hear another word. 'We must rest,' he said, whistling to Dog and Wolf to stop. By that point, the longer-legged creatures knew the whistle commands too, and they turned back to the small party without being coaxed to come rest beside the dogs.

"'It won't be much longer,' Liná said when Atsá's hand on her stomach was greeted with a strong kick.

"Tibah came to Liná's side and touched her stomach as well, and then wiped at the younger woman's brow. 'The little one inside her is strong, and our journey is preparing him. He will come soon,' Tibah said, turning to Atsá and then urging him, 'We must make preparations. This is not a good place for the baby to come. There is no protection here.'

"'I know, Grandmother. We must travel a little longer,' Atsá responded.

"'I will find a place ahead of us,' Niyol declared. 'I will send the prayer song. In a little while, follow that song. It will come from the wind.' He turned to smile in Dibé's direction. 'You will know it when you hear it.'

"Atsá let him go, knowing he would find a safe place. Yet his worried eyes still traveled upward to search the late afternoon sky. Right then, the small group found themselves in a widening respite on the narrow pathway, with sheer rock on one side and a drop off on the other. His view regarding what was before them was limited but focused. Searching for something, possibly a sign that they were truly on the right path, his eyes came back empty, even though he had no time to dwell on it.

"'We must move on. We will hear Niyol's song carried by The Right Way if we move in the direction he went.' Atsá was already walking toward Dog and Wolf. And, without a word, Doli and Dibé steadied Liná as she rose from her resting place.

"Liná smiled down at the girls. 'How little and young you are, my daughters, yet you are showing such strength, courage, and love. The Yei are pleased with your thoughtfulness.'

"Tibah, meanwhile, assisted Ooljee to her feet. With the support of a staff and Ahiga, who came to help, they moved forward again as a clan.

"For his part, Niyol was wasting no time as he moved from where he'd left his people to the winding and jagged path ahead of him. It seemed to him that the Creator had been a bit mischievous in carving the mountain's landscape.

"He thought of the creatures and the Ever-changing Woman, who had helped to create and walk the trail before the two-legged, even though at times the path was very narrow. The four-legged would have to be very cautious and surefooted to not slip and fall here, he recognized.

"With that in mind, Niyol quietly sang a song of thanks to the Creator and the Ever-changing Woman. Then he asked the Yei to provide safe walking for himself and his clan that would soon follow.

"At other times, the path changed from being a very narrow and treacherous path to a smooth and even one as it ascended upward. The Yei and Ever-changing Woman must have traveled this part of the trail many times to make it so easy to walk. And then there was the twist that brought him right up against a stone-cold wall of granite, looking for all the world like it was the end of Creation.

"Niyol stood as still as the rock he was staring at, letting his mind rest so his spirit might invite the Word Speaker to listen. With confidence, he began to sing another prayer song, this time asking the Word Speaker to give the wind a voice and open his eyes so he would see the way.

"He sang for some time while standing a short distance from the mountain face until it seemed he was moving beyond the path into a vision. After his song grew quiet and he had stood in silence for many breaths, the Trickster suddenly appeared, flying right toward the mountain wall just a short distance from where Niyol stood. In a vision just before their journey had started, he had seen the Trickster flying toward the mountain wall and disappear, only to reappear in a short while as if he had somehow gone into the granite wall and came out again. His vision had given him confidence their small party would be safe, but something that had not been answered and still troubled him was the presence of the wind wearing a face and chasing after the Trickster.

"Now the Trickster called out to Niyol with raven's words that were still somehow understandable. 'Look! Look!' the Trickster cried, 'Don't step out into the sky, but turn toward the wall and follow me. Take the step, and you will see the place that you and all should be.' With those words, the winged being flew right into the mountain—and disappeared.

"Niyol moved slowly toward the wall to see what had happened, only to discover the granite face had taken a slight turn that could not be seen from where he had been standing a few feet away. Yet when Niyol took those additional steps, the path opened up to a small mesa, which seemed to rise from the center of the mountain.

"Niyol had seen this place once before. It came earlier in the vision he had before they left the village, but until now he had not fully comprehended its mystery. In his vision, the opening was a burning path he was walking on, but his feet were not even warm. He rubbed his eyes to be certain he was not back inside the vision, as well as reassure himself that the Trickster was not playing with his mind. Despite those concerns, when he opened his eyes, everything was as he'd last seen it.

"A few cottonwood and piñon trees were standing without sound despite how Niyol both felt and heard the wind whispering around him: a beautiful and peaceful scene. Suddenly, something brushed against the left side of his face, causing him to be startled. Turning as quickly as he could, he found himself even more disturbed to find the Trickster perfectly paused in mid-air.

"'Stay, stay!' it cried without human speech. 'Sing and pray! Sing and chant The Evil Way to be gone so no harm comes to you today.'

"With the message delivered, it flew back through the crack in the granite wall. Awed as he was, Niyol's mind tried to process how the raven could understand that The Evil Way chant held the sacred words honored by the Yei to ward off evil. Yet, despite the confusion, his mouth was already moving to obey what he had heard. When he was done, he next sang a request to the Creator, asking that his small clan be brought safely through the crack in the wall.

"Then he picked up a handful of the mesa's spirit, lifted it into the air, and let it dribble from his hands. While he continued to sing, the whispering wind lifted the mesa's spirit to carry it through the same opening the Messenger had departed through. With that sign accepted, Niyol went on to work at making an open-sided shelter from brush, piñon, and cottonwood branches, all the while re-chanting The Evil Way and asking the Creator, 'Bless this small place, free from fear. Protect those who come to find shelter here.'

"It wasn't the hogan, but it would nonetheless provide protection from Ever-changing Woman's behavior, as it looked like rain was coming in. In which case, Ooljee, the children, and especially Liná would certainly need a safe place. That realization kept Niyol moving to ready the place.

"As the night seemed to close up the sky, he caught the sound of Wolf and Dog panting shortly before he saw Atsá and Ahiga through the crack in the wall. 'You are riding the wind, my shiyes,' he told them. 'I did not even hear you enter. It was only the sound of the dogs that gave you away.'

"'It might be that night covers our walk, Grandfather.' Atsá smiled as he and Ahiga helped Liná and Ooljee through. Before long, the two women were resting under the shelter. Dibé and Doli guided the churro to the very small but sufficient corral Niyol had fashioned out of brush tied together with strips of rawhide he carried in the sacred pouch tied around his waist.

"'There is little left to eat,' Tibah said while unpacking a small bundle she had taken from the travois.

"'I collected some piñon nuts when I asked the pine for her branches.' Niyol handed them over, yet his gaze was already traveling over to the long-legged churro.

"Liná shook her head. 'No, Grandfather. We will do fine with a meal of corn and piñons. Atsá has found Ever-changing Woman's tears in a small pool, which has given us enough to drink our fill. We will feast, and our bellies will be full, leaving the churro to provide us with fine blankets and clothes instead.'

"'They are too bony to eat anyway,' Doli said, surprising everyone with her clever words.

"After they had eaten, Niyol made a painting for healing with the help of the fire's light. He then sang a prayer song for Ooljee and the Blessing Way for Liná.

"It appeared she would need that sooner rather than later when he awoke to the sound of her sharp cry. Rising quickly, he found Tibah and Ooljee were already awake and tending to her.

"'The baby will come,' Tibah told him. 'Maybe he will come before dawn. Liná's time is hard, and it would be good if you sang the Blessing Way again.'

"'I will,' he assured her, then he took a few steps into the darkness. 'The Yei will help me open wide the heart of the Word Speaker so Liná will be safe.'

"The children did not wake until a burst of thunder broke loose from the mesa's roof, chased by a jagged horse that hit higher up on the granite wall and rode away, only to come back again and again. In its light, Doli and Dibé found their way to Liná's side, while Ahiga took his place with Atsá.

"In the custom of their ancestors, the Athabaskans, Tibah untied Liná's hair to give the baby an easier path into the Glittering World. She sent Doli out into the falling raindrops to loosen the rawhide straps that held the corral's brush gate shut. As it opened, the three long-legged churros stepped forward. For a few seconds, they stood still before moving, not out of the enclosure as would be expected. Instead, they crowded beneath the shelter near Liná.

"Without knowing—or maybe they did know—the churros offered warmth and protection to the expecting mother.

"The waiting wasn't easy. Waiting is never easy, but it is often necessary. It is a time for preparing. Rushing life is like rushing the Blessing or Evil Way songs and chants. You can easily miss the spaces in between, which are meant for thinking and experiencing. You then fail to see through the heart's spirit window into places where thoughtfulness unfolds toward The Right Way. Even for the small clan clustered together on this journey, waiting would take its time—time enough to prepare and embrace what they thought was to come.

"It seemed the Ever-changing Woman was very disturbed. Her words continued to ride the streaking horses through the dark sky, crisscrossing time and again to hit the mesa's floor or its granite walls, filling the Diné ears with deafening sounds.

"Atsá folded his concerns into his own words and gave them to Niyol. 'Grandfather, what does it mean?'

"'I am not sure, my shiye,' Niyol answered as they both turned to look through the falling rain again. 'We must be careful. This is all I know.'

"An hour or so seemed to pass into the night, but it did not take Ever-changing Woman's presence with it. She seemed to hold the skies under her command, but for a few minutes she allowed the rain to dance more lightly. And then, unexpectedly, she let out another thunderous roar, unbridling the jagged horses once again so their lances of silver flung even more fiercely, signaling the Ever-changing Woman's tantrum was still wide awake.

"With the hours passing on, Liná finally let out a loud and long pressing cry, followed by a soft and tender moan. During all of the noise Ever-changing Woman was making, it was a brief comfort for all of them to hear the final birth pangs of a human.

"Atsá, Niyol, and Ahiga's ears soon heard shouts of joy and a chorus of words exclaiming, 'It's a boy!' Liná's heart eyes knew before his birth. 'She is blessed. The Creator has rested a hand over her shiye. He too has been blest.'

"Atsá moved to Liná's side, embracing her and his new son while Niyol sang a prayer song thanking the Creator.

"That's when Tibah left Liná and went to Wolf's travois, quickly returning with a small woven blanket. Liná looked very surprised as the older woman took the small baby and carefully wrapped him in the woolen cloth.

"'It's a gift from the churro,' Tibah said. 'I don't think they noticed their own body blankets are shorter now.' Finishing with a smile, she laid the boy child next to his mother.

"'How? Time?' Atsá's disjointed words accompanied his puzzled look.

"'Ooljee, Dibé, Doli, and I found the spaces of time where no one else was looking,' she said with a mischievous grin.

"In their joy and excitement, no one noticed the Ever-changing Woman had settled into a calmer mood, allowing the first moment of real peace they had experienced in a long time. It was followed by a blanket of security that wrapped itself around their tiny mesa. Yet, as peace and security can sometimes be, the moments they held were fragile and all too brief.

"The first sound to alert Atsá's ears was the bleating of the long-legged as they turned from the shelter and looked out into the darkness. Then Wolf and Dog turned in the same direction to cautiously growl, telling him of unseen danger coming through the kinds of sounds and smells that creatures always understood before their masters did. As Atsá moved into the darkness toward the crack in the wall, he began to hear the familiar clanging of metal and the neighing sound of weary horses.

"'Grandfather!' he exclaimed. 'The Nakai! They have found their way. How were they able to—?' Atsá asked in a distressed tone.

"'It is not for us to know, my shiye.' Niyol's words brought no comfort. 'We must find a way to protect Liná and the others,' he added, understanding full well that Atsá was thinking the same.

"'We, too, have heard the noise the Nakai and their horses make,'" Ahiga said as he came to stand beside Atsá and Niyol while, behind him, the grandmothers were helping Liná to her feet as she tightly held their newborn son. For their part, Doli and Dibé went to work tying rawhide straps around the necks of the long-legged and fastening Dog to his travois, leaving Wolf with Atsá and Niyol.

"'I will fight with you,' Ahiga said while clenching the lance he had been using as a staff.

"Niyol began a prayer chant to The Evil Way and then, without questioning the ways of the Creator, sang the Word Speaker's presence to stand in defense of their small group.

"As the sounds of the Nakai grew louder, they must have stirred Ever-changing Woman's rest because she once again broke the darkness with her confusing words and streaking light, though not in the body of horses this time but with lances. She hurled them against the north wall of the mesa while the crack in the granite wall stood to the west.

"'We have no way to escape,' Ooljee said, more out of reason than fear.

"'Liná is too weak to walk. She cannot even travel with help. The baby needs nursing,' Tibah said. Yet they all knew staying where they were meant certain death.

"Even in the earlier days of their escape, there were no answers as to why the Nakai destroyed their village and killed its people. Still, no answers came to help them in their present danger, and no words were brought to their understanding to give them peace. Even if the answers had come, the immediate danger would not have given them ears to hear what they had to say.

"Strange as it was, Atsá saw him first—the Messenger, who truly seemed to be the Trickster at the moment. He was circling above the first Nakai rider and horse to come into view. The horse's breath was much labored, and it seemed it was blowing its very spirit out of its body as it started to come through the crack in the wall.

"Without hesitation, Niyol pulled a few colored precious stones from his sacred pouch and, with all his might, flung them toward the north wall. Their clattering sent his prayers and those of his clan to the ears of the Creator and the Yei. As the stones began to fall toward the mesa's floor, the Yei swooped down to gather them and then, with one breath, blow upon the tiny rocks.

"In an instant, a rainbow-colored cloud enveloped the stones. The grandmothers stood calmly on both sides of Liná as she held her new son tightly in her arms while Dibé and Doli hid behind the grandmother's skirts. The small girls shivered as they each dared to peek from behind the skirts to see what was happening. For his part, Ahiga felt himself standing tall between Atsá and Niyol. His curiosity and willingness to surrender his young life to defend his new family made him ignore his own fear.

"The clan stood motionless while the Nakai continued to move through the crack in the wall. Time seemed suspended as they watched what was happening before them. It started with a heavy breathing that came from inside the cloud and then progressed to a pounding like the stamping of a hundred horses. Only one streaking riderless silver horse came out of the cloud. But what a horse it was!

"Its feet moved so swiftly they could barely be seen with human eyes, but they all heard the loud but not intrusive clattering of his hoofs beating upon the granite floor. It looked confidently toward Atsá with the gentle eyes of a steed that stands before his master, then it rocketed from their view upward into the heavens like a winged warrior. Yet even before Atsá could look to Niyol for its meaning, the majestic silver horse reappeared, only this time coming quietly and gently by Atsá and Liná's side.

"While calling up to the heavens, the raven reversed its course to head back toward where the jet horse came into their view. In the power of the Spirit, Atsá heard the raven crying out to Ever-changing Woman to help him, and her ears were open to the sounds he made. She answered his cry by taking aim and splitting a streaking lance in two through the air. One side of the spear headed toward the clan, landing directly in front of where the horse stood by Atsá. The other struck the granite floor in front of the first Nakai. Both rider and horse burst into an eye-blinding ball of fire, causing the Nakai who followed great confusion and halting their advance through the wall.

"Yet, on the other side of the fire, the raven and clan were not affected by the bright light. The raven swooped down over Niyol's head, calling with sounds that came only to his ears before heading toward the canyon wall once again—this time, however, through a new opening in the north wall.

"'Come quickly!' Niyol said, seeing this. 'The Yei and Creator have truly heard our prayers a hundredfold. We must go while Ever-changing Woman blinds the Nakai. Hurry!'

"He did not need to say more. Atsá carefully lifted Liná and their son onto the horse. Because the powerful creature's back was long and narrow, he also placed Ooljee and the sisters there. Tibah held tightly to the horse's tail with one hand, grasping Ahiga's hand with the other. In that way, the small group made no retreat but advanced without fear through their new passageway out of sight of the Nakai.

"Surprisingly, the path felt very smooth under their feet.

"Atsá stayed behind to make certain there was time for his family to put some distance between themselves and the Nakai. He did realize there was no clapping of hoofs, clanging of armor, or marching of feet in front of him, for which he was grateful. But he also knew it would only be a matter of time before the Nakai would be free of their obstacles.

"*Changing Woman has other business to tend to,* he thought. And the Yei exist to help, not to coddle us into states of helplessness.

"He knew it was not a time for them to let down their guard, and he had no intention of doing so. Yet the miracles that had come alive for them this night were filled with such wonder. When he caught up with the others, he found them to be filled with the same awe. They all seemed quicker on their feet, and the horse appeared to be full of energy. Even the sounds from Atsá and Liná's new son did not seem to be those of discomfort; instead, they were sounds filled with peace.

"As they had so many times already on this journey, Atsá's eyes were drawn to the skies. He was pleased to see that Ever-changing Woman's tantrum had remained on the other side of the mountain. On this side, she had even allowed a few eyes of the heavens to shine out from behind their pillows upon the group, with one standing out in particular.

"'Is it possible that you are one of the precious stones Niyol offered to the Yei?' Atsá asked quietly at this sight. The shining eye appeared to be the same color as the jet horse. Its silver radiance twinkled as it moved slowly forward. Spellbound, he became even more amazed to see the Messenger glide in from the same direction until it appeared to be riding on top of the twinkling eye.

"Understanding the sight to be a sign for him to follow, Atsá turned his group's steed in the same direction. The jet horse neighed as if giving his approval to the decision, and Wolf and Dog quietly nuzzled his leg as they moved forward obediently as well.

"It was with the first golden ray of dawn light from the eastern sky that Atsá saw a lone walker moving toward them. The stranger was not a Nakai; his dress was that of a Pueblo. As such, Atsá motioned for the clan to stop while he went out to greet the lone walker and see if he was on his way for good or harm. The two spoke a while from that distance, and then they kept walking, this time together, back toward the group.

"'I am Bisahalani,' the man said respectfully to Niyol. And then, in an unusual practice, he turned toward Liná and the baby, his eyes searching for something in the child's presence. 'I came before you. I was born of your people when my parents were very old: That is why I have a Diné name given to my mother by the Yei. Your grandmothers and grandfathers passed many days behind us and lodged with our families when the Nakai came for their first kill and slave trapping.'

"The clan listened to him speak.

"'The Pueblo taught the Diné how to plant corn, and your grandmothers shared their wool with our people. I am Diné in my heart and Pueblo in my walk. The Creator has sent me to bring you to our

84

lodging in the cliffs, where the Nakai have no eyes to see for now. Come, you will be safe with us.'

"When Bisahalani finished speaking, the horse gently nudged Atsá closer to the Pueblo.

"Niyol spoke as the mouth of the clan. 'We will follow you,' he said clearly. 'Your words sound like the Yei talking in my vision. I believe they have sent you to us.'

"The grandmothers and Liná nodded in approval. Atsá affirmed the words of the group with, 'We will follow as Niyol has spoken, my shilah.'

"As they went forward, Bisahalani led the way while Atsá and Niyol readily shared all they had experienced. Throughout this, Niyol could not help but notice that Ooljee no longer seemed to favor her bad leg. In fact, she appeared to have been healed of the wound.

"Seeing him watching her walking tall, she smiled. 'It's your healing song. You sing it strongly.' Then she tenderly called him 'Grandfather' even though they carried the same years.

"Niyol heard the word and let it into his heart.

"Bisahalani took the path that led through a small arroyo, which wound across the Little Colorado River several times. But in every crossing, there was no trouble for the party. They walked upon a shallow river trail and then passed through a tunnel burrowed in the east wall of the arroyo. It opened on the other side upon an upper valley with stone houses built into the mountain wall.

"'This will be your new home for as long as you desire,' Bisahalani said to the group. 'Here the Pueblo and the Diné are the same. You are now our clan, and we are yours.'

"'It is good,' Niyol said.

"After several Pueblo came to greet them, Bisahalani led them to stone houses already prepared for them. This made Atsá look to Niyol. 'How could they know we would be coming?'

"'It is a mystery, my shiye,' was all Niyol could say.

"After Liná, the children, and Atsá had time to rest in their new hogan made of stone, they heard a soft bleating at their doorway. The sound was followed by Bisahalani entering, followed by a young Pueblo girl carrying a male long-legged. Standing in front of the baby's cradle, the child said, 'The churro is a gift for you. The lamb will grow to lead your flock.'

She carefully put the lamb on the stone floor, where it stood for a few minutes. After nuzzling the baby, it found its way to where the female churro had been waiting to welcome it into their family. As was the custom of their people, Liná gave her the staff that had supported her on their journey.

"'This staff was passed down to me by my grandmother. I have used it to help guide and protect the churro,' she told her.

"The girl looked to Bisahalani first. 'May I take this gift?'

"He nodded. 'Yes, you may. Now take your sisters and brother to meet more of the children in our village. They are waiting to greet them.'

"As the children walked out onto the path again, everyone heard the familiar sound of the Messenger. They all moved to see it too, not knowing what he might do or say. Before them, the raven swirled, circling ever so tightly upward as in a spiral maze. Just before he was out of sight, he was engulfed by a small cloud and was lost. As they continued to look upward, a strange wonder occurred. At the very spot where they had last seen the raven, a beautiful dove came into their view. The dove descended toward them and came to rest on the cradle of the baby, and then before their eyes, it disappeared altogether.

"Filled with awe, the children turned to Atsá for an answer, only to find Atsá looking in Niyol's direction. And, in his turn, the elder's face showed the same surprise and amazement. Even so, he did not pause in saying, 'I only know the dove is a symbol of peace and goodwill. Still, the mystery of his appearance and disappearance of the raven belong to the Creator and the Word Speaker, our Talking God. In time, they and the Yei will reveal to us what is needed. For now, let us sing the prayer song of praise, for we have found refuge and safety.'

"In the peace that followed, the baby slept while the Yei kept watch. Atsá, Liná, Niyol, and the grandmothers held the treasures of the miracle in their hearts while Doli, Dibé, and Ahiga explored their new world, played with new friends, and watched tenderly over their new brother. In their daily council with the village elders, both Atsá and Niyol continued to listen very carefully to what was being said, hoping to hear the words that would help them understand the 'mystery yet to come.'"

With that, Tsé finished his story. "Are your ears full, Yiska?" he asked his grandson.

"My ears and my heart, Grandfather," Yiska replied, even though that didn't stop him from pressing on. "But who is the baby with no name? Did the dove—I mean, the Messenger—ever return? Did Liná and Atsá have more children? And what about—"

"More questions?" Tsé asked with a gentle smile.

"Yes, Grandfather," Yiska answered quietly.

"Yiska, your ears and heart are full of words for now. Use what you have learned from our story wisely," Tsé told him. "In time, there will be another story. When your ears and heart are ready, the story will find its way."

REFERENCES

Calloway, Calvin G. *One Vast Winter Count.* Lincoln: University of Nebraska, 2003. *Social customs, beliefs, rituals, history, and origin.*

Josephy Jr., Alvin M., ed. in charge. *The American Heritage Book of Indians.* Rockville, MD: American Heritage Publishing Co., Inc, n.p., 1961. *History, culture, beliefs.*

Navaho-names.html. *Navaho names and meanings.*

Pasqua, Sandra M. *The Navaho Nation.* North Mankato, MN: Bridgestone Books, 2000. *Family ties, beliefs, culture.*

Santella, Andrew. *The Navaho.* Chicago: Children's Press, 2002. *Beliefs, myths, and history.*

Sherman, Josepha. *Indian Tribes of North America.* New York: New Line Books, 2006. *History.*

Underhill, Ruth M. *The Navaho.* Norman: University of Oklahoma Press, 1956. *History and culture.*

Chapter 4

A Morning Called Christmas

"I'm scared, Paulie," Sara, Paul's six-year-old sister, whispered, moving closer to her brother as the train came to a stop at the station.

Putting his arm around Sara's shoulder to pull her even closer, Paul turned to press his nose against the window and blow on the frosted window pane. His warm breath succeeded in clearing a small hole that was just enough to give him a good peek outside.

The other children traveling with Paul and Sara were younger than ten-year-old Paul; in fact, two of the boys were only five years old. They had a habit of trying to copy everything they saw Paul do. When Paul made his peek hole, they immediately followed suit. One even tried to clear the window with his tongue, only to shiver and yell out, "Hey, this window is cold!" His sudden outburst brought ripples of giggles from the girls and hee-haws from the two other boys on the train.

"Mal-vern," Paul read out loud enough for Sara to hear above the engine's hissing. "We're in Mal-vern, Iowa." Paul continued to look out onto the platform through his small peek hole and saw an all too familiar sight—a small group of soldiers dressed in blue standing guard at the train station. At the moment, Paul did not think it was necessary to tell Sara about the soldiers he saw. Paul had also noticed Union soldiers at the station in New York City, where they had boarded the train. Their escort told the children the soldiers were there to guard the depot against saboteurs. From reading day-old newspapers he found, Paul also knew they were there to protect people, even though their escort did not say anything about that. Paul reckoned it was because such news might frighten the children.

"Mal-vern," Sara pronounced it exactly as he had. "Paulie, where is Mal-vern?"

"I don't know," he said. "But it's somewhere in Iowa, I guess."

"Paul told his sister we were in Iowa," one of the girls said matter-of-factly to her seatmate, who had been straining to hear what Paul and Sara were talking about. She simply continued to look at Paul with dreamy eyes and muttered in reply, "Oh, that's nice."

Sara looked like she was about to ask another question when Miss Esther Arthur, their Children's Aid Society escort, came bouncing into the coach.

"Children! Children! We're here!" she said with a jovial tone and a very big smile.

"Just where are we, Miss Arthur?" Paul asked, despite what he'd seen outside the train window.

"In Malvern, Iowa! We're in Malvern." Then, in a softer tone she added, "Imagine that. We've traveled all the way from New York City to Malvern, Iowa."

It grieved her very much when she looked at her young charges while thinking, *This Civil War . . . so many orphans.* It also caused her pain when she accompanied children on such trips and heard people muttering, "Those are the children from the Orphan Train."

For her part, she tried very hard to encourage her young charges while staying hopelessly positive. As hard as she tried, she couldn't help but feel anxious for her charges about what might be waiting for them in their new homes.

"We're in Malvern," she repeated the town's name, only this time sounding more relieved than excited.

"Why?" Sara's question was almost a whisper.

"Why?" Miss Arthur was a little surprised to hear the question, only because it was coming from Sara, who had not spoken to anyone except Paul during their journey. "Why, Sara, we came all this way to find you a new home and family," Miss Arthur answered, repeating words she had said so many times to one child after another as they were leaving New York City, heading for what she hoped for all of them to have—a new and better life.

"I have Paulie." Sara's explanation was filled with fear. "He's my family."

"We have each other, Sara," Paul whispered in her ear.

Not really knowing what else to say, Miss Arthur gave Sara a gentle pat. And then, glancing around at blank faces and searching eyes staring back at her, she forced a smile once again and said, "Now, now, children. Bundle up your things."

Except for the five-year-old boys, who went back to staring out the window, the other children looked around and under their seats, including in the racks above them, as if their bundles of clothes or small brown suitcases—each provided by the Society—had somehow increased.

"All right now, children," Miss Arthur went back to practicing words straight from the office. "Remember, there are people here who will care for you. They want each and every one of you. You all will have a family."

She was still looking at her nine charges when a series of concerns flashed through her mind. *What will happen to my dear ones? Will they truly be loved? Will they be safe?*

While they were still on the train, a voice called out from behind her, "Miss Arthur! Miss Arthur!" Coming down the aisle, Reverend Myron Thomas strained to be heard over the engine's mumbling and hissing, along with the anxious and chattering voices of people waiting on the platform for their new wards.

"That's me!" Esther exclaimed, looking up at the young pastor.

"Oh! Hello," he said, startled. "I was expecting . . . I mean . . . you don't look like . . . uh . . . ." It was quite obvious he was a little lost about what to say next.

"You mean you were expecting someone older," she said with a slight smile. "Maybe with a stern, unpleasant look?"

By now, Reverend Thomas's face had turned red and his mouth was gaping as if he wanted to say more but just couldn't.

"Oh, I'm so sorry." Seeing how flustered he was, Miss Arthur started to worry she'd made a bad first impression. "Yes, I know I'm on the young side for this position. I was under the care of the Children's Aid Society for several years, you see, and then I was adopted by the director and his wife." She tried another smile. "So, it was just a natural calling for me to become a social worker after college."

"Oh." Collecting himself, Reverend Thomas was just about ready to say how pleased he was to meet her when they were interrupted by a still, small voice and an equally little hand pulling ever so slightly on Miss Arthur's coat.

"Miss Arthur?" Rachael, a red-headed girl with no last name on her name tag, timidly inquired.

"Yes, dear?" Rather thankful for the distraction, she knelt down to better address the little one. "What's wrong?"

Without looking directly at Miss Arthur, Rachael continued, "Me, Sara, and Paul . . . well . . . we were wondering . . ." Rachael took a deep breath. "We were wondering what's going to happen now?"

"Maybe I can answer that." Reverend Thomas leaned over to touch Rachael's shoulder. "All the people on the platform are from the Malvern community. We've been waiting for you children to come and live with us."

His enthusiasm did not seem to impress Rachael, however. "Why?"

Paul did not expect Rachael to include him or Sara in her questioning. While Rachael and Sara whispered back and forth to each other over their seats on the train, she had barely said a word to Paul since they left New York City. Still her question seemed very appropriate to him, so he also said "Yeah," inching closer to the trio. "Why?"

"Now, Paul," Miss Arthur gently chided, "let's not be disrespectful." Seizing the opportunity, she pointed Paul toward the exit door and asked him, "Will you please help me get the children off the train? You lead, and I will pick up the end, making sure we all depart." Paul gave her an obedient nod and took Rachael, who was clutching her brown suitcase, by the hand and headed back to where Sara sat. Hand in hand, Rachael and Sara, holding tightly onto their suitcases with Paul following right behind them, went down the aisle toward the exit.

With each small step, he glanced from side to side while giving the command, "Follow me." The children did as they were told until he came to the two five-year-old boys who still sat there, fixed on looking out the window. Paul stopped, put a gentle arm on each of the boys' shoulders, and said, "Come on now, Sam and Harry. We don't want to be left behind." Without a word, the boys picked up their bundles and followed behind Paul, Sara, and Rachael.

When it was Paul's turn to depart from the train, he was grateful for the side bars on the steps. With the limp he had had since childbirth, he was always a little unsure of himself when going down steps. The sidebars made it easier for him, however, and the situation was handled without any difficulty.

Finally, when all of the children and Miss Arthur were off the train and gathered on the platform, Reverend Thomas almost apologetically said, "Miss Arthur, the people are waiting in the church. They are most anxious to meet you and the children. They all wanted to come down to the depot, but I thought it best for them to wait at the church. I thought it might be too overwhelming for the children to just arrive and try to make sense of it all in that instant."

Miss Arthur looked up at Reverend Thomas and gave him a reassuring smile of agreement. "Thank you. I do think the walk to the church will be a chance for the children to stretch their legs and, now that we're here, have a minute or two before meeting their new families."

Hearing her words, Reverend Thomas returned the smile and said confidently, "Okay, children, the church is located up that hill." As he spoke, Reverend Thomas pointed at the small town's main street leading to the hill.

As they headed in the direction of the church and passed by the town square, Paul read aloud so all the children could hear him. "Moore's General Store, Malvern Post Office, Crank's Bootery, Ralph and Hazel's Good Food Restaurant." A small group of people standing on the sidewalk silently watched the children, more out of curiosity than for any other reason.

At the corner of the square stood several statues. Pointing to them, Reverend Thomas explained, "Those are the founding fathers of Malvern." None of the children seemed too impressed by the statues nor were there any questions asked, so Reverend Thomas continued the march up the hill to the church.

It only took a few minutes before they were all inside. The late morning mid-October air had just a slight chill, which made the wood stove's warmth welcoming to everyone who entered. While the adults found their seats, Miss Arthur walked the children up to the front of the sanctuary, where they stood almost as stiff as the statues they had passed by on the town square.

Through previous correspondence with Reverend Thomas, the Society understood that farm families and a few merchants from Malvern would accept a total of nine children. But Miss Arthur knew from experience that there were always some last-minute changes, surprises, and even a few heartaches.

Couples and a few children who were waiting for the arrivals filled the first two rows of the sanctuary pews. As the children passed by, those anxiously expecting them rose to their feet.

Rachael's new family was the first to come forward. They identified her by her large name tag pinned to her coat. The lady was lean and tall, with coal-black hair laced with streaks of silver gray. She wore a plain black dress, and around her neck was a string of pearls. A stout man a few inches shorter than she walked beside her with a clean white apron tied around his waist and his shirt sleeves rolled up to his elbows. His appearance gave one the impression he was taking only a very short break from his duties back at the general store.

"Rachael," the woman said, "I'm Mary Moore, and this is my husband, George. We own the general store, and we're so happy you'll be coming to live with us."

When she put her arm around the little girl, she could feel her shoulders stiffen. But Rachael otherwise slowly and silently let herself be led back to the pew where the Moores had been sitting.

One by one, the children met their families with varying greetings and reactions until only Paul and Sara remained. In the hubbub of questions and answers, no one else seemed to notice Reverend Thomas pulling Miss Arthur aside.

"We've had a problem," he said. "It seems the family who was going to take them decided to move back east. They just couldn't make a go of farming." He looked utterly apologetic. "I'm so sorry, but I just found out as we were coming into the church."

"Oh no!" Miss Arthur glanced over at her two wards still standing in the front of the church.

His tone was both sincere and sympathetic. "I know this is very hard, and I'm sure Sara will be heartbroken. But there is a couple sitting in the back—Isabelle and Howard Canfield—who have opened their home for one boy. Their only son was killed in the war." The reverend hurried on. "Their farm is mostly hardpan soil and they aren't well off, but they're good hard-working people. They keep mostly to themselves."

Miss Arthur's face had already filled with sadness and remorse. "How many times?" she asked. "How many times have we failed these children?" She couldn't keep the thoughts to herself as a tear fell down her cheek.

Reverend Thomas didn't know what to say to that.

Forgetting the social etiquette she had been taught at the orphanage in earlier years and experiencing the need for some support herself, she said, "Myron, I promised Paul and Sara they wouldn't be separated." Her eyes brimmed with emotion. "I promised." When he said nothing, clearly uncertain how to fix the problem, she did her best to pull herself together. "Well, maybe we can find another home for Sara. At least maybe they could be together in the same community."

Following her lead in using first names, Reverend Thomas answered, "I don't think so, Esther." His words seemed to tumble out of his mouth. "I tried—no one, not now anyway—I'll keep trying. I promise."

Unsure what else to do, he motioned Howard and Isabelle Canfield to come up to the front of the sanctuary. As they approached, Miss Arthur instinctively put her arm around Sara, trying to protect her from what was about to happen.

"Are those the people?" the little girl whispered to her.

"Well—" she started, bending down close.

Mr. Canfield unintentionally interrupted her. "Hello. I'm Howard Canfield, and this is my wife, Isabelle. We were a little late finishing morning chores because one of the cows got out, so I had to repair some fence before we could come. But . . . I see . . ." His eyes flashed back and forth between Paul and Sara while reading their name tags. Reading Paul's name tag once again and looking directly at him with sympathetic eyes and what sounded to Esther like a caring voice, he continued, "Uh, oh . . . yes. Paul, we are happy to meet you."

After an awkward moment of silence, he reached his hand out toward the boy, who didn't look too sure about what to do with it. No one had ever shaken hands with him before. But after a pause, he accepted the gesture from both Mr. and Mrs. Canfield.

"We'd better get started," Mr. Canfield said, looking at Miss Arthur and Reverend Thomas, and then glancing down at Sara even while he avoided talking to her. "We have chores to do later. When you have cows, you milk in the morning and again in the late afternoon. It's a ways to the farm. Cows will be lined up at the barn." He danced from topic to topic in his awkwardness. "We live on the other side of Malvern, you see."

Beside her husband, Mrs. Canfield sighed deeply while she bent down to pick up Paul's bundle of clothes. But Paul snatched it up quickly and tucked it under his arm. He seemed to have picked up on the fact that they were only taking him.

So had Sara. "What about me?" With tears streaming down her face, she cried out, "Paulie! Paulie, no one wants me. No one wants me, Paulie."

Yet Paul refused to move away from her, his free arm wrapping around her shoulder.

Looking helplessly at them, Mrs. Canfield quietly tapped her husband's shoulder.

"No!" he responded, correctly interpreting the motion. They had talked it through several times already. They could only take one child, as he had reasoned and clearly explained to Reverend Thomas. Now, in the moment, he had to remind himself, "One child."

They needed help on the farm. They needed a boy. At least, that's what made sense to him, and she sadly accepted her husband's wishes.

Miss Arthur, meanwhile, was confused, angry, and stuck all at the same time. No one had ever prepared her for something like what was happening before her. She had always brought children to communities across the Midwest, and they were always received into homes—that was that. Afterward, she returned to New York City and resumed her work in the Society's Home.

While it was true she had warned herself time and time again there could be problems, heartaches, and mix-ups, the ones that had come up usually could be fixed before the day was out. As for people deciding not to accept a child after all, it seemed like there was another couple always waiting to take their place. She even had couples expecting one child but graciously accepting two when, at the last minute, someone decided not to take a child. For her, problems along with the unexpected disappointments that came her way always seemed to be worked out. Then she would calmly find a small respite on the journey back to New York, where her daily challenges awaited her until it was time to take another train ride. As she stood there wondering how to resolve the current problem with compassion for both Paul and Sara, her thoughts were interrupted by the sound of Sara's voice.

"No one wants me," Sara continued to cry, keeping her arms wrapped around her brother's waist, squeezing tighter and tighter.

"I want you, Sara. I want you." Paul was trying so hard to soothe her fears. But uncertain of the outcome himself, he had no idea if he could really protect her.

After quieting her own thoughts and hearing Sara's words of pain, Miss Arthur, with a calm, firm voice, spoke to the little girl while stroking her hair. "Sara, I want you. You'll go back with me to New York City, and I'll watch over you until we get this all sorted out. I promise I'll watch over you."

Sara's young mind found it very hard, however, to understand what grown-ups meant by promises, especially ones they made to children. So, instead of responding, she focused her light blue eyes on Paul's presence as if, should she dare blink, he would disappear.

Miserable about the whole thing, Reverend Thomas worked hard to compose himself. "Paul, I wish I could make it better for you and

Sara right now, but I can't. I'll keep trying, though. I won't give up." He struggled to find the right words. "The Canfields are nice people. They'll provide for you. But for now, this is the best we can do. I'll come out on Saturday to see how you are."

Paul politely acknowledged him, and then bent over and carefully whispered in Sara's ear. "Remember, I love you. Remember, it's you and me. You and me."

With those words echoing inside his thoughts, he gently pulled away from her tight grip. Wanting to be brave for Sara's sake, Paul turned and, without looking back at her fearful face now flooding with tears flowing freely to the floor, walked out of the church with the Canfields.

Yet, as he climbed into the back of the wagon, for the first time he could remember, a stream of tears easily flowed. Now he did not have to be brave for Sara. Desperately not wanting anyone—including the Canfields—to see him, he tucked his face into his elbow, comforted only with the thought that by volunteering to ride in the back of the wagon, he was alone with his pain—something he had years of practice doing at the orphanage.

It seemed like a long journey out to the Canfield farm, and it was—long enough for him to pull himself together. Turning sideways on her box seat and a distance from town, Mrs. Canfield tried to talk to Paul several times. But when she wasn't able to solicit any response, she turned and stared ahead instead, gazing at the horizon that always looked to be a hill away.

"Whoa!" Mr. Canfield pulled on the team's reins, speaking for the first time since they left Malvern. Wrapping the reins around the wagon wheel's front brake, he climbed down from his seat. "Paul, bring the bucket and come with me. Pat and Pet need watering. We still have a ways to go. We always stop here for a rest and water going to and coming from town. Now Pat and Pet have come to expect the stop. I suspect they would stop on their own even without my coaxing."

With those words, Paul was introduced to the team of draft horses pulling the wagon.

Filling the bucket from a running stream was a new experience for Paul, only to be outdone by trying to balance the pail to keep the water from sloshing out onto his jeans. He also discovered that walking with a limp added to the challenge. Mr. Canfield came up behind him to watch as the bucket swung back and forth, water splashing out in the process, first on Paul and then on the ground. Walking right up in front of Pat, the boy put the bucket down, which turned out to be the wrong move. Frightened by someone unfamiliar coming into her line of vision, which was narrowed by the blinders on her bridle, the horse instinctively reared her head, lifted her left leg, and kicked the bucket over.

"Get another bucket of water, Paul," Mr. Canfield said calmly even while he started to look over the harness. "Only this time, don't fill it so full. And talk to Pat when you approach her."

Paul was surprised he did not receive a scolding as he might have gotten from some of his teachers back at the orphanage when he made a mistake. He was also comforted by the thought that Mr. Canfield did not call him "Clumsy" or "Limpy" as some of the boys in the orphanage often did. How Mr. Canfield had responded to him made it easier to ask, "Talk to her?" He was curious despite himself. "What do you say to a horse?"

"Hmm . . ." Mr. Canfield murmured as he thought about it. "Well, I guess I don't really know. I haven't been asked that question before. Guess that's just what you do so the horses—or cows, for that matter—aren't afraid when you approach them from behind."

"Oh." Paul turned back toward the stream to refill his bucket. And this time, when he came up alongside Pat, he started to sing an old English lullaby.

It seemed to work because she didn't lunge forward again.

Mrs. Canfield had been busy spreading out a lunch for the three of them on a canvas cloth she had brought along. She was just about ready to call them over when she heard Paul singing, and she also noticed her husband had stopped inspecting the harness to listen carefully as well.

After Pet and Pat had drunk their fill of water, Paul dropped a small bundle of hay in front of each of them as Mr. Canfield had previously asked him to do. When he had finished, they both walked over to where Mrs. Canfield was waiting for them.

"That was lovely, Paul," she said, motioning him to come and sit on the canvas. "Where did you learn such a beautiful song?"

"I don't know." He genuinely didn't. "Somewhere on the street, I guess. I used to sing it to Sara before we were picked up by the Society."

"Well, it is very lovely and you sing it so beautifully," she said again while she handed him a cold roast beef sandwich.

Neither she nor her husband were halfway through their own before Paul had finished his, along with the lemonade she'd poured into a small mason jar for him.

"Do you want another one?" she asked, putting another sandwich and a piece of chocolate cake in front of him without waiting for a reply.

Paul looked at the food before him and then anxiously turned toward Mr. Canfield as if he was expecting him to say something, or worse, take the food away altogether.

Mr. Canfield did reach, but only for the last sandwich in the basket. "I'd better help myself before you give this sandwich away too," he told his wife.

"I've never known you to go away from my table hungry, Mr. Canfield," she said, meeting his look with her wit.

After their lunch was finished, Paul went with Mr. Canfield and watched closely as he checked over the harness one more time. Then they were back on the road long enough for Paul to fall asleep in the back. It wasn't until several hours later that they arrived at the Canfield farm.

"Whoa, Pat. Easy, Pet," Mr. Canfield said to his team while pulling tightly on the reins, bringing the two draft horses to a stop, which caused Paul to awaken from a deep sleep.

Holding on to the back of the wagon seat and standing up, Paul was able to take in a quick sweep of the farm. He saw the whitewashed farmhouse and a barn shaped like a narrow house covered by a pointed roof with what appeared to him to be the outline of a possible door. Later, he found out the *door* on the second story of the barn opened into the hay mound, where hay was stored for the livestock. Connected to the barn was a corral where the livestock were free to roam and stay when they were brought in from the pasture and not yet herded into the shelter of the barn. There was a lean-to on the north side of the barn housing gadgets that Paul assumed were farm machinery.

His last visual stop was a smaller shed with a high wire fence on its south side. He had never seen that type of wire before. It consisted of octagons from top to bottom. It didn't take long for him to find out the fence was designed that way to keep predators out of the chicken pen and the chickens safe on the other side. Paul's eyes stopped its survey when they espied Mrs. Canfield.

"We're home, Paul," she said while giving him a big smile.

"Oh," Paul said quietly. Favoring his good leg, he jumped down from the wagon, once again holding tightly to his bundle.

"Paul, you take your things into the house," Mr. Canfield told him, "and Mrs. Canfield will show you your room. When you're settled, you can come out to the barn. I'll show you around." Before slightly jiggling his lines to once again set the horses in motion, he added, "In a little while, we'll have to do chores."

"Chores?" Paul called out, remembering that chores at the Home usually involved scrubbing floors, cleaning bathrooms, and sometimes having to go out and work for people in the city. He could only guess that the work on the farm would be something different than what he had experienced in New York City. "What kind of chores?"

"Whoa," Mr. Canfield called out to Pet and Pat.

As they stopped, Paul stopped also. Looking up to where Mr. Canfield sat on the wagon seat, he received a warm smile from the man.

"Well, evening chores are a little different than morning chores. We milk the cows and give them fresh hay and bedding for the night, and then feed the calves and the pigs. Next, we shut up the chicken house to keep foxes that prowl around our place at night from climbing in and carrying off a tasty meal. I suspect by the time we get to the chicken house, Mrs. Canfield will have gathered the eggs and fed and watered the chickens, so we won't need to bother about that. Now go on and put away your things. I'll see you in a bit." With that being said, Mr. Canfield once again gave Pat and Pet a gentle slap on their rumps with the lines he was holding in his hands and headed toward the machine.

When Paul entered the house, he went into the kitchen where Mrs. Canfield was starting to fix their supper. As she wiped her hands on her apron, she smiled at Paul and said, "Paul, let's go upstairs and I will show you your room." The small upstairs had three rooms. Mrs. Canfield stopped at the door of the first room and said, "This is our bedroom, and across the hall is the storage room, but we can easily turn it into another bedroom if needed." After pointing toward each room, she continued down the short hallway, and Paul followed without saying a word.

At the end of the hall, Mrs. Canfield opened the door to the last room and motioned for Paul to come inside. "This will be your room, Paul. It belonged to our son, Samuel. Now it is your room." When she mentioned her son's name, her voice quivered a little. Paul was quick to hear how her voice changed, and he wondered if there might have been more she wanted to say, but the only thing that followed was silence.

"You mean I don't have to share the room with anyone else?" Paul asked, interrupting the silence.

"No, it's your room now," Mrs. Canfield replied after regaining her composure.

"Oh . . . thank you," he responded, not quite sure if he should say any more.

"Well, I'm going back to the kitchen to make our supper. You go ahead and put your things away. The trunk and the small dresser are for you to use. When you are done, I am sure Mr. Canfield would appreciate your help." With those words, instead of leaving as she said she was going to do, she stood quietly at the doorway.

There wasn't much for Paul to put away, so it didn't take very long. But he took his time looking around the room, peeking into the small closet and examining the chest of drawers where he had carefully laid his clothes in the top drawer. Then he stared at the bed.

He had never had a room that was just his before. In fact, he had never had a chest of drawers or a closet. Usually, he stored his clothes and treasured items at the foot of the bed or in a small locker that rested at the end of his bed.

"My room," Paul reflected on the words. "I wish—I wish I could share it with Sara."

Tears filled his eyes, catching him off guard yet again. Not knowing what she would do or say, Paul turned away from Mrs. Canfield so she could not see him crying, even if she was going to hear him regardless.

It broke her heart. She wanted so much to move over to him and wrap her arms around him. She wanted to think of some way to make his life happier. She wanted to tell him, *Sara is okay. It will be all right.* But those words were not hers to give away. So, in the silence, she listened to his hushed crying until she wondered if he wished she wasn't there at all.

Taking a few steps toward Paul, she reached out to touch his shoulder while searching for something to say. Finally, with a voice of assurance, she spoke. "Yes, Paul, this is your room. *Your* room." She put every ounce of compassion and warmth into the words. "When you're ready, Mr. Canfield will be waiting for you out in the barn. Paul, sometimes words are hard for Mr. Canfield to find, but I know he is excited about showing you around the barn. He might even want to start chores a bit earlier this afternoon. We both know this is all a new experience for you and you have had a long day." She really didn't know what else to say, but seeing Paul grieve so, she felt the need to say something—and say it with kindness.

Mrs. Canfield gave him another warm smile and then turned to leave. But Paul did not respond to her last comment, nor did he return her smile. He sat there on the bed in the silence of a room that was larger than life in the moment—just not large enough to contain all his fear, hurt, and aching for his younger sister.

Thinking he would be scolded if he lingered too long, Paul did find his way back downstairs, where Mrs. Canfield gave him a woolen coat to wear before he went down to the barn. Mr. Canfield was already there, putting out some cracked corn in front of the milking stanchions. After shaking a small pile of cracked corn at the third one, he looked up at the silent, waiting boy.

"What are these?" Paul asked as he put his hand on top of one of the stanchions.

"They are called stanchions. When we bring in the cows, they each walk up to one, putting their heads through the openings so they can reach the grain. Once they are muzzling down on the grain, I can walk up from behind and lock them in—like so," said Mr. Canfield as he demonstrated how the stanchion locked. "Locked in, regardless of how tame our cows are, they won't back out while we are milking."

"Oh," Paul said, not sounding too convinced the cows would stay in place.

"When I call the cows in, I think you will be able to understand better how it all works. Next time we milk, I will let you lock them in, Paul. We have three cows. They answer to their names: Betsy, Brownie, and Spotty. You'll find that most of our animals have names. It's just easier to talk about them that way."

Saying nothing, Paul took it all in.

"I can't tell you for certain," Mr. Canfield continued, "but I imagine Mrs. Canfield has names for her ten laying hens, too. I know she calls the rooster Chester. Don't ask me why. Oh, and we have one sow and a boar. They have names also, but you don't really need to know all of this right now."

As he listened, Paul tilted his head as he usually did when learning something new. Unsure if he was supposed to ask questions, nod his head, or what, Paul waited. It wasn't long before the silence was broken by the sound of milk cows sloshing through the mud as they made their way from the barnyard to the barn door.

"Step back a bit." Mr. Canfield walked over and opened the door, swinging it out before he also stepped aside, out of the cows' path.

Paul watched them make their way to the stanchions and the cracked corn waiting for them there.

"Move over, Betsy." Mr. Canfield pushed on her rump until he could navigate beside her and lock her in. Turning toward Brownie, he spoke again. "Easy, Brownie. Easy there, girl." Without any problems, he locked her into a stanchion, too.

Watching all this, Paul was a little surprised to hear Mr. Canfield address him in the same tones. "Move up beside Spotty, Paul, and lock her in just as you saw me do with Betsy and Brownie. Put your hand on her rump, and speak to her as you walk."

If he hadn't been so afraid, Paul would have giggled at the words he heard. As it was, he moved very cautiously to do as instructed. "Move over, Spotty. Easy, Spotty. Easy there, girl."

To his surprise, the cow didn't put up a fuss. But, as she moved over, she put her head down so her thick pink tongue could lick up some more cracked corn. Mr. Canfield didn't speak up again until after Spotty was locked in.

"You did good there." He reached for the t-shaped stool he sat on when he milked, grabbed the milk pail, and started to milk. Once he had a rhythm going, he looked over his shoulder at Paul, and with a smile said, "There is a trick to sitting on one of these stools. You have to keep your balance, but I have a hunch you'll catch on pretty fast."

Once again, Paul didn't say anything. He just watched. It was all so new and strange to him. On the one hand, it was exciting, but on the other, confusing. And he was still very much guarded and afraid. There were noises he'd never heard before in a place he'd never seen with unfamiliar people who were now part of his life. But for how long?

And then there was Sara. He was afraid for himself, yes, but even more for her. Missing her hurt so much, which was made worse by not being there with her, wherever she was, to care for her like he always had.

Listening to the streams of milk hitting the side of the pail, Paul leaned against the barn's wooden wall. The chill of the evening wind slipped through the cracks, and he tightly wrapped the collar of the woolen jacket up around his neck.

Mr. Canfield didn't say another word until he was pouring the milk into a cream can standing near Paul. "What's wrong?"

"Nothing," Paul answered.

"Must be something," he said. "You've been standing there all the while I've been milking. Haven't seen you move a muscle. So, something's wrong. Are you scared?"

"No." Paul didn't want to give away how he really felt, yet his next words came out as if he had no control over them. "I just—I miss Sara. I'm responsible for her! And now I'm not there for her." The words hurt to say, but he couldn't stop them. "You don't know. Miss Arthur doesn't know. Even the Reverend and all his promises. No one knows. Only me."

He began to shake. "No one really cares. No one. Not anymore. And now I'll bet Sara thinks I don't care, either. I know she does."

That was too much for him. He didn't really know where he was going or why, but with those words, Paul unlatched the barn door and darted out into the darkness. Falling down in the mud, he picked himself up to sprint farther out into the pasture, where he finally came to rest in a pile of leaves beneath a large maple tree.

In the twilight, amidst the confusion, he found himself doubled over with sobs.

Watching from one of the barn's windows, Mr. Canfield could actually see Paul hunched over. Yet with no idea about what to do, he let the cows out of the barn and closed it up behind them. With his cream can filled with fresh milk, he made his way to the house where the smell of frying chicken wafted out.

Mrs. Canfield turned from the stove, a smile on her face and a greeting on her lips, both of which quickly disappeared when she saw her husband standing there alone. "Where's Paul?"

Mr. Canfield's expression was one of honest bewilderment. "He's out in the pasture still, I think. I really don't know."

"What happened?" Utterly distressed, she moved the chicken from the stove as fast as she could so she could give him her full attention. "What went wrong? Did you say something to hurt that boy?"

"I don't think so," he answered, although he didn't look so sure. "He seemed to accept everything I said regarding the cows and the names we had for all the animals . . . but then he just . . . changed. He started talking about his sister and his responsibility and how we didn't know or care." He sighed. "I thought everything was going okay until he started talking like that."

"Oh, Howard." Losing her fierceness, Mrs. Canfield called her husband by his first name, reserved for times of sympathy and intimacy. Without another word, she put her arm around his shoulder. "Do you remember how you felt when we heard about Samuel?" she asked. "Remember how you just went off and were gone for hours? When you came back to the house, I asked where you'd been and you just said, 'Oh, out in the pasture checking fence.' You didn't say anything more."

"But I was—" he replied.

When she interrupted him, it was with the utmost tenderness. "Yes, I'm sure you were. And later that day, you just started talking about how it was all your fault he went to war, and it was your fault he died. Remember?"

"Yes, I guess I do." His next sentence sounded like he was speaking to himself. "I guess I do."

Without another word, he picked up the unlit lantern from the cupboard shelf. "I'd better go find the boy," he declared as he set the wick ablaze. "I'll go find him. You just mind the chicken, Isabelle." He looked at her, returning her love, and then added, "I know he'll be hungry." As he trailed off into the darkness, Isabelle heard him say again, "That boy will be hungry."

It didn't take him long to reach the maple tree, where Paul's silhouette was rising from a pile of leaves the boy had apparently built around himself. Expecting the worst, Paul stood in silence as Mr. Canfield approached.

"I thought I'd find you here, Paul," the farmer said gently. "This is my thinking tree, you see. I've come here often when I wanted to think stuff out, too."

When he got nothing from the boy, he went on. "Samuel liked to come here as well. See, you didn't know you were in such good company, did you?" He tried to put a smile on his face as he lifted the lantern a little higher to see Paul better.

Not responding to any of that, Paul only bravely replied, "I'm sorry for running off, Mr. Canfield."

"Running off?" he asked. "Oh, I thought you were just taking a walk around to see how things looked in the dark."

The boy didn't respond to the joke either.

"Both Mrs. Canfield and I were worried." Mr. Canfield was not too sure of what exactly to say, so he simply told Paul the truth. "We can't make you like it here. We can't make you happy. You'll have to decide if you want both of those things on your own."

Paul sniffled.

"We do want you here, boy. I had a son. He was killed in the war, but I'd like another try at it. I'd like to have you for a son if you'll let me be your father. We just want you to . . ." Giving up for the moment, he took a hold of the boy's shoulder, and the two of them turned and headed for the farmyard.

"I would like to be happy," Paul said almost in a whisper, staring out into the distance at the light shining through the farmhouse window on top of the hill. But, as he fixed his eyes on the light, he concluded, "I can't be, though. I don't deserve to be happy. Not without Sara."

He heard Paul's words, but for the time being, he let them linger. His mind was racing back to the conversation Mrs. Canfield and he had when Reverend Thomas asked them about accepting both children. Howard had reminded everyone, including himself, that he and Isabelle could only take one child.

They only had room for one child, he had said in his mind again and again.

In the following weeks, Paul learned how to pick corn and drive Pat and Pet. He also gathered the eggs, even though Chester the rooster was always chasing him around the chicken pen. In spite of the limp that partially caused him to slip and slide through the pig pen, he fed the animals. He liked feeding the pigs the least because they were always pushing and shoving him as he tried to dump milk and cracked corn into their trough.

On more than one occasion, he slipped and fell during the process, resulting in a stinky mess. Whenever that happened, Mrs. Canfield would make him take off his overalls and scrub himself down good on the back porch before coming into the kitchen.

He was picking up the other chores with much more ease. It had taken several slow starts, but Paul was now able to milk Spotty while balanced on his own milking stool he had made himself.

As for attending church, which was to be expected in his life. Children's Home had always included Sunday worship, and now he was even going to choir practice at Malvern Community Church with Reverend Thomas. The reverend had kept his word by coming out that first Saturday, and through the weeks that followed, he used their time together to tell Paul about the community and the Canfields. On one of their visits, Reverend Thomas even told Paul about his own parents, who raised him in a big town back east.

On two occasions so far, the reverend had shared with Paul how he had received letters from Miss Arthur. She always asked about him and wanted him to know that Sara was moved into her own small apartment at the Home so she could especially watch out for her as promised.

What Reverend Thomas didn't tell Paul was that the little girl kept mostly to herself and was having frequent nightmares. That last piece of news was too sad for the adults involved, and neither of them wanted to share it with Paul.

"I'm going by train to New York City tomorrow afternoon," the reverend told him after the Harvest Sunday Celebration, as the Canfields were leaving. "I'll be having Thanksgiving there. So, if you want to write Sara a letter, I'll take it with me."

"I don't know what to say," Paul said, not looking up at him as he quickly walked down the steps.

Mrs. Canfield stepped in with another question. "Are you going to see Miss Arthur, Reverend?"

"Well, I have business and a board meeting at the Society's office, so I'm sure I'll see her." A twinkle in his eyes betrayed the excitement he'd tried to muffle in his answer. Now, Mr. Canfield had seen the reverend's expression but didn't say anything at the time.

Mrs. Canfield directed her next words to Paul. "I can't help but think little Sara would want to hear from her brother," she pointed out before smiling at the reverend again. "I'll help him think of something to write. Mr. Canfield will be coming to town tomorrow for supplies, and he'll bring the letter with him."

"That will be really nice. Thank you, Mrs. Canfield," Reverend Thomas said with a smile he then redirected at Paul. "I know you'll write a good letter."

"We better scoot." Mr. Canfield said. Being the man who usually tried to be first out of the church door, he was more than ready to leave. All the same, he'd been keeping an eye on Paul, who was staring out the door at Pat and Pet.

Later that day, after they had eaten, Mrs. Canfield went about cleaning up the kitchen. Since Sunday-evening supper was always very simple, it didn't take her long before she was ready to join her men. By then, Mr. Canfield had pulled the rocker close to the table, where the kerosene lamp rested, to read the almanac. Paul was sitting at the table, deep in his own thoughts and doodling on a piece of paper Mrs. Canfield had given him.

"What have you written so far?" she asked as she pulled a chair over next to his. "Hmm. Well, nice doodles. That's a start. How 'bout turning your paper over, and we'll begin again."

Paul obeyed but then immediately put his pencil down on the paper.

"Why don't we start out by talking about what you want to tell Sara?" she encouraged.

"I don't want to tell her nuthin'," muttered Paul.

"Nothing," corrected Mrs. Canfield. "You must want to tell her something. How about telling her about the animals? Or how you've learned how to drive Pat and Pet? Or about sleigh riding out in the pasture? Or—"

"I can't," Paul declared, moisture already forming in his eyes. "Don't you see? I can't! She's there, and I'm here. That's that."

In his self-imposed silence, tears dropped on the piece of paper, making it officially impossible for him to write the letter.

Mrs. Canfield wasn't quite sure what to do whenever he got like this. She just wanted to hold him, but she found herself recalling what Howard had told her the night he found him under the maple tree out in the pasture. Her husband had said Paul would have to decide if he wanted to be part of their family or not. If he wanted to be happy or sad, it would be up to him.

Sometimes, on similar occasions, Howard would simply say, "Come on, Paul. We have work to do." And they would go clean the barn, chop wood, or fix a fence because that's just what men and boys did. But there had to be more, something she could do, as well.

"Paul," she said, deciding to be firm rather than sentimental. "Maybe you can't because you won't. It hurts me to say this, but I think you're being very selfish. I remember Sara saying she thought no one wanted her. That means now more than ever. She needs to know you care and you love her very much." She stood up. "She needs to hear from you whether the two of you can be together right now or not."

With that, she picked up the pencil, put it in Paul's hand, and left the table.

"Sara, you have to eat. You're almost as skinny as you were when you first came to the Home," Esther said, trying very hard to coax Sara to eat the sandwich on her plate.

The other children had already eaten and been excused, but not this one. The little girl sat in her chair with her legs tucked under her, sucking her thumb.

"Please, Sara," Esther coaxed some more, but her words didn't seem to do any good.

When Miss Arthur moved Sara into her apartment, she had truly hoped the child might feel a little safer and believe she was, in fact, loved. For a few days after she arrived back at the Home, she did seem to be returning to her normal self. But in a few weeks, she began to change. Every morning and often throughout the day, she would run and look out the window or put on her coat, and then she'd stand outside looking up and down the street.

When asked what she was doing, she would reply, "Oh, Paulie's coming. I know he is. He's coming back for me. They want me."

But as those days passed by too and Paul did not come, her expectant smile vanished and with it, what appetite she had. Most days now, whenever possible, she retreated to her small bed and sat on the edge, sucking her thumb.

Mrs. Martin, the nurse, came around while Esther was still trying to think of ways to get Sara to eat. "The doctor is coming this afternoon to check on her, Esther," she said. Although the nurse did give the little girl a warm smile, Sara's non-responsive actions ultimately made her too uncomfortable, so she didn't linger long.

When the doctor arrived, he ended up spending a good amount of time talking to Esther and the nurse about the troubled child. First, he tried and tried to visit with Sara, but in the hours since her non-existent lunch, Sara had also stopped talking. It was as if she had little energy or will to do anything. As such, after a complete examination, Dr. Wylie motioned for Esther and Mrs. Martin to go out into the hallway with him.

"There doesn't seem to be anything physically wrong with Sara," Dr. Wylie offered.

"What is it then? What can we do?" asked Mrs. Martin.

"I'm not sure." Dr. Wylie shook his head slowly. "I'm just not sure. Children Sara's age are still developing a sense of purpose, identity, and community. Their world is supposed to be filled with play." His lips twisted in sad contemplation. "But prior to coming here, most of your children missed out on that part of their childhood—out there." He waved his arm in a sweeping gesture and said, "Out there, life hits them in the face. They feel there's no room for them. Instead of being able to play, they're used, abused, and abandoned. They have to fight to survive."

"But we're supposed to change that," Esther said, feeling like a failure as the words left her mouth.

"Here, you do the best you can with what you have," the doctor reassured her. "Routine. Rules. Order. Food. Shelter. You offer safety. You spread love out further than most people would ever dare or imagine could ever be done. You give children a place to belong—a minute in their life to play—so they're valued for more than what others can take or profit from them."

Esther felt no better, however. Not at all. "But Sara," she pressed. "What about Sara?"

He shrugged helplessly. "Maybe taking her out to Iowa and then separating her from her brother was just too much for her. This isn't the Home's fault. Personally watching over her, Miss Arthur, and caring for her as you've done demonstrates love. Whether she will actually allow herself to receive it remains yet to be seen. You continue to demonstrate Jesus' love for her through your love for her. In spite of what I have just said, the idea that someone out in Iowa couldn't love her, too, might have been too difficult for her to handle."

"So, because there was no room for her," Esther said, "there is no love for her."

"I'm sorry," Dr. Wylie remarked sadly as he put on his coat. And then, since there seemed to be nothing else to say, he excused himself.

Esther found herself moving too, but only to stand by the window. It was already mid-November, and in ten days, Myron would be in New York to have Thanksgiving at the Children's Home. In the meantime, the city's first snowflakes were already falling softly on the window ledge and the walk outside.

"Each flake so different, so unique," reflected Esther. "Each snowflake so loved. It should be the same for our children, especially for our Sara."

Later, as Sara curled up in Esther's arms and sucked her thumb, her eyes were becoming heavy as her caretaker gently sang over her, "Jesus does love you, and I do, too. The stable has room for Jesus and you."

When the little girl was officially asleep, Esther carefully laid her in her bed. And then, with pen and paper in hand, she sat down in her rocker and began to write.

My Dearest Myron . . .

Even though Mrs. Canfield seemed to be very busy with her cleaning, Paul went from staring at his blank paper to looking up in her direction, hoping she would see his silent cry for help. If she had seen him, she gave no indication that she had and continued to go about her own chores while softly humming, "What a Friend *You* Have in Jesus." And so, Paul did something he previously thought he couldn't. He picked up the pencil and started to write.

Once he started, he found he couldn't stop. He wrote, and he wrote, and he wrote some more. He told Sara about the farm, Malvern, and Nodaway, a smaller community where the Canfields often went for some of their trading and harness repair. He also told her about Reverend Thomas and the church. He introduced her to all the animals: Brownie, Betsy, and Spotty, the milk cows; the sow, Gerts; and the boar, Hercules. He did the best he could explaining what sows and boars actually were. He told her about the hens whose names he always got confused and the mean rooster, Chester, whose name he never forgot. He delighted in telling her about the collie dog, Slim, and the cat, Charlie. And he saved a half-sheet of paper to specifically describe Pat and Pet, and how, by standing on a small four-legged stool, he could now harness them, hitch them to the wagon, and—after much practice—drive them. He had to admit, though, his arms were really tired after driving a short distance.

As if she were right there sitting next to him, close enough to see the words he was writing, he continued to write—heavy heart and all. Whether he meant this as a P. S., an afterthought, or just did not want to stop writing, he took another piece of paper and once again wrote a greeting and started as if it was another letter altogether.

My dear Sara,

I miss you very much. When I go to school, do my chores, and say my prayers, I imagine you are here with me. Remember what I told you: "I love you." The world may not have room for us, but we have room for each other. Someday, I will come and get you. Someday, I will be able to take care of you and protect you again.

Until then, please, please, please, stay close to Miss Arthur. Do what she says. I think she will keep you safe until I get there. And somehow, I will. The Canfields talk about Thanksgiving and having roast duck and turkey, but I remember Thanksgivings with soup and bread. Soup and bread would be okay if we were together, but I wish you could have some turkey. Mrs. Canfield is a really good cook.

The Canfields are also talking about Christmas, and Reverend Thomas asked me if I would sing at the Christmas Eve service. Do you think I should? I know it's silly to ask. I'm supposed to be the big brother with the answers. But without our being together, what does it matter?

I guess I have to believe someday soon we will be together. Yes, I dare even to pray, if God will listen to someone like me, that somehow, someway, we will be together at Christmas. And maybe, somehow, I have to hope. And maybe, by singing, Jesus' stable will have room for you and me. I guess that is what I believe. We have to believe, and we have to hope. Anyway, that's all I can say. I know: Maybe you and I could live in the empty stall next to Pat and Pet. Maybe I can ask the Canfields.

Until then.

Love,

Your brother, Paul

With those words, Paul put his pencil, along with his head, down on the table. In a few minutes, he was fast asleep.

"Do you have everything, Mr. Canfield?" Isabelle asked fondly as she watched her husband prepare for his trip to Nodaway and Malvern.

"I have your list of supplies to pick up in Malvern, I have the outline you somehow were able to procure, and here is the bag you just now gave me. I will take those to Nodaway." With these final words, he held the bag and its contents up in his hand so she could see them.

"Mr. Canfield, you are the silly one this morning," she said as she handed him his hat and coat. Then with a gentle peck on his cheek, she moved him toward the door.

As she moved him forward, he continued, "The cookies you made for Reverend Thomas's trip, too. Eggs to trade when I arrive in Malvern . . . harness to drop off for repair in Nodaway, outline . . . Yes, I have everything. I'll go to Nodaway first and then to Malvern." Howard said these words more to himself than to her. It didn't matter, though, because her thoughts were somewhere else and she told him so.

"What about this?" Mrs. Canfield asked, in a tone she would often use when Mr. Canfield forgot her list of supplies. When he looked up at her, he saw her holding up Paul's letter in front of him.

"Oh . . . well, yes." Howard smiled. "I knew you would be giving it to me. Did you read it?"

"Why, of course I didn't." she declared. "And don't you dare either!"

"I wouldn't think of it," Howard said. Taking the folded letter, he carefully placed it in the inside pocket of his coveralls and was on his way.

Isabelle hadn't exactly been honest, although she rather figured he knew that already. She had read Paul's letter. After all, that is what a mother does when she frets over one of her children. She tries every way she can to protect them.

Since it was still very early in the morning, Isabelle decided she would let Paul sleep a while longer. And when he woke up, she would tell him to bring in some black walnuts. He could crack the shells and pick out the nuts. They would taste pretty good in cake, and she would have enough for Christmas divinity candy as well.

Just maybe, with that inducement before him, he would open up to her a bit more. Just maybe.

In Nodaway, Howard went directly to the harness shop to drop off a leather strapping that needed a new buckle, along with the outline Mrs. Canfield had drawn. Handing the drawing to the shop owner, Jas Jordan, he asked him, "Do you think you can do this, Jas? Everything else is in the bag."

"Hmm . . ." was all he said as he examined the drawing and the bag contents. "Might need to talk to Joe over in Malvern, but I think it can be done. Never done it before. Maybe Joe has, but I think it can be done. Come by in about a week. How does that sound?" he asked as he finally looked up at Howard.

"Sounds just fine, Jas. Thank you," Howard said as he extended his hand. After they shook hands over the agreement, Howard went on his way to Malvern.

By the time Howard reached Malvern, Reverend Thomas was already packed for his trip and waiting for him at the church.

"I'm sorry I'm late," he called out, hitching Pat and Pet to the rail.

"Oh, you aren't really late, I guess," the reverend said. "I'm just anxious to get going is all. Even so, I was hoping we could walk over to Millie's Café and have a coffee before I head out. There's something I want to visit with you about."

Howard needed no second invite as he was already walking toward Millie's. He never turned down a good cup of coffee and maybe a cinnamon roll.

As they sat down in the corner of the café, Reverend Thomas told Howard about the letter he had received the day before from Miss Arthur and her grave concern for Sara's emotional health and spiritual wellbeing. "Sara still believes no one has room for her, even though Esther has taken her under her wing," he explained. "I'm afraid her young mind thinks Esther did so as just a duty."

He went on to stress how much Sara wanted to see Paul. Yet both he and Esther believed it would be more traumatic for her to come and visit, only to have to leave her brother all over again. "Maybe after Christmas, with your permission, I could take Paul to New York instead."

Reverend Thomas studied Howard's face for his reaction.

"Maybe," Howard said with minimal expression. But then he took the letter from his inside pocket and handed it over. "Read it, please."

Reverend Thomas started to put it in his briefcase.

"No," Howard said a little more forcibly. "Read it now."

Without a word and making sure no one was sitting nearby, Reverend Thomas read the letter loud enough for Howard to hear. Afterwards, he very carefully folded it again and this time put it in his briefcase without a word. They both sat in silence until he shook his head.

"Oh my! Oh my!" the reverend moaned.

"What have I done?" Howard asked, almost to himself. "What have I done? Live in an empty stall next to Pat and Pet. Is that the answer?" Looking straight at Reverend Thomas, he looked desperate for some type of an answer, maybe even a miracle.

"May I share a secret with you?" Reverend Thomas put a hand on Howard's arm. "Esther and I have . . . well, we've been sort of courting through letters, and the few times I've been in New York City, I've gone to see her."

"Courting? Miss Arthur?" Despite his heavy heart, Howard couldn't help but be amused by the admission. "That's not really a secret. Most everyone knows you're sweet on her. And according to Mrs. Canfield, Esther likes you quite a lot, too."

Reverend Thomas blushed. "Well, the other part of the secret is Esther's idea that, when we get married, maybe we could adopt Paul and Sara. It would be hard at first, but I think we can do it."

"Reverend, I believe you and Esther can do about anything you set your minds to." But he wasn't finished yet. "I'll tell you this, though: I'm not sure that's the answer regarding these two. I know you both would love them dearly. So, yes, it solves a problem, but I'm not sure it's the answer." He squinted in contemplation. "Let's both think on it and talk again when you return."

Reverend Thomas was both surprised and puzzled at Howard's answer, but he agreed to do as he proposed. A few minutes later, with a letter in his pocket and cookies on the buggy seat next to him, Reverend Thomas waved goodbye and set out for the livery stable located next to the train station, where he had made plans to board his horse while he was gone.

By the third week of Advent, snow was falling in regular intervals. After each new round, Paul would wake up early in the morning, bundle up in the coveralls Isabelle had made for him shortly after his arrival, and slip on an old pair of Howard's work boots that—with the help of the thick woolen socks Mrs. Canfield had bought him at the Bootery—fit snugly on his feet. And then out he would go, shoveling paths from the house to the barn to the chicken house and from the house to the privy.

Dressed in that kind of weather-appropriate clothing to protect him from the cold wind and dampness, Paul enjoyed the freedom he found outside. He often thought of the contrast between the Canfield farm and New York streets he used to roam, along with the warmth of the inviting farmhouse compared to the unsettling feeling he always seemed to have at the Children's Home.

In many ways, even though he was just ten, Paul understood how fortunate he was to live with the Canfields. That was part of his aching feeling. Although still very leery, he did feel that since he was under their care, he had a responsibility. Before Paul left New York, he, along with Sara and all of the other children who were being sent to live outside of the orphanage, had been told by the superintendent many times to behave, mind their manners, and do as they were told. No back-talking and no getting in trouble, or who knew where you would possibly be placed next.

What Paul discovered at the Canfield home and Reverend Thomas's church respectively was that the Canfields were a warm and welcoming couple and all the church members seemed to accept him with open arms, even though he still held some of them at a distance. The treatment he received from the Canfields and people at the church was nothing like the horror stories told by children who were sent back to the Home when a placement didn't seem to work out.

For Paul, his deeper ache came from imagining what Sara was going through, wondering what she thought of his letter, and wishing he could make her world and his safer. If he could take her place, he gladly would have. However, imprinted in his memory was the fact that the Canfields only wanted one child, and that child *had* to be a boy.

As much as he wanted to believe they really did care for him, he held their emotional openness, demonstrations of kindness, and concern for his wellbeing still at a distance most of the time. He also held his own warm feelings for these two people—who probably had given him more love and support than anyone ever had before—buried beneath his suspicion and fear that sooner or later, they'd grow tired of him and send him away when he was no longer needed. It was only once in a while, when he hurt so much, that his pain seeped through the cracks in his armor of self-protection.

That happened again during the fourth week of Advent. Up earlier than usual, he was fumbling for his clothes in the dark of the December morning when he overheard Howard and Isabelle talking. Quietly moving closer to the door, he opened it just a sliver to hear what they were saying.

"It won't work out," Howard said. "It's asking too much of two people. I'll tell Reverend Thomas about our plans when I see him."

Isabelle responded, "It grieves me greatly to say this, Mr. Canfield, but you might be right. They're good intentions, but with so many hurdles to face? Your suggestion is best. You need to be honest with him."

"I know, I know," Howard said. "I will."

With the conversation at an apparent end, Paul closed his door, sat down on his bed, and buried his head in his hands. It had happened. Just as he was waiting for, they'd decided to get rid of him. His one consolation was that at least he'd be back with Sara, no matter what.

No matter who cared about them, he'd care for her. He'd have room for her.

With that resolution, he finished getting dressed and then sat on the edge of his bed until someone knocked on his bedroom door.

"Paul," Howard called. "Paul, you awake? It's breakfast time."

"Okay," Paul said. And that was all.

Other than the most basic of responses, that was all for the whole morning. And it stayed that way when they were chopping wood and Reverend Thomas came up the winding lane.

"Hi, Paul." He waved before stepping down from the buggy.

"Hello." Paul's voice was less enthusiastic than he'd ever displayed to the reverend.

That made the visitor pause, but he didn't comment on it. Instead, he only turned to greet Howard and said, "Can we talk in the house for a minute?"

"Of course."

As the two men retreated, Paul paid no attention to them. He simply continued to chop wood, swinging the axe over his head and hitting each log. Working faster seemed to be the only way he could keep from running down the lane to take off to nowhere. For Sara's sake, he had to stay until they told him he would be leaving. Then, sadly leave he would.

On his way back out, Reverend Thomas tried to make himself heard over the noise of one very focused orphan boy. "Remember Christmas Eve, Paul."

But Paul didn't look up to acknowledge Reverend Thomas. In fact, he even turned away so he wouldn't be able to see the reverend while he stepped into his buggy and took off down the lane.

The three days 'til Christmas Eve became a blur for Paul. He did not know which day it was, nor did he care. On more than one occasion,

Howard or Isabelle asked if something was wrong, and he would simply shrug his shoulders. Moreover, his normally healthy appetite was stifled severely, so when Isabelle tried to coax him to eat, he would just ask to be excused. Paul also thought about the past few times Mr. Canfield went to Nodaway. Usually, he would ask Paul if he wanted to ride along, but on those occasions he didn't ask. It seemed to Paul that was another sign they were displeased with him and he would be going back to New York.

When Howard gave him chores to do, Paul still did them. He wasn't disobedient, only distant. Despite his best attempts to not care about anything, though, he couldn't help but be curious about one detail: why Howard had stopped helping him so much. Paul would watch from a distance as Howard went alone to the work shed, where he did woodworking.

His ultimate conclusion was that Paul was no longer welcome at the Canfields. That soon, probably after the Christmas Eve service, he would be sent away. For him, there would be no Christmas. His only heartfelt joy was knowing he would be reunited with Sara. They would make their own Christmas, even if it was nothing but being in each other's presence. Turning his attention back to his thoughts about Sara brought him a few seconds of joy. But the joy quickly disappeared as his heart became heavy once again. Now, no one wanted *him*.

It was a miserable thought, worsened by the exact realization of what Sara must have felt—and what she must still be feeling—when she cried, "No one wants me, Paulie."

It was Christmas Eve, and Howard had gone into Nodaway, leaving the silent Paul to finish the milking. He didn't think anything of it until his return, when Isabelle wasted no time calling him into the house. "Mr. Canfield, come here. I want to show you something."

That something was up in Paul's room. Laying on the bed there, neatly folded, were all the clothes and items they had bought or made for Paul since his arrival. At the foot was a small bundle.

"I went through it," Isabelle said as her tears fell down her face. "It holds nothing more than the clothes he had with him when he came here."

"What?" Howard shook his head. "What brought this on?"

Isabelle had no response to that.

"Paul's been slipping backwards for weeks now, almost to the place he was when he first arrived." He might have said the words out loud, but they were almost spoken to himself as he tried to sort through the problem before them. "He's quiet, jittery, and sullen, and he must be hungry. He has to be hungry. He hasn't eaten much for a while."

"We need to talk to him," Isabelle said, determined to find out exactly what was wrong.

It was late and getting later, with chores left to do and the Christmas Eve service to attend. But he nodded in agreement. "Yes, before chores and before we go, we need to talk to him. Before we—"

The sound of boots stomping against the back porch steps broke into his statement. This was the familiar noise indicating Paul was cleaning snow off his work boots before taking them off and entering the house.

They headed back downstairs into the warm kitchen, where Paul was standing on the large rug, taking off his coveralls.

"Are you hungry?" Isabelle asked him.

"No."

"Sit down, Paul." Howard did his best to couch it as a request, not a command.

Paul just stood there, inching slowly toward the wood-burning stove to warm himself.

"Please sit down," Isabelle tried next, placing a cup of hot chocolate down on the table for him.

This time he did, but he looked stiff and emotionless the whole time.

Howard cleared his throat. He found it took a great amount of effort to begin. "Paul, we know something has made you terribly upset, angry, or hurt. Maybe all three, but we don't know what it is."

"You won't tell us, and it deeply hurts us." The look on Isabelle's face spoke as loudly as her words. "We thought you were finally feeling like you belonged here. We know you're upset about Sara, but—"

Before she could say anything more, Paul broke, spilling out everything he had been holding on to. "I heard you talking," he accused them with hot, angry tears. "I heard you say it wasn't working out—that it was too much to ask of two people."

Howard and Isabelle stood there, too surprised to say anything.

"I know you talked to Reverend Thomas about sending me back to the Children's Home," Paul cried. "Just after I sing in the Christmas Eve service or something. I heard you say 'there were too many hurdles.'" His slim shoulders were shaking. "I tried. I thought maybe you did care, and I tried!"

He started to rise from his chair, but Isabelle stopped him by the heartfelt act of wrapping her arms around him. Kissing his cheeks, she was crying too, which made her own speech difficult to get out.

"Oh, Paul! Paul, we want no such thing," she said. "We want you to be our son. Remember? Howard told you that weeks ago."

"Paul, you misheard us entirely." Coming over as well, Howard gripped the boy's shoulder. "Reverend Thomas and Miss Arthur wanted to adopt you and Sara both as soon as they're married. You know they're fond of the two of you," he said. "But I told Reverend Thomas to wait, and we all would discuss it some more."

Both Paul and Isabelle were still crying while he spoke.

"You see, I was wrong," Howard admitted. "I said we only had room for one child, but I was simply looking at the space we had. You and Mrs. Canfield and Miss Arthur have shown me that love is as deep and wide as we want it to be, regardless of the physical space we have."

"What Mr. Canfield is trying to say—" Isabelle started. But she didn't get to finish, thanks to some sort of commotion outside, followed by a very loud knock.

"Go answer it," Howard said with a hint of anticipation.

As always, Paul did as he was asked. However, he had barely started to open the door when it flung open so hard he was shoved up against the wall. And he had to wonder if he'd knocked his head harder than he thought, considering the familiar voice in his ears.

"Paulie! Paulie, it's me! It's Sara! I'm here!" Sara, unaware she had slammed her brother behind the door, called out, "The Canfields want me too!"

Her absolute joy was evident enough to affect the whole room, and to convince Paul he had not heard wrongly.

"Sara!" He stepped into her line of vision. "Sara, it's you! It's really you!" Hugging his sister, he let her go only to hug her again.

"Reverend Thomas came to New York this morning," the little girl explained while he smiled at the scene. "We . . . all of us—you know, Miss Arthur, Reverend Thomas and me—ate sandwiches on the train. Miss Arthur and I made them for our trip. I ate two of them because

I was really hungry." She didn't stop to let anyone else get a word in edgewise. "I saw Malvern 'cause Reverend Thomas drove the buggy right down Main Street and showed Miss Arthur and me the whole town. Oh, Paulie, is it true? Do Mr. and Mrs. Canfield want me?"

Paul had no time to answer since Isabelle and Howard wrapped both of them in their arms, exclaiming together, "Yes! Yes! We want you. We want both of you! This is where you belong now. There will always be room for you here."

As soon as there was a brief calm to the excitement, Reverend Thomas told Paul and Sara about Esther, er . . . Miss Arthur . . . and their plans to be married in the spring.

Howard was the one who specifically added the details. "We've already talked to the lawyer to start filing for adoption for both of you." He regarded both of them with shining eyes. "That is, if you'll let us be your mother and father."

Sara and Paul looked at one another, then at their proposed parents. "Yes! Yes!"

"And we'll be your godparents," Esther said with a big smile.

"Folks," Reverend Thomas said as soon as there was the chance, "Esther and I had better get going since we have a certain Christmas Eve service to hold in just a few hours." He directed his next statement solely to Paul. "Paul, you will sing, won't you?"

"I said I would." Paul's whole face was still beaming.

"Can I sing too?" Sara clapped her hands together. "Can I sing too? Miss Arthur says I sing better than Paulie does."

"Oops," Esther's face turned red.

"She does," laughed Paul. "She sings a lot better than I do. Maybe we can sing a duet."

"That would be great!" Reverend Thomas exclaimed. "What a night this is turning out to be."

132

"Yes, it is," agreed Howard, turning practical despite the joy he still radiated. "But before we can be off too, we have three cows that need milking. Oh, Paul, I almost forgot . . . wait here a minute." Everyone but Isabelle seemed to be wondering where Mr. Canfield went off to and for what reason. They did not have to wait too long.

When Mr. Canfield returned, he was carrying a sack. Handing it to Paul, he said, "I suppose you've been wondering why I went off to Nodaway the last couple of weeks and didn't take you."

Paul nodded his head and said, "Well, I thought . . . yes, I was wondering."

"Well, look in the sack and you'll see why," Howard answered.

At the mention of the word "look," Paul opened the sack and pulled out a shining pair of work boots, with one of them featuring an elevated heel. "What?" he exclaimed. "I haven't . . . I mean I never thought I would . . . for me?" he asked, hardly able to contain his excitement.

"Yes, Paul. They are for you," Mrs. Canfield answered.

"For you, Paul. Mr. Jordan at the harness shop made them, and the shoe repair man at the bootery helped," Mr. Canfield said with a smile and added, "try them on."

He really didn't have to tell him to do so because Paul was already busy throwing off his old boots and, with little effort, putting on the new ones. While he walked around, his broad smile let everyone know how happy he was.

"Paulie, your limp is gone!" Sara cried out, and as if he hadn't heard her, she repeated again and again, "It's gone! It's gone!"

"Yes, it is! It really is! Thank you, Mr. Can . . . I mean, thank you, Dad and Mom!" Paul shouted with a sound of glee in his voice. But after a few more steps, he sat back down and immediately took off the new boots and reached for the old.

"What's wrong, Paul?" Howard asked.

"Nothing, nothing at all. I'm not wearing these out to the barn. I want to wear them to church tonight, so we'd better get moving. We have cows to milk."

"That we do, son. That we do!" agreed Mr. Canfield.

"Yes, we do!" Paul reached for his coveralls on instinct, then turned to Isabelle. "Ah . . . before we go milk . . . May I have a sandwich? I'm really hungry."

"Me too," Sara added. "I'm hungry again."

"Of course you can," Isabelle said, beaming. "I might as well fix some for everyone. Otherwise, our stomachs will be growling before church is over. And I don't want to hear any racket while our children sing."

Everyone laughed, their joy feeding off of each other's until the whole room seemed to shine.

As Reverend Thomas had said, it was quite a night—a beautiful night with so many messages of hope and reminders of love. During the service, Rachael, who had been adopted by the Moores, read Luke 2:7: "And she laid Him in a manger, because there was no room for them in the inn."

Hearing that, Howard looked at Paul at his side, then Sara next to Paul, and finally Isabelle beside Sara. She intuitively looked toward him too, and they both smiled as if to say, *If it was our inn, there would have been room.*

Just before the candles were lit, their two children slipped out of the pew, just as Reverend Thomas had instructed them. Right behind them, Esther sat at the piano to accompany them in singing "Jesus Loves Me," while watching the siblings hold hands and look out into the congregation at Howard and Isabelle.

The moment was beautiful in every way.

It was really late by the time all the Canfields arrived back at the farm, but there was one more thing left to do. While Isabelle and Sara went into the house, Paul helped Howard take Pat and Pet to the barn and bed them for the night. They worked in happy silence, for the most part, until the moment they were leaving the roomy structure.

"Come with me," Howard told him, leading the way to the woodworking shed, where he lifted the lantern toward the bench.

"What is it?" Paul asked, curious.

"It's a trunk bed," he explained. "We'll store it under your bed when Sara isn't sleeping in it until I build you a room in the attic."

"So, that's what you were making in here." Paul's young voice was filled with remorse, regretting all the thoughts he'd had about what might be happening in here.

"I'm sorry I couldn't tell you, Paul." Howard's own words held the same apologetic tone. "I didn't want you to have another disappointment if, for some reason, Sara couldn't come back with Reverend Thomas and Miss Arthur."

"I understand now." Paul stopped for a moment in thoughtful contemplation. It seemed like he had a whole conversation in his head before arriving at a worthwhile conclusion. "Yes, I know. I know you really do care."

Unable to speak past the lump in his throat, Howard picked up one end of the trunk bed, watching while Paul reached for the other end as if they'd always been working together. Then they carried it to the house, where a very, very sleepy Sara was waiting and ready to jump into it for a good night's sleep.

✳

"Is it morning already?" Sara yawned as she came into the kitchen after Paul.

"No, it's not morning," Howard answered, "It's Christmas!"

"It's Christmas! It's Christmas!" Both Paul and Sara shouted back, their eyes very open now to take in the beautiful decorated evergreen standing in the small sitting room, where a number of presents were placed underneath, tagged with clearly written names.

Their names.

"It's Christmas!" Isabelle repeated joyfully, handing them hot chocolate and homemade cinnamon rolls.

"Is this Tuesday?" Paul asked, remembering how recently he had lost track of the days.

"No, silly." This time it was Sara who answered. "It's Christmas!"

Chapter 5

MOO News Is Good News

Was there more or less bad news
At the time of Jesus' birth?
Was evil more pronounced
When Jesus walked the earth?

When Tabitha arose,
And a mother served her guest,
Was her joy in a stranglehold
When someone criticized her best?

And how about you or me,
When our joy is cut off at the knees
By some sneaky bit of bad news
That keeps us in a squeeze?

When you add up the daily ledger
Just before you fall to sleep,
Isn't it really good to know
It's Good News that measures deep?

"Momma! Momma!" Sally yelled as she headed down the hallway to the living room. "Momma!"

Rachel Richards looked up from her iPhone.

"Momma, Joey won't play bank with me." Sally came to a stop right in front of her mother. "Make him play with me, Mom."

Racing right behind Sally was her brother, Joey. "Mom, I don't want to play bank with Sally. She's too bossy, and she wants to be the president. I'm eight. I should be president and—"

"Am not bossy."

"Are, too." Joey made a face at her.

"Momma, Joey just made a face at me," Sally tattled, hopping onto the couch to try to block her mother's view of her brother. "Make him stop and play with me. I'm six, and I like numbers. I should be president."

"Sally." Rachel put her iPhone down. "Hush for a minute, and be still. Joey, stop making faces at your sister." Her eyes moved back and forth with the magical ability to catch both their attention at the same time. "Now, what's the problem?"

"I said—" Sally started.

"I don't want to play bank with her," Joey repeated.

"Well . . ." Rachel looked thoughtful. "What would you play with Sally?"

"Huh?" The question threw him off, making his mind race with possibilities that wouldn't interest her. "Well, uh—"

"How about café?" Sally was determined for her mother to make Joey play with her.

"I'll play café," sighed Joey, "if I'm the cook and you're the truck driver."

138

"What can we have to eat, Mom?" Sally asked her mother, thinking about what might be on the menu.

Pleased that her children were able to work out their differences for the time being, she volunteered. "I'll cut some apple slices for you, and you can have some graham crackers. Then I have some work to do."

"Okay, Mom," the children said in unison.

Joey rushed to his room and sat down at his desk to write out a menu. In a short while, he was back at the play area he and Sally shared to take on the respective roles of truck-stop cook and truck driver. Pretending to be wiping down the counter and rearranging chairs, he looked up as Sally came through the imaginary door. A truck driver now, she had on a ball cap and one of her father's old shirts, which was six sizes too big for her.

It got in the way a little as she majestically plopped herself onto a counter stool.

"What'll it be, Mac?" Joey mumbled, acting utterly unenthusiastic, which was very easy for him to do.

"Name's not Mac," Sally said loudly. "Name's Sal." She grabbed the menu from her brother's hand to look it over.

MENU	
Pop	$ 6.00
Coughee	$ 5.00
Toasted Chees	$ 3.00
Sallid	$ 9.00
Tip	$10.00

"Hmm . . ." Sally broke the silence and looked up. "Give me my usual."

"Look, Mac—er—Sal, I don't know what your usual is."

"Clara knows what my usual is," Sally said, gazing over his shoulder to look for the imaginary individual. "Ask her."

Joey looked over his shoulder as well. "Clara, huh? Oh yeah, Clara. She's not here. She won something from a magazine and doesn't have to work for ten years now. She left me without any help."

On a roll, Joey would have continued if not for her rude interruption. "Look, I'm hungry." Sal barked without expressing any interest in Clara's fortune. "Just give me the toasted cheese and a salad."

Joey and Sally played just long enough to empty out the café food pantry. By then, Rachel had finished her work and came over to see how they were doing.

"We're done playing," Sally reported matter-of-factly.

"She ate all the food," Joey added.

"Hmm, it looks like the cook might have had a supper break, too." His mom's fingers traced the graham cracker crumbs falling from his shirt.

"Ah, Mom," Joey gently protested.

"Now that you're both fed, go grab your coats and bundle up tight. It's cold outside. Joey, remember you have your reading lesson with Miss Kate. Sally, you can go to the real bank with me."

As the family drove to Miss Kate's home, Joey was thinking of all the times his father had told him about how she had also been his reading teacher.

"I remember," Dad said, "Miss Kate wearing spectacles perched lightly on her nose. I always thought they would fall off, but they never did. She wore her brown hair in a bun even when she was a younger lady. When I went to her home for extra reading lessons, they were always held at her kitchen table. She always wore a colorful apron tied around her waist and a house dress, but only in her home. At school, she wore a very smart business suit just like your grandmother does when she's at the dress shop working." Before he ended his description of Miss Kate, he started to laugh and said, "I think she enjoyed the cookies she made for me when I went to her home for Saturday lessons as much as I did."

To which Joey replied, "I think she still does." He giggled as he said it, adding, "Wow! Dad, Miss Kate still looks just like she did back in the old days when she taught you."

A half hour later, Joey was sitting at Miss Kate's kitchen table. He enjoyed being at her place. She always decorated her house for the holidays, and the Christmas season was extra special with all of her mangers and stable animals. Sometimes, after he had finished his lesson, they would play with one of the displays. In his opinion, she was really good at pretending—almost as good as he was! Joey had been coming for reading lessons since he was in first grade. He knew from experience that when Miss Kate said, "It's time to read," it was indeed time to read, especially if he wanted to play with the animals and a manger afterwards. The manger he usually picked to play with was the one his tutor's father had made for her when she was his age.

And here he was, reading for real.

"Now, Joey." Miss Kate spoke fondly but with authority. "Read it again, and pronounce each word slowly."

For the third time, Joey looked at the sentence, his index finger underlining each syllable as he went. "The el-e-phant ran fas-ter than all the o-ther an-i-mals."

"Pretty good." Miss Kate smiled. "You'll need to watch those syllables, though."

"Huh?" Joey gave her a puzzled look.

"Well," Miss Kate explained, "you pronounce this word 'oth-er,' not 'o-ther.' And it's 'fast-er,' not 'fas-ter.'"

"Oh," Joey said, not very convincingly, but he let her guide him to the next sentence and then the next until his mom was back to pick him up.

As they were eating supper that evening, his father turned to him. "How did your reading lesson go this afternoon, son?"

"Okay, I guess." He took another bite of his pasta, calmly ignoring the drip of sauce that fell from his fork onto the table.

"What did you read?" Jacob prompted, since he had been hoping for more of a conversation than that.

"Oh," Joey stalled, his face flushing as he tried hard to remember how he and Miss Kate had practiced pronouncing the words. "About el-e-phants and o-ther a-ni-mals." He didn't think he was doing a very good job of it at the moment.

"Hmm . . ." His dad put his hand to his mouth and his elbow on the table. "Hmm . . . "

"Miss Kate is helping me pronounce words," Joey volunteered. "I'm working on o-ther and fas-ter right now."

"Sounds like you're doing pretty good, son. It takes a while," Jacob said. "You'll pick it up. Believe it or not, Miss Kate was my reading teacher in school, too."

"I know, Dad. You told me that before and another time." Actually, Joey had lost track of the number of times when his father had told him, but it didn't matter. His father only smiled.

Rachel looked at her husband and smiled. "Your dad is a pretty good reader now, Joey."

"Yeah, he can read all those numbers in the paper." Sally turned to him for reassurance, though. "Can't you?"

"Well, as a matter of fact, I guess I can. You know what? I can even read them better when the two of you are sitting in the chair with me." That took a second to wink at Rachel.

"Oh," the children said in unison. "You're just teasing."

Joey shifted in his chair. "Did you and Miss Kate ever play with her stables and animals?"

"Ah, wow! It's been a while. But—" his father had to stop and think about it. "Yes, I think we did. I remember playing number games more with Miss Kate. After my reading lesson, though."

"Yeah, I know." Joey was very well aware of the rules. "She says we can't play with the animals until after I read."

"Well, it sounds to me like Miss Kate has the Richards men all figured out." Rachel looked across the table at her daughter, who seemed to be waiting for a chance to say something as well. "Wouldn't you agree, Sally?"

"She sure is smart!" the little girl blurted.

"She certainly is!" they all exclaimed.

Thanksgiving weekend was filled with football and family visits, along with the days seeming much shorter. Yet the Richards still found time to put up their Christmas decorations. Likewise, when December officially hit, they found themselves falling back on their family traditions, including a game their parents called "Where Is Santa?"

Each week, Santa was hidden. After the Advent candle was lit and the Advent reading completed, the children were given reindeer clues to help them search for Mr. Claus. Sally especially liked that game, while Joey's favorite was "The Trip to the Manger," which always preceded "Where Is Santa?" As he or his sister would light each new Advent candle, the other sibling would move the shepherds, sheep, donkey, Mary, and Joseph closer to the stable. By Christmas Eve, they would all be in place for the Christ candle to be lit and the baby Jesus to be put in the manger.

Early Friday evening, a week after Thanksgiving, Jacob was reading the paper in the living room while Joey was playing on the floor with his action figures. With a sigh, he put his paper down, muttering to himself. "Sometimes I really wish I didn't know how to read. All there seems to be is bad news these days."

That got Joey's attention. "What do you mean, Dad?"

His father instantly regretted not speaking more softly. "I'm sorry, Joey. I didn't know you heard me."

But it was too late. Joey was already rising from the floor to slide onto his father's lap, crunching the newspaper as he landed. "Yeah, but why?"

"It's rather hard to explain, I guess," his father admitted, puzzling over his own words again. "You know I work with numbers all day long?"

Joey nodded.

"I know that—regardless if it's cold and there's a blizzard outside, or if it's hot and sunny; if two countries are at peace or war; or if a person is happy or sad—two plus two will always be four, and six divided by three will always be two."

"Yeah." Joey was trying very hard to follow where his dad was heading. "But what does that have to do with reading? Or people being happy or sad?"

"I guess it is a little confusing." Jacob smiled and pulled his son closer. "What I'm trying to say is that number problems always come out exactly how they should, regardless of how people act or feel, or what they think or believe. People are much more confusing to understand than numbers, though. I didn't really mean I don't want to read. I was just expressing—"

Joey weighed in when his father paused. "I think I understand." He cocked his head to the side. "Hmm. Yeah, I sorta get it."

His father gave him a squeeze. "Well then, someday you'll have to explain it all to me."

The next morning, Joey came through Miss Kate's front door with a very determined look on his face. Without his usual greeting, he sat down at the kitchen table and blurted out, "I don't think I want to learn how to read any better than I do now."

His comment really surprised Miss Kate. It took her a few seconds to come up with a suitable response.

"Why, Joey, whatever do you mean? You're doing so good, too."

But he just sat there with the same determined expression.

Having dealt with stubborn children for a very long time now, Miss Kate would have none of Joey's monkey business. She turned his chair sideways, put her own right in front of his, and sat down to look him straight in the eye.

"Now, Joey, you listen to me. Reading is too important to be ignored. You're going to be a good reader. Look at all you'd miss if you couldn't read."

"Like what?" Joey was just a little curious about that last comment.

"Well, for starters, you wouldn't be able to read menus at restaurants. You would have to point at the pictures and say, 'Gimme that' or 'Gimme this.'"

Joey let a slight giggle slip out while he watched her point at imaginary items.

"Reading and writing go hand in hand," she explained. "How would you know what to write if you couldn't read? You would be grunting and pointing your whole way through life."

She now illustrated her point with grunts and finger-pointing, and Joey burst into peals of laughter.

After they were both settled down, she added, "And if you can't read, you won't ever be able to read the Good News for yourself."

"That's just it," Joey stated matter-of-factly. "My dad says there isn't much good news in the world anymore. He says there are so many problems and bad things happening, he wishes he'd never learned how to read."

Miss Kate took her time responding. "Well, I've heard some pretty good excuses from a lot of kids. I can even remember a few your dad gave me when he was in my class. But this takes the Christmas cookie. I have to say, it's pretty lame."

"Lame?" questioned Joey.

She nodded. "When I say lame, I mean some people can make up some pretty creative excuses why they don't want to or don't like to read, or why they don't have their homework done. But this is a first!"

146

Both her hands went out, palms up. "'I wish I didn't know how to read because of all the bad news.'"

"Are you mad at Dad, Miss Kate?" he asked, worried now.

"No, of course not." The smile she gave him was reassuring. "But you and I have to think differently about this problem and come up with a different solution. Let's see now." She intentionally trailed off, leaving room open for him to chime in.

Listening really hard, Joey wanted to say something. He just wasn't sure what it should be. Fortunately, he didn't have to wonder too long because Miss Kate started to speak again.

"Now, you're eight years old, right?" she quizzed her student.

"Uh, yes," Joey said hesitantly.

She continued, "You've seen a lot in your lifetime, I suppose."

Joey didn't answer, too busy trying to come up with things she might consider important, just in case she asked him.

It was a good thing too, considering her next words came in the form of a question. "What's the worst thing you heard, read, or saw this week?"

"Huh." Once again, he thought hard. "I guess a picture of a boy. The words with the picture said he was starving because there was a war. I asked Mom about it."

"Oh!" Miss Kate exclaimed. "I think I saw a picture like that. It was of a little boy in Europe during World War II. Is that the same picture you saw?"

"I don't think so." Joey tried to be just as serious as she was when he responded, "It was a little boy in Africa."

Miss Kate shook her head. "Wow! Bad news. Bad news." She shook her head again. "Never seems to stop, does it?"

"I guess not." He looked down at his lap.

"Okay, now what's the best thing you saw, read, or heard this week?" All seriousness was gone from her face, replaced with encouraging delight.

"That's easy," Joey said. "I heard on the radio a little boy was given a kidney, and he's doing great. And Dad helped me read how they're giving backpacks filled with food to kids. So, we filled one up, too. And then there's a man who gave this family a house, and—"

"Whoa, there," Miss Kate teased. "I just asked you about one thing."

"Oh, I'm sorry."

She laughed. "Don't be sorry, be happy! I just asked for one good thing, and you told me about several good things. That's good news!"

Joey digested that for a minute or two. "Miss Kate?"

"Yes?"

"I think I get it." He came across as solemn and thoughtful once again. "We can't ever stop bad things from happening, but we can make many more good things happen if we really want to."

"I think you're right," said Miss Kate. "And I believe that was God's idea when He gave Jesus to us."

"That's why we say Christmas is about Good News, isn't it?" he asked.

"Yes, I believe you're right again." Miss Kate wasn't finished with the little lesson yet. "What do you think we should do to help your father see just how strong the Good News is?"

"Well, I have an idea." Getting up from the table, he went over to collect one of the mangers and the animals. "Let's make up a play with animals, people, and angels. Then we can put it on! Maybe we can get the other kids you teach to help us, and—"

"Well," Miss Kate said a little guarded. "We only have about three weeks until Christmas. Since I'm on the education committee, though,

I know we can get the church basement the Sunday afternoon before Christmas Eve." She seemed to be talking to herself more than him. "Hmm. But we don't have a play to present. What to do? What to do?"

"I know!" Joey said enthusiastically. "I'll tell you the story, and you write it down. And then we can call the kids and set up a time to practice. And—" The more he spoke, the more enthusiastic he became. "You can even be the director! Will you? Can we?"

"Yes, and yes!" Miss Kate answered, pretending to roll up her sleeves. "We'd better get started."

And so they did.

Maybe it was because of the season. Maybe it was because Miss Kate was doing the asking. Maybe it was because of all the enthusiasm the children involved brought to the first practice. Their excitement continued, even though they had to practice four nights a week. Whatever it was, everything seemed to fit into place. Three weeks later on Sunday afternoon, the church basement was packed with family and friends.

Finding his mom and dad sitting in the second row, Joey went over to see them before he went up on stage.

"Hi, son." Jacob grinned at his son.

"Hi, Dad! Hi, Mom!" Joey replied. "Dad, I really hope you like the play. I remembered what you said about two plus two and people and reading. I thought really hard about it all, especially about good news and bad news." He took a deep breath, his shoulders straightening with the kind of importance only a child can pull off. "I hope you hear the Good News today."

"Thanks," his father responded, even though he was a little confused.

It was a condition that intensified when, after their son scooted off again, his wife leaned over to whisper in his ear. "Actually, I think two plus two is more than four." And then, without saying anything more, she squeezed his hand.

A few seconds later, the lights blinked a couple of times. Then Miss Kate greeted everyone and motioned to Joey, who came out from behind the curtain and took his place at the podium. For a few seconds, everything and everyone was very quiet. Then Joey spoke.

"Good afternoon," he said. "We are very happy to present a play written by Miss Kate and Joey Richards. That's me."

A light chuckle ran through the room.

Unfazed, he continued, "The title is 'MOO News Is Good News.' One of our cows came up with the title."

That got an even bigger laugh from the audience, and this time Joey smiled right back.

"Oh," he added after the levity died down, "My dad gave Miss Kate and me the idea for this play. We hope you all like it, especially you, Dad!"

The curtain rose. Pretending to clear his throat once again, Joey waited for everyone to take their places on the stage. Once they were ready, he began by stating the title and introduction, and then the list of characters.

Moo News Is Good News
(A Four-Act Play)

A four-act play, counting the sneak preview, presented by the barnyard animals of the Bethlehem stable, a few people, a very important baby, and some other guys:

Cast of Characters

Narrator: Joey Richards

Mary: Maggie Burns

Gabriel (an angel): Marybeth Spangle

Joseph: Gabriel Gonzales

Donkey: Hope Simmons

Innkeeper: Aaron Sharpe

Patsy (a cow): Molly Peterson

Betty (a cow): Gracie Godfrey

Baby Jesus: Sally's doll

Charlie (a bull): Charlie Godfrey

Mrs. Innkeeper: Ruth Archer

Gabby (a sheep): Sally Richards

Whitney (a sheep): Marcus Humphrey

Shorty (a shepherd): Tom Carter

Slim (a shepherd): Michelle Joiner

Cyclone (a shepherd): Charity Love

Corky (an angel): Mickey Spangle

Miracle (an angel): Faith Thomas

Other angels: Jimmy McGregor, Jeremy Gonzales, Sandra Jones

Other sheep: Audience

Director: Miss Kate

Clearing of his throat, Joey started the narration from hours of careful memorization. "Sneak Preview," he said loudly and clearly.

— ACT I —

Narrator: This story actually begins about eight months earlier when, one day, Mary was minding her own business and an angel appeared right out of the blue.

[Joey remembered they had practiced what would happen at this point, and he was very happy that Mary and Gabriel had remembered, too.]

[MARY and GABRIEL walk onto the stage, pretending they don't see each other until Gabriel speaks.]

Gabriel: Hi, Mary! My name is Gabriel. God sent me to check on you. Make sure everything is going fine in your life. AND you're going to have a baby!

[Right before Mary spoke, Joey held up a cue card he wrote out on poster paper, turning it toward Mary, not the audience. It read, "Remember to act shocked and surprised, or whichever one you can do."]

Mary: What? Who are you? What? Gabriel? God? A BABY! Oh my! What will my mother say? I'm not—

Gabriel: Relax, Mary. God and the Holy Spirit have it all figured out. You and Joseph will be married. Corky, another angel, talked to Joseph in one of his dreams. That's all taken care of in another book of the Bible to be written later. Oh yes, I almost forgot. You're to name your baby Jesus.

Mary: Joseph is okay with all this?

Gabriel: Hey, when an angel of the Lord talks to you, how can you not be okay with it?

— ACT II —

Narrator: And so Mary was pregnant. There wasn't any doctor in their small town, so she and Joseph were going to Bethlehem to take her to the doctor, see their tax lady, and be counted by the census workers. They started out late because Joseph had to finish working on Grandma Murphy's roof before the rains came. And he had a hard time catching the donkey and finding blankets for Mary to sit on. But now, they were on the road with Mary sitting on Hope, the donkey.

Mary: I'm tired, Joseph. I mean really tired. My back is killing me, and this donkey is no easy ride.

Hope: Hey, what do you expect? They haven't fixed this road for ages. I'm tired too, you know. Come on, Joseph, give us a break. We need to stop.

Narrator: I forgot to tell you that our animals can talk, but people don't understand what they are saying.

Joseph: Just a little longer, and we will be in Bethlehem.

Mary: Did you bring a map? Does this donkey have a GPS? We should stop one of those shepherds and ask for directions. Ow, my back! Ouch! Joseph, this is a rough ride.

Hope: I'm trying not to step in the potholes. You should have to try getting four legs to all go in the right place at the right time!

Joseph: I know the way, Mary. We have been on this road a lot of times. We just have to follow the North Star. I wish it wasn't so foggy!

Mary: Why couldn't we have registered in Nazareth? Why couldn't the tax lady have come to see us? I just hope Baby Jesus doesn't get the hiccups from this bumpy ride. *(Mary rubs her stomach.)*

[Joey held up another cue card, reminding Mary to rub her stomach, but thinking she might not read fast enough, he imitated what she should be doing.]

Joseph: We're almost there. Come along, donkey. *(Pulls on the donkey's rope.)*

Hope: *(pretending to whisper, though loud enough for the audience to hear)* Ouch! Not so hard, Gabe—er, Joseph.

154

Narrator: After a long, hard ride and walk, Joseph and Mary and the baby-to-be—who everyone knows is named "Jesus"—came to Bethlehem. Joseph quickly learned that with the census being taken, the state basketball tournament, and a plumbers' convention in town, there was no room for them at their favorite inn. So, Joseph finally found an innkeeper who might give them a stall in his stable.

[MR. INNKEEPER enters.]

Mr. Innkeeper: I'm all booked up for the night, Mister. You should have come earlier.

Joseph: Yes, I know, but—

Mr. Innkeeper: Wow! Your wife is really pregnant.

Hope: Amazing! He noticed.

Mary: We'll take anything you have open for the night.

Mr. Innkeeper: Hmm. Well, I guess—it's against the city code, you know. People inside the inn, animals outside in the stable. But okay. Come on. I'll show you to the back. I'll just have to double up a couple of my cows. (*He walks toward the stable while mumbling about needing more space and how the city won't let him expand his stable.*)

Mary, Joseph, Hope: Thank you. Thank you. Thank you! (*Mr. Innkeeper leads PATSY, a cow, alongside BETTY, another cow.*)

Patsy: Move over, Betty. I'm coming in!

Betty: Oh no, you aren't.

Patsy: Oh yes, I am! (*Betty turns to see the innkeeper coming up with Patsy. He shoulders Betty to push her over.*)

Betty: Hey, what's going on here. This is my apartment. You can't just move her in. Don't I have rights?

Patsy: Yes, he can. No, you don't. He's people. We're animals. We don't have rights yet. Hey, you're hogging the space. Move over.

[At this point, Joey held up another cue card, big enough for all of the cows to read. Betty and Patsy, push each other—but only a little bit. Patsy, remember the last rehearsal? You pushed Betty down on the floor. Be careful this time.]

— ACT III —

Narrator: In a little while, everyone was settled down. Patsy and Betty were gazing at Mary and chatting away. Hope was nibbling on some grain Joseph had bought for him, and Mary was—well, let's get back to the story.

Patsy: She looks like that baby is coming really soon.

Betty: She sure does! *[CHARLIE, the bull, pokes his head out of his stall.]*

Charlie: Hey, what's up?

Betty and Patsy: Where have you been for the past hour?

Charlie: Huh? I was napping.

Patsy: Isn't that just like a bull?

Betty: Yes, just like a bull. You'd think he was out to lunch or—

Charlie: I said I was napping. And anyway, why are you two sharing an apartment?

Betty: We have company!

Patsy: You *have* been out to lunch!

Hope: No, he's been sleeping.

Charlie: Hey, there's a lady and a man and—

Hope: Yup, you got it. We're having a baby!

157

Charlie: Oh my! OH MY!

Narrator: While the donkey and cows were catching Charlie up on things, Joseph and Mary were settling in for the night, but not for long.

Mary: Joseph! It's time! I think the baby is coming.

Joseph: Oh my! Oh my!

Patsy and Betty: Where have we heard that before?

Joseph: *[starts to stand and shouts]* I need to do something!

Patsy: I'd say!

Betty: And quick!

Joseph: Maybe I should boil some water.

Mary: Maybe you should go get the innkeeper's wife. I think she'll know what to do.

Joseph: Yes! That's a good idea. I'll be right back! *[He exits stage, and then returns with the innkeeper and his wife, MRS. INNKEEPER.]*

Mrs. Innkeeper: *[rushing over to Mary]* Okay, are you ready? *[to Joseph and her husband]* We're going to have this baby! You men go outside and talk about the weather. *[Joseph and Mr. Innkeeper exit.]*

Patsy: Now we're getting somewhere.

Hope: If you ladies will excuse me, I think I'll take a walk around the corral and keep an eye out for coyotes.

Charlie: I'm going back to sleep.

Betty: Go, donkey! Get out of here!

Patsy and Betty: Good night again, Charlie! *[DONKEY leaves, and Charlie goes to sleep.]*

— ACT IV —

Narrator: And there were some shepherds up on the hill with a bunch of sheep. Two of the sheep had been watching all the coming and going down at the stable.

Gabby: *[baas]* What's happening down there?

Whitney: *[baas back]* Maybe there's a party.

Gabby: Let's go see.

Whitney: Can't. The dog will just chase us back up here.

Gabby: Let's make a lot of noise and get the other sheep to make noise. Then we'll make a run for it.

Whitney: Good idea!

[Just as Sally and Marcus started to "Baa! Baa!" again, Joey lifted up a cue card, only this time, he turned it toward the audience and asked them to "Baa! Baa!" as well. In a few seconds, there was a lot of noise in the room.]

[Shepherds—SHORTY, SLIM, AND CYCLONE—run around looking out into the audience.]

Shorty: Why all the racket? I don't see any wolves.

Slim: Hey, look! There go two sheep running down toward that stable! Where did the dog go?

Shorty: What! The whole flock is running down the hill. We'd better go get them.

Cyclone: There goes a nice, quiet evening—help! Look at that star! It's right over that stable where all the sheep are going!

Narrator: As the shepherds—Shorty, Slim, and Cyclone—gathered their stuff and prepared to start down the hill, people who appeared to be angels came from the direction of the bright star. The

160

shepherds stopped and stared at their visitors. *[Angels GABRIEL, CORKY, and MIRACLE step up to the shepherds.]*

Corky: Don't worry about your sheep. Our crew will round them up. Go down and see Jesus. He's the Lord!

Gabriel: This isn't the way the script is written. We're going to confuse these guys. *[Other ANGELS enter and begin singing, "Here, sheep! Here, sheep! Don't run away. Christ, the shepherd, the blessed shepherd, is born today!"]*

Gabriel: Oh my! Are we in trouble.

Miracle: You shepherds go ahead and see Jesus, and praise God. We'll take care of your sheep 'til you get back. *[Slim, Shorty, and Cyclone look at Gabriel.]*

Gabriel: Hallelujah! What can I say? Go!

All angels: *[singing]* Hallelujah! What can we say! Christ the Lord is born today!

Narrator: So, Jesus was born, and the crowded stable saw a lot of traffic that night. Sheep came. Shepherds came. Angels came, and went, and came again. Patsy and Betty mooed and mooed—first with joy and then to calm things down.

When the evening grew late, the shepherds went back to the hillside to find their sheep sleeping soundly. Baby Jesus slept on the hay in the manger, and Mary and Joseph finally fell asleep to the soft mooing of Patsy and Betty's duet. Gabriel shooed the angels back to the heavens while staying watch through the night.

And Charlie slept through it all.

The End

Joey cleared his throat one more time, a cue for Miss Kate to join him on stage, which she did.

"Joey," she asked, "what do we want our audience to really stop, listen, and think about this evening?"

He turned to the audience with utmost solemnity. "There will always be problems in the world. People won't always be nice to each other, even though they could be if they wanted to."

When he paused, Miss Kate encouraged him to continue. "Anything else?"

"Oh . . . yes!" he said. "When you think about it, we all need good news. When we think of the Good News that came with Jesus' birth and when we practice what Jesus taught, the world can change. It can be better."

"Yes, it can." She put her hand lightly on his shoulder. "So?"

Joey looked down at the stage, thinking carefully. "So, we must never tire of hearing how it is with the world and everyone in it, even with all the problems and bad things that happen." He raised his eyes to her again to see if he had answered correctly.

Her lips turned upward when she prompted him one more time. "Because?"

That did it for him. Knowing precisely what she was looking for, he smiled right back, and then turned to the audience to lock eyes with his dad. "Because with the Good News, we can listen differently and make a difference in this world!"

Someone behind the curtain handed him a cue card, and he held it up so everyone out there could read it while it simultaneously flashed on the screens at the sides of the stage:

> Stop!
>
> Listen!
>
> Think!
>
> Believe!
>
> Act differently!

That got a lot of "Amens" from the crowd, who were dismissed a moment later. It took a while longer before the Richards began their walk home.

Hugging her doll close to her, Sally let out a short stream of commentary. "That was fun. I'm tired. I liked it when the cows were mooing."

Her mother agreed. "It was very good, Joey. Did you really write all of that?"

"Of course not," Joey said, embarrassed. "I told Miss Kate what Dad said about the bad news in the world and—"

Hearing what Joey had to say, his father stopped walking. "Wait. I seem to remember saying something about numbers and—"

"Yes!" Joey interrupted. "And then I didn't want to learn to read anymore because I wanted to be like you. But Miss Kate taught me different."

His father looked at him, a little bewildered and very humbled by his logic. "What did she teach you?"

Sally and is mother looked on, waiting to hear his answer as well.

"Well, she said if I can read, learn, think, and write better, just maybe I can help change some bad news to good news. You do that, Dad."

There was a moment of silence while is father thought that one out.

"Miss Kate said it was good for me to practice my reading," Joey added.

"And she was right!" his father said. "From what we saw and heard this afternoon, I don't think I'll ever forget that no amount of bad news in the world can measure up to the Good News we've got in the Christmas story. And when I'm feeling down—"

"I'll read you the story again." Joey wrapped his arm around his dad.

While his father returned the hug, he said, "And then we can both laugh when we talk about how 'MOO News Is Good News.'"

Sally's resulting giggles turned into a yawn. "I'm tired," she said.

"I'm more tired than you," teased Joey.

"Are not," Sally said, smiling.

"Are, too!"

Chapter 6

A Christmas Harvest

The fallen leaves had long lost their colors. The air was cold, and evening was coming earlier and earlier. In short, fall had worn its welcome out. The dampness, freezing drizzle, and late morning and early evening fogs all left their marks on the landscape and human spirit.

The harvest was nearly complete, but a so-far elusive freeze was necessary for farmers to gather the remainder of the corn. With a sigh, Thomas Williams unhooked the feed wagon and prepared to drive the tractor between the separate parts of the two-row corn picker.

"Sam!" he yelled to be heard over the tractor. "Sam!"

His thirteen-year-old did not answer.

Where is he? Tom's eyes traced the many boot prints up the small hill to the farmhouse. With another frustrated sigh, he put the tractor out of gear, locked the brake, and walked up the hill to find Sam on the back porch starting to take off his jacket.

"What are you doing in here? I need your help, and it's chore time. When are you going to quit running into the house as soon as I'm not looking?" He raised his arm to strike him, but Sam ducked out of the way and left quickly through the back door.

Outside again, neither of them spoke to the other as they put the picker back on the tractor. And there were no words given or received when they were finished and Sam headed out to the field for the milk cows. Not until he was out of hearing range did the boy teared up.

In the stillness shrouded by the evening fog, he cried quietly. Why did his father always yell? Why did *he* always have to be the one to help? Of course, Sam was the oldest son and more than old enough to help on his own. But for what? "If I just had something of my own." Some guys and girls he knew who lived on farms all seemed to have calves, a sow, and pigs, along with their own chickens—and some even had a horse. He didn't.

When he asked if he could have his own animal to raise or maybe an acre of corn or beans, his father always told him, "We can't afford for you to have your own livestock. And besides, after we give the landlord and the bank their share, we barely have enough money from the crops to cover our expenses and keep you, your brother, and sisters in clothes and food." His father was usually pretty good at talking about what Sam couldn't do or had to do, but when it came to offering him something or just talking, his dad was usually short on words.

When his father thought his words sunk into Sam's brain, he continued, "Besides, you probably would soon grow tired of whatever you were given." It seemed to Sam that was usually the end of the conversation, but as his father turned and walked away, Sam often heard himself say to his father's back, "I wouldn't either . . . if it was mine."

The truth was Sam knew his father was mostly right, at least the part about not being able to afford it. He knew the calves from the milk cows were sold after they were weaned to help pay the farm rent. The profit from yearly crops was divided between the bank, landlord, and their financial needs. Sometimes, when he was listening to his parents talk at the kitchen table while they drank their after-supper coffee and Dad smoked his cigarette, it seemed to him they always came up on the short side of dividing up the money. Yet all of this knowing did not stop him from wishing.

As he came up on the backside of the small herd and turned them in the direction of the barn, in between his, "Hey, hey! Get up, get up!" he purposely muttered to any cow that was listening, "I hate farming! I hate you all! Why do we have to be so poor?"

By the time he came back with the small herd, his father was already calling for them. Without coaxing, the first five Guernseys moved through the open barn door into their stalls, leaving Sam to close the door behind him. It took him until that moment when his father was sitting on the stool and milking before he could summon the courage to speak up.

"Dad? Dad, I was wondering."

"What, Sam?" His father had not lost the disappointed tone Sam had come to know so well.

"I want to make some money for Christmas. Do you suppose I could possibly receive something for doing my chores?"

Mr. Williams was quiet for a moment, wondering how many times his son would ask that question. "Where do you think this money would come from?" he asked. "The cream check goes for groceries. The egg check is for you and your siblings' school lunches and clothes. Where would I get the money?"

"I don't know," Sam almost whispered. Again, tears were sliding down his mud-stained cheeks while he slipped out into the night to feed the pigs.

"Nothing is mine," he cried. Out of frustration and hurt, he once again exclaimed, "Other farm kids have calves or pigs. I get nothing."

As far as his "nothing" went, it also seemed to Sam it extended even further into their relationship. Sam could not remember the last time he received a father-to-son grasp of affection, whether it was receiving a smile or fatherly hug, sharing a laugh, or playing checkers (or any game, for that matter) with his dad.

The last time he believed something resembling a twinge of closeness ever happened was on an occasion when Sam and Mary, his closest sister, were much younger. After his father put the milking machine on a cow, he would go out to the cornfield and hide. Sam and Mary always went out to find him. It was their version of hide-and-seek. They would never find him, so they returned to the barn. And there he'd be, putting the milking machine on another cow. When they came into the barn, he would chuckle and ask, "Where have the two of you been?"

Those memories were now only a part of "Once upon a time . . ." *It would seem strange if my father embraced me now, shared a joke, or actually listened to my ideas,* he thought as he scattered the corn and mash into the pig trough.

The sad truth was that Sam and his dad were becoming strangers at a time when a son desperately needed a father and a father desperately needed a son. His father constantly reminded him he didn't take care of things and was always in a hurry to get to the house, to which Sam always thought he would care more about his chores if something were actually his.

By then, however, Sam knew enough not to say his thoughts aloud. The few times he had, his father got angry and told him just to go in the house so he could finish the chores all on his own.

Sam knew his father tried hard. He knew they were just barely making it on the farm. But to Sam, it seemed his father was far away in

168

another world and so hard to please in this one. Instead of doing as his father said when he got angry, Sam always went ahead and finished his chores before he went in the house.

By the time his father came into the house, Sam had already gone off to take a bath. So, when he sat at the kitchen table, it was his wife, Mary, who greeted him with a cup of coffee.

"Sam was crying when he came in," she said, wishing her husband would open up more to their oldest son. Maybe it would help Sam know his father better.

Tom accepted the cup. "He's always crying about something."

"Tom," she protested, unwilling to leave the subject alone. "He wants to please you, but he just can't seem to do it on his own. He needs your help."

"Mary, I've told you before—I can't leave what I'm doing to help him." Tom's gaze showed his weariness from saying what he had already said before. "He has to learn to do his own work. He never seems to stick with a job. It's always hurry up to get inside to play, read, or watch TV."

Mary was also weary from hearing him say what he'd already said before. She was almost sorry for bringing it up, but these were people she loved. And she knew in spite of those difficult words or feelings communicated in the moment, beneath that layer was a solid foundation of love they had for each other. She also knew that somehow their love needed to be expressed before one of them thought it was too late to give or accept.

It got her wondering why it was so hard to love under the skin. If God and all His goodness could bring His Son into the world of human existence, why couldn't He bring a father and son together who were already here?

She shook her head to clear her thoughts and shoved her chair away from the table. "I have supper to get ready."

Tom sat at the table while Mary moved around him. The kitchen was small, so it was obvious he was in the way. Nevertheless, it was as if he needed to be in the way for someone to notice him.

There was the added issue of him knowing full well that Mary was right. So, long after supper was over, he sat there drinking cup after cup of coffee and smoking cigarettes. His thoughts moved slowly through a history of hard work and trials, including his own two hands gripping around a wrench or some other tool, fixing—always fixing—one broken piece of equipment after another. How much he wished his son wanted to be like him—to love farming, the land, and the work involved.

His thoughts shifted only a little to reflect on his childhood, one that was absent a father. Raised by an older brother, he'd had to earn his own way, an upbringing that had led him to once vow that he wouldn't raise his own son that way. Yet it seemed he was doing just that.

For a moment, he forgot to hide the pain, and his eyes teared up unselfishly for a young boy he might never know.

"Sam, come out here." Tom turned his head toward the living room, where he knew his son was.

Sam came out thinking he'd probably forgotten to turn off the cow tank or the yard light.

"Yeah?"

"I know you'd like to earn some money for Christmas," his father said. "We don't have it, though."

"I know," Sam said, feeling ashamed, as if his father had seen him crying earlier.

"But I want to make you an offer," he went on. "That old picker drops a lot of corn when I'm picking. I'll take the empty wagon out, and you can go out after chores and pick up the corn. I'll buy what you pick up and pay you when we go Christmas shopping on the twenty-fourth."

"Would you, Dad?" Sam's entire face beamed with excitement. "That would be great! I could have my own money for Christmas."

He reached over to hug his father, something he hadn't done for a while. Yet his enthusiasm died down a bit with his father's reminder.

"I'll only pay you for what you pick. I know how excited you get about things and then quit halfway."

Sam wanted to explain that had happened because he kept hoping his father would help him, but he stayed quiet.

The next evening, the oldest son carefully hurried through his chores without messing up. Even though darkness was quickly approaching, he went out to the corn field dragging a gunnysack behind him. After just starting, Sam thought, *Golly, it won't take me very long to fill this wagon.* He worked hard to pick up ears of corn, carefully searching along the hillside so he would miss as little as possible.

As the days kept passing, corn-picking became a normal part of his routine. And when Saturday came along, Sam spent all afternoon at it, even though the payload from the partially filled gunnysack of small and big ears of corn he dragged through the field now hardly seemed to make a dent on the wagon floor. Despite his father's concern, however, he was becoming more excited rather than disinterested.

Allowing his imagination to be as wide as the field itself, he made a game out of believing each ear found was a silver coin robbers had long ago dropped from their saddle bags when a sheriff's posse was chasing them after they had robbed a bank. It was especially nice, he had to admit, when his father came out several times to move the wagon and then stayed to help him find an ear or two. In his imagination, he gave his father the role of a special federal agent being called in to assist in finding the coins.

One evening Tom began milking, only to pause and look across the barnyard to the field. Night was coming down on the small valley, but

Sam could still be seen looking intently out there, first to the left and then to the right.

Normally, Sam would find reasons to ask for help, or he might simply lose interest in such things since it was easier just to be yelled at. But that was "normally"—this time it was different. Turning the task into a game or mission, and then knowing he would be earning something for the value of his work, made all of the effort worthwhile; however, deep inside his own mind, he realized there was more. This was something he had to do for himself—and to show his dad he could accept responsibility when there was something of himself to give.

This was something to which he was entirely committed.

The day before Christmas Eve, Sam and his father drove out to pick up the wagon. Looking inside, Tom could see it was half full, which was somewhat surprising but also impressive. It had him musing about the difference he had seen in his son and the reasons behind that difference, leading him to conclude he'd just been giving his son jobs before this. Not vocations, not callings—just jobs with no greater incentives added.

Clearly, though, picking up the extra corn had been more than a mere job to Sam. And maybe just as clearly, Tom could learn a lesson from his son's example. Maybe he could start putting all of himself into truly being a father to him rather than just treating it like a job.

With that in mind, he smiled at the boy. "I'll give you forty dollars for the load. Will you take it?"

Sam's eyes widened. "Forty dollars! Sure!"

All of Sam's efforts had paid off. He would not only have enough money for presents, but he'd even have some left over. But the best part yet, he couldn't hear any disappointment in his father's voice like he had heard so many times before today.

"You did a good job," his father said, putting an arm around Sam's shoulder. "It would cost me at least fifty dollars to buy this much feed. I really am proud of you."

The two of them stood there for a few moments. The field didn't seem so large now. The wagon didn't seem so big either, and Sam didn't seem so alone.

The next day the whole family went shopping, as was their tradition. Christmas Eve was always exciting for the Williams family.

The rush of city traffic, the cold air and traces of snow, the hamburger-and-french-fries lunch were all part of a beloved routine that had captured many memories over and over for the Williams's. This time around, Sam treated it with special consideration, picking out presents for each family member based on hints and clues they gave—some intentional, others not so much.

When it came to his father's gift, though, Sam just could not decide until he remembered how hard it had been putting the two-row picker together and then uncoupling it whenever grinding feed was necessary. That made his decision a whole lot easier.

Tradition in the Williams's home called for all family members to have their chores done by supper time, as well as presents wrapped and under the tree for the evening's festivities. It seemed a little silly to have just wrapped all the gifts just a few hours earlier, only to unwrap them so soon. But silly or not, no one in the Williams family seemed to mind.

And so, following supper, the family gathered around the tree. Mrs. Williams passed each present out to its corresponding recipient, and they each took their turn finding out what was underneath all the wrappings.

When Tom came to Sam's present, he passed up the card to open the small package first. The present inside, a small model of a combine, seemed a little unusual.

"Well . . . thanks, Sam," he said anyway, holding up the combine for Mary to see.

But Sam shook his head. "Read the card, Dad."

So, Tom opened it up, only to see a ten-dollar bill fall out. Grabbing at the currency, he chose to read the accompanying handwritten note out loud. "Father, I may not be able to always do as you wish or be what you want, but I do want to be your son and for you to be proud of being my father. This might not buy the combine you'd like to have. But together, we can make a good start at saving for one. Merry Christmas. Love, Sam."

For Tom, it seemed like the whole room was still, warranting only whispers. That was a good thing, especially since he didn't know if he could manage anything louder than that when he stood up to hug his oldest child.

"Merry Christmas, son," he said. "I love you."

Sam's ears opened wide as his father's words registered and then traveled to his heart.

Sam felt his father's strong arms around him, which didn't seem strange anymore. It was the right thing for a father to do.

"I love you, too, Dad." The words were just as natural. "Merry Christmas."

Chapter 7

BEN'S CHRISTMAS APPLES

"There are just too many apples! I'll never get them all peeled and cooked into applesauce before they rot." Nonetheless, Ann Thomas's wrist was flicking, and her paring knife was speeding around and around the fruit in question.

"What will we do with them, Mom?" Ann's ten-year-old son, Ben, asked as he lifted the pan of peelings from the kitchen sink to feed the chickens.

"Do with what?"

Her thoughts had already wandered off to concerns about bad weather, bad crops, and bad egg and cream prices. Even though the question had brought her right back to the overflowing pail of apples sitting right in front of her at arm's reach on the kitchen counter. The kitchen was coated with a rich, warm smell from the ones already simmering on the stove in liquid, sprinkled with a bit of sugar and a few spices.

She turned toward Ben and smiled. "I'm going to cook as many of these into applesauce as I can and maybe freeze some slices for apple pie. As for the rest of them, what you don't eat, we'll feed to the chickens."

"I can eat a lot of them." Already making good on his word, Ben bit down on an apple while he tried to balance the pan of peelings on the back of the chair.

"Ben's spilling peelings all over the floor," his seven-year-old sister Kelly teased as she came into the kitchen.

Mrs. Thomas did not respond. Her thoughts had once again wandered out the window to the leaves falling from the wild plum, walnut, and apple trees in their small orchard. Soon it would be chore time, and she simply had to finish this bushel before doing anything else.

Besides, her son was already out the door.

Kelly put on her coat and ran after him yelling, "Can I help?"

She caught up as he reached the chicken house, where most of the fowl were still outside despite the sun dropping over the hill.

"Open the door." Ben nodded at the gate, glad she had followed him.

He didn't care much for chicken chores, especially when the rooster, Grouchy (as he and his mother called him), was in the pen. That creature always seemed to enjoy chasing him. Even now, while his sister complied, he watched the mean, old bird warily.

"Come in and keep the rooster away while I empty the pan," he instructed next.

Only too happy to be helpful, Kelly picked up a stick and began to yell, "Shoo! Shoo!" while running around the pen, scattering the chickens in all directions—including outside of the pen.

Catching sight of that, Stu Thomas came running out the barn door, a look of alarm and irritation on his face. "The chickens are getting out!"

In a few seconds, there was complete chaos. Sparky, Ben's dog, went off barking and chasing the chickens. Kelly ran around shooing and waving her stick. Ben tried to force a hen back inside he'd managed to catch between his leg and the pen door. Stu was busy yelling at Sparky, Kelly, and Ben all at the same time.

It took a few minutes, but Kelly finally decided to collar the dog, at which point her father sent the two of them back to the house while he and Ben coaxed the chickens back.

"I'm sorry, Dad," Ben said. "I forgot to latch the door, and then Kelly came in—"

Stu cut him off. "Go out and get the cows." It seemed his son was always doing something that caused more work for him.

Later, after the chores were completed and supper was over, Ben lingered a few extra minutes at the table. His mom and sister were working on Kelly's arithmetic assignment in the living room, but his dad was still in the kitchen, reading the paper and drinking coffee.

"Are you going to the sale barn tomorrow, Dad?" Ben asked, hoping his father would answer.

A room away, Ann could feel the burden of silence between her husband and son even while she read out the equation, six plus four, to Kelly. How much easier life would be if fathers and sons knew how to do that kind of simple math. If only life was as easy as simple math, where all Stu needed to understand was if he was open and loving with Ben, he'd solve the problem of having a son who felt accepted and loved for simply being instead of trying too hard to prove himself worthy of love.

"Ten, Mom!" Kelly pulled at her arm. "I said the answer is ten!"

She snapped to and said, "You're right, dear. Now what's twelve plus twelve?"

"If you are, can I go with you?" Ben asked in the kitchen, unwilling to let go of the possibility of going with his dad.

Stu looked up from his paper. "You have school, Ben."

Since that was the end of that, Ben climbed the stairs at bedtime wishing the evening had gone differently. He often wished his dad would write an excuse for him to be released from art class Friday afternoon so he could walk down to the sale barn and meet his dad. Sometimes he wished his dad was an airplane pilot so he could ride in one of the planes he saw flying over the pasture when he went out to bring the cows home. He wished he had a twin brother, or if not, perhaps he could be five inches taller so he could be a good shot in basketball. He also wished he wasn't so scared of Grouchy, or else his mom would pop him in the frying pan and get a new rooster for the hen house.

Daring to wish really hard on just one thought, he wished he and his dad had a chore to do together and he wasn't just told what to do. So many wishes had been lost in the evening darkness, making it silly to wish anymore. Yet wish he did—hard enough for the fall wind whistling around the old farm house to carry his hopes deep into the night.

Since no one actually heard his wishes, before he jumped into bed, he knelt and said his prayers. Ever since he was five, his evening prayer always began the same way: "Now I lay me down to sleep . . ." In the early years, his "God bless" and "Please" lists were shorter and more basic. Not until he became older did he broaden his prayers.

The next morning when Ben awoke, he rubbed the sleep from his eyes, dressed, and tramped down the stairs to the kitchen. He was surprised to see his dad still at the kitchen table. Filling his bowl, Ben sat at the table and began to eat, crunching down on corn flakes soaked in cow's milk fresh from the mason jar his dad brought to the house from milking the night before. He was even more surprised to hear him say, "Ben, if you do your chores in a timely manner, you can run to the lumber yard with me to pick up a roll of plastic we'll need to weatherproof the windows for winter. When we return, I think your mom will want you and Kelly to finish picking the rest of the apples."

"Okay!" Ben said with a crunch of excitement as he swallowed down an oversized spoonful of corn flakes.

Ben enjoyed the trip into town with his dad. It seemed to him that the conversation Dad had at the lumber yard with the clerk was just about the same conversation he heard lately between him and the driver from the creamery when he came out to pick up the cream and leave a pound of butter. Or when the salesman came to the farm to deliver feed and tried to sell him another type of vitamin or supplement for cows, calves, or chickens.

"How's it going, Stu? How's the missus?" they would ask.

He'd always reply, "Goin' fine. Ann put on a pot of coffee and made some cinnamon rolls if you want to stop in."

"Sounds good," they'd say, but then they would talk with his dad for another fifteen minutes before they went up to the house. Of course, the part about coffee and cinnamon rolls wasn't mentioned at the lumber yard 'cause they always had coffee brewing and a plate of store- bought rolls on the counter for all their customers. The rest of the conversation, though, was very familiar.

"Almanac says we're going to have a mild winter," they'd mention.

"Wish you'd tell my arthritis that," my dad would reply.

"How's the crop look? How's pickin'?" they'd wonder aloud.

"Good as expected, considering the lack of good rains and too hot of an August," his dad would answer. That part of the conversation would vary depending on the weather, but it never seemed to be just right for his dad—or any other farmer he ever knew.

When the helpers finished loading their pickup with the weather plastic, roofing nails, and slats to hold the plastic on the windows, and he and his dad finished their not-homemade sweet rolls, they were back on the road again. They were home in plenty of time for he and Kelly to scour the orchard and yard for the apples and do other Saturday chores his mom and dad had for him to do. By Saturday evening, he was tired. After he had polished his Sunday school shoes, he only ate three cereal bowls of popcorn before he climbed up the stairs for bed.

It came as a surprise. Usually when Stu did his best to winterize the old farm house, he would give Ben a chore like cleaning out the calf pen or hog house. Whatever the chore was, it would take him a good deal of time and not require his attention until Ben had the manure spreader full (or at least, his son thought it was full). But the second Saturday of November was different. As soon as breakfast was over for Ben and his dad had swallowed down his third cup of coffee while listening to the farm news on the radio, he said, "Ben, I need you to help me stack straw bales around the west and north side of the house. Uncle Chris and I put weather paper up, but we still need to put the bales around the house. When we're done, we need to start putting the weather stripping on the windows."

"You mean I don't have to clean the hog house again?" he asked.

"No, son. You did fine the first time," he answered.

"That's great, Dad. Thanks!" Ben responded excitedly. As he went out on the back porch to put on his coveralls, his mind wandered back to his wish list. *Gee, one of my wishes is already coming true. Dad and I are doing something together. I think I'll like this, and my shoes won't stink like they do after I clean out the hog house.*

After loading the lowboy with straw and driving it up into the yard near the west side of the house, it did not take them long to stack the bales two high in the proper places. The next task was a bit harder. After they had gotten out the roll of weather plastic, slats, nails, and a hammer, it took the two of them to manage the long extension ladder needed to reach the second story.

"We'll do the second story first," Stu said as he leaned the ladder against the wall, moving it upward while Ben guided the end of the ladder. Once they were all set and had the plastic cut, Ben took the materials far enough up the ladder for Stu to reach them. Ben's next task was holding the ladder to make sure it stayed put so his dad wouldn't come tumbling down.

As they started on the first-floor windows, Stu realized the small step ladder they had gave him more height than he needed, so he nailed the slats from halfway down. Then, he climbed off the ladder and handed the hammer to Ben. "Now, you finish this window, and I'll start on the next one."

Wearing a big smile on his face, Ben did exactly as his father requested, not really noticing the cold north wind starting to blow its way across the yard. He had the hammer, so he could do his part of the job. He was happy.

Even though their work on the windows was distracted by other necessary tasks including lunch, they were finished by chore time. Climbing off the ladder and arching his back, Stu gazed upward and said, "Well, son, I think we have done the best we can to prepare this old farmhouse for winter. What do you think?"

Ben felt so proud to hear his father ask for his opinion. He arched his back, mimicking his father's actions, and said, "Yup. I think we have. Now I'd better go and do my chores."

"Good idea. I'll start chores as well. Best we get them done before supper time," Stu said.

It only took a long Saturday for the farm house to be winterized. So, besides school and homework, the next few weeks were very busy with harvesting. Shortly before Thanksgiving, Ben and Kelly picked the last of the apples.

"Where should we put them, Mom?" Ben put the bushel down on the back porch and walked into the mudroom, where his mother was washing eggs and putting them in the egg box.

"Bring them inside," Ann said. "It could get cold enough to freeze tonight. When I have time, I'll wrap them in newspaper and put them down in the cellar. I hope we can use them before they rot."

"Can I wrap them?"

"Sure!" She reached out to give him a kiss on the top of his head. "Go ahead and wrap each apple, and then put them in the spare potato bin."

He was busy with his task when he heard his dad come in the house and call out, "Where's Ben?"

After Ann responded that their son was in the cellar, he quickly went down the stairs. "Hmm . . . it looks like your mom has put you to work. Maybe I can help." Without waiting for an invitation, he picked up an apple.

"I really appreciate how hard you've worked at helping me get things ready for winter," he said.

"Thanks!" Beaming, Ben kept on wrapping apples.

"I'm going to the sale the Saturday after Thanksgiving, son." Since he made a statement not expecting a response, he continued, "They are selling a load of feeder pigs, and the bank said they would loan us the money to buy some. So, I'm selling Mabelle. I think we can buy another milker to replace her. I can use a second opinion before I make a decision. Do you think you'd like to come with me after the chores are done?"

"Okay!" Ben was too excited to say much more, considering the rarity of going to the sale with his dad and not having to stay home and do barn or hog house cleaning. On the few occasions he had gone to the sale barn with his dad, he really liked listening to the auctioneer and watching the animals being sold.

The opportunity to go to the sale barn with his dad made it hard for him to wait for Saturday to come around. But since he had no other choice, waiting is what he did. Giving it another thought, he guessed the waiting wasn't really that hard. What came right before that weekend was a stop on the calendar for Thanksgiving.

Thanksgiving was always a wider family affair. This particular Thanksgiving was at his Uncle Chris and Aunt Martha's. Just like in years past, this Thanksgiving he had cousins to play games with or bundle up and go sledding with in one of the pastures. There was more food passed around than what he or Kelly could ever put on their plates. He had seconds of dessert, and both helpings were the apple pie his mom had made from the ones he and Kelly had picked. No one left the table with empty stomachs, and as Uncle Chris always said every year,

"If you leave the table hungry after a holiday meal with the Thomas's, it's your own fault." Ben went to bed that night with a happy stomach.

The next few weeks flowed by with a routine typical for the school year. There were tests, normal assignments, and a few kids absent because of colds, flu, or a bout of playing hooky. When December sixteenth came around, Ben was more than ready to see the school week end because it meant only one week left before Christmas vacation.

Mrs. Larsen's fifth-grade class always spent the last school hours of the week doing fun projects with language, writing, and art. This Friday afternoon held even greater anticipation for the students. Whenever a holiday was coming, the last period was even used to plan parties. As such, Ben was just finishing some greeting card designs when Mrs. Larsen announced all the desks should be cleared.

"Class, we need to plan our Christmas party!" she called out in a sing-song voice. "School is out on Friday, December twenty-third, and that's next week, so what would you like to do?"

"Let's play games," several children shouted.

"Let's sing carols," others added.

Mrs. Larsen immediately began writing on the blackboard, talking out loud as she did. "Games. Carols."

"We want to have treats, don't we?" one of the boys asked.

"Well, of course." She wrote that down too, and then prompted the students to pick specific games and caroling spots. After that, as three o'clock drew ever closer, it was on to the topic of treats.

"I'll bring cookies," Linda offered. Everyone knew her mother made great-tasting cookies. So, no one argued with her about her suggestion.

"My dad said he'd order us some peppermints and peanuts." Tommy's dad owned the supermarket and was always willing to help out the class when he could.

Ben wanted to offer something too, but he wasn't sure what. He knew the cream and egg money went for groceries, and school clothes always came from the crop money. He'd heard so many times before that he didn't get an allowance because there wasn't any extra money. As such, there wasn't much he could volunteer. *There must be something I could bring. I mean, something that won't cost my mom and dad any money. Something we already have. Something my mom doesn't have to go to the grocery store to buy.*

Then he thought of the winter apples he and Kelly had gathered that were now being stored in the fruit cellar and how his mom knew they couldn't eat them all before they rotted. "Mrs. Larsen, I'll bring apples for everyone!" Ben smiled. He was pleased he could offer something.

"Are you sure?" Mrs. Larsen couldn't help but be concerned over his generous offer.

"Yes." He was quite sure he could bring the apples, remembering what his mother had said. Since they would not cost them money, his conscience was clearing the way for him to feel very confident, and he stayed that way on the school bus drive home.

When he and Kelly walked into the house after the bus dropped them off, his dad greeted them as he was sitting at the table doing bookwork trying to juggle figures around.

"Hi, Dad!" and before his dad could say anything, he continued, "I volunteered to bring apples to school for our Christmas party next Friday!" He smiled.

"Apples!" His father frowned. "That's a lot to volunteer. Where are you going to get the money to buy apples for your class?"

"We don't need money, Dad. I was thinking of that already. That's why I felt so good about volunteering." Ben didn't understand why he had to explain. "Dad, we have all those apples in the cellar. We don't need to buy any."

His father didn't answer right away, too busy having an imaginary conversation in his head. *You just weren't thinking, son.*

Frustrated that Ben would put them in such a situation, he shook his head. Someone would have to tell Mrs. Larsen they couldn't afford to buy apples for the class. It was bad enough having to struggle and make things stretch for your family, especially after just borrowing more money from the bank for the feeder pigs and milk cow. Even though he rationally knew buying apples wouldn't cause them to go broke, it just wasn't good timing and then, on top of that, he would have to explain that to someone else.

"Those apples are for us," his dad finally said. "People in town don't eat apples like those." He pictured the red delicious apples at Tom's Supermarket in town and then imagined Ben's friend Tommy holding one of the farm apples in his hand at the party.

"Why not?" Ben was utterly confused.

Stu had all kinds of practical adult reasons to give him. "They have worm holes. They have blemishes. They're too small. They're not good quality."

"We eat them," Ben interrupted.

"We eat them because we can't afford to buy apples in town."

"You mean we're poor?" Ben had never thought of himself as poor before. Yes, he had less than his friend Tommy, but he was pretty sure he had a lot more than the Smith family down the road.

Stu didn't answer this time, which his son knew was answer enough. In his father's mind, at least, it was clear they were poor.

Ben wasn't quite sure what being poor really meant. Was it having to do without things you wanted, like the items on the wish list he put in his prayers at night? Did it mean having to save for galoshes in the fall and heavy coats in the winter rather than just going to town and buying them? Did it mean you didn't eat in town on Saturday night when you went grocery shopping, or did it mean you just didn't eat?

If we're poor, why do we have more apples than we can eat, eggs for breakfast whenever my dad wants them, and fresh milk every day?

Neither Ben nor his dad said much during supper. But it wasn't until after Ben had excused himself to go and do his homework that Stu told Ann what their son had done.

"I thought he was quiet." She shook her head, understanding now why Ben had left so quickly. "He didn't once mention the sale."

"By selling Mabelle, our cream check will be cut this month because even though I bought a younger milker, she won't be coming for three weeks." Stu stared down at his coffee.

"With cold weather here to stay, the chickens aren't laying as well. I know he was eager to volunteer, maybe too eager. I just wish he had talked to us first," Ann added.

But after a brief pause, just long enough for a little more thinking, Ann looked up at Stu and said, "You can't begin to guess how many times I've told him and even teased him a bit about hurrying and eating all those apples before they rot."

Stu simply shook his head.

"You know," she continued, the concern in her voice coming out just as clear as her actual words, "maybe we're thinking more about how things are than Ben is. I mean, he sees us give. How many times have you dropped everything to go help a neighbor? Remember when Charlie was in the hospital? You volunteered us to do their chores so

187

Alice could stay late at the hospital with him. And you didn't even ask if I minded being 'volunteered' because you knew I would say okay. He sees us giving of ourselves, so maybe this is just one of those times he wanted to give something. He tries so hard. And maybe we don't open ourselves enough to the real gift our own son is giving."

He looked up at her. "You mean, 'maybe *I* don't.'"

She took a while to respond. "I have some grocery money set aside for Christmas presents. I think we could use some of it for the apples."

"I don't think so," he said. "I think we just need to say 'no,' and Ben will have to tell—no—I'll tell Mrs. Larsen."

"Stu, do you really want to say no?" Ann touched her husband's arm ever so gently.

Despite everything, it made him smile. "Well, maybe we could find a way. Such a simple thing."

Sure enough, they were able to find a way. Ben's parents planned on picking up the apples during a shopping run on Thursday afternoon before the class party.

For the children, it was already an exciting day since they'd both saved money throughout the year. Ben had saved some of the money he had earned when a neighbor asked him to help gather hay in early September, and he also had money from the time he and his dad went to help his uncle shell corn. If he planned it right, he would have just enough for presents. The little money Kelly had saved came from cashing in on pop bottles she found in the old wash house last autumn, and of course, her Aunt Anna always paid her generously when she helped her wash windows in the fall and spring. She was a better saver than Ben.

So, they both were satisfied with what they had earned and saved and proud of the fact they didn't have to ask their parents for money to buy their presents. Always eagerly anticipating the yearly trek to town for Christmas shopping, they had many ideas about what to give each other, and they were also not shy about giving out hints for things they were hoping to receive. So, their enthusiasm was unstoppable, even when they were back at the car putting presents in the trunk.

Ann let out a happy but relieved sigh. "Shopping can be tiring."

"I'm not tired!" Kelly was still bouncing on the balls of her feet as she handed her sack over to her mom.

"Neither am I!" Ben jumped into the back seat.

Both of their parents laughed as they got into the car and started off, with the ride to Tom's Super Value short and sweet.

"Come on, Ben." After parking, Stu opened up his door. "Let's go in and get your apples for the party."

But that came as a surprise to the boy. "But Dad, I want to take our apples!" To his parents' ears, his words were heard as a protest.

"Now, son," Stu began as he looked at Ben through the rearview mirror, "we've been over this already. We have the money to buy the apples. Don't worry about it. Remember what I told you? Town kids don't eat our kind of apples. And besides, your mom and I don't want you to be teased or laughed at if kids in your class make fun of you."

"Our apples come from our orchard, not a store. We can go home and find some good apples. I know we can. I guess I'm not afraid if anyone makes fun of me. I want to give everyone something special. Our apples are special. I remember when I was a little kid and we planted those trees. Uncle Delbert gave them to us out of his orchard. I helped you and Mom plant and water them. They're part of us, Dad. The store apples aren't."

Surprised as well by the concern in his son's voice, Stu sat in silence as he continued to look in the mirror at his son. He had heard it in Ben's voice, and now he saw it plainly on his face—confidence and determination. Dropping his eyes from observing his son to staring down toward the floorboard, he felt Ann's hand touch his arm. Her gentle touch caused him to think back to his conversation with Ann, even though it was more than two weeks ago.

Maybe we don't open ourselves to seeing the real gift. Maybe the real gift is what comes from our heart and what sacrifices we are willing to make for the joy of giving.

He turned to his wife. "Did you say you needed some sugar, Ann?"

She smiled, "Why, yes. Ben, go help your father. Will you please?"

"Sure!" With that, he jumped out the door and walked into the store with his dad. They were both laughing.

Kelly, sitting on her knees and leaning over as far as she could until she was just about ready to fall into the front seat, asked, "Why is Ben laughing?"

Ann had only to turn slightly sideways toward Kelly to wrap her arms around her daughter's shoulders. Once she secured her embrace, she said, "I think he's just happy."

"Are you happy, Mom?" Kelly asked as her mother kept hugging her shoulders.

"Honey, I'm very happy."

As soon as they arrived home, they placed the groceries on the table and left them there while the entire family went to the cellar and started to cull the apples for Ben to take for party treats. Ben and his dad unwrapped the newspaper from around the apples, picked out the biggest ones, and handed them to Ann.

"These are good," Ann said and promptly handed them to Kelly. For her part, Kelly gave the acceptable apples a dunk in the pan of fresh water and a good cleaning with a kitchen towel. Then she completed the assembly by wrapping the apples in fresh tissue paper and placing them in a cardboard box.

The assembly continued under Ann's careful inspection. "Nope, nope, hmm . . . maybe this will do for pie tonight," Ann said after placing the "nope apples" off to the side of the bin and the "apple pie" apples on the floor.

To every one's delight, there were more "yes" apples than "nope" ones.

"That didn't take too long," Ann said, smiling at Ben.

"I had the hardest part—didn't I, Mom?" Kelly claimed while pulling on her mother's apron.

Without hesitation, her mother turned to her and responded, "Yes, you did, dear, and you did a very good job. Didn't she, guys?" Ann asked her son and husband.

In unison, Stu and Ben replied, "Yes, you did!"

After Stu stretched his back, with Ben and Kelly imitating his actions, he said, "Well, now that this job is done, we have chores to do. Right, son?" he asked as he turned toward Ben.

"Sure, Dad. Let's go!" Ben answered. But before leaving, he stopped to give his mom and even Kelly a quick hug accompanied by a quick word of thanks, and up the stairs he went.

The next morning, Stu drove Ben and Kelly to school so the apples could arrive safely. For his part, Ben was delighted to have his dad come into the classroom. Stu, meanwhile, felt a little uncomfortable; but when Mrs. Larsen saw them, her warm smile made him feel very welcome.

As Ben excused himself to go out and see some of his friends before the bell rang, he only heard his teacher say, "Why, Mr. Thomas, it's good to see you," and then he was out the door. While Mrs. Larsen helped Stu with the box, she continued, "Ben told the class how you all wrap your apples with newspaper and then cover them partially in sand so they would keep in the winter."

"Did he also tell you they aren't very good quality? I thought we should buy some from the supermarket, but Ben was very, very insistent that we bring some from our orchard. In fact, he said, 'Dad, we eat 'em even if they do have worms.' So, here they are. I didn't think you would appreciate the newspaper wrappings. We bought some tissue paper yesterday to wrap them in. The whole family worked on making sure we brought the class the best ones we had. We thought the kids would enjoy them more than eating around any worms they might find in some of the ones we still have at home," Stu honestly said.

"No," Mrs. Larsen laughed. "Ben said we needed to eat them or they would rot. I didn't think it would have troubled him to bring wormy ones to class."

"Well, he has a point there about rotting and I think you're right about him not being bothered by the worms," Stu said as he joined in the laughter.

Before he left, Mrs. Larsen said, "Mr. Thomas, I sometimes think we make things too complicated. We worry too much. We sometimes aren't willing to accept a gift that comes our way, regardless of its wrapping. I think most of the kids in the class would have eaten the apples in spite of their appearance. After all, they are a gift."

"Hmm . . . I guess you're right. Sometimes I think I forget. Maybe I need to embrace the joy I saw in Ben's eyes when he told us about his volunteering apples as a gift as well. Thank you." With those words, he gave Mrs. Larsen another smile and left.

Stu put the conversation he had shared with Ben's teacher out of his mind for the rest of the day, even though come supper time he let his curiosity decide the conversation.

"How did the party go?"

"It was great!" Ben beamed. "Tommy said his apple was really good. He said the skin wasn't hard like the ones his dad brings home from their store. He said our apples are juicier and easier to eat. Tommy really likes our apples, but I didn't tell him Mom had to give a 'yes' to the ones we took to school. Do you think I should have?"

Before his father could answer, he continued, "I had some left over so I gave Tommy another one, and Joyce asked for another one so I gave her one, too. The last extra one went to Mrs. Larsen. She said she would take it home to her husband. Mrs. Larsen even asked me if next year I might pick her a basket of apples, and she would buy them from me. I told her if we have enough, I'd just give them to her—whether I pass history or not. I know that is what you and mom would want me to do."

He stopped talking, but only to take a breath, and then asked once again, "Do you think I should have?" Before Stu could say a word, his daughter interjected, "I helped too, Ben. Didn't I, Mom?"

Looking at her daughter, Ann replied, "Yes, you certainly did, and a very good helper you were."

"Ya, Kelly, you were a good helper. Dad helped too, and I'm glad you did, Dad." The conversation they shared made Ben forget all about the question he had asked his parents about whether or not he should have told Tommy about the inspection.

Stu reached over to tousle Ben's hair. "I'm glad he liked his apples, son. I'm also thankful you wanted to share what we have with your class.

Thank you for that. You helped me see what we all have to share in a way I hope I never forget."

Ben was a little confused about why his dad would be thanking him, but he liked the feeling. It made him feel just as good on the inside as the affectionate gesture his dad gave him made him feel on the outside.

"Oh," he added before he forgot, "Tommy wanted to know if he could come out and help pick apples next fall. Could he?"

"Well, I suppose," his father said. "That is, if you both don't eat them all before your mom has a chance to can some for applesauce."

"And for apple pie," added Ben.

"And for apple cider," Ann chimed in.

"And candy apples for Halloween," Kelly said in a loud voice, not wanting to be left out.

Everyone laughed. Ben's apples were a Christmas gift from the Thomas family, a treat to share with friends and his class, regardless where the apples came from. As the laughter softened, with a broad smile on her face, Ann surprised her son by saying, "Gee . . . now, I don't know . . . . Let's see . . . . hmm . . . applesauce, apple pie, apple cider, apples for Mrs. Larsen, apples to eat. Maybe we won't have enough for your class next year. You know you and Tommy are growing boys. Tommy will probably want to eat three at the party next year."

"I'll save seeds from the apples I eat," Kelly offered, and then reflectively added, "Then we will have more apples and enough for me to take to my class."

"Mom, remember . . . you always say, 'I don't know what we will do with all of these apples!'"

"That's correct, son." Stu added, "And we have already planted the seeds for next year's crop in our hearts."

Hearing what her father said, Kelly just sat there scratching her head, trying to figure it all out. Still not wanting to be left out, she added, "If we plant the apple seeds I'll save, we will have plenty of apples. Right, Mom?"

Ann turned to her daughter, smiled once again, and answered her in a way to be said to everyone, "Yes, darling. If you and Ben, and Dad and I plant those seeds with the new apples and the ones we already have, there will be more than enough. Our apples are a gift that can be given again and again because their seeds were planted deep in our hearts."

Chapter 8

THE CHRISTMAS SALE

The hill sloped evenly between the chicken house and the north side of the big red barn. By this time last year, so far into December, there was snow on the ground for Mitch Williams; his brother, Michael; and sister, Melissa; to sled on after chores were done. If they started with a strong running push, they could make a left curve right at the corner of the barn and continue down another slope to the water tank. Better yet, when the tank ran over and there was a hard freeze, ice could boost their speed all the way down to the end of the feedlot.

This year, though, it had yet to snow. The brown earth was frozen but bare, which was probably for the best. Snow would only get in the way. That was the unspoken consensus as Bruce Larsen and several other neighbors stood at the old washhouse gate, their eyes peering across the farmyard, feedlot, and surrounding landscape.

"We'll line the farm machinery in two rows, Charlene," Bruce said.

"Thank you." Charlene did her best to smile. "In the meantime, Nancy and I will make a pot of coffee to go with the cake she brought."

196

"Can I help, Mr. Larsen?" Mitch asked, knowing full well it was his responsibility to help.

Most ten-year-olds would rather be spending Saturdays out in the pasture riding their horses, sledding, or watching television. However, in his own mind, Mitch wasn't ten anymore. He'd stopped being ten last summer when his father died unexpectedly from a heart attack. Since then, he had seen their small herd of Holsteins being loaded up and taken to the Tuesday-evening dairy sale, and later he spotted the sadness in his mother's eyes as she looked at the check registering the amount she received from their sale.

"It won't go very far," she had said to herself, but he heard it anyway.

He had also seen the car with the out-of-state license plates drive out of their lane back in September when he got off the school bus. It belonged to the landlord, who drove all the way from California to Iowa for his yearly visit and inspection of the farm. After the usual greetings and a general walk around, his mother had invited him in for coffee and cake. As he stood to leave, with no explanation, he told his mother the bad news. That same evening, she shared the news with Mitch and his siblings. With her tears mingled into words, she said, "The landlord told me we have to move."

"Why, Mom?" Melissa asked.

"The landlord said he was selling the farm, and we had to move out before Christmas. For now, we will move into town. I'll find us a place to live. Don't worry, everything will work out okay," her mother answered, closing with what she hoped were reassuring words at a time of uncertainty.

Now Mitch was helping to get everything set up for the final round. Just three days remained until the last sale. He would have to watch the rest of the equipment leave the farm—objects he had always identified with his father and being a farmer—either driven or carried away by strangers.

I don't know why the farm bill the auctioneer posted around the county says, "Williams Farm Sale." It's not our farm. All we have are worn-out tools, broken-down equipment and machinery, some grain and hay, mom's chickens, this year's calves from the milk cows, a few sows and their pigs, and yes, my horse. Really, it's all we have, but still it meant so much to my dad. So much, but now . . . Mitch had such thoughts over and over when he would see "Williams Farm Sale" bills scattered around the small community where he and his brother and sister went to school. So, yes, he had seen and heard too much to remain ten years old.

"Mitch, why don't you carry the tools out of the machine shed and put them on the lowboy." Mr. Larsen pointed to the lowboy Bill Johnson was bringing around the corner of the barn.

As Mitch moved toward the place he knew Mr. Johnson would stop, he allowed himself a few seconds to muse.

I wonder why they call it a lowboy? It's just a hay wagon. The only difference between it and other hay wagons is it sits a lot lower to the ground and has two wheels instead of four. He also knew from going to farm sales with his dad, that it was easier for prospective buyers to view and handle items such as farm tools and odds and ends from a lowboy rather than a hay wagon.

Stirring from his musing and watching the moving lowboy, he turned toward Mr. Larsen and replied, "Sure, I can do that." He took off, happy to have something to do.

It was better when he was busy because "busy" was normal.

It seemed the Williams family was always busy. Ever since Mitch could remember, he'd had chores after school. Saturdays were always times to help his dad clean out the side of the barn where they milked. Either that, or they would pitch manure from the sow pens and put down fresh straw. The smell of the clean straw was something Mitch believed he would remember forever. Just like he would remember his father.

"How can pigs be so messy?" he had asked his dad.

Mr. Williams gave him a wink. "I guess to give ten-year-old boys something to do on Saturdays."

Mitch laughed. "That's what you told me when I was nine."

The happy memory made his eyes tear up a little, knowing he'd never see his father's wink or hear his laughter ever again.

"Are you done, Mitch?" Mr. Larsen came around to help him pick up the big bucket of nails he was struggling to lift onto the lowboy. With that accomplished, Mr. Larsen suggested, "Why don't you come with me for a few minutes and check out the stalls for the livestock."

Besides their small milk herd, now departed, the Williams family had always managed to keep a few calves each year to add to their herd. But those would be gone soon enough, too, as would the sows and pigs. Still, Mitch followed along to the place where several men were putting together some makeshift pens, pounding steel posts into the hard ground at the corners.

"Are you selling your horse?" Mr. Larsen asked.

Mitch's eyes watered. *No, I'm not selling my horse. My horse is being sold.*

Once again, though, he swallowed his tears. "I can't keep Jasper since Mom's new job is in town. We'll be living just off Main Street in the Carlson home since they're off to Texas." He stopped, unable to continue.

The resulting silence came as hard as the pounding of the posts into the wintry ground.

Mr. Larsen wasn't sure what to say when he knew Mr. Williams had not been in favor of his son having a horse for a 4-H project. His friend had told him that Mitch had saved his hay money earned from helping neighbors during haying season to help pay for the horse. He would have much rather seen Mitch buy some chickens or rabbits. Mr. Williams's exact words had been, "They cost too much, eat too much, and don't produce enough." Yet he still signed the bill of sale for his son to buy the horse and paid half of the cost.

"I worked for Jasper," Mitch managed to get out. "I couldn't have a calf because half of our yearly calf crop went to the landlord to help pay the farm rent, and my dad always said our half was needed for expenses. It was the same thing with our newborn pigs. Dad said we needed our share just to make ends meet. So, I saved money by driving the tractor and baling hay in the neighborhood. Remember when you paid me for baling at your place, Mr. Larsen?"

"I remember, son," Mr. Larsen answered, and added, "you worked hard for what you earned."

"Thanks," Mitch responded, but said no more. Yet, in his mind he couldn't help but remember those Saturday afternoons after he was finished with his work at home—how he rode his bike to Mr. Larsen's place and cleaned out the farrowing pens for his pig operation. He felt good that he was able to make enough money to pay for half of what Jasper cost.

"You were only nine then, Mitch," Bruce said with a tone of amazement.

"Yup, I guess I was, but I wanted Jasper," he answered.

"He's sort of skinny, isn't he?" Unsure of what else to say, Bruce reached out to pet Jasper as the horse came up to the fence.

"He's all right." Mitch climbed the fence rail to stroke Jasper's mane. "I haven't been able to feed him much ground corn. Since we sold the cows, we don't have much grain left on the place. Mom says we need most of it for the chickens and pigs. I've been feeding him mostly hay."

Mitch did not know how to tell Mr. Larsen they always seemed to be running out of feed, long before it was decided there would be a sale. Grinding with their old grinder was a full morning's chore on Saturday, and the feed never seemed to last the week. That"s why his dad had always said, "The cows, pigs, and chickens are fed first—then Jasper."

By the time he finished what few chores he had left, the neighbors were getting ready to leave. Full of coffee and cake, Bruce Larsen waited behind the group of men to visit with Mitch a little more.

"Your mother said you're coming to the service tomorrow," he said.

Mitch slipped off his work shoes and replied, "Mom said we would be in church, and then I have to help her line up some stuff in the garage for the sale."

"I need someone to help me usher," Mr. Larsen explained. "I'd appreciate it if you could help me out."

"Okay." Mitch looked up now, accepting this new responsibility right along with all the other ones. "I'd be glad to do that. I haven't ever ushered before."

"Don't worry," his neighbor reassured him. "I haven't done it too many times myself, but I'm sure we can help each other out."

As it turned out, Sunday morning's service was a little more involved than expected, if only because the fourth Advent candle had to be lit and its original lighters were absent. The Jackson family had originally volunteered for the honor, but on Saturday evening Mrs. Jackson had called the pastor to say the Jackson family Christmas dinner was on Sunday, and they had forgotten that when they made the commitment to light the Advent candle. She also explained the dinner was always held at the Legion in a small town up in northwest Iowa. "It will take us over three hours to get there, but only if you pray for good weather, Pastor," she told him. She ended her conversation by saying,

"I'm sorry, but you know how it goes. The holidays are such a rush. You understand, though, right?"

Pastor Thomas had been explaining this to Bruce when Charlene and the children came into the country church.

"Don't worry, Pastor," Mr. Larsen said reassuringly. "Mitch and I will light the candles and read the Scripture for the day. After all, we're ushering, so we're supposed to handle emergencies."

So, they did, and beautifully, too. The ceremony went off without a hitch, for which Pastor Thomas was very grateful.

"Mitch," he said afterward, shaking the boy's hand, "you and Mr. Larsen were really life-savers this morning. I'd like you to read the Scripture for Christmas Eve, too. Would you?"

Watching her son nod his acceptance, Charlene smiled. Even though they were moving to town immediately after the sale, she had decided they would continue to come out to the country church as long as they were able. *It would be good for Mitch to have something to look forward to after the sale*, she thought as they left the church. It was going to take a lot out of all of them physically and emotionally to leave the farm and neighborhood, especially now with their father—and her husband—gone.

On Monday after school was out and the chores were done, Mitch helped his mother, brother, and sister finish last-minute projects for the sale. Charlene had been very grateful for the assistance she also received from a group of neighborhood ladies who arrived shortly after the kids went off to school. They helped her pack some items and mark household furnishings she wanted to include in the sale. The men, under the direction of Mr. Larsen, finished last-minute outside projects for the sale. Even Melissa and Michael put a lot of effort in helping to make things ready. By Monday evening they had gone to bed with a lot of yawns and no protesting. Charlene was pretty tired too, but she nonetheless poured herself a cup of hot tea to drink while finishing some signs for the sale.

"Do you want me to help, Mom?" Mitch asked, coming up behind her.

Charlene gave him a fond smile. "Aren't you ready for bed?" she asked. "Tomorrow's going to be a big day, you know."

She had already written a note to his teacher to excuse him from school so he could help out, even though her first thought was he needed to be in school. Keeping him on a routine as normal as possible would be for the best. After talking the whole situation through once again in her head, she realized that the children, particularly Mitch, needed to be part of the process. He needed to be present. It was important for him to be able to say his "goodbyes." He needed to be there for a final "goodbye" to Jasper. He needed to be able to let loose of the old machinery, junk, and well-beaten pathways from the house to the barn, pasture, hog house, and chicken house.

Charlene didn't exactly know how all of this was embedded in his brain, heart, or soul. She only knew the sorrow, pain, and loneliness he had shared—and continued to share with her—in the death of his father as well as a way of life that now brought them to all of these "goodbyes." Yes, she resolved that he needed to be here at that time, which had also been at his sincere request. She also admitted to herself it would be nice to have her helper there with her.

All of her thoughts held her in a present state of limbo. She had almost forgotten her question to him regarding being ready for bed until he exclaimed, "No!" He looked solemn, as he did far too often these days. "I don't think I can sleep. I'd like to help."

He didn't need to say more. She understood.

"Here." Charlene handed him the magic marker. "You can make some menu signs. The morning circle from the church is going to serve lunch in the garage, and we'll plug in a heater."

"Yeah," Mitch agreed, "they'll need it." Mitch had heard the forecast. "Cold and colder" was the weather prediction for the day, according to channel 7.

"I know." Charlene frowned, and then moved on in the next breath. "Say, how 'bout some tea?"

"Okay," he said with more boyish enthusiasm than usual, waiting until she poured the beverage before squirting some lemon in the cup.

"Remember when we used to make hot tea after you and your father would come in from doing the chores?" she asked. "My goodness, the two of you would flavor the stuff with spoons of sugar. I think you used the tea as an excuse just to satisfy your sweet tooth."

Without his boyish reluctance, Mitch leaned over to hug her. "I love you, Mom."

"I love you, too, son." Charlene tried hard to hold back the tears, but they found their way into the moment, leaving a lot of silence while the two of them finished up for the night.

Mitch had long since recognized that the old farm house had a difficult time insulating him and his family from the winter's chilling winds. So, he made sure to snuggle deep under a pile of covers when he went to bed. Even so, there was not much he could do against the roar of the north wind as it beat upon the plastic sheet covering the window pane above his bed. He would have gone back to sleep, but the crackling noise only grew louder as the wind rushed along the side of the house.

It was intense enough to make him jump out of bed and hurry downstairs to check the time. The kitchen's linoleum floor felt like ice piercing through the heavy woolen socks he had worn to bed to keep his feet warm, and a glance at the clock showed him it was really too early to rise. Yet he still went over to turn on the outside light and peer out the window, where snow was swirling around in the front yard. Already he could see drifts across the lane.

"Is it bad?" his mother asked. She was just a minute behind him.

"It's across the bottom of the lane, Mom," he said. "I can't see much farther than the mailbox."

She shook her head in distress. "It won't be easy for people to get here for the sale."

Mitch felt just as helpless, but he strove to overcome that feeling for his mom's sake. "Remember what Dad used to say: 'You can only do so much, and then you just have to have hope.'" He pulled for more memories to keep going. "God seems to have a way of making a bridge with our hope across our fears and struggles so we don't feel alone."

"How did you get so wise, young man?" She leaned down to kiss the top of his head, and then sent him off to bed. As he'd said, they could only do so much.

With the first sign of the sun shivering through the storming sky, neighbors came over and were plowing out the Williams's lane. The auctioneer's truck was right behind them. In spite of the snowdrifts, the sale was going to take place.

"You could postpone it, Charlene." Ray Timmons, the auctioneer, was already making some bid starters on his sales sheet as he spoke. "I'm sure your landlord will give you a time extension." He had already explained how the county snowplow was just ahead of him on the highway.

Charlene frowned. "I wish we could, but I'm afraid it would just be too much. Besides, what is there to postpone?" She tried to stretch a smile across her face. "Most of what we have is nickel-and-dime stuff: machinery held together by baling twine, along with livestock that all look like they've been put on a crash diet."

As such, the sale started at ten o'clock, while Melissa and Michael were playing in the house with one of the neighbor children. Charlene helped the clerk pass out numbers for bidders, even though there really was no need for such things, considering how a mere twenty or so neighbors and friends had come along the various paths cleared by the snowplow and tractors.

"I know just about everyone here, Mom." Mitch smiled.

Charlene wasn't so thrilled about that fact, though. No matter— she didn't let on to her son. Knowing everyone was not a good start for a farm sale when she knew most of her acquaintances were in the same financial position as she and her husband had been before he died. *When you can't even do your part, what happens? What do you have to offer?*

Mr. Timmons started calling out, "What will you give me for this John Deere tractor here?"

Noticeably, he left out the word "old." The weathered piece of equipment had seen a lot of field hours, and most recently it was used for grinding feed.

"Who'll give me three-hundred?"

That was the last sentence Mitch understood until the auctioneer yelled out, "Sold for two-hundred and ten!" Looking over at his mother, he could tell by the expression on her face that the tractor hadn't sold for enough.

Whether the final bids were enough or not, the sale kept progressing with the inanimate objects on up to the livestock, which started to sell in the afternoon. When it was time, Mitch led Jasper out of the pen and walked him around the small group of farmers still bidding.

"It's a fine pony." Mr. Timmons smiled at Mitch. "Who'll start the bid? Who'll give me a hundred for this pony?"

The low price horrified Mitch. *A hundred dollars? This is Jasper, my pony. He's worth a thousand!*

Despite Mr. Timmons continuing to receive the bids, all Mitch heard was the "hundred" over and over again in his head for the next minute until a voice broke the auctioneer's beat.

"I'll give you five hundred."

Knowing full well that was way more than where the auctioneer had started, Mitch turned to look. Mr. Larsen was standing there looking certain, and it seemed everyone else there was too: No one was going to bid any higher.

"Five-hundred going once. Going twice. Sold to Bruce Larsen for five hundred dollars!" Mr. Timmons nodded at the clerk, who recorded Bruce's number.

Charlene smiled at him as he took the halter rope, but Mitch couldn't help but feel devastated. Jasper had been his last hope—his bridge across all the hurt that came from not always understanding why any of this had to have happened.

His father was dead.

They were leaving the farm.

And now, Jasper was no longer his.

A few hours later, the sale was over, and Mitch was watching Mr. Larsen saying goodbye to his mom. Before he left altogether, though, their neighbor made sure to catch his attention.

"I'll meet you at church for Christmas Eve," he said. "Remember, you're going to read the Scripture."

"I'll remember, Mr. Larsen." Tears started to form in his eyes despite his best attempts to keep them at bay.

"Don't worry, son." The man just put his arm around Mitch's shoulder. "Things will work out."

After everyone had left, and later as Mitch was preparing for bed, the silence of a December country night came and settled in deeply. There was no wind or anything else to distract Mitch from mourning over the farm and all the memories it held. He found little comfort in remembering the happier times. For him, there was only aching pain.

Turning on the light beside his bed, he opened his Bible and read for a while until he heard his mother in the kitchen. And so he decided to join her.

"Mom," he asked, "if Christmas is supposed to be a happy time, why was everyone so afraid?"

Surprised, Charlene turned to her son. "What do you mean?"

"Well," he squinted in thought, "I've been going over the Scripture passages I'm supposed to read tomorrow evening, and everyone just seemed to be so afraid. First it was Zechariah. Then Mary. Then Joseph. Then the shepherds."

"They were also filled with joy," his mother added.

"But why were they afraid?" Mitch persisted.

"Maybe it's because they just couldn't see beyond the moment." Now it was her turn to think it over. "You know how it is. Like when Jasper was sold this afternoon. You felt very sad because, in the moment, you couldn't see or feel anything but the hurt. And hurting took up all the space you had."

Her words gave him a definite understanding to work with. "So, they couldn't feel joy at first because fear took up all of their space?"

"I suppose so." She gazed at him with a mother's love. "Yet in spite of their fear, because they had hoped for a king, they were able to make enough room for hope and joy to continue."

"So, their hopes were bridges." Mitch wanted so hard for the hurt to go away.

"Sweetheart, your hope will always bridge your fears, even if—in the moment—hope doesn't seem likely."

He nodded, taking a deep breath and squaring his shoulders in acceptance. His courage and faith helped her get back to building her own bridge, a beautiful reminder she desperately needed herself.

The following day was Christmas Eve, and there was little to do around the farm. It seemed strange not to have chores. As the sun began to disappear over the horizon, Mitch caught himself looking at the barn more than once. He could almost hear the cows and see Jasper's head hanging over the fence. Yet after speaking with his mom the night before, he was determined to focus on bridges instead of hurts.

After a light supper, they were off to the candlelight service, where Mitch made sure to read the Scripture carefully. He wanted people to know that, even though hardships and fear seemed to abound in the world, there was also hope and love.

It seemed as if he succeeded in touching more than one person because they came up to tell him so later while refreshments were being served. Mr. Larsen was among them.

"You really did a nice job," he said, handing him a glass of punch. "Say, if you have a minute, I want to show you something."

Mitch dutifully followed him up from the church basement and outside. Heading toward Mr. Larsen's pickup, he was a bit confused by what he saw. "Hey, you have your horse trailer."

But the man just smiled. "That's what I want to show you. Now you wait right here."

Disappearing into the trailer, he came out in a minute with a horse saddled and bridled.

"It's Jasper!" Mitch exclaimed.

Mr. Larsen was flat-out beaming now. "Merry Christmas!"

His young friend was already climbing into the saddle when those words began to register in his young brain. "What?"

"Well," Mr. Larsen said, "I need someone to exercise Jasper, at least. So, I thought we could be partners. You could come out and work for me during the summer and make a little money by taking care of him, too. What do you say?"

He handed over the reins.

"That would be wonderful!" Mitch's face radiated his happiness. "I really will take good care of him."

"I know you will," Mr. Larsen said confidently. "Merry Christmas, son."

"Merry Christmas!" Mitch called back as he and Jasper circled the churchyard, joyful in the knowledge that bridges really could bring about a more hopeful perspective to life.

Chapter 9

THE ORDINARY

"Well, I believe that about covers it, unless you have other questions." Brian Johnson swallowed hard, put down the coffee mug, and let out a conspicuously tired breath.

He seemed to do all three things simultaneously, at least according to Ellen Jane Carson.

"But I do have other questions," she said as Mr. Johnson, the agency caseworker who had recruited her and her husband to be foster parents again, started to rise from his seat.

"Oh." He paused, knees bent inches above the cushion. "I thought—"

Carefully ignoring his awkward pose, she turned to her husband, Michael. "It just seems like so much has changed since the last time we did this."

Michael understood her concern, so he picked up where she had left off, even while Mr. Johnson settled himself back onto his seat.

"Twenty years ago, when we first became foster parents, we mostly had young pregnant girls coming to live with us. We didn't have children at the time and, while those girls became a part of our family, we always knew they had their own. They were here for a while, and then as things improved, they either went back home, on to school, or got jobs." He shook his head. "But now? Now it seems these kinds of children have a lot more issues, problems, and crises to resolve."

Ellen chimed in, remembering the conversation around last night's supper table as clearly as if it was still happening. "And we have a seven-year-old daughter and a nine-year-old son now who aren't necessarily pleased with the idea of a foster child sharing their home and parents."

Michael took her hand. "Although Mary Katherine did think having an older sister would be nice."

"And I guess Jeffrey thought an older brother would come in handy when it came time to do chores around the house," Ellen recalled.

With a crisp tone in his voice, Brian brought them back to the here and now. "You're right about things that have changed. Changed a lot, in fact. Most of our children, especially the adolescents, are coming into the system from families with conflict, crisis after crisis, and more things than you want to know about."

If that was supposed to allay their fears, it failed.

Nor had he finished just yet. "A child might bring one physical suitcase with him or her, but they're often dragging a mental trunk full of negative and painful feelings they might very well unpack while staying with you." His matter-of-fact attitude never shifted. "But you can do the job. That's why we're asking you to consider being foster parents again."

Then there was silence. When neither Michael nor Ellen broke it, he rose from the chair and grabbed his coat.

"Well?"

The Carsons stood up too, looking at one another while they did. Despite how little actual encouragement they'd just received, Michael nodded, and Ellen spoke up.

"I guess we'll give it a try. I hope you understand our hesitancy, though. I mean, we consider this more than just 'a job.'"

Mr. Johnson ignored the last comment. "I'll call you as soon as I have things set up. We'll have case reviews this afternoon, and I'll know more in a couple of days."

Together, the couple watched him depart not saying a word. Without a cue, they embraced, each knowing the other had an inner strength called perseverance to share in the commitment they had just made.

Brian Johnson, meanwhile, was striding toward the office of Martin Case, director of Foster Children's Inc. At the time, Martin was sitting across from one Samuel Mason, a stocky, short, brown-eyed fourteen-year-old with unkempt curly brown hair who had already been in and out of two foster homes, not to mention in and out of his own home several times as well.

"May I come in?" Brian stuck his head through the open door, entering without actual permission. The question had been a formality anyway.

"Are we ready?" Case quizzed him, still staring at the teenager.

"Everything's ready at the Carson's," he declared, no matter that he'd implied to them they had a day or two before anything happened. "I'll call them in an hour, and then Sam and I can go out there this afternoon." He turned to Sam. "Are you packed?"

As Mr. Case looked over at the corner of the room, Brian's eyes followed his to a travel-worn brown suitcase that rested against the office wall.

Sam said nothing.

The Carsons had barely stepped in the door before the phone was ringing. They were greeted by the sounds of two children racing to answer it, each no doubt hoping a friend was on the other end.

Mary's long arms won, but her voice revealed disappointment as she answered.

Jeffrey smiled a little smugly as he interpreted the signs correctly. "Mom, it's for you."

Sure enough, Mary handed the phone over to her mother before heading down the hall toward her room. Yet she stopped when she heard the gist of the conversation.

"This afternoon! About an hour? But I thought . . . well, I guess it will be okay. Yes, see you in about an hour. Okay. We'll see you then."

"A boy or girl?" Mary asked. In spite of thinking she might like to have a sister, she had really been holding out hope until now that it wouldn't work out.

"Samuel Allen Mason will be coming soon," her mom responded with a knowing smile. "He likes to be called Sam."

So, just like that, the wheels started turning. Brian and Sam arrived at their house and received the usual greetings and introductions. On his part, there was an overall sullen silence—from the new family member. When Michael tried to engage him in small talk, the teen contributed little or kept silent altogether. And when Jeffrey and Mary Katherine showed him to his room downstairs near the family room, he sat on the bed and paid no attention to their invitation to come back upstairs for cookies and milk. After those attempts failed, they tried to respect his wishes and give him some space.

Sitting there, Sam could hear the front door close, which meant that Mr. Johnson had left. It didn't matter, though. He was here but he wasn't, already preparing for a short stay and another disappointment.

214

His heart had never even made the trip.

Not knowing what else to do, the Carson family went about their usual Saturday routine. Michael thought it best they leave Sam alone for a reasonable amount of time, so he ran errands while Ellen went back to the work she'd brought home from her office the previous day. When Mary went out to play with her friends, Jeffrey, forgetting what his father thought was best, hung around a bit, hoping Sam would appear from his room and be eager to go out and play catch. He waited. Nothing happened, so he went down and knocked on Sam's door. No answer. He knocked again but still no answer. Jeffrey knew Sam was on the other side, so he was disappointed when Sam did not respond. Disappointed, hurt, and a little put off, he left to also go find some of his friends.

Suppertime was different, though, especially since Saturday evening was always pizza night at the Carson's. So, while Ellen took the fresh pies from the oven, Michael asked Jeffrey to go down and bring Sam to supper.

It only took a moment for his son to return, frowning in confusion. "He said he's not hungry." Because of what Jeffrey felt as a rejection from Sam earlier in the day and now his refusal to join them at supper, it caused him to have some doubts regarding Sam stepping up to the plate to be the big brother he never had and wanting to spend time with him. These particular thoughts definitely did not confuse him, and he was beginning to feel a little apprehensive about Sam being in their home.

Already moving toward the stairs, Michael shot Ellen a deliberate glance. "That's okay, Jeffrey. I'll go see what the problem is."

Ellen bit her lower lip in concern, praying her husband would find the right words to say.

As he entered the basement room, Michael was praying the same thing. "What's wrong?" he asked, taking a seat on the bed.

Sam did not answer, nor was he greatly taken aback by the intrusion, polite or otherwise. *Why doesn't the guy just yell? I'm more used to that.*

"Nothing," he said after it was certain that this man—this Mr. Carson—wasn't going away.

"It's time to eat, Sam," Michael tried again. "If nothing's wrong, then you need to come to supper."

"I'm not hungry." His tone was just as obstinate as the words themselves.

"Well, one rule in our home is that people come to the table whether they're hungry or not. It's a time for fellowship. You know, to catch up on the day with each other." He offered a friendly smile.

"What other rules?" Sam asked wryly.

"One thing at a time," Michael responded. "The one thing right now is supper. Come on." Getting up to leave, he paused to indicate he wasn't taking no for an answer and then started up the stairs, making it clear that Sam should follow.

As usual, supper was filled with a lot of chatter, most of it coming from Jeffrey and Mary. Whenever Sam was asked anything, he usually mumbled. He did eat, though, devouring four pieces within minutes.

It's a good thing I made two pizzas, Ellen said to herself as Sam reached for his fifth slice.

"Ahem." Michael pointed at the bowl in front of Sam's plate. "You haven't even touched your salad yet."

"Oh, is that for me?" Sam's surprise was exaggerated, to say the least.

Mary gasped and Jeffrey giggled, but one look at Michael convinced Sam to take his fork and stab it into the lettuce.

"Hmm," he commented obnoxiously. "That's good."

Ellen tried to redirect everyone's attention. "Tomorrow is the first Sunday in Advent, Sam. So, we're going to go to church school and the service and then pick out a Christmas tree in the afternoon."

"What's Advent?" Sam quizzed her during his last mouthful of lettuce.

"Sam doesn't have to go, does he, Dad?" Jeffrey interrupted, startling both his parents.

"Why, of course he does," Michael said. "What makes you think he doesn't?"

"He's not really part of our family," Jeffrey stated, seeming to mean every word of it.

With a look of defiance quickly appearing on Sam's face, he stared at Jeffrey, but the nine-year-old met his eyes in triumph.

"I thought you were hoping we would have a foster son," Michael reminded his actual child.

"Not Sam," Jeffrey said honestly. "He eats too much pizza." With that remark, he left the table. He wanted to say more regarding how Sam had avoided him that afternoon, but he didn't.

Silence followed, a vivid reminder to both Michael and Ellen that this was not going to be easy.

As for Mary Katherine, she felt extremely awkward sitting there. "May I be excused?" she whispered.

"Yes." Her mother tried to give her a reassuring smile. Then, as much for herself as for Sam, she said, "I think Jeffrey just needs some time."

"I think he was hoping you would enjoy having a little brother," added Michael.

"I have a little brother." Sam stood up. "He's a brat. I don't need another one." He stomped off to his room.

"He tells us more in his anger than he does in his calm," Michael said poetically.

"I don't know." Ellen looked near tears. "Is this a good thing? I mean, the idea is right. We agreed the commitment was something we wanted to make, but—" She struggled to find the right words. "I mean, if just getting through a meal is going to be this difficult . . ." Ellen said no more.

Despite how she'd addressed her husband, she was talking to herself more than looking for answers from him. For the moment, she really didn't need to hear an answer she knew would only make her feel worse.

Unfortunately, Sam's behavior at church the next day did nothing to alleviate her concern.

"This is the first Sunday of Advent!" Reverend Marvin Mitchell proclaimed enthusiastically. "It is a Sunday filled with prophecy and preparation. The very word, Advent, is a way to announce that Christ is with us again!"

"Big deal." Sam rolled his eyes.

"Shh," whispered Mr. Carson.

Sam rolled his eyes again and then fidgeted the whole service long. In his opinion, it seemed to last forever. Even so, every so often, something seemed to catch his attention.

It doesn't matter. It's all the same. The bitter, sarcastic thoughts were his shield. Words. Just words. Preparation to be bounced on the street again. Now, there's the Christmas spirit.

"Well, Jeffrey, what is your joke for this week? I believe it is your turn," Reverend Mitchell asked Jeffrey, who had pushed his way in front of his father and Sam to greet him following the service.

"Okay, why did Santa go out to his garden before Christmas?" asked Jeffrey.

"Hmm . . . you got me there. Why did Santa go out to his garden?" Reverend Mitchell responded.

"So he could 'Ho! Ho! Ho!'" Jeffrey relished imitating a Santa.

"Jeffrey, that is lame," Reverend Mitchell said as he chuckled. "I'll work on one for next week, okay?"

"Sure," Jeffrey yelled over his shoulder as he scampered off to meet up with friends and help himself to cookies at the refreshment table.

"I don't know where he comes up with his jokes, Pastor. I was just about ready to introduce you to our new foster son when we were so enthusiastically interrupted." Then, turning toward Sam, he said, "Reverend Mitchell, I would like for you to meet Sam Mason. Sam, this is our pastor, Reverend Mitchell, and he will be your pastor as well."

"Pleased to meet you, Sam." He reached out his hand.

Sam didn't take it.

The reverend went on anyway. "I hope you will be joining our youth group. Would you like for me to give you a call this week to tell you about it?"

Sam paused only a second before walking away, muttering something about how M&Ms really do melt in your hands when you add hot air.

"In time." Michael couldn't help how uncertain he sounded as he touched Reverend Mitchell's shoulder in apology. "In time."

But the time still hadn't come to go out to find a Christmas tree. Noncommittal as he was, Sam didn't seem to mind either the trip there or back, just as long as no questions were asked of him nor attempts made to draw him into conversation.

After unloading the tree, Michael had the teen help him carry it into the family room, where they'd secure it in the stand.

"Can I help?" Jeffrey was all over it in his attempts to be useful. "Can I help?"

But Michael, preoccupied with giving Sam directions, didn't pay him any attention. For the moment, he continued addressing Sam. "Hold the tree straight up while I tighten the screws into the trunk." The next second, he was on his knees with his back arched down so he could duck under the tree and tighten the screws. Looking up from the trunk, he could see the tree starting to lean toward the right. "Sam, move it a little to the left," he called out from under the tree. Sam gave out an apathetic grunt that was barely audible, but at the same time, he did as he was told.

"Can I help? Can I help?" Jeffrey went from standing to bending down with his face directly in line with his father's, wishing he would have asked him to hold the tree instead of Sam. Jeffrey knew he would be doing it the right way. "Can I help?" he asked for the third time.

But Michael was still so focused on giving Sam more directions so the tree would stand aright that he seemed to be paying no attention to Jeffrey's pleas.

When it became obvious to Jeffrey that his father was giving his attention to Sam and the tree, forgetting all about his presence or what he was asking, he stood directly in front of Sam and gave him another one of those stares he saved for a person who definitely was not one of his favorites. Sam could not help but notice Jeffrey's stare, yet he chose not to say anything.

Even though the task took a little longer than Michael thought it would, the tree was finally standing tall and straight.

"Cocoa time!" Ellen called from the kitchen.

"We're done here at least for now," Michael said with both Sam and Jeffrey in his sight, but not eyeing either of them directly. "Come on, let's go have some cocoa."

Sam sat at the table, expressing what might appear to be little to no feelings of enjoyment. That did not stop him, however, from quickly downing his mug of cocoa.

Ellen offered him another mugful. "We don't start decorating the tree until next Sunday, Sam."

"We add a little more each Sunday afternoon," Mary chimed in. "Except for the china angel. She doesn't get put on the tree until Christmas Eve!"

"China what?" Sam asked, sarcastically of course.

"Angel, Sam." Michael winked at him. "An angel."

Sam was not amused.

"It's an heirloom," Ellen said. "It belonged to my great-grandmother, and our family has always put it on the tree the last Sunday before Advent."

"What's an heirloom?" Sam was quick to add, "Like I really care."

By then, Jeffrey had most definitely had enough. "You'll see," he snapped.

But as for Mary, his surly attitude made her wonder the rest of the evening until bedtime, so she stopped by Sam's room. Since the door was ajar, she peeked in to see him lying on the bed.

"What do you want?" He didn't look at her.

"Can I come in?"

"You already are, aren't you?" Sam still avoided staring in her direction.

"My friends call me Katie," she explained. "You can if you want to."

"I'm not your friend." Sam's sharp words caused her to step back as he rose from the bed. "I didn't ask to come here. I was perfectly fine taking care of myself."

"Don't you have a mother?" Even though her parents had told her about Sam, Mary Katherine really didn't know much about her new foster brother. And for the time being, her curiosity was simply stronger than her fear.

"Sure, I have a mother. Doesn't everyone?" Sam really wished she would just go away, but he didn't know how to tell her to leave except by being meaner than even he wanted to be.

"Do you have a dad?" she hung on.

"My dad's gone. My mom doesn't want me." Sam stood in the middle of the room, wishing the instant tears away but not succeeding. "So there! Are you happy? Now you know a kid whose mother doesn't want him. Ho! Ho! Ho!" He swiped at the lone tear that slipped down his cheek. "Some Christmas."

Even though his rudeness failed to intimidate her, the vulnerability was too overwhelming for her. With an "I'm so sorry, Sam," she ran out of his room.

Not wanting to regret anything he'd said, Sam immediately closed his door as she left. Wrapped in the familiar embrace of loneliness, he took off his armor of toughness and let himself cry. He knew they all cared. He even felt twinges of caring for them. But the cost was too high and the risk too great.

Finding the way to her bedroom, Mary Katherine plumped herself on the side of her bed. It took only a few seconds, but she eventually felt a sense of calm. Not peace, just calm. She began to allow her mind to ponder about what it must be like not knowing where your father is, or maybe even worse, knowing your mother didn't want you. Deep inside herself, her heart voice said, "I'll share my mom and dad with you, Sam. They have love for all of us."

The Second Advent Sunday came and went, with Reverend Mitchell trying to initiate another conversation with Sam during fellowship time. He even extended another general but personal invitation to youth group. Sam simply pretended he didn't hear the invitation and went over to the table where the cookies were.

This time, Michael assured their pastor that he would try to intercede.

Ellen, however, had an idea of her own. "You know, Reverend, the senior high youth are going Christmas caroling next Sunday afternoon. Why don't you have Laura give Sam a call and invite him?"

"Do you think that will work?" he asked, doubtful that a girl—even someone as pleasant as Laura—could accomplish such a thing. "I mean, I don't want him snapping her head off or something like that."

"Trust me." Ellen's lips pursed in amusement. "Adolescents have a language of their own. Besides, just a few minutes ago, Laura's mother was asking me about Sam. It seems Laura told her about a new boy in her class. She said he was introduced to them by their homeroom teacher. She also said Laura is in some of the same classes Sam is. I'm really not sure how Laura found out he's living with us."

Back home again, the family spent the afternoon trimming the tree with tinsel and Christmas ornaments. After declaring his aversion to participating, Sam watched from the easy chair until Mary Katherine got stuck with tangled globs of tinsel and was desperately trying to unwind it all. He was somewhat amused to see her trying to work out the tangles. As her fingers fumbled through the tangles, without saying a word, she would look up at him as if to say, "Help me." He did not move. When her facial expression changed from accepting the challenge to what he interpreted as a look of overwhelming helplessness coupled with tears beginning to appear on her bottom eyelids, a strange wave of warmth washed over him—something he hadn't felt for anyone for a long time. Sam had thought he would have no problem avoiding her dilemma.

It was all a mystery to him, but his own feelings and memory took him back to the children's home. He remembered the Christmas tree being put up on the afternoon he was brought back to the home after his first foster home failure. A new resident, a young girl named Anna about Mary Katherine's age, was there. For some reason, she immediately took a liking to him. That afternoon, he tried hard to avoid her, but it didn't work. As she helped some of the other kids decorate the tree, she would often say to him, "Won't you come help?" His answer was always a negative head-shake.

When they finished with the tree, Anna picked up the storybook she had brought into the room with her and carried it over to Sam. "Read to me, please," she asked with enthusiasm. When he didn't answer but did not leave the room, she stuck the book out toward him and said, "My name is Anna. I know your name is Sam. Read to me, Sam . . . please." She was persistent. The third and fourth time, he said nothing, but he still did not leave the room. Yet she was not discouraged by his refusal. Before she asked again, looking up at him, she surprised him by saying, "I like you, Sam. Do you like me? Will you read to me?"

Even though he wasn't sure why, his tough resistance was worn down by her determination not to be discouraged, along with her unfailing optimism. From then on, not only did he read to her on a regular basis, but he also taught her how to play checkers and even helped with her reading. But then he had to leave again. When he was brought back to the home from failing to measure up in his second placement, Anna was gone. Unlike Sam, she never returned.

Now, in the Carson's living room, watching Mary Katherine and the dilemma she was in with the tangled mess of tinsel, his past experience with Anna and the feelings he had locked up in his own emotional dungeon all came to the surface. *I wish I had treated Anna a little nicer. A few seconds passed before he reflected, I wish I had treated Mary Katherine nicer earlier.* Still eyeing Mary Katherine, he thought, *I can help her now.* To everyone's surprise, he went over to help her with the mess.

Afraid that bringing attention to his kindness might set Sam right back, nobody said a word about the matter. While they held their surprise in check, the topic of conversation picked right back up where it had left off.

"Next week," Ellen said for Sam's sake, "we'll put on the garland and decorate the dining room. Then, next Sunday, we'll put on the lights and take the china angel out of her wrappings. She'll be put on the tree right before we go to the candlelight service on Christmas Eve. For now, she will rest here on the hutch, where she will await her throne," Ellen said with a voice exaggerating the whole ritual.

"Mom says she's Fra—what's her name, Mom?" Mary Katherine had worked hard trying to tell Sam the angel's name, but she just couldn't pronounce it correctly.

"Honey, we haven't named the angel. I told you, she's fragile. That means if she's dropped on the floor, she will break, so we have to be really careful. So, we will just leave her for now." Ellen touched the angel that still rested securely on the hutch.

Unmoved by this conversation, Sam seemed more focused on what had been said earlier. "You mean you go to church on Christmas Eve, too?" Sam sighed. "We've been to church every Sunday I've been here."

"What would you normally do?" Michael asked.

"Oh, I don't know." Sam made it sound like anything would be a better choice. "Go to a movie. Watch TV. My mom usually worked, so I hung out with friends."

"What about your brothers and sisters?" Ellen asked.

"My aunt usually watches them. She has them more than my mother does." The second he said that last line, he wished he could take it back, especially the melancholy tone that had slipped in without his permission.

Once again, nobody said a word about it, even though they did notice his silence was much less sullen for the rest of the day—just sad. He didn't say much the next morning either. By then, however, his old attitude had slipped back into place.

As if he timed it, Mr. Johnson called the Carsons as soon as Sam walked in from school. Michael talked to him for a few seconds, and then he handed the phone to Sam.

"Mr. Johnson wants to set up a time when you can see your brothers and sisters."

"Big deal," Sam replied as he took the phone and demanded, "what do you want?"

Unfazed by his rudeness, Brian got right to the point. "I talked to your aunt, and we've arranged for you to meet her at McDonald's near the mall at three o'clock on Saturday afternoon."

"I don't have a way to get there," Sam interrupted.

Disregarding his remark, Brian said, "I talked it over with Mr. Carson. He'll make sure you get there."

"That's it?" Sam questioned.

"That's it," Brian confirmed. "Your brothers and sisters want to see you. I hope you have a good time."

"Oh, sure. A good time at McDonald's." And with that, he hung up.

Watching Sam from the kitchen, it wasn't difficult for Michael to figure out what had just happened, yet he chose to let it go. "Well, Sam, either Ellen or I will take you over on Saturday. You'll probably want to buy your siblings something, right?"

"I don't have any money."

The phone rang again behind them, but someone picked it up in another room before the second ring.

"You have an allowance coming for your chores, and I'll pay you ten dollars if you clean out the garage." Michael extended his hand. "Deal?"

Sam didn't accept the outstretched hand, but he also didn't hesitate to reply, "Okay, I'll do it."

Ellen, who was working in the den, yelled out, "Sam, it's for you!"

"Probably Mr. Johnson wanting to remind me not to heist the golden arches," he said while marching over to the phone. "Yeah?" and then, "Who?"

Michael decided there was something in the paper behind him he desperately needed to look over again.

"Oh," Sam said. "Sure I remember you."

Michael kept pretending to read.

"What? Has Reverend Mitchell been talking to you?" A pause. "Well, okay, I guess. Just a minute."

Sam put the phone down and turned to his foster father, who made sure to look up as innocently as he could, a task made easier by the fact that Sam refused to meet his gaze. "This girl wants to know if I can go to the senior high caroling party on Sunday night. Can you take me to church?"

"Girl?" Michael frowned, pretending confusion.

"Laura Thompson." Sam felt stupid asking for permission when he was used to having no supervision at all. "You know—she's always at church like we are. I'm sure her parents make her go."

"Sure. I guess we can add this week's decorations to the tree before you go and—"

"The tree?" Sam interrupted. "You mean I have to still help even if I go?"

"Yes, you still have to help." Michael chuckled. "And yes, you can go."

The teen turned his attention back to the phone. "Yeah, I can go. I'll see you at school." This time, he added, "Goodbye," before he hung up the phone.

With schoolwork and chores, there wasn't much free time before Saturday. Also, Mary Katherine always seemed to find some excuse to stop at his room, even if just to say "Hi." Depending on his mood, Sam either ignored or tolerated her. As for his other so-called foster sibling, he didn't let it trouble him that Jeffrey usually seemed angry whenever they had to be in each other's company.

That included on Saturday afternoon when Michael and Sam were heading to the car.

Jeffrey poked his head out the door behind them. "Where are you going, Dad?"

"I'm taking Sam shopping to pick out some presents for his brothers and sisters, and then we're going over to McDonald's so he can spend a little time with them," Michael replied.

"I thought *we* were going shopping!" He thundered down the stairs after them.

"I told you," his father reminded him, "we'll go Wednesday evening after Cub Scouts. Remember, just you and me. After we go shopping for your presents, I said we would go to the Burger Deluxe and have supper."

"I want to go now!" he yelled defiantly.

"Jeffrey, stop that." Michael was already opening his car door. "Go in the house. Now!"

After hearing his father's last words, he turned to leave, but not before giving Sam one of the stares he'd become good at using whenever it seemed Sam came between him and his father. In the past few weeks, there had been more and more of the "Jeffrey stares." Even though Sam was aware of them, he decided not to turn them into a big deal.

But Michael didn't see it because he was too focused on getting his foster child off to the mall to do a little shopping and then to McDonald's to meet his brothers and sisters. So, he didn't address the situation like Jeffrey so desperately wanted him to do—not that evening, not the following morning, and not for the rest of the day. Still, it was impossible not to notice the tension altogether. So, it didn't surprise him when it came up in a conversation Sunday night after the kids were all in bed.

"Guess what?" Ellen asked Michael after he joined her at the kitchen table.

"The President called you and wants you to be chief of staff," Michael teased her.

"No, silly." She rolled her eyes. "That was last week, and I told him he couldn't afford me. Guess what happened?"

Michael took a sip of his coffee. "Do tell."

"Sam told me all about the caroling party this evening. He talked to me!" Her face was a study in joy. "It sounded like he had a nice time, too."

"Maybe we should have had Laura invite him to youth group instead of Reverend Mitchell," Michael mused aloud.

"He also told me about shopping and the trip to McDonald's," Ellen said. The joy was still there, but her eyes moistened as she reflected on what Sam had shared with her regarding his siblings. "He really seems to care for his brothers and sisters."

"I know, El." He reached out to accept the hand she'd given him. "The boy has some hard places in his personality, but I really do think he wants to do what's right." He frowned. "I just wish—"

"You wish he and Jeffrey could work things out," she said.

"Yeah. I do."

"So do I, Mike. So do I." She gave his hand an extra squeeze. "I don't really know if we can be a family if they can't at least be civil to one another."

Unfortunately, Jeffrey had yet another reason not to be civil the following Sunday, when Reverend Mitchell asked Sam to be another candle lighter on Christmas Eve.

"How much does it pay?" Sam inquired.

"About the same as ushering," Reverend Mitchell replied, "and Michael will be doing that, so you'll both be divinely employed."

"Well, if I have to come anyway," Sam said.

The reverend was disappointed that his humor had been so thoroughly slighted. Yet there was a far greater victory when he extended his hand and Sam actually shook it. He shook it quickly, but he shook it nonetheless.

Overhearing the whole thing, Jeffrey slipped off to go talk to his friends instead of trading a joke or riddle with Reverend Mitchell like he usually did.

"The tree is completed!"

Looking at their handiwork, Ellen beamed. They had spent an overall lazy afternoon with the kids alternatively doing homework and puttering in their rooms. So, when it came time to work on the tree, no one really complained, not even Sam.

"Tomorrow night is Christmas Eve," Michael said by rote as he did every single year at this time. "We'll go to church, come home, and—"

"Put the angel on the tree," Mary Katherine added.

"Then you can open the presents your grandma and grandpa sent. And possibly the ones we got for each other," Ellen chimed in, trying to stir up just a little more excitement from her younger guy.

After his mother mentioned presents in years past, Jeffrey would usually shout a "Whoopee!" but tonight he said nothing.

"The next part is really hard," Mary Katherine said. "We have to go to bed and wait for Santa Claus."

After a light supper, Michael and Ellen gathered a few gifts they'd purchased for their dear friends, the Cannons, who lived next door. "We'll be gone for about an hour," Ellen said.

After she put on her coat, she once again turned toward the children, who were all standing in the hallway, and gave them all strict instructions to call her and Michael immediately if they needed them. "Mary Katherine and Jeffrey, bedtime is in a half hour. Remember when it's time, no fussing. Sam, you can stay up until we return home."

"Okay, Mom," Mary Kathrine said sincerely while Jeffrey simply frowned. Sam stood and listened but did not respond. Even though Jeffrey knew the neighbors, Michael gave Sam their names and phone number he had written down from the address book.

"Call if you need us," he said to Sam, echoing Ellen's words.

This time, there was a response. "I will," Sam said as he folded the paper and put it in his pocket.

Sam and Mary Katherine opted to watch TV in their absence while Jeffrey played with his Power Rangers, an activity that apparently called for a good deal of sound. His action voice grew louder and louder until Sam demanded that he quiet down.

"Make me," snapped Jeffrey.

"Stop it!" Sam barked back.

"I can do anything I want. You aren't the boss over me."

To prove as much, he began running around the room, accentuating his storyline even more by picking up things and throwing them into space like Power Ranger projectiles.

"Knock it off!" Sam tried again.

Not surprisingly, Jeffrey did no such thing. One item after another flew through the air—first a couch pillow, then a magazine, and finally, a shoe.

It was the shoe that did it, going wild while Jeffrey spun around, resulting in a very revealing crash that stopped him with arms suspended in mid-air.

Mary Katherine only watched her brother at first, not thinking much about his antics. She had seen his spinning game with the Power Rangers before, but not with the turbulence he was now presenting, especially adding to his visual effects by throwing objects. When she heard the crashing sound, all she could say was, "Oops!"

232

That's all she could manage, and her brother said nothing at all. Neither did Sam. All three just stared at the china angel laying on the tile floor after being knocked over by the flying shoe—helpless and broken into quarters like a carved-up chicken at a barbecue.

It took several painful seconds before Jeffrey's eyes swelled. "I hate you!" he shouted at Sam. "I hate you!" And then he ran up the stairs to his room.

The TV kept playing in the background, but neither of the remaining children paid it any attention. Instead, they were silently dreading the worst to happen yet—for Mr. and Mrs. Carson to get back and see the damage done.

It was a suspended, agonizing length of time, similar to that terrible period between the moments the dentist takes the drill in hand and actually hits your tooth with it. It was a terrible time, like the silence before the principal asks if you really were the one caught running in the halls.

Sam simply looked at the pieces with no idea about how to handle the situation.

Finally, it was Mary Katherine who came up with a solution. "I have some glue."

"Thank you, Katie." Sam's voice sounded odd in his own ears. "Will you go get it?"

Despite everything, she smiled at the nickname, which he'd never used before. Then she went to get the glue while Sam put a newspaper on the table and carefully laid out the pieces to analyze. As far as he could see, they were clean breaks.

Katie came back with the glue. "Can you fix it?"

"I think so." He hoped so. "I glued my mom's lamp back together once. We broke it playing football."

At her prompting, he went on to recount the incident while he carefully set about his very important task, interrupting himself every few sentences to instruct Katie on how to help. With her holding on to the angel pieces and Sam doing the actual gluing, they finished the painstaking job just in time.

"Now we'll just have to wait and see if it holds," he said.

The front door opened before he could close his mouth, and they could hear Michael and Ellen putting their coats away and starting down the stairs. Sam and Katie both looked at each other, unsure whether they should move back to the couch or 'fess up right away.

"How were—" Michael said as he reached the family room.

His wife's cry stopped him short as she took in the children still standing over their project. "What happened?" Moms always seem to be the first to know when something has happened. At least the Carson mom always knew.

"It broke." Sam didn't offer any explanations. "We glued it back together. I think it'll stay."

"Oh, Sam." Ellen started to cry. "How could you do this?"

Between that and Michael's frown, Sam figured he should leave. So, without saying anything else, he went into his room and quietly closed the door to pack up for his imminent departure.

What seemed to be hours passed before Sam heard feet shuffling in the family room, followed by a knock on his door. He didn't answer, not even after the second knock.

"Sam, can I come in?" Ellen asked.

"It's your house," he said with neither bark nor bite to the statement.

She turned the knob and started to walk in, only to stop short at the sight of his brown suitcase on the bed and his clothes folded inside. "What are you doing?"

"I know you'll be calling Case." He shrugged, his voice quiet and his eyes looking down at the rug. "I guess I lasted longer here than I did at the second house. The first kicked me out because I broke a window playing baseball."

"We're not sending you away, Sam." She sat down on his bed. "This is your home for as long as we can have you. If anyone from the agency, Mr. Case included, wants to prematurely take you away, they will have to deal with the Carsons first—all of us, Sam. You're our foster son," she explained. "We care very much for you, regardless of how you behave."

"You're not angry with me?" Sam asked, looking up.

"I'm very hurt," she acknowledged. "That angel is very precious to me. It's been in my family for a long time. I think you and Mary Katherine did a wonderful job patching her up. I think she is good for a lot more years."

"I've never had anything for a long time." It was almost a whisper.

"Well, you do now." Ellen meant every word of it. "You have us."

Now someone else was knocking on the half-open door, which opened wider to admit Michael and Jeffrey, one of them looking understanding and the other miserable.

"Mom." The miserable one walked over to stand by her. "Sam didn't break your angel. I did. I was mad at him, so I wouldn't listen, and I accidentally broke your angel."

Tears raced down Jeffrey's face well before he got through the monologue, prompting Ellen to wrap him in a hug. Without a pause, Michael reached over and pulled Sam over, too, so they were all hugging one another at the same time.

After Ellen reminded her foster son to unpack everything, Jeffrey made sure to look up at his foster brother before leaving the room. "I'm really sorry, Sam."

"Thanks, Jeffrey." There wasn't a single bit of attitude there to find.

Sleep came easily that night for everyone. And while things were maybe a bit more hectic the next day, it was only because Sam, Jeffrey, and Mr. Carson had some last-minute shopping to do. A casual observer watching them would have identified the threesome as a father and two sons out together without giving it another thought. At the same time, he might have also noticed how careful the younger one was around the older, as well as how very courteous the older was toward the younger. There wasn't the normal sibling display of affection or irritation on either end.

Then again, there was further progress to be made that weekend. When they arrived at church for the Christmas Eve service, Reverend Mitchell met them in the foyer.

"Well," he said. "I'm glad to see all the Carsons and Mr. Mason this evening. Merry Christmas!"

"Merry Christmas!" they echoed.

"We do have one little problem, though," he said. "Our other candle lighter came down with the flu this afternoon."

Sam and Jeffrey both responded with, "Yuck!" at the same time.

"So, we need someone else to step in," the reverend continued. "Do you have any ideas?"

"How about Laura?" Ellen offered.

Sam rolled his eyes, complete with all the typical teenager sounds of dismissal to an embarrassing parent.

Michael and Katie laughed.

Jeffrey stayed quiet this time, but Sam tapped him on the shoulder. "Do you want to help me?"

"Could I?" Jeffrey asked the adults.

"If Sam will help you get ready," Michael answered.

"Sure, I will." Sam's smile was small but sincere. "That's what big brothers are for. Right, Katie?"

"Right!" she agreed, and then proceeded to follow her two brothers as they walked off to rehearse their tasks with Reverend Mitchell.

"What do you think now, El?" Michael inquired, watching them the whole way down the carpeted aisle.

"Well, it's a start, and it does have possibilities." She volunteered thoughtfully, "I think we're grateful and will continue to be so for every little step that's taken."

"And tonight in particular?"

"I wouldn't trade tonight for a hundred china angels." She squeezed his hand. "Because tonight, our children are growing. All three of them."

She squeezed his hand and then went to save five spots for them to sit together and worship as a family.

Chapter 10

THE BOY WHO MISSPELLED
CHRISTMUS

"Russell, sound the word out and try it again." Myra Jackson looked up from the spelling list, which she then carefully covered with one arm.

"Ac-shun. The Lone Ranger and Tonto see a lot of ac-shun." Russell smiled, pleased with his use of the word before he began the hard part. "A-c-s-h-u-n." After spelling the word exactly as he had pronounced it, he thought his mother would be pleased. The skinny brown-haired, brown-eyed nine-year-old waited for his mother's response.

Last year's T-shirt that he wore revealed arm muscles disproportionate in size to the rest of his body. His muscles were a dead giveaway regarding the type of farm work he was used to doing even at his young age. Yet, along with his delay in learning how to spell correctly, his coordination also had a ways to go to catch up with the rest of his body.

In the moment he thought, *Having to scoop oats into the grain bin, even if it is cold outside, would be better than studying my spelling words. I think I know them good enough.* Without saying a word, he continued to wait. Frowning as she looked up from the fourth-grade McGuffey spelling book, his mother said, "Russell, that's the same way you spelled it the last time, and the time before that."

"Isn't it right?" he questioned, his face pleading for some sign of relief.

"No," his mother said and handed him the book so he could see for himself.

"Oh." Russell paused as he put the book down. "I remember now. Action: A-C-T-I-O-N. Did you like my sentence, though, Mom?"

"I'd like for you to concentrate harder." Her face showed sincere concern for her son. "How are you going to be ready for the spelling competition if you don't know some of the tougher words?"

Russell's head dropped. "But Mom, I *am* concentrating."

Mrs. Jackson had previously seen that look apparently indicating her son's easily hurt feelings. "I'll tell you what. Let's stop for now, and you run outside and do your chores." She smiled as she closed the spelling book.

Russell slipped away from the kitchen table and out to the back porch, where he got ready to go out.

It really was cold outside, and the farmer's almanac for 1955 predicted a cold winter and lots of snow. The early December gray sky was determined to prove it right, after already stirring up a cold spell and now starting to spit snow. Russell hurried through his chores of gathering the eggs and then went to get water from the pump. As was his habit, he ended up filling the bucket far too full, spilling a decent amount down his pant legs as he walked toward the calves' pen. So, by the time he reached the calves' trough and finished chopping through a layer of ice in the trough, Russell was shivering badly.

Mark Jackson had been walking toward the hog house when he saw his son staggering across the way to the calf pen with a pail of water. His winter dress was not unlike that of any other Midwest farmer. The only difference was he usually stood an inch or two higher than most of his neighbors. Protected in his bib overalls, a winter jean jacket, and well-worn work shoes, he felt very comfortable working outside in the winter season.

"Son." The tenor voice coming from behind Russell held a note of concern and maybe a little exasperation. "I told you before not to fill your bucket so full."

"Hi, Dad!" Russell grinned as if he hadn't heard a word his father had said.

Mark let it go, turning around to get back to his own work. "When you finish watering the calves, go collect some firewood and put it on the back porch as usual. You might bring a little extra tonight since it will be a cold one. Meanwhile, I'll call the cows to the barn for milking."

When the boy didn't reply, he turned and once again looked toward his son to see him with his back bent and head down, watching the water pour into the trough. "Russell!" Just to make sure he heard him this time, Mark touched his son's shoulder, too.

"Yes, Dad?"

With a sigh, Mark repeated himself, making sure that Russell was pulling his wagon to the woodpile before he went out to call the cows for milking.

Since it was Sunday evening, supper was going to be either leftovers or pancakes. Tonight it was pancakes, which was just fine with Russell. Chores were usually done by 5:30 on Sunday evenings, and supper followed as soon as Russell and his father were in the house for the night. He liked that because as soon as he was finished eating, he'd rush into the living room to watch *Lassie*, and of course, he had to sit through *The Ed Sullivan Show* with is sister and his parents before *Alfred Hitchcock* came on.

"Can I have more, please?" He passed his plate to his twelve-year-old sister Sheri. Sheri followed the Jackson family trademark by being a skinny-boned energetic girl, but unlike anyone else in the family, her face was colored with freckles that matched the dark red color of her hair. Her mother had told her, "You inherited your freckles and red hair from my mom, your grandma Franks." Sheri usually didn't respond to her mother's comment but secretly wished she had inherited anything but the freckles.

When Sheri took Russell's plate, she rolled her eyes as she passed his plate on to her mother. "You sure eat a lot," she said to her brother, disgusted.

Mr. Jackson looked up and smiled.

Mrs. Jackson hushed her daughter, and then turned to her son. After putting two more pancakes on his plate and passing it back to him, she said, "Now, Russell, I'll pick you up at school tomorrow about 12:30. That should give us time to get to the city and find the doctor's office before your appointment."

"What?" Russell looked up while stuffing his mouth with another big bite of pancakes.

"What?" Mrs. Jackson mimicked her son. "Don't you remember? You have an appointment to get your ears tested."

"I already did that." His furrowed brow showed several fault lines. He remembered when he was called out of class to have his ears tested. It embarrassed him to have to walk out of class in front of all the other kids. They all knew he was going to be tested because the principal had announced that the hearing people would be there that day. If that wasn't bad enough, they called him out a second time later that day to be retested. When the last bell rang for the day, some of the kids came up behind Russell, gave him a few catcalls, and in a singsong voice they chanted, "Russell has dirty ears, dirty ears, dirty ears . . . ." He was embarrassed, humiliated, and angry.

"That was just the preliminary test," she tried to explain. "The doctor has to do a more thorough one to see if you need a hearing aid."

"A what?" Russell cringed.

"A hearing aid," Mr. Jackson echoed his wife.

"I'm not going to wear one!" Jumping up from the table, he ran upstairs crying.

"I just don't understand how he can get so emotional over something like a hearing test." Looking at Myra, Mark spread his hands in confusion.

"It's the hearing aid, Dad," Sheri said quietly.

Later that evening, just as Ed Sullivan was telling his audience that tonight he had a *really big show* lined up for them, one long and two short rings came from the phone.

"I'll get it," Sheri shouted as she jumped up from the table where she had been doing her homework and quickly moved to the phone. "Hello? Oh hi, Mrs. Jones. Yes, Mom's here. Just a minute, please."

"It's for you, Mom," Sheri said in a voice revealing her disappointment that the call wasn't from one of her friends.

When Myra came over to accept the call, Sheri sat back down at the table near her mother, hoping to pick up on the conversation.

Myra turned away from her daughter in an attempt to discourage her from listening. "Hello?"

242

"Myra, this is Thelma Jones."

"Oh hi, Thelma. I was going to call you this evening to see about rides for the spelling competition next Saturday."

"Well, that's partly why I called." Thelma realized she had to speak louder because the Jacksons were on a party line. Because she lived in town, she had to acquaint herself with the rural phone system. She quickly learned that a party line meant that four and even five neighbors shared a common phone line. While each had a different number transmitted over the phone line in a sequence of long and short rings, whenever someone in the neighborhood received a call, others on your "party line" could pick up the phone and listen in on your conversation. The Jackson's ring was one long and three shorts. Invariably, there would always be individuals in the neighborhood who liked nothing better than to listen in on other people's conversation. Usually, the more neighbors who picked up their phones to listen in, the louder you had to speak.

"I think some people are not too pleased with Ed Sullivan's really big show this evening. Apparently, there isn't much else on they're interested in watching. So, I guess we're the entertainment," Myra chuckled as she heard another neighbor pick up the phone just to listen in on their conversation.

"I can tell," Thelma replied.

There were several clicks off the line, and then they were able to hear each other much better. So Thelma continued.

"I was thinking about the competition Saturday. We have six children in our third grade. Mrs. Craig has three from Carson, and Mrs. Malley has two from Center Point," she said. "I thought we could have a practice competition on Wednesday at the church, and Reverend Lewis agreed to call the words. Do you think Russell would want to participate?"

"Why, yes, I think he would." She didn't say a word about her son's earlier reaction. "In fact, it will be a good chance for him to try out his hearing aid before the competition."

"Hearing aid?" Thelma inquired.

"Well, I have to take Russell into the city for some more tests tomorrow afternoon. I'm almost certain the doctor will have him fitted with one." Now she did let it slip. "Even if Russell isn't exactly receptive to the idea at the moment."

"Oh." Mrs. Jones hesitated. "Well, I hope things go okay. I'll encourage him to give it a try as much as I can at school."

"Thank you, Thelma." She meant it because she knew Thelma did. "He really thinks you're a great teacher, and I'm sure your comments will help."

She was still hopeful the next morning when she heard her husband walk to the head of the stairs, his coffee cup in hand. "Russell, Sheri, it's time to get up!"

"Okay, Dad," both children answered. It wasn't too hard getting the kids up and downstairs on a winter morning when the only heat was from the registers built into their bedroom floors. Besides, it was Monday morning, and both Sheri and Russell enjoyed school. That was the norm, anyway. This morning, however, Russell seemed a little less excited.

After breakfast and a quick homework check, the boy sat down in front of the kitchen window to watch for the school bus. He was withdrawn, to say the least, refusing to meet his mother's gaze. And it wasn't hard to determine why.

"Now, remember," she said. "I'll pick you up at the principal's office at 12:30."

244

"There's the bus!" Russell jumped up to put on his coat and gloves as if he hadn't heard his mother.

Mrs. Jackson turned his way to make sure he got the message. "Twelve thirty, young man."

He heard her. But he had already determined to pretend for as long as he could that it wasn't going to happen. Besides, school wasn't too hard for him. He heard most of what the teacher said, and he could always ask her questions or talk to his friends when he missed something. Why couldn't his parents just leave things alone?

But they didn't just leave things alone. At 12:30, as promised, he was informed that his mother was at the principal's office waiting for him. It was a clear day, so there was no chance of canceling the trip because of snow, even if it did take about an hour to drive to the city.

Russell sat in the front seat with his mother. Yet he didn't say a word, and she didn't press him for a while. Since the car radio was broken, that meant all he could do was stare out the window.

Finally, about halfway there, his mother tried to engage him after all. "Mrs. Jones says you have a very good chance of winning the competition."

"Uh-huh," Russell answered.

"If I remember, the prize is *fifty dollars*." When that elicited no response whatsoever, she tried again. "What would you do with all that money?"

"Buy Christmas presents." That question had gotten his attention despite his best efforts to ignore her. "I already have my list, but I don't think I have enough money right now." In fact, the last time he counted, he had exactly four dollars and twenty-seven cents.

"Well, I'm sure you wouldn't spend the whole fifty on presents. Would you?"

"There's a sled at the hardware store I'd like," Russell added.

Actually, it was hard for him to imagine how much fifty dollars would be. He'd never had more than five dollars at any one time. And unlike Sheri, who was a saver, money just burned a hole in his pocket.

"Christmas presents." His mother smiled at him. "That's very thoughtful."

"I would give some to the church too," Russell said matter-of-factly, as if he'd thought this whole thing through long ago, "and some to Dad and some to you and maybe some to Sheri."

"Oh, so you'd want to share your money?" Mrs. Jackson pressed, enjoying the conversation.

But they were coming to the outskirts of the city now, and Russell took that as his cue to fall into melancholy silence once again. He might have also simply allowed himself to be distracted by the Christmas lights and decorations already up for the holiday. However, if you are a nine-year-old boy gazing at Christmas decorations in store fronts and decorations strung across Broadway, you are not distracted—you are amazed! The evergreen garland overhead seemed to have a melodious sway, making the small white lights embedded in the greenery appear to be flickering. Store windows were outlined with red, green, and gold garland, as if they were frames holding different pictures.

In the first store front, he saw a lovely young lady dressed as Snow White with children dressed as dwarfs standing or sitting beside her. All of them were waving at pedestrians on the sidewalks or motorists driving by in their cars. One store window featured child-sized mannequins dressed in winter clothes, complete with hats and gloves. Each one of them clutched a sled in their hands. Another window had a live Santa with children dressed as elves waving to those passing by. Still another window portrayed a nativity scene. When Russell looked more carefully, he realized Mary, Joseph, the baby Jesus, and the shepherds were actually real people, and a live donkey and one sheep were with them. "Mom, look!" he shouted.

Sitting at a red light at the moment, Myra was able to look over through his window and saw the nativity scene. "Wow! Will you look at that!" she exclaimed.

After parking the car in a lot, they walked the two blocks to the doctor's office. While Myra checked him in, Russell found an empty chair and immediately started to read a comic book he found. Eventually a nurse came to the outer office and called out, "Russell Jackson."

Russell did not look up. Myra did, however, and smiled at the nurse. As she rose from her chair, she gently took a hold of Russell's elbow and said, "It's time to go, Russell." He silently followed his mother's direction. It wasn't so difficult to discern his innermost feelings in the examining room when Dr. Hanson came into the room carrying an object.

After introducing himself, he said, "Russell, after going over your hearing tests and reading the reports sent ahead by the school, I think it's best that we try to fit you with a hearing aid," he said, looking cheerful about the announcement.

Russell stiffened, and became even more rigid when the doctor fit the device in and around his ear and then turned up the volume. "How's that?"

"Okay," the boy replied with no enthusiasm whatsoever.

"Hmm." He waited patiently until he saw that his patient was not about to give up any further information without prompting. "I need you to talk to me, son, so we can adjust your aid to what you hear and how you hear yourself."

"It's noisy." Russell volunteered no more.

"Okay. If it's too loud, just turn the volume down—like this." He bent over the boy's shoulder to show him. "Your mother says you have a very important engagement this Saturday. The fourth-grade county spelling competition! So, I'm going to let you take this model to wear this week, and we'll have your aid next Monday. How's that?"

Russell just stared at the floor.

"He's not a happy young man," Dr. Hanson reported after the glum patient excused himself to go use the bathroom.

"Yes, I know." Myra sighed. "It's hard on him. This year has been especially hard." She tried to smile. "He's usually a very determined boy, but I wish he would use some of his determination to realize how a hearing aid would help him."

Russell gave no indication of being ready to bend the whole ride home, and he was still obviously down at supper. By the following morning, he flat-out tried to leave the implement behind, busying himself with various distractions while his sister watched for the bus.

Despite his best efforts, as soon as Sheri yelled, "The bus is coming," Myra looked his way and saw what was most definitely missing. "Where's your hearing aid?"

"Aw, Mom." Russell protested.

"Put it on! Hurry, or the bus will leave." Myra scooted her son into the bathroom and watched him put the harness on under his shirt and then push the hearing aid into his ear.

And so, his fate was sealed.

Just as he'd feared, the bus ride was an absolute nightmare. The high school boys spotted his new attachment right away and began to taunt him until even the younger kids were clamoring, "Hey, Russell! Can't you hear?" It got so bad that the bus driver even pulled over to the side of the road at one point and glared into the overhead mirror until everyone got quiet.

Sheri was embarrassed, but she hurt even more for her brother. Turning to the high school student with the loudest mouth, she said, "Hey, pug mouth! Shut up or I'll cram your tongue down your throat!" The loud mouth was shocked to hear the normally quiet and polite Sheri make such threats. It probably wasn't the cramming business that stopped the boy but most likely the pug-mouth comment. A name like that could stick with a person, especially on a school bus where there were high school kids. In fact, as soon as the older boys heard that, they too were first amazed and shocked that a girl with Sheri's personality would be so blunt. Instantly, they redirected their attention to the loud mouth and started to tease him.

Still experiencing the awful feeling that goes with humiliation, Russell sank down in the seat with tears streaming down his face. As soon as he got to school, he ran into the bathroom to remove the hearing aid before going to class. Since a girl named Allison, a member in the same 4-H club as Sheri, was the only person in his class who rode his bus, no one suspected anything. Allison was not the kind of person who would carry on the teasing or tattle to others about what had happened to him.

After they arrived home and Russell had gone outside to do his chores, Sheri went to the kitchen to help her mother. While they were busy preparing supper, Sheri said, "Mom, the older boys on the bus really gave Russell a bad time. They teased him about his hearing aid."

"Oh my, I was really hoping that wouldn't happen. I guess I put too much stock in people being considerate of others, at any age. What did Russell do?" she asked her daughter.

"Well, Mom, he really didn't say anything. He just sat there, but I could tell it was really hurting his feelings," Sheri answered.

"And . . .?" Myra, knowing her daughter was good at sometimes holding back important information or more of the story, waited for more information.

"Mom, I just couldn't stay quiet. I can't always do that. I called one of the boys a pug mouth and told him what I would do if he didn't shut up," Sheri emphatically answered.

Myra thought perhaps she didn't hear her daughter right because this behavior was so out of character for Sheri. So she asked, "You said what?"

"Yes, Mom, you heard me correctly. I called him a pug mouth," Sheri replied.

"And?" Myra once again asked, but now in disbelief.

"Well, Mom, he shut up. Boy, was I glad he did, but I believe I probably would have socked him right in the mouth if he dared to say anything more to Russell," she said, convinced she would have followed through.

"Honey, I'm glad you didn't. You saved me a trip to the principal's office," she said, now with a smile on her face. Putting her potato-peeling knife down, she wrapped her arms around her daughter and gave her a motherly hug. And no more was said.

The following morning, on Wednesday, Russell removed his hearing aid just as soon as he was out of sight of the kitchen window. A few kids still teased him a little when he walked down the aisle of the bus, but Russell made sure to sit by himself.

For her part, Sheri wasn't sure what to do. She knew her brother should wear the hearing aid, but she also didn't want him to be teased. Pug Mouth and the other boys didn't say a word. They had experienced enough of Sheri's wrath in defense of her brother. The little teasing Russell received was from younger boys who tried to copycat what they had heard the day before, but when they didn't hear a repeat of yesterday's chatter from their mentors, they quickly quieted down. Sheri was relieved and had an enjoyable time talking to her friends while keeping a watchful eye on Russell.

Mrs. Jones, of course, knew—or she thought she did. Privately, she certainly asked Russell what had happened at the doctor's office, but he simply told her he didn't know. Puzzled, she figured she'd get the whole story from Myra that evening at the practice spelling session.

Russell might not have been ready for a hearing aid, but he was ready for the spelling bee. He'd been practicing hard for the contest, memorizing those words he had problems with and studying his lists over and over again.

In fact, that's how Russell learned all his words—not by hearing them, but by memorizing them. He was the top speller in the class as long as it was a written test. But he knew this would be a little more difficult. Also, there would be new words, as he found out on Wednesday when the new list was passed around. These were words each speller in the class had heard often enough, but his particular age group was not expected to know how to spell such words quite yet. As such, Wednesday evening would be the first time Russell would have to spell some of them.

After supper, Mark went to the bathroom door to check on his son. "Hmm," he said. "Hair combed. Shoes on the right feet. Aid in ear. Yep! You're all ready. If you don't knock 'em over in spelling, you can always charm 'em to your side."

"Dad!" he protested, blushing.

The Jackson's farm was only about fifteen minutes from church. Somewhere along the way, Myra turned to tell Russell something, only to notice there was no hearing aid in his ear.

She turned to her husband, making sure to use a low voice. "Mark, I thought you said Russell put his aid on."

"He had it on when he was in the bathroom," Mark replied, looking into the rearview mirror at their son.

Gazing out at the stars, Russell had no idea his parents were talking about him.

"He must have taken it out when he got into the car," Myra said. "Sheri told me today how badly he was teased on the bus, and how he slipped the aid in his pocket this morning when they left the house."

"Let's not say anything," Mark suggested. "Let's just wait and see how tonight goes."

"All right," Myra said hesitantly. She reached over and touched his hand for some reassurance. "We can wait. I just don't want him to be disappointed."

There were fifteen chairs up on the stage area—one for each contestant—and Russell quickly found a seat while Reverend Lewis took his place at the podium. If it weren't for his black and gray wavy hair, Russell wouldn't have recognized his minister because he wasn't wearing his usual Sunday garb, a black robe. After some brief remarks about the practice competition and then a prayer, Reverend Lewis started things off. After he pronounced the word, he would use it in a sentence for the contestants. One student after another would stand, pronounce the word given, and then spell the word.

When it was Russell's turn, Reverend Lewis said, "Your word is 'enjoy.' I enjoy school."

"Enjoy." After repeating the word, in a very serious tone, he said each letter clearly, "E-n-j-o-y."

"Good job. You may be seated." Reverend Lewis said, "Good job" to all the contestants. Russell thought, *He's just being nice to us.*

That cycle kept going until only two students were left—Sara Main and Russell. "We are now going on to the 'one hundred' word list," the reverend told everyone, and then turned to the remaining female contestant. "Sara, you'll have the first word: Tuesday. Tuesday always follows Monday."

Sara repeated the word and spelled "Tuesday" correctly. Russell spelled his word correctly as well. They both aced their second-round and third-round words, too. So, next up, Sara spelled "testament" correctly.

And then it was Russell's turn again with "Christmas." Reverend Lewis said with a grin on his face, "I can hardly wait for Christmas to come."

"Christmust." Russell paused before continuing. He wanted so much to say, "Me neither," but catching a cue from his mother when he just happened to look her way, he thought it best not to do it and just spell the word. "C-h-r-i-s-t-m-u-s-t."

"I'm sorry, son. You pronounced the word correctly, but you spelled it incorrectly." Reverend Lewis was about to say more when Russell interrupted with certainty.

"But Christ must come at Christmust! That's why we celebrate His birth," Russell explained, forgetting all about the spelling bee.

"Yes, it is," Reverend Lewis replied, surprised by Russell's rush of words and excitement. "However, it is spelled how, Sara?"

Sara Main smiled as she stood. She said, "Christmas," and then, without even a pause, she spelled the word, "C-h-r-i-s-t-m-a-s."

"Correct," said Reverend Lewis.

And with that, the parents applauded.

Everyone went into the next room for coffee and cake except for Reverend Lewis and the Jacksons. As they approached Russell, he was still mumbling that "Christ comes at Christmust."

"Russell, this is just the practice," Reverend Lewis tried to remind him.

"How could I miss?" Russell sulked.

"Could it be, son," his father said, "you might have spelled the word correctly if you had worn your hearing aid at home and practiced seeing words such as *Christmas* while hearing yourself pronounce them? I remember from my experience in spelling class that hearing and seeing words at the same time when I said them out loud helped me to remember the silent letters and loud letters in a word."

"I don't know what you mean," Russell responded.

"I think your dad is trying to say that if you were wearing your hearing aid when you practiced at home, you might have heard and recognized words with silent letters. 'T' can be very tricky when it comes to hearing it and spelling it. Even then, memorizing how to spell some words is also necessary. I hear you have tried to memorize some of your words. By the way, son, you did spell 'Christmas' just as it sounds, but not how it is spelled," Myra added.

"Huh?" He tried to ignore that. Most of what they were saying was too confusing, especially for the moment. "I tried to memorize everything, but I guess that didn't work," he said, mostly to himself than to anyone else.

"I have an idea," Reverend Lewis said, jumping back into the conversation. "Myra, why don't you and Mark go ahead and have some refreshments? I'd like to talk to Russell for a few minutes."

When it was just the two of them, he turned to his young student. "Why did you want to win the spelling competition, son?"

Russell did not hesitate to answer. "So I can win some money to buy Christmas presents."

"Is that important to you?" Reverend Lewis asked him.

"Yes," Russell nodded. "I like to give people gifts—that's why we celebrate Christmas. And I know God gave us Jesus because He loves us."

"You definitely get an 'A' for your church school lesson." The reverend smiled. "How about right now, though? What kind of gift do you think your parents and maybe even God are trying to give you?"

Russell might have only been nine years old, but he knew a set-up when he heard one. "But you don't understand. Kids tease me."

"And that does hurt," he agreed, switching tactics. "But remember what you said earlier? Why did you enter the competition?"

For a while, there was silence between the two of them. It wasn't a bad or good kind of silence—just a thinking kind.

"To win money for Christmas presents," Russell finally said.

"And if that's the most important thing, wouldn't you want to hear everything correctly so you could do your best?" He waited again, though not nearly so long this time. "Even if it means you have to try to not let your hurt feelings become bigger than your goal?"

"I never thought of it that way before." Russell looked truly surprised.

That led the reverend right back to his original tack. "You know, a lot of us forget that God has feelings, too. What if He decided that He'd be lonely after sending Jesus to be our Savior? Or that Jesus wouldn't like Him anymore because of what God was asking Him to do?"

"We sure wouldn't be having Christmas," Russell said, pronouncing the word correctly.

"Probably not," Reverend Lewis agreed. "You know, your hearing aid was a gift from your parents. They know you're good at spelling, and they were willing to sacrifice their money so you could do your best."

"Just like God sacrificed so we could do our best," Russell contributed.

"Why, yes," Reverend Lewis' lips turned upward again into a smile and his eyes sparkled. "Can I show you something?" And then he pulled back his wavy black and gray hair to reveal a hearing aid connected to his glasses.

Russell's eyes got wide. "I never saw that before."

"Well, I have worn mine since I was about seven. I practiced pretending it wasn't there until I just didn't care what people might say. Now I can hide it beneath my wavy hair," he joked. "However, I think people notice it less because I put it on and still pretend it's not there. I don't think about it because I have more important things to consider."

"Oh." The boy looked down at the floor. And he only looked up again because he could hear someone coming down the aisle—his father.

"Dad," Russell said, "Reverend Lewis and I have been talking. I think I'm ready to wear my hearing aid now. I'm going to wear it tomorrow so I can practice pretending it's not there."

"Oh . . . okay." Mr. Jackson looked pleasantly surprised, but he didn't say another word.

Russell, however, was more than ready to continue talking when they started their walk out to the car. "Did you know Reverend Lewis has a hearing aid? Did you know God has feelings? What if Jesus had said, 'No, Dad, I don't want to be a baby'? I mean—wow!"

Mrs. Jackson squeezed Russell's hand, happily listening to his chatter, particularly when she could see very well that he'd put the hearing aid back in his ear.

While "Christmust" had come in the past, Russell knew for certain now that Christ came at Christmas. As such, he went to the competition on Saturday and out-spelled even Sara Main. And do you know what word he had to spell in the winning round? No, it wasn't Christmas. It was "enlightenment."

With his hearing aid turned on, he heard the word correctly. He also remembered that those silent letters could be tricky, and the word did not start with an 'n' but an 'e.' In fact, it had another silent 'e' as well. He had studied words, looked at them, and at the same time, pronounced the words he studied out loud with his hearing aid turned on. And he won!

He didn't have to wonder what he would do with the money that came with the trophy. After all, it was Christmas!

Chapter 11

THE ROYAL TAILOR'S CHRISTMAS

"It's time! It's time!" said the chambermaid
While scurrying through the halls as if afraid.
"The royal tailor, where is he now?"
She questioned soft. She questioned loud.
With kerchief in hand, she wiped her brow.

"I'm here, my maid. Don't be alarmed!
I just came from where the socks are darned."
The tailor spoke with confidence,
For when he darned, 'twas darned just once!

"No time for socks! No time to darn!
It's time! It's time! Sound the alarm!
You need to bring your measuring tape
To the queen's room, and don't be late!"

Now the royal tailor in the king's domain
Was the measurer for those who reign.

258

He measured up. He measured down.
He measured wide and all around
For kings, and queens, and princesses,
For chairs and beds, and bright dresses.

For princes who travel royal grounds,
To ride their steads and run their hounds,
He measures for britches and jackets fair,
Then he measures for hats to cover their hair.

But the job he really likes to keep
Is to measure the time royals need to sleep.
So, when night falls or royal naps are due,
Not just any rest for a royal will do!

It's his work regardless, though some might fret,
He's not lost his head, no, not yet!
He finds great joy to do it right,
So, each royal can have a good night.
He fills his quill with proper lead,
To measure right for a perfect bed.
It's the silliest thing, but you know it's true:
A tailor who measures is a carpenter, too!

For just as soon as the new prince is born,
He measures him for gowns that warm!
And then he measures again from rib to rib.
To his workspace he goes to build a crib.

It's time! It's time for a princely birth!
One who comes to bring peace on earth.
He wasn't to arrive until next week,

But now he's due right as we speak.
There was to be time to find royal wood,
And for the tailor to do as he should.
But now it's late; the time is near.
"Oh no!" the maid corrects. "The time is here!
Soon we will dance, and clap, and give our cheers,

No, not yet, not yet, my dears."

"Oh my! Oh my!" the maid repeats.
"He's here! He's here! It's time to greet.
His mother calls the tailor's name.

I heard her call. I heard her plain!"
As chambermaids go, I'm sure you can tell
This one talks to herself so very well!

From her mistress' room, she runs down the hall.
When she reaches his shop,
She gives out a call.
But he doesn't answer,
No, not at all.
Again, she starts her search,
Looking high and low,
"He was to be in his shop,
'cause he told me so."

When she stops in the kitchen,
Guess who comes through the door?
The tailor comes tramping,
Leaving snow on the floor.
"It's snowing, it's winter," he says with a shake,

The chambermaid ignores the mess he makes.
"You weren't in your shop!"
She says, shaking her head.
"'No time for the forest,'" that's just what you said,
So I found the fine wood, in the tree-cutters shed."
"Now, don't you remember, my sweet chambermaid?
'A crib and a gown, from my work must be made.'
So now I am here, I'm here once again."
"Ah, that you sure are," the cook says with a grin.
"To eat my fine stew and my apron to mend."

The chambermaid frets, and her face grows a frown,
"No time to be eating, no time to sit down.
No time for the apron, no time for fine stew,
My goodness, fine tailor, just what will you do?"
And when she was finished, he smiled and said,
"What you spoke, my dear maid, you know is quite true,
I must make a gown and I must make a bed.
For I know how to sew and I am a carpenter, too.
To dress a new baby,
Who someday is King,
And to make him a fine bed,
For rest and for dreams."

Turn around, turn around,
Barely an hour goes by,
When the tailor returns,
Both cook and sweet maid,
Give out a quick sigh.
"The gown is all made, without a hitch,
It's color deep purple, sewn stitch by stitch."
The tailor, now carpenter, puts on the frown,

261

As he hands the sweet maid
The new purple gown.
But his words are not finished,
There is more to be said,
"I have not finished the crib for his bed.
No time to dawdle, not even a bit,
No time for a snooze, no time for a sit."

The royals expect their bed in an hour,
So I had to think fast, with fast-thinking power.

Then I remembered the first Christmas night,
When a choir of angels gave shepherds a fright!
A royal was born, a miracle birth,
A herald of angels sang peace to this earth.

I remembered how special the thrill and the joy
Of those who gave witness to that little boy!
"And where were the cedars of Lebanon then?"
Prompted the tailor, his face in a grin.
Then turning around, his arms made a swoosh
As he grasped at a manger, then gave it a push.

"A cow's trough is for hay, how well do I know."
Now there on the floor, the manger He lay.
"This night its bed, where the new royal will go."
The words had been spoken. Now his mouth he did close.
Then the chambermaid said, "It will do, I suppose."

"My tailor!" the lady meanwhile began.
"Now where can he be? What's keeping that man?"

262

'Til softly at first came a knock at the door,
Then louder it grew as the tapping came more.
"It's the tailor, my lady, and your chambermaid, too.
He comes with a bed for the royal who's new!"
"Well, come in! Come in! Don't wait one more minute!
Bring the prince His new bed so He can sleep in it."
The lady was quick but so very polite.
For her baby, she wanted what would be just right.

"Beg your pardon, m'lady," the tailor began,
Hoping by grace that she'd understand.
"The baby came fast. The baby came quick.
Then came me a thought, by golly and wit.
I came up with a crib that won't fit quite right,
The cow gave it on loan, just for the night."

Then he retold the story that had been told before,
Of the baby boy Jesus who came through earth's door.
While He was laid in a manger, the heavens gave shout:
"Kneel down to the baby, a royal, no doubt!"
When the tailor was finished, his lady did smile.
"Please hold Him," she said, "for just a wee while."
Then she made ready the manger; she made ready the bed.
And there the tailor did rest the royal's sweet head.

"Oh my, does He fit? Is it large or too small?"
Asked the chambermaid, twisting her hands in a ball.
The lady just smiled and said not a word
But her head gave a nod to what her ears heard.

"Be still, dear woman," the tailor quietly said.
"See how the royal fits deep, fits deep in His bed.

Sleep now, Your Highness. Lay Your head on the straw,
While to Your manger the world calls, the great and the small.
It takes not a measure, this bed for a king.
For its width and its breadth has its own measuring."

It's a simple reminder, this birth of a child.
Each birth a new wonder, so fragile, so mild.
In the eyes of our Maker, more precious than gold.
Before coming to earth, the Maker does hold.

For the arms of our Maker, become a manger to rest
Each prince and each princess, before earth is their quest.

Regardless how big. Regardless how small.
Regardless how wide. Regardless how tall.
We all should remember and need to recall,
In God's loving arms, one size will fit all.

Chapter 12

WHAT EVERY CHRISTMAS NEEDS

It was just another morning as Nicole climbed over the end of her bed onto her toy chest and jumped to the floor. Wearing her My Little Pony nightshirt and crunching into her Cabbage Patch slippers, she grabbed her Smurf doll and was out of her room like a flash, hoping her mom would let her eat her favorite cereal, Trix, for breakfast instead of oatmeal. It took her until she reached the stairway before she remembered it was Saturday. That meant no school, and for a first-grader, it also meant cartoons. So, off she ran to the TV room.

"Where are you going so fast?" her mom, already dressed in denims and a brown blouse, asked as Nicole turned the corner from the kitchen.

"To watch *The Smurfs*," she replied. "Can I eat my Trix in here?" She didn't stop to wait for an answer.

"No, young lady." Mom pulled on the back of Nicole's nightshirt and turned her around. "In fact, hurry back upstairs and get dressed. We have to go shopping."

Now, normally, Nicole liked to go shopping with her mother. But early on Saturday morning just wasn't the time. "Oh, Mom! Let's watch *Smurfs* first."

"No, we need to get Grandma and Grandpa's presents." She looked up at the ceiling. "There are so many things to do, and I have to get some stuff for extra baking and—"

"Why do we have to get extra stuff?" Nicole sat on the kitchen chair, waiting for an answer.

"Because it's close to Christmas, and I have to bake more cookies, bread, and fruitcakes." Her mom sighed while mentally making out her shopping list.

"Are we going to eat it all?" Nicole's eyes were wide. It was no secret she had a sweet tooth, but even she had a limit.

"No, silly." Her mother's words were framed in a smile as she continued, "We'll have some for parties, some for gifts, some for snacks, and some to take to Grandma's house."

"Why do we have to do all that?" Nicole wondered out loud.

"Because it's Christmas," Mom said, pushing her toward the stairs again.

"It seems like Christmas comes with a lot of stuff to do," Nicole murmured as she went to get dressed. Quickly, she put on her Snoopy sweater and the pair of girl's denims her mother had placed on her dresser last night after she had fallen asleep. Even though she was really in a hurry before leaving her room, she paused to take out the tablet and pencil from her My Little Pony school bag. Hopping on her bed, she carefully printed out her own Christmas list that included friends, the postman, and Arthur, their next-door neighbor. She was deep in thought working on her list in a language only she could understand when her mother called out from the bottom of the stairs.

266

"Nicole, what are you doing up there? It's time to go!"

Tucking her list into her pocket, she yelled as loud as she could, "I'm coming, Mom!"

Nicole always seemed to be awake, and she'd be up before her eight-year-old brother, Nathan, especially on school days. This morning when she scampered by his room, she shouted, "Mom and I are going shopping, Nathan. YOU can't come 'cause you aren't awake!" Then she scurried down the stairs.

The mall was already busy when they arrived, even if it should have been Saturday morning cartoon time. There was a lot to see and a lot to buy and, coming from Nicole's level, a lot of legs going in all kinds of directions to skirt around.

"Why don't we give Grandpa a Care Bear and Grandma a Cabbage Patch doll?" Nicole suggested as they strode into one department store.

"Well, we could," her mother replied, "but I think your grandfather would rather have a tie and your grandmother might like a nice silk blouse."

That did not impress her. "I think we gave them those presents last year. I remember, Mom, 'cause every time Grandpa wears the tie we bought him, he tells me we gave it to him at Christmas. That's how I remember we did!"

"Oh, well, let's see now. What else could we get them?"

Mrs. Clark was thinking about the possibilities of other gifts while looking at the shirts on the rack next to the ties. With her back turned away from Nicole, her daughter took a few steps down the aisle, attracted by two ladies she had seen earlier walking up the next aisle. Normally she would not have paid much attention to them, instead interrupting her mother's browsing by asking her question after question, but she thought the ladies were wearing the most unusual hats. She was just close enough to hear the women talking. The rack gave her the cover she needed to eavesdrop. She listened in on their conversation and waited, hoping they would move farther down the aisle so she could eventually see their hats once again.

"Boy, I'll be glad when this season is over," one of them said. "I swear, the prices on these things! It's enough to make you poor. My grocery bill went sky high this week with all the extras."

The other sighed in agreement. "Yes, and my daughter is singing a solo at the candlelight service. I really hate saying this, but that service really messes up our Christmas Eve supper. This 5:30 business—who ever heard of having a Christmas Eve service that early? We've never done it that way before."

While Nicole slowly peeked around the corner still unnoticed, the one lady looked like she was going to say more, but she ended up picking out a silk tie and complaining about its price instead.

The other lady didn't say anything, but she shook her head the same way Nicole saw her mother's head shake when she meant "yes." Nicole almost laughed when it seemed to her the lady's head wouldn't stop shaking as she said to her friend, "I know, I know. What a racket."

As they walked toward her, Nicole stepped back to avoid being noticed but still be able to see the ladies. Only now, one of them wore a great big red hat with a very large white feather that hung over the brim and flopped into her friend's face every time she shook her head. The second woman would then politely smile, showing her polished white teeth through rose-red lips, and blow a puff of air at the feather while continuing to shake her head in agreement.

"Hey, Mom." Nicole pulled on her mother's blouse.

"What?"

"Look at the chicken feather in that lady's hat." Nicole still hadn't learned to talk too softly before Mrs. Clark could shush her.

Looking up toward the ladies, she was relieved they didn't seem to have heard Nicole's comments, but she still shushed her daughter anyway and then made sure to move elsewhere, just in case the ladies decided to turn and come back their way.

Nicole went along with her for a minute, but in no time at all she was pulling—only this time on her mother's slacks.

"Yes?" Mrs. Clark asked.

"Are we going to church before Santa Claus comes?"

"I suppose so."

"Why?"

"Well, for one thing, because your dad's the minister, and for another, because we should." Mrs. Clark usually had more than one reason.

"Oh," said Nicole. "But why?"

"Come on, sweetheart." Mom tugged on her. "We have to pay for Grandpa's tie and Grandma's blouse."

"Will the baby Jesus be at church?" Nicole asked.

"Yes." Mrs. Clark smiled, whimsically thinking how sometimes she bet He thought He'd be the only one.

While they were walking toward the cash register, Nicole suddenly remembered the list she was carrying in her pocket. Pulling it out, she stopped and pushed the piece of paper toward her mother. "Mom, what about my list?"

"Your list? What list, dear?" her mother asked, looking down at the paper.

"You know, my list of friends I want to buy gifts for," she answered, a little surprised that her mother would not already know.

Realizing the meaning of her daughter's words as she quickly glanced down the list, she stopped and bent down in front of Nicole. Choosing her words carefully, she said, "Honey, we don't have the money to buy presents for all of your friends on this list. Maybe when we do our baking, we can make some extra cookies for you to give to your very special friends."

"Okay, Mom," Nicole said hesitantly, but all she remembered was her mother's words, "We don't have enough money."

The days passed quickly from there. December fifteenth, December sixteenth, December seventeenth, December eighteenth . . . And with each one, there seemed to be a new activity. There was the school program for one, and then came several invitations to dinner. Nicole only liked those dinners if they were at her friends' homes.

Then came baking—lots and lots of baking—on December nineteenth, twentieth, and twenty-first. Those days also saw Dad taking Nicole and her brother, Nathan, to see Santa Claus. And then all four of them, following a family tradition, hung up their Christmas stockings.

Two days before Christmas, school was officially out, and Nicole was going shopping with her whole family this time. There were a whole lot more people out in the mall, with everyone pushing and shoving, moving and complaining, and looking just plain tired, worn out, and broke. It all gave Nicole a lot to observe, but the lady dressed in red and ringing a bell still caught her attention. Standing next to a red bucket perched on a stand, she kept saying, "Merry Christmas" as people passed by.

"What's that, Dad?" Nicole asked.

"That's a bucket to put money in," he explained, "so poor people can have a merry Christmas, too."

"You mean us?" She had often heard him say they couldn't afford this or that, and even though she was only six, she came to the conclusion they must be poor. Once, she even asked her brother if they were poor, and he responded, "Uh . . . I guess so. Dad told me I couldn't have a telescope I saw in *Boy's Life* because we couldn't afford it. So, I guess we are." So, if her brother said so, they must be poor.

Her father's answer to her question, now interrupted her thoughts. "Well, no, not exactly," he said. "Poorer people than us."

Nicole stopped right by the lady. "Are you going to put some money in there?"

"Well, actually I gave at the office," her dad laughed.

The lady didn't laugh, though, as she kept the bell going "ding-a-ling," and Nicole didn't even smile. So, Reverend Clark took a dollar bill out of his wallet and placed it in the pail. He was used to seeing those at church find their way into the collection plate.

Just then, Nicole saw the lady with the red hat. And she saw Nicole, too.

Nicole's eyes got very wide when the lady started to come toward them. "Dad," she said, "that lady with the chicken feather was here when Mom and I came to the mall before."

He immediately shushed her. "That lady is Mrs. Thompson. She's in our church." And then, since that individual came right up to them, he added, "Hello, Mrs. Thompson."

Reverend Clark happened to look up just as the feather was looking down, and so, he got it right in the eye.

Nicole giggled, but fortunately for her father, she didn't say a word about previously sighting Mrs. Thompson and her hat.

Mrs. Thompson paid no attention to her giggle. "Why, hello, Reverend Clark. Is this your sweet little daughter?" She reached down to pinch Nicole's cheeks.

"Ah, yes." He prayed Nicole wouldn't bite the woman's hand. The poor girl had been accosted by more parish pinchers than any child he knew. He could understand why she did not recognize his daughter.

When she came to church, that is, *whenever* she came to church, Nicole was already in the church school class her mother helped teach.

"Well, I see you're shopping. So am I." Mrs. Thompson gazed back up at him, still holding on to Nicole's cheek and swooshing the feather into Reverend Clark's other eye. "I must be going. I have about twenty more presents to get yet. Everything is so expensive."

And then she was off again without a goodbye, but fortunately she had finally let go of Nicole's cheek.

Nicole acted like the whole event was very boring, so she immediately changed the subject when Mrs. Thompson left. "Did they do all this at Christmas when Jesus was born?"

Realizing she was referring to the entire hubbub around them, he shook his head. "Oh, no. Jesus is why we have Christmas."

Nicole knew her father was very smart, so she took him at his word. But she still didn't get it. "Then why isn't Mrs. Thompson and everyone else happier?"

"Well, I guess we just sometimes forget the Jesus part of Christmas," he said. "Now, have you bought your presents to put under the church Christmas tree?"

"No," she said.

"Do you have any money left?" he asked.

"Yes." She had a very determined look on her face. "But I want to get them later."

Long after they arrived home from shopping and the kids had gone out to play, Reverend Clark started across the lawn toward the church study. Passing by the plastic nativity set, he noticed the manger was empty. Baby Jesus was gone.

He closed his eyes in mild frustration. "I told the committee they should use some of the swaddling clothes to tie him in the manger."

Yet he still had hope, first checking behind the plastic brown cow. And then, when that failed to yield the plastic piece, he decided the janitor must have taken it out to fix its light bulb. Otherwise, they'd have the only plastic baby Jesus that winked on and off at night.

The thought of a winking Jesus did make him smile. So did his children the next morning at breakfast, starting with Nicole.

"Dad, will the poor people really get our presents?"

Before he could answer, Nathan replied, "Sure. Santa Claus gets Buzz Lightyear and G. I. Joe, and the reindeer, and they take presents to all the poor people."

"What about us?" Nicole quizzed her brother.

"Oh, we get ours first." He looked at his father just to be sure he was correct. "Right, Dad?"

"Well—" Rev. Clark tried to clear the peanut butter toast from his throat. "Well, I'm not sure who gets what first, but we take our presents to the church to share. It's very important to share."

Nicole jumped in. "Nathan helped me wrap the present, Dad."

"Good. It sounds like we are all set for tonight, then." He smiled, and went back to reading the paper, thinking nothing more about it.

Now, the church where Reverend Clark was the pastor had a very old tradition, which was exactly what Nicole had prepared for. Even though she really didn't understand what the word "tradition" meant, the whole Clark family knew it was a tradition because no pastor had been able to change it. Each year, people brought gifts for the less fortunate, whoever they might be. These presents were then put under the church's tree. Before the service was over, everyone would stand up and say where they hoped their gift would go. It might be to the county home, a family down the street, or the "Army," as Nicole had begun to call the Salvation Army people. Then, they would deliver their presents before they went home, and this year was no exception.

When evening came, Nicole, her brother, and mother walked to the church. Her dad always went early to make sure the lights were on, talk to the ushers, and just generally be there so people would know he was doing his job.

When Mrs. Clark and the kids arrived, it was just in time to hear the lady with the big red hat and the floppy feather ask, "Reverend Clark, where's the baby Jesus? He's not in the manger. You know, my Aunt May gave that crèche and the holy family to the church." She sounded very matter-of-fact and maybe a little like a know-it-all, too. "It's been used for twenty years now. I do hope you know where it is."

"Well . . ." said Reverend Clark, not too sure of himself, "I do think the janitor is probably putting another light in him."

"Mom, is Dad in trouble?" asked Nicole.

"No, of course not. He's just not sure where the baby went. That's all," she replied.

"Is that lady going to wear that funny hat in church?" Nicole whispered—or what she thought was a whisper. Mrs. Clark immediately shushed her but, fortunately, the woman and her hat were already in a pew far enough away to be out of earshot.

The service started just fine. The children sang and the candles were lit, including the Christ candle, which was seen to by the Smith family. All eight of them had something to say, which did take some time. But finally, it was time to tell where the presents were going. One by one, a child, a grandma, an aunt, a mother, or sometimes a whole family would come up to say where their present was going.

Nicole wanted to get up twice. But when she wiggled to get out of her seat, she saw her dad frown from the pulpit and remembered what he'd said at supper: "Now, Nicole, we have to be last. After all, I'm the minister. We must let the others be first."

When it finally was their turn, Nicole, who had been very insistent that the gift she brought stay with her and not be put under the tree, slid out of the pew with her brother. Nathan carried the present the family had bought when they went Christmas shopping. Up the aisle they went. Usually, her brother made the speeches, but tonight, Nicole's mouth opened first. "Open the present, Dad."

She handed it to her father.

Reverend Clark smiled in some confusion. "We aren't supposed to open the presents. We're supposed to say where we're taking them."

But Nicole was very persistent, still holding it out to him.

"Oh, well," he said as he accepted the gift. There was some chuckling in the pews, making him consider how people always thought it was funny when it wasn't their child taking the awkward spotlight.

Everyone waited while he worked his way through the assortment of strings, tape, and leftover wrappings Mrs. Clark had given Nicole to use. But as he opened the lid to the box, he looked utterly puzzled.

"It's the baby Jesus from outside. You're the one who took it?"

"It doesn't belong outside, Dad. It belongs right here," she explained. "The lady with the chicken feather said she was poor. And Mom said we couldn't afford to get presents for all my friends. But that's okay if we give everyone Jesus, right?"

There were a few blushes throughout the pews but a whole lot more smiles and nods and murmurs of agreement.

"So, I think He belongs here with us this Christmas," Nicole said with the simple childlike logic that sometimes adults really need to hear.

"Yes, Nicole," her father agreed, despite his blushing face and watery eyes. "I think you're right." Turning to the congregation, he smiled as he exclaimed, "Merry Christmas, everyone."

"Merry Christmas," the congregation echoed, renewed by a little girl's reminder that they already had what they needed right there.

Chapter 13

CASPAR AND THE ELUSIVE STAR

"I know you've studied the stars for many years, Balthasar." Nevertheless, Caspar looked up at his friend with a doubtful glance. "And you know the heavens like a shepherd knows his sheep. But how can you be so sure?"

Balthasar was slow to speak.

Even though he was from Persia and Caspar from Babylon, the two astrologers had known each other for many years. Over that time, they had shared many stories about the numerous stars journeying across the vast span beyond them. But this? This was not a story. And so it required even more careful consideration to convey it correctly.

"I tell you, Caspar," he finally said, "this star is different! You've seen its brightness. You already told me you saw it first that same night I spotted it from my tower." He stroked his beard. "There has to be a reason."

His friend grimaced, a good indication of how he felt about his next words before he even uttered them. "In my books, the legends speak of Abram, father of the Jews, who came from Ur. Today, their nation is no more. That is to say, it's no longer its own sovereign entity. It has suffered under many rulers and now awaits a king whom their prophets say will rescue them."

"What does this Abram have to do with anything?" Balthasar asked.

"They say Babylon was once Ur. If so, we gave the Jews their father," explained Caspar.

"Did you also give them their god?" asked Balthasar.

"No, I'm afraid not." Caspar smiled. "Though I've sometimes wished we had. Their God seems to be beyond the works of the gods we know, and His people seem to have such faith in Him as a merciful God." His expression turned more solemn. "Yet all the while, they suffer. Their Scriptures say they wait for their Deliverer—their Savior—who will rescue them from their suffering. They have been defeated in battle, conquered by tyrannical powers, and enslaved. Through it all, however, they hope. They believe in a god whose judgment is forthcoming when they stray, but who is always merciful, forgiving, and loving when they call upon Him."

"You've studied this very well, my friend." Balthasar had a very contemplative look on his face. "Would you dare go with Melchior and me to see this strange sight that rests over their home?"

"No!" Caspar sounded adamant because he was. "Why should I give up my comforts when I can study the star right here as it moves across the heavens? What good can be found among a broken people?"

But Balthasar smiled. "What good can be found in anyone whose heart has not been broken from time to time?"

278

"What if the star doesn't move like a regular star?" Melchior winked at his friend. "What if it doesn't move at all?" As he often did, Melchior had been listening quietly to his friends' conversation. He usually joined one of their many conversations, but only after he had time to listen and reflect.

"I tell you, it will." Caspar was officially annoyed. "You go off on this meaningless trek if you dare. I, however, will have no part of it."

Making sure to have the last word, he walked off and did not engage his friends again that evening. In silence, they all retired for the night. Even so, hours later, while they were sleeping, Caspar found himself awakened by thoughts racing through his mind. Not wanting to disturb the others, he silently slipped up the stairs to the rooftop garden and stared out into the distant heavens.

Caspar knew he was wrong. He had watched the star night after night even while his two friends were traveling from Persia to meet him. The celestial light had not moved. It stood in the same place in the sky—so mysterious and unmovable, but so bold and real. And yet so out of reach.

Isn't that the mystery of all life? All the good in the world is so often just beyond our fingertips, waiting to be grasped?

After awakening and seeing that Caspar was absent, Melchior knew the one place he was sure to be. As he came up the stairs to the rooftop, he found his friend peering out into the heavens. He did not have to ask what he was looking at or waiting to see because he already knew.

"Have you been here all night?" Melchior asked, coming up behind his friend.

"Why, yes, almost . . . I guess I have." Caspar turned to his friend, somewhat embarrassed to be caught sleepless like this.

"For someone who resents the stranger's intrusion in the heavens, you have kept a watchful eye on our friend," he said as his words turned his head upward toward the direction of the star.

"Friend? I am not sure the star is my friend," Caspar grumbled while still looking out into the night sky. "Sleep slipped by me. I came up here so I wouldn't disturb you and Balthasar."

Caspar spoke words that seemed to be awkward. Maybe the awkwardness came from being found out by his friend seeing him with eyes wide open and gazing out into the heavens, once more fixated on the unmovable star. As he turned toward Melchior, he felt the need to explain further.

"In spite of my earlier remarks, I have been held captive by the star."

Now, with both of them looking upward once again, he continued, "It defies all scientific understanding of the heavenly bodies. Furthermore, I feel uneasy because of its presence. No heavenly body—absolutely none, I tell you—has made me feel this way before. It just hangs there, absolutely radiant, almost like it is lighting the way to a journey unknown. I sometimes think it is trying to tell me something. No matter how I look or from what position, it sparkles and shines as if it is looking right at me. You and Balthasar can call it a friend, but I am not so sure I can."

"Ah, maybe you can't . . . or maybe in time you will," Melchior said. "But tell me, Caspar, if the Jewish legend is true, would you hope for the same?"

"The same?" He wasn't following him one bit. "The same what?"

"Someone." Melchior looked very wise standing there. "Someone who could give hope to your people. Someone who could be as God among us: a deliverer—powerful, swift and mighty—who could conquer our greatest enemies."

"No," Caspar said, and then again, wanting to make sure he was understood, explained, "Yes, I would certainly look for someone who gives us hope. As I have said before, a god, as the Jews proclaim their God to be, someone who is merciful, kind, and loving, someone who is beyond the use of force, someone who does not hold their subjects captive by power or fear. I would want a deliverer who leaves his magic at home and moves by mercy and lives with love."

Caspar shook his head as a cautious look crossed his face. Thinking he should not say any more, he stopped and would have fallen into a contemplative silence if it had not been for his friend's next request.

"Ah, Caspar, I know it has been some time since we have visited, but I have always known you as true as you know Balthasar and myself to be. I can sense you have more to say and I need to listen. Please continue," Melchior encouraged him.

Not waiting to be asked again, Caspar continued, "When I study the history of the Jews, the beliefs they have in their God, and the promises they hold onto for a Messiah or Deliverer, I am conflicted. I believe their God is like I said before—a god who is merciful, kind, and loving, but I also see . . ."

Then he stopped, his thought suspended somewhere in a maze of confusion. He took another breath and started again. "But what are we talking about? What does this have to do with the star?"

Balthasar had been standing on the stairs for some time. When his two friends were silent, he finished his climb and moved into the garden toward them, showing no remorse at all for listening in on their conversation. "What if—like you say, Caspar—the star is the guide and wherever it rests there is the Mighty One? The Deliverer!"

"Impossible," Caspar protested.

281

"Oh." Balthasar cocked his head to the side in gentle mockery. "And why not? You Babylonians are somewhat mystical. Even you, a priest, understand magic as having knowledge. And yet you can't believe anything magical about this star?"

"I am a scientist. I cannot speak for other mystics, but my magic, as you call it, comes from study and reason. I see logic where other people see wizardry. I find truth in what can be proven. Such is the way of my studies of the stars."

This was a point Caspar was very firm about. "There is nothing to this star. And even if there was, look at this world! It's already had its share of conquerors and magicians. Yet are we not to be better? I am going to finish now what I did not say earlier. I am still conflicted. I do not understand how the Jews can still believe in a merciful, kind, and loving god. I, too, want to still believe the one true God is such a god. Nevertheless, for century after century, they have been defeated or betrayed by the words of false prophets, conquerors, and even their own leaders. For some reason, they have continued to trust in the God they call Yahweh and their belief that a Messiah will rescue them. Why and how do they do it?"

"It is my understanding, friend, that they do so by their faith and hope," Melchior answered.

"But my friend, what does faith mean to them? What is the meaning of their hope?" Caspar now sounded less skeptical, instead searching for a better understanding.

"Friend, faith believes beyond all our learning. It can defy reason. It cannot be bullied into action. Faith believes that the impossible can happen. The weak can be strong. The blind can see. The lame can walk. The child believed to be dead can rise and eat. And the worst, most despicable action or behavior, as the Jews might call *sin,* can be forgiven by their God if the people call upon Him and their hearts are fully sorry," Melchior explained.

Without challenging his words, Caspar spoke again. "And hope? What is *hope?*"

"I have learned that when there is nothing left, when there is no reason to believe that the promise will come true, there is still hope. No one can take it away from you; only you can give it up. Even a defeated people, as we have known the Jews to be and still are, can hope for their Messiah, their Savior." Again, when Melchior had finished, Caspar seemed more thoughtful than contrary.

Looking to his friend as if needing more explanation, he waited, but when Melchior fell silent, Caspar finally said, "You think this star, this immovable star, has something to do with what the Jews hope for, what they believe is possible—the Messiah, the Deliverer. I don't know. I still don't know. How can it be?"

Melchior could tell that his friend was not asking further questions as much as he was experiencing an arm-wrestling match taking place between his mind and beliefs that had not yet been proven by reason. He patiently waited, and then with conviction said, "You will never know, friend, not unless you come along with us."

Melchior might have been a bit smug with this declaration, but he knew his friend well enough to know he'd already hooked him. If for no other reason, Caspar's curiosity would draw him to the journey. Sure enough, he was right. Before the morning sun could rise from the hillside, Caspar was ready to go.

Inside the bundle of clothes they took with them, they each carefully put a gift. The Magi had a belief that gifts for a baby or child had their own story to tell, along with certain powers. What those powers were, however, could only be brought to life by the way the baby or child lived out his life and the individual decisions made along the way. It was as if the direction that each recipient took unfolded, and the gifts were either used for good or ill. The gifts they took would be given to whomever they might find at their personal journey's end.

When the Magi finished packing, they climbed atop their camels to ride out between the city gates and into the unknown, drawn by the mystery of the star. Their trip took them a great deal of time, and with it came many conversations, much silence for personal contemplation, and very few moments of extreme excitement or enlightenment. One of those moments happened, however, when they were well within Judea and came across a group of shepherds who told the most wondrous story, but only to Balthasar and Melchior.

Caspar had not been with them because when they originally approached the shepherds and the sheep, "Achoo! Achoo!" came from Caspar, along with a runny nose and watery eyes. At the sound of Caspar's sneezes, the startled sheep turned and tried to make a fast getaway. It was possible they had never heard an "achoo" before this. Most likely, if it had not been for the two collie dogs circling the flock and holding them tight while gingerly moving them back toward the shepherds, they would have scattered to the hills.

"I'd better stay—'Achoo!'"—behind, far—'Achoo!—far behind," Caspar explained as he turned his camel around and headed a distance away from the flock and the shepherds. He was relieved that his "achoos" were his reason for staying behind, not the horrible smell he assumed came from the wooly critters. Thinking he had a good idea, if for no other reason than preventing another sheep run, Melchior and Balthasar went on ahead to meet the shepherds.

It took him until the next evening to stop sneezing from the scent Melchior and Balthasar had carried back with them to their camp the previous night. Caspar wore a miserable look throughout the day. His friends decided not to tell him the details of their visit with the shepherds until after night had fallen when they came to rest upon a hillside where the ever-present star hung before them.

Balthasar looked into the dancing flames of their glowing fire. "Those shepherds last night said the star rests over the town of Bethlehem."

"Bethlehem?" Caspar knew of the place—a pitiful little town, to be sure. "Such a place for their Messiah . . . Deliverer . . . King," he muttered.

"One of them said he knew a shepherd who had been there that night," Melchior said. "He spoke of strange men like angels calling from the heavens and declaring that their Savior had been born."

"And the star?" Caspar stared into the darkness.

"The star led them to a place—a stable—and there He was, in the solid form of a baby! Imagine that, an infant!" Balthasar laughed. "Some conqueror, eh? They also told us rumor has it the boy and his parents still live in Bethlehem. His father, they say, is a carpenter."

"Ah, but infants grow up." Melchior was not so amused by the idea, taking it in stride. "Or have you forgotten?"

An infant. A stable. Mercy and love. Caspar had learned from his studies of people and their societies that conquerors who showed such qualities as love and mercy, forgiveness and grace, honesty and generosity, and trust and freedom opened themselves up to betrayal. The cost of caring too deeply for another was much too great, and the goodness to which they believed all could aspire was simply unthinkable. In a world where people enjoyed control, power, greed, and subjugation, the qualities of the conqueror he had mentioned were very rare. Despite how the words came to his mind, he shook his head to refute them. *Do you suppose this baby could be a king? A conqueror? Who would ever guess that God would care to become man—and as a child, no less! If it is so, He would truly learn the bitter cost of caring too deeply for another.*

"But could He still love? Could He mend the hearts of others by His own brokenness?" Caspar sighed, and at the same time, he looked beyond the fire into the faces of the others.

"Is that for us to know, my friend?" asked Melchior.

"Yes," Caspar said. "We must know, or there is no mercy. No hope. There was a prophet of the Jews who wrote of their God, 'Once you were no people, but now you are My people . . . . Once you had no mercy, but now you have My mercy.' The hope of the ages must rest on this one Deliverer being able to show the highest form of God in the simplest of human ways. He must not be like the star—so visible, yet so out of reach. He must be tangible and real!

"But how can a baby, no matter what he will be when he grows up, take on such a mission in the world we live in today? I understand the prophet's words. I believe this is what the Jews hold on to, even to this very day. This is where their hope and faith is. He is the One who will deliver them and still they wait—but a baby? And what about us? Are we to believe their Deliverer, the world's Savior, will be presented to the world as a baby? Can a child alone do all they expect? Is not such hope a foolish thing?"

Melchior could tell his friend's thoughts were still burdened by the questions he presented to them, so he replied, "Let us go see for ourselves, my friend." Melchior rose up. "We are not very far from this Bethlehem. Let us finish our journey tonight."

Having heard himself speak, Caspar quietly admitted to himself that he needed to see, too. He needed to know. Was he right, or was he wrong? So, he joined his friends packing up what they had unpacked and loading up what they had unloaded, and then they rode the remaining distance in silence.

The star did not lead them to a stable as it once did for the shepherds but to a small house on the outskirts of Bethlehem, where they were greeted in a friendly manner by a carpenter named Joseph and his wife, Mary. Both wondered what had brought such distinguished men to their home.

"May I ask," Joseph said, "why you have come to our home? We can tell you have traveled a long way to come here."

After introducing themselves, Melchior explained, "Because of our studies, even though we come from different countries, we often confer with one another as we search the heavens. A little over two years ago, we each saw this magnificent star in the sky. It always seemed to appear as bright as the noonday sun. The strangest thing about this star is that it never moved. Desiring some explanation, we searched the holy books and found once again that the Jews' hope and faith are firmly planted in the promise from their God they would receive their Deliverer—a Savior, a King. We began to wonder if the star we had been studying was somehow connected to this prophecy. Rather than continue to go on wondering, we decided to find out for ourselves. We were not sure exactly what we would find."

Balthasar added, "A couple of nights ago, some shepherds we met told us about seeing the same star we had been following. They went on to say that they were visited by heavenly beings who told them 'a Savior was born who would save His people.' The shepards then directed us to a stable in Bethlehem."

Caspar began where Balthasar had stopped. "They also said all they had experienced regarding the baby they met that night was about two years ago. So the baby would now be about two." He went on to say, "They probably would not have mentioned it if it weren't for the immovable star and the probability that we would not find the boy at the stable any longer. After all, a stable is a place for cows, horses, and sheep, not a place to raise a child."

"It is another miracle," Mary said, without telling more about her story and the child's birth.

"What do you mean?" Melchior inquired.

"I can answer that," said Joseph. "Shortly after our son was born, we were warned by an angel to flee to Egypt. For some reason, King Herod was hunting Him down to kill Him. His soldiers killed so many baby boys, so many."

The visitors could tell Joseph's words were filled with grief; however, he still had more to say.

Joseph continued. "We came back to Bethlehem after a heavenly being appeared to me in a dream and told me we could return. But we will be here only for a very short time. Tomorrow, I will move my family to Nazareth, where we will raise Jesus as a Nazarene." When Joseph said "Jesus," it was the first time the visitors had heard His name.

The visitors could tell that he had no more to say. Out of politeness, they allowed the quiet to settle between them, all the while casting their eyes on a young boy who appeared to be about two years of age, hiding behind his mother's long dress. Seconds passed by, into a minute or two, and then Balthasar handed Mary his gift. Caspar and Melchior followed their friend's lead.

And so it was, just as the shepherds had said. Once there had been a stable and a manger. Now, instead of a manger, there was a house. The baby who once fit into the manger was now a shy two-year-old, who, along with His parents, had already faced imminent danger from those

288

in power. Yet it made no difference to the Magi. As Mary and Joseph had said, it was a miracle. For the three visitors, it was still a miracle. The child was so very young that Caspar couldn't help but feel a need now to protect him. Without coaxing, the shy little boy came forward and embraced Melchior and Balthasar. When He came to Caspar, He did not embrace him but instead held his arms out in an upward fashion.

Caspar smiled at the lad and then looked toward his mother and said, "My lady, He is so young. It's been a long time. So long ago . . . I am not too—"

But somehow or another, the young boy was in his arms, and he found himself becoming quiet as the child nestled into his warmth. A certain peace came over his soul, even while his mind acknowledged this most definitely wasn't a mighty warrior he held in his arms but rather a child—a helpless, little child.

"If this is the Deliverer," Caspar wept, "He comes in a way I can believe. He comes for me as well."

Tenderly kissing the child, he gave Him back to His mother and knelt before Him. Balthasar and Melchior lowered themselves to their knees as well. Each one of them, in their own way, came to believe this boy, Jesus, somehow had the power to hold a star out of the steps of time.

Caspar gazed upon the child and said to Mary and Joseph, "Our gifts were meant as tokens and peace offerings. They are filled with power that will come to life as your child lives by the choices He makes. But He needs no such gifts, for I think the choices He makes will be out of the love, hope, and mercy He has for all humankind. So, please take them as gifts from our hearts instead. Their value is little compared to the joy my soul feels at this moment. I have received more than my mind can measure or my spirit hold."

Mary smiled as if she understood him exactly. "Surely then, you can give some of the joy you have received to those you meet from this day forward."

Caspar couldn't agree more with that sentiment. As they set out again from Bethlehem, her words held him spellbound for some time. It was not until Melchior prompted him that he truly spoke again.

"So now, Caspar, was the journey worth your time?" his friend joked.

"Yes, I believe it was." He smiled because he couldn't help himself. "But not so much for this moment, for it has begun a journey I will travel for the rest of my life."

As it turned out, he realized that star—goodness, but that star—was like the young boy. It was not so elusive after all when properly sought and held and treasured within one's heart.

Chapter 14

His Majesty's Tree

"If you want to grow to be big and majestic like we are, you'd better eat your nitrogen!" The one they called Spike bent over and shook his branch in the littler fir's face.

"No!" Little David said defiantly. "I'm not going to!"

"You are 'not going to' what?" Spike bent over further, now staring right in Little David's face.

The fir gulped. "I'm not going to eat my nitrogen . . . sir."

"Ah, leave the kid alone, Spike," Annabelle swished coolly. "It will be no snow off our backs if the kid doesn't get picked to decorate the king's banquet hall this Christmas."

"Eat up, you little sap," Bert insisted from the other side of Annabelle. "There has never been a tree in the king's majestic forest that's refused to eat. It's our duty. It's our right."

"It will get my trunk cut off," said David softly.

291

"But think of the glory." Spike clearly thought nothing of getting hacked. "The king doesn't choose an elm or maple—or even a spruce. He chooses the majestic fir to be the center of his Christmas festivities."

"Wait!" he interrupted his own dialogue. "What's this trying to crawl under my branches?"

Swooshing his lower branches repeatedly, he shooed out a family of eight rabbits who went streaking away from him in fear.

"Come in," David told them. "Come in."

"Thank you, thank you," the father, mother, and six little ones said as they scampered deep inside.

"I don't know why you bother with them pesky creatures." Bert blew a breeze of disgust down toward David. "Next thing you know, you'll let cardinals sing from your branches."

"Maybe I will." But David said it too low for any of his fellow firs to hear. He knew they wouldn't listen anyway.

As the stars came out that night, he couldn't stop thinking about why Spike, Annabelle, and Bert ignored the little creatures of the forest. They always had a huff, a howl, or a whine to scare them away, never offering a soft breeze of welcome or comfort.

Meanwhile, away at the castle, the torch-lighter was lighting the hall for the evening when he met the prince coming from the royal stables. He had always known the prince to be a handsome young man who was well mannered, but for a young man who would soon be sixteen years old, he seemed very small for his age.

"Good evening, Your Highness." The torch-lighter bowed, almost dipping the flame into the young sovereign's hair. "Oops! I'm sorry, Your Highness."

The prince almost giggled but then caught himself. "That's all right, Samuel. It's good to see you."

"And I am always pleased to see you. Oh, before I forget, your father wants to see you in the banquet hall." said Samuel.

Prince Michael sighed. "What did I do wrong now?"

"What day is today?" Samuel grinned. "Hmm, let's see. It's Monday." He shook his head. "Nope. Too early in the week for trouble. Maybe he just wants to see how being a prince is going."

"Will you come with me?" Michael never liked meeting his father alone in the banquet hall. It seemed so much like business.

"Well, I don't know, Your Highness." Samuel was cautious all of a sudden. "I mean, I'm not royal." Because of the prince's request, Samuel spoke carefully, understanding the situation perhaps better than the prince—as adults sometimes do.

"It means you're going as my friend," Prince Michael said with sincerety which was nothing short of natural. "Besides, I need moral support."

"I guess I could take some oil along and say that one of the lanterns in there is running low."

"Good. We'd better get going, then. The king doesn't wait for anyone," he said, feeling much more confident now as he led the way to the banquet hall.

"Hello, Father." Prince Michael bowed to the king, as even a prince must do.

"Your Majesty." Samuel bowed even lower.

"Hello, my son, and hello to you as well, Samuel," the king said as he allowed a smile to cross his face. And then he asked, "Did I summon a torch-lighter?"

Before Samuel had an opportunity to explain the reason for his presence, Michael said, "I made him come with me."

"I brought more oil for the lanterns, Your Highness," Samuel added.

The king nodded toward Samuel while giving him the same smile he had offered his son. He then turned his attention back to his son and with a gentle expression said, "Michael, I want you to do me a favor tomorrow and go with the royal axeman to select a Christmas tree for this room."

"You mean just me and the royal axeman?" Prince Michael tried not to show his alarm.

His reluctance came from how his very creative mind ran with the stories told by the castle servants. They would often tell younger servants about the wild creatures and strange, mystical people in the dark forest. Some servants even told about the rumors they heard regarding the axeman's father, who had held the position he now cherished. They said he would take people out into the forest, and when he returned, those individuals did not come back with him. When they told such things to young servants, they would almost always exaggerate the right words so the hairs on the back of their listeners' necks would stand straight up.

Of course, Michael always heard these stories from someone who was told the story by someone else who heard it from another servant. He still believed the possibility of the stories to be the truth. After all, the axeman, even without the tales, was a bit frightening in appearance with his shaggy black beard, bushy eyebrows, deep voice, and muscular arms on a towering frame. Yet it never occurred to Michael, nor anyone else for that matter, to ask the storyteller why the people didn't return.

Prince Michael was able to hide his fear far away from his father so the king never knew how his son felt about the axeman. The only person who actually knew how he felt was Samuel, and he was sworn to secrecy. After all of these thoughts went through Michael's mind like a fast- moving stream of water, he asked again, "You mean, just me and the axeman?"

"Well, of course," replied his father, but giving it another thought when he saw the look on his son's face, he said, "You and Samuel, that is."

Hearing the name of his friend marked a change in the prince. "I can do that, Father. You can count on me to select a grand tree! I promise."

And so the king dismissed him, watching the young man bow gracefully and turn to walk away.

"Samuel," the king called as the torch-lighter started to leave as well.

"Yes, Your Highness?" Samuel quickly turned and bowed again.

"Watch out for my son." He knew he didn't have to add the rest, but he did anyway. "He has a tender heart and might be too easily cowed or frightened by the axeman's strong will."

With confidence Samuel responded, "Sire, believe me when I say your son has a will of his own." He smiled, and then added, "His will and strength are just shown differently."

"Well, it won't be long before Christmas," Spike grunted. "If it weren't for the chance to be in one's realm of glory standing in the king's banquet hall, it would just be another day of human indulgence."

"*When isn't it?*" Bert declared, bristling while giving more thought to human indulgence. "Humans think they own the place, and they aren't the only ones. The same goes for those birds and all their chirping. Blue jays, cardinals, sparrows, chickadees—even a crow or two—get in my branches and spire, and then all day long, it's 'chirp, chirp, chirp.'"

"You would think it was their Savior that'd been born," said Annabelle as if she was a tree-in-the-know.

"Maybe He is," Little David whispered thoughtfully. "Maybe He is a Savior for us as well as the animals and the humans."

"I wouldn't know about those things." Spike swished his bottom branches. "I just know when that axeman comes riding my way, I want all of you dumb birds, squirrels, and all you other things to be quiet so the human can gaze upon my glory without interruption." He glared at David's branches when he said that last part.

"In your dreams," said Bert. "He's going to see me first."

"I doubt that, big boy." Annabelle preened with confidence. "I got you both beat by a branchful."

It wasn't until mid-morning when Spike alerted everyone that they had visitors. "Hush. Someone's coming."

And so they were. Prince Michael rode his horse alongside the ox cart Samuel was driving. Riding ahead of them, the axeman stopped his horse right in front of Spike.

"See? I *told* you," Spike whispered to the others, but even his whisper was loud enough for them to hear. "He's looking right at me. This is it. I'm coming into my realm of glory!"

The axeman looked around, sizing up one tree after the other—first Spike, then Bert, then Annabelle. All were considered. While he was looking at the trees, he bumped into Little David.

"You measly little stub," he blurted out as he regained his balance. "I'll fix you for getting in my way." Little David shivered, not because of the cold, but out of fear. His branches quickly folded toward his trunk as he tried to protect himself from what he instinctively knew was soon to come.

With a scouring look fixed onn his face, he took his axe and lifted it above his shoulders.

296

But just as he was about to swing, Michael, whose eyes had been moving from the axeman to Little David, read the fear that was coming from the little fir's actions. Without hesitating, he quickly dismounted from his horse and called out, "Stop! Stop, I say!"

"What? Are you telling me to stop?" The axeman squinted at the small prince.

"Yes, he did say, 'Stop!'" Samuel said as he scrambled from the cart and rushed to the prince's defense.

"Sir, it is my father's wish that I select a tree. We aren't here to do any of the others harm," the prince protested.

Those simple words further enraged the man. "You know, I've had just about enough of you and your father's kingdom. See this axe, Your Highness?" He stuck it far too close to Michael's face. "It cuts off heads just as quickly as it cuts down trees."

In less than a second and having no fear for his own safety, Samuel jumped in front of the prince. "Are you forgetting to whom you're speaking? This is your prince! Have you no respect?"

"Look, you puny twig," the axeman snapped, "I'm not going to let you and this half-pint tell *me* what tree to cut or not to cut. I've been at this business for twenty-five years. Twenty-five years!" he repeated. "The nerve of the king—sending a kid to tell me what to do!"

With those angry words, the axeman demanded, "Now, stand back both of you and let me do my work."

Leaning the axe against one leg, he gave both Michael and Samuel a bit of a push. Now, a push from the axeman is no gentle thing, whether it is meant to be or not. Stumbling into each other, they both hit the ground hard, too dazed to struggle to their feet very quickly. The axeman once again lifted his axe, and even though Little David felt frozen in fear, he was able to tell the rabbit family, "Run for your lives!"

"Oh, for the love of Christmas," Spike muttered.

"And for other things," yelled Bert.

Together, they swung their branches down hard on the axeman. With one swoop and a strong gush of wind, they knocked the axe out of his hand, and he tumbled to the ground. They even went so far as to hold him down while Samuel, already back on his feet, bound his hands and feet with the rope they'd brought to tie down their chosen Christmas tree.

"Did you ever see anything like it before?" exclaimed Samuel after he finished the troublesome task. "It's as if the trees came to the little fir's rescue."

"And to ours as well. Thank you, all of you, my friends," Michael said, as his eyes once again moved from the surrounding firs to gaze upon Little David.

Little David looked right back at the prince. With a quiet sway, he bowed ever so politely.

That gave Michael an idea. "Let's dig around its roots."

"Ah, okay." Samuel reached for the shovel that always seemed to be a standard tool carried in the palace ox carts for the servants, but that didn't mean he was following the prince's train of logic. "I thought we were supposed to be selecting the Christmas tree for the banquet hall."

"We are." Michael smiled fondly at Little David.

"Would you believe it?" Spike mused to the others while they watched the two humans taking turns digging carefully around Little David's roots. "The prince is really in trouble now. I was willing to rescue the half-pint from the axeman, but there certainly isn't anything majestic about him."

"There is now," Annabelle quietly said as she bowed before Little David. "Your Highness, we really aren't half as bad as we pretend to be. Remember us, please."

"I will. I will." Other than that, he could hardly speak as Michael and Samuel freed his roots from the ground and then wrapped them ever so gently in Samuel's outside cloak he had dipped in the nearby brook.

Just before they were ready to close the back end of the ox cart, Michael happened to notice the family of rabbits all standing there, looking up at the prince with plaintive eyes.

"Please! Please!" they squealed.

Looking down at his little friends and then out toward the prince, Little David echoed the request in his own language. "Please!"

The commotion got Michael's attention. "I think this rabbit family wants to go with us. We must have taken their home from them." With a sweep of his hand, he beckoned them forward. "Come on, then! Hop into the cart."

Without hesitation, they scampered back beneath their fir's warm branches.

"Thank you," Little David said politely, with a sway of his branches.

"You're welcome," Michael replied. In some magical way he seemed to be able to hear the voice of the fir, so he responded, feeling a sense of joy and peace believing all would be well.

"What?" Samuel asked as he put the shovel back into the cart.

"Oh, nothing," smiled Michael.

With the axeman in tow, David, Michael, Samuel and, we mustn't forget the rabbit family, were off for the palace. They hadn't taken too many steps before Samuel shook his head.

"Just one question," he said.

"Yes?" Michael was almost certain he knew what his friend wanted to say.

"How are we going to explain all of this to your father? He's expecting a majestic tree, yet we're bringing in a small fir instead, roots and all, plus a family of rabbits." Samuel gave a helpless shrug.

But Michael remained outwardly unfazed. "Aren't I supposed to make a royal decree on my sixteenth birthday that the king will honor?"

"Hmm . . . yes . . . well, within reason of course," Samuel answered.

"Don't worry. I have a plan. I'll do the explaining, and you fill in the blanks."

"I believe this journey has not been as I thought it would be, Your Highness," Samuel said. "I just hope everything works out when we come before the king."

So do I, Michael said to himself, and then for his own comfort repeated, "*So do I.*"

It was late in the afternoon by the time they reached the palace. While Samuel ran to fetch a guard for the axeman, Michael helped a servant remove the fir from the ox cart. Just then, the king entered the courtyard.

"Isn't it a beautiful tree, Father?" the prince asked.

Waiting for Samuel's return before speaking, the king repeated over and over, "hmm, hmm, hmm." With the sound of footsteps quickly approaching, he finally said, "Right now,"—he threw Samuel a frown to affirm his remarks before continuing—"I'm much more interested in hearing what all has happened today." The king did not look happy. "I sent you off to find something majestic, yet you come back with this shrub and my axeman bound like a criminal!"

So, Michael followed through with his plan, explaining the majority of their adventure. Samuel filled in the blanks, adding in a few words wherever he felt that Michael was being a little too hard on himself for not selecting a more majestic tree.

"At first, I didn't notice the little fir. The majestic firs towering around almost hid the little one from my view. I saw it for the first time when the axeman nearly stumbled over it and out of anger raised his axe to give the fir a swift end to its life. I thought, *Even at a very tender age, its beauty radiates. Then, beneath its branches, I saw this family of rabbits sheltered from the winter's cold.*

"We are a lot alike, Father, this fir and me. I am still young and have a lot to learn, yet you see in me the potential to become a king. Although I am small in stature and tender in shoot like the fir, with the responsibilities you give me, I find people seeking me out for advice and help. You have provided me with Samuel to watch over me, and I know him as a friend who offers me very wise counsel. I believe the fir you see before you has the desire to grow as majestic as the firs that surrounded him in the forest. Maybe it is my foolishness, but I seemed to have heard him speak.

"In just this short time, I have seen him provide care, shelter, and protection for a young family of rabbits and birds of the forest. I believe he has a kind and gentle heart. I selected it out of all the majestic trees in your forest because of its strength, but I also see its present and future beauty. And Father, if we cannot see the true beauty and have a heart for the youngest in age or stature in your kingdom, how can we see the true beauty in and have trust in the older?"

Taking a quick breath, in conclusion Michael continued, "From the moment I saw this tree, I understood how precious little things really are. It's very humbling to walk through the Royal Forest with all its majestic trees and view their splendor, but I believe it's even more humbling to see the majesty in the little things."

Michael was quiet for a moment. In the stillness that encompassed the room, the rabbit family must have thought it safe to hop out of the cart. In so doing, they found themselves right at the feet of His Royal Highness, the king himself.

"What in the—?" the king began.

"Aren't they beautiful and precious, Father?" Without waiting for an answer, Michael reached down, picked up the father rabbit, and handed it to the king.

"Michael, we can't—I mean, even if we could—this tree won't live—and how can it fill the banquet hall?" While he spoke, he held firmly but gently onto his furry subject. "I told Samuel I had a plan," Michael reassured him with a smile.

"That he did, sire." Samuel hadn't shaken his doubts that the prince was about to get into trouble. Even without knowing the plan, but wanting to protect him, Samuel added, "And, I agreed with it."

Michael smiled at his friend before turning back to his father. "Didn't you say on my sixteenth birthday that I could declare a royal decree?"

"Yes." His father looked slightly wary now. "But you said you weren't interested in doing so, and even though your birthday is soon, you have said nothing more about it."

"Yet, I can still do so. Is that correct?"

"Yes, my son. It is your right to do so, and yes, you still can," the king answered.

"I do want to make a decree for this Christmas and for Christmases to come." Michael's tone, attitude, and posture were all very bold. In fact, he was so bold that it amazed his father, for he had never heard such confidence from his son before.

"I decree that this fir shall be our royal Christmas tree—not for one year, but for years to come. And from its seedlings will come the new royal tree."

"But, son—" the king said.

Michael wasn't finished, however. "This tree will be planted in the palace courtyard, which will be called 'The Commons' from now on because it will be open to all people. Every year, during the Christmas season, this tree will illuminate the commons with its beauty, reminding us of how precious life is meant for all of God's creatures."

"So be it," the king announced without further protest. "It is a decree. I place upon these words my royal seal."

That's why, under Samuel's watchful eye, Little David was planted in The Commons. When the task was completed, Michael and the king came to inspect the work and, of course, to give the rabbit family back their home.

"You have proven yourself to be a wise and trusted friend, Samuel," the king said while they looked at his work. "Going forward, you will be the royal caretaker of The Commons and all the trees in the Royal Forest."

"By the way," the king continued, "the axeman has been exiled to the wasteland, where he can swing his axe and chop away at all the dead tree stumps he so desires."

Samuel smiled and bowed respectfully. And so all was right for the rest of the day and many days going forward.

On Christmas morning, there was something of a to-do when Samuel came running into the prince's chambers. "Your Highness, Your Highness! Come and see! Come and see!"

"You've decorated the tree?" Michael inquired. "You know I wanted to help you do that."

Yet that wasn't it. When they came skidding into The Commons, they were met with the most dazzling sight. During the night, water drops had frozen upon Little David's branches and now sparkled like crystals. Birds of every color were perched upon his limbs, and at the sight of the prince, they began to sing softly.

"It's beautiful!" Michael couldn't take his eyes off the tree. "Please, Samuel, go and bring my father so he can see this beautiful sight!"

Before Samuel could turn, the king placed his hands on both of their shoulders. "I'm here," he said. "I saw the most amazing light from my window, and when I came down to see what it was—" He stopped himself short, and then redirected his words. "You were right, Michael. Even in little things, royalty can be found."

"Thank you, my friends." The birds kept singing as Little David bowed and whispered, "Thank you, my friends."

As the years went by, both Little David and Michael grew to be outwardly majestic as well as inwardly, each in their own way. Michael was known throughout the kingdom as the prince who became a king who cared for his people, even the needy and helpless. And it was said of Little David, the royal Christmas tree, that beneath his branches the little creatures always found a home, and upon his limbs the birds a nesting place.

Chapter 15

Everyday Divinity

"Walter!" Marie called to her husband from the kitchen, even though he and their granddaughter, Laurie, were in the dining room just a few feet away.

"Yes, Marie!" Walter responded with the same volume, giving Laurie a wink.

Marie, wiping her hands on a kitchen towel, walked into the dining room and was now in direct view of her husband. "You don't have to yell, you know. I can hear you." She looked at the computer screen, where Walter and their granddaughter were playing a game from the past called checkers. With an amused tone, she asked, "Who's winning?"

"I am," Laurie, their perky, brand new jeans-and-T-shirt clad nine-year-old, said confidently. Her words were carried by a radiant smile, and her long blonde curls bounced when she looked up at her grandmother.

"Well," Walter said, hoping to disarm his competitive opponent. "I do have a few more checkers on the screen than you do."

"Yeah, but watch this!" Laurie moved the mouse across the screen with surprising ease. "There go your checkers, Grandpa. I win again!"

Standing up to do a victory dance around his chair, she raised her hands in the air while singing her favorite football team's fight song. Then, without any hesitation, she patted his bald spot in consolation.

"Do you want to play again?"

"He would love to," her grandmother replied, "but he needs to go and find me some black walnuts so I can start making divinity for Christmas."

"Can I go?" Laurie was right back to jumping up and down. "Can I go with you, Grandpa?"

"Gee, I don't know." Walter squinted at her as if in deep thought. "You just beat me—unashamedly—three times in checkers. Are you sure you want to spend more time with me?"

Laurie put her arms around his neck. "I'll let you win next time."

"For a nine-year-old, you sure know how to twist me around your finger," he said. "Okay, you can go with me if you promise to let me win next time."

"Listen, you two," Marie teased. "I'd like to have those walnuts sometime before Christmas Eve."

"Then we're off!" Walter exclaimed, jumping from his chair and taking hold of Laurie's hand.

It wasn't long before the pair were riding down the street in Walter's old Ford pickup. Laurie was listening to a song on her iPod, not paying much attention to where they were going until, out of the corner of her eye, she saw the store where her grandmother went for groceries.

"Grandpa, you missed the store," Laurie announced, turning off her iPod.

"We did?" Walter questioned.

"Yes." Her answer was matter-of-fact. "Grandma always goes there for groceries."

"Well, those store nuts are *very* expensive," Walter explained. "We get our walnuts somewhere else."

"Where?" Laurie asked.

"Out at our church," her grandfather answered.

"What?" This line of reasoning was clearly confusing her. "I didn't know there was a store at your church."

"I never thought of it that way before, but I guess there is a store." Walter chuckled at that, and then took the opportunity to continue the conversation since he, not the iPod, had Laurie's attention. "You know, if you look closely out the window, you might see some deer on this stretch of the road."

Sure enough, not two minutes later she was exclaiming, "Grandpa! I see one! No, two! There are two deer. Look!"

She jabbed her finger toward the ditch up ahead, even though there was no need for her to point because the animals were walking toward them, coming closer and closer to the edge of the road.

Walter slowed the pickup almost to a stop, allowing the deer to dart out safely onto the road and then escape into the woods on the other side.

"Wow!" Laurie's face was lit up with delight. "That was really neat. Do you think we'll see any more?"

"I'm not sure." He hoped so, if only to get another reaction out of his granddaughter. "I guess we'll have to keep watching."

So, they did just that until they reached the church driveway, where they parked right in front of the sign.

"I can read that," Laurie said proudly, then proceeded to sound out the words without any prompting. "Hopkins Grove Com-mu-ni-ty Church."

"You're becoming quite the reader." Getting out of the pickup, Walter handed her a gunnysack. "Now let's see how good you are at gathering Hopkins Grove nuts."

His words diverted her attention from finding something else to read. "I thought you said we were buying them, not picking them off the ground."

"Oh, hmm . . . I did, didn't I?" Walter pretended to look thoughtful. "I guess you can say we're purchasing them from nature's store. And there must be a special on walnuts 'cause they aren't going to cost us a penny but they're as precious as gold nuggets."

Not quite content, Lauri angled her head while she continued to regard him. "But these are squirrel nuts. People don't eat those," she said, quite sure of herself as she pointed to the nuts lying on the ground without losing sight of her grandfather.

"Your grandma and I do," Walter explained. "So does your mother. That is, she did when she was growing up. You eat them, too, every time you take a bite of your grandmother's famous divinity candy."

"I do? Well . . . okay." Laurie still looked doubtful, but she complied anyway.

Once they started, it only took a little while to fill their sacks. There were black walnuts all over the parking lot and church lawn. At first, Laurie tried counting them as she picked up one after another after another to put into her sack. But she became stuck when, in her way of counting, she arrived at a thousand.

"Grandpa," she called as she walked toward him, dragging her sack full of walnuts. "What comes after a thousand?"

Walter stood up and arched his back a bit. "Hot chocolate."

"There are a lot more nuts. Don't you think we should pick some more?" Laurie asked, no matter how happy her grandfather's words made her. The mid-afternoon weather seemed to be much colder than it had been when they'd driven into the church parking lot, and the wind was blowing harder.

"We have to leave some nuts for the squirrels," Walter reasoned out loud, "or they'll be coming to our house for lunch. Besides, I'm not as tough as you are. I'm really feeling cold out here."

"Okay, Grandpa." Laurie tried to sound sympathetic. "If you think you're ready to stop. I guess I'm pretty cold, too."

Walter turned on the heat as soon as they got back into the pickup.

On the way back to town, they took turns humming their favorite Christmas songs while the other tried to guess what song it was. Once they arrived home, Walter found a couple pairs of old gloves and handed Laurie a pair as he put his on.

"What are these for, Grandpa?" she asked.

"We need to take the husks off the walnuts so they can dry faster," he answered.

Still not sure of why they should wear the gloves, she asked again, "But why are we wearing gloves?"

"I'll show you," he said. As he picked up a walnut and started to peel off the husk, a dark brown stain rubbed into his gloves. "See!" he exclaimed. "Now, you wouldn't want to show up in school tomorrow with this stain all over your hands, would you? Besides, I would really be in big trouble if your mother saw your hands stained with this stuff. It takes about a hundred years to wear off," he said with a grandfatherly smile.

"Ya, I think you're right." Needing no further instruction, she quickly put on the gloves he handed her, and the two of them immediately began rubbing and peeling husks off the walnuts. In no time, they had the work bench full of black walnuts.

"Are we done, Grandpa?" Laurie asked as they both surveyed their work.

"Just about. All I need to do now is turn on the heater so the hot air will help to dry the walnuts faster, and then, the really hard work comes," he said as he reached over and turned the heater and fan on. Next, he took a hammer from the nearby tool rack and handed it to Laurie.

"This is yours," Walter said as her fingers closed around the metal end.

"This is really neat!" She reached up to pull on his shoulders and then gave him a big kiss on the cheek. "It even has my name on it: 'Laurie's walnut cracker.'"

"Well, now." Walter grinned. "Let's go see your grandma."

After putting their hammers on the bench, they found their way into the kitchen, where three steaming mugs filled with hot chocolate and tiny marshmallows sat waiting. When Marie set a plate of cookies down on the table next to the hot chocolate, she was pleased to see her granddaughter make a run for the table. With half a cookie in her mouth, Laurie barely waited for her grandparents to sit down before she proceeded to give Marie a detailed report of their afternoon. It wasn't until Laurie finally paused to sip her hot chocolate that anyone else got a real word in edgewise.

"Sounds like the two of you had a full afternoon," her grandmother said. "Good thing you got back when you did because your mom should be here in about fifteen minutes."

"Ask her to come in," Laurie suggested. "I bet she'd like some hot chocolate."

"I will. But I—I don't think she'll have the time." Nevertheless, she looked across the table at her husband, her gaze asking if he'd give it a try anyway.

Walter gave her a quick, reassuring smile, even if he didn't think it would do any good. Yet when they heard Ann honk her horn outside— normally a signal for Laurie to come out—the girl didn't move. Since she was obviously waiting for one of her grandparents to do something, he took a quick but deliberate sip from his cup and stood up to head out the back door.

"Hi, Annie." Walter gave her a sincere smile as she cracked her window.

"Hi, Dad. Where's Laurie? We need to go." She went right on. "Tell Mom thanks for watching her. You, too."

The brief narrative sounded more like one of those automated voice messages at your doctor's office than something from a real conversation.

"We were wondering if you'd like to come in for some hot chocolate." Walter made sure to keep his tone light, not showing any hurt in the process.

But she didn't even hesitate. "I can't. Tom's out of town on business, and I have office work to do just as soon as we finish supper."

"Annie—" Walter began.

A twinge of human emotion—annoyance—crept into her voice. "Dad, not now. We really need to go."

Turning away in defeat, he went back inside to hug his granddaughter goodbye, thanking her for making sure to leave him a cookie or two. Seconds later, she and her mother were pulling out of the drive and down the road.

Walter sat down across from Marie. "What happened? When did life become so busy you can't even enjoy a cookie break?" He took a bite of a cookie to prove his point. Then he sighed and reached for his hot chocolate.

"I'm not really sure, Walter," Marie said. "I'm not really sure."

In the weeks left before Thanksgiving, whenever Laurie was spending the day or after school with her grandparents, Walter made sure they spent time at the kitchen table using their walnut crackers to crack the hard shells, along with the nut-pickers to clean out the meat buried within the shell.

"This is really hard work," Lauri noted. "I didn't know it would take so long to do."

"It does take time," he agreed. "But I guess if it didn't, you and I wouldn't be sitting here visiting and drinking so much hot chocolate at Marie's Diner."

"You're funny sometimes," she giggled.

"That's just what your grandmother says."

Then there was the whole weekend Laurie spent with them while her dad was away for a conference and her mother was out of town on business. Since they brought her to church with them, she heard the Sunday school teacher remind everyone that the practice for the Christmas program would start on Saturday, five days before Thanksgiving.

According to a certain nine-year-old, it sounded like too much fun to miss, so Laurie pleaded with her parents until her mother finally agreed, but "only if Grandma and Grandpa will take you." And that was no problem since Marie and Walter always volunteered to help. Taking Laurie with them this year would just make it extra special.

The first Saturday-morning Christmas program practice brought with it clear skies and some instant chaos.

"Okay, let's all come down to the front." Marie spoke with her experienced teacher's voice—firm but not demanding. "It's time to get started."

"I don't know." Millie Samson shook her head, frowned, and then shook her head again. "I just don't know. All we have is nine children. We need twenty, and we have nine."

Marie opened her mouth to speak, but Millie went right on. "I almost called you to say we probably wouldn't have a program this year. I called all the parents." Another shake of her head. "The Larsons are going skiing in Colorado. The Leonards said their kids just don't want to participate. And the Thomases decided they wanted their children to be in the Christmas pageant in town. They are using a real camel in their pageant." She blew out a heavy sigh of consternation. "I wish we could use a camel."

Walter's eyes held a light touch of mischief. "Maybe we could use a Guernsey and put a sign on her that says 'camel.'"

"Now, Walter," Marie softly scolded, "stop that." Then to Millie, she said reassuringly, "We'll make it work. We'll just adapt the program to nine kids."

"Yeah," Walter added enthusiastically. "You can have three wise men and three shepherds, Mary and Joseph, and one angel. What more do you need?"

"You forgot the innkeeper," Millie said.

"Okay." He gave the issue a single second of contemplation. "Maybe we can say that one of the wise men stayed home with the flu."

"That's not in the script." Even her reproof sounded distracted, though. "I don't know. I just don't know."

"Well, I don't think the flu was diagnosed in Jesus' day, but Walter does have a good point. I suppose we could just have two shepherds instead of three. Yes, I think that will do just fine," Marie said. As an afterthought, she added, "Who really knows how many shepherds there actually were, anyway?"

"But the Bible says—" Millie began but stopped as she looked at Marie.

"I believe the Bible tells us, 'There were shepherds out in the field,'" Marie replied. Then she calmly sent Millie to the third pew, where she could prepare to give assistance and pull herself together while she herself distributed the speaking parts. Offering no reaction and possibly relieved for not having to figure it all out, Millie went and sat down without any further comments. "Tony and Jenny, you're the oldest, so you'll be Mary and Joseph. And Clara, I think you would be good at playing the angel."

"But I want to be the angel," Kurt blurted out. "My mom said Uncle Charles would come if I was someone important."

"Oh, but you are someone important." She used the perfect voice to pacify him. "You're a shepherd."

Edward was the next child to pipe up. "My dad's a carpenter, and my Uncle Sam is a carpenter. So, I want to be a carpenter, too."

"Joseph's the carpenter," Clara said while sending Tony a girl-crush look.

"Anyway," Walter said, trying to take some pressure off his wife, "Edward, you would make a great innkeeper."

"Innkeeper?" Edward appeared to think it over with much somber consideration. "Is that like running a motel?"

Since that sounded like a good thing in the boy's book, Walter capitalized on it without hesitation. "Yes, it is."

"I like motels." Yet he still looked thoughtful and shrewd, like he was brokering a business deal. "Will we have a swimming pool and sauna?"

"It's your motel," Walter assured him.

"Great!" Edward grinned. "Then I'm the innkeeper."

Millie could still be heard repeating, "Oh my, oh my," from the third pew.

"Yes! That will work out perfectly," Marie said. "And JoAnn, you can be a shepherd, too."

"Girls aren't shepherds." JoAnn sounded very matter-of-fact.

"Really?" Fortunately, Marie knew a thing or two about the girl, just as much as she knew all of her charges. "Didn't you take a lamb to the state fair this year? And didn't you get the grand-champion ribbon?"

"Oh yeah." It was JoAnn's turn to reconsider her role. "I guess I can be a shepherd."

"Laurie, Janet, and Sally," Marie said, turning to the last children in line. "The three of you will be the wise women."

The way she emphasized those last two words made the girls giggle and the boys howl with laughter.

"Mrs. Godfrey!" Kurt waved his hand high in the air. "Mrs. Godfrey!"

"Yes?" Marie answered.

"The wise men were guys! How can the girls be wise men?"

"Good question." Not that it was going to get him anywhere. "I guess we'll just have a contemporary play. Is that okay with you?"

Looking genuinely surprised and then pleased that anyone would ask for his blessing, Kurt gave in. "Well, yeah. I guess."

"Wonderful!" Marie was quick to seize on the moment of agreement. "Let's set up the stage then and just walk through our places and parts. Then we'll have treats."

"Can we have the treats first?" Edward asked.

Walter stepped in with admirable ease. "I think not. We need to work up an appetite."

"But I'm hungry now." Perhaps capitalizing on his role as a businessman, Edward stood his ground.

Yet once again, he got an offer he couldn't refuse, this time from Walter. "One cookie now, or three cookies later."

"Three cookies?" The boy rushed to the stage, ready to go. "That's more than my mom lets me have. Let's get going!"

Thanksgiving came to the Godfrey home with all its warm and mouth-watering scents of turkey, fresh-baked rolls, pumpkin pie, salads, and apple cider. The full spread was just one more sign of how much Walter and Marie delighted in entertaining out-of-town family members as well as Laurie and her mom and dad.

After table grace, there was the clatter of food being passed around, along with the chatter that always comes during a holiday meal: plenty of talk about football, and catching up, and telling and retelling funny stories. Then when dinner was over, everyone talked about eating too much, going on a diet until Christmas, and needing to walk around the farm before the game began.

Like the years before, no one really did go for a walk—and nobody would actually go on that daunting pre-Christmas diet—but some people did take naps while others helped clean or set up their traditional

Thanksgiving game of tile rummy. Most of the cousins, meanwhile, played computer games while comparing their Christmas wish lists and hoping it would snow.

Also as usual, the days after Thanksgiving went by really quickly for the moms and dads, grandmas and grandpas. It was only for Laurie, her friends, and fellow young people that time took on the habits of a snail.

All the same, the Christmas play was coming along—unexpected challenges and all. One Friday, they had a hard rain and freeze that lasted the whole weekend. School, practice, and even church had to be canceled, which meant Laurie was unable to spend any time with her grandparents that weekend. On another Saturday, four kids had the flu, leaving only five to rehearse their lines. Yet all the kids and adults seemed to take things in stride. Even Millie Samson had come to peace with her worries by the time the last practice rolled around.

"Okay, children," Marie called out before the children could go their separate ways after the final line was given in the final scene for the final rehearsal. "Let's come down to the front, and we will go over what you'll need to bring."

In spite of some good-natured but not exactly obedient shoving, the boys found their places. After Clara squirmed her way between Tony and Jenny, Walter stood and gave the group a loud grandfatherly, "Shhh."

Everyone quieted down.

"Mary and Joseph." Marie looked at Jenny and Tony while pretending not to notice Clara. "Do you have your costumes? Did you find everything you need?"

"Yes," they said in unison.

"Good." She nodded in satisfaction. "Walter will make sure the manger has straw."

"What about the baby?" Kurt asked.

"Oh yes." Marie realized she hadn't addressed substituting a baby prop for a live infant like she'd meant to. "Jenny, do you have a doll?"

"I've never had a doll." Jenny may or may not have looked a little snotty as she said it. "I play with Legos."

"Okay." Marie tried to keep her expression appropriately solemn, which wasn't easy considering the childish pride on display before her. "Let's see. Does anyone have a doll we can use?"

"A doll is not a baby!" exclaimed Edward.

"I know, but this year a doll will have to do."

Tony came to her rescue. "My sister has a doll. I'll ask her if we can use it."

"Thank you, Tony." Marie moved on down the list. "Shepherds—oh, wait. I guess we have your staffs in the attic near the manger."

"I want to use my 4-H cane." Judging by the tilt of her chin, JoAnn had already given this some serious consideration. "It's my sheep, and those long staffs might scare him. He knows my cane, though. Can I use my cane?"

Millie opened her mouth to say something, looking very doubtful.

"Of course you can." Unlike Millie, Marie didn't see the point of arguing about this one. The play would proceed just fine with one cane-carrying shepherd and one staff-carrying counterpart.

Manger. Doll. Staff. Cane. Gifts, Marie said to herself. After reviewing the list, she suddenly remembered. "Oh no!" She turned to Walter and Millie. "The pastor accidentally threw away our gold, frankincense, and myrrh last year. Walter, I'm going to need you to make some new props for the wise women."

Walter looked doubtful about his ability to perform the task. But this time, it was Millie who came to the rescue.

318

"If we're going to have a contemporary play, why don't we just ask our wise women to make gifts?" Millie seemed very pleased with herself.

"That's a great idea!" More than willing to grant her credit for that good idea, Marie turned to their contemporary astronomers and said, "What do you wise women think?"

Janet shrugged her shoulders, figuring she could give the baby Jesus the picture she'd painted for her 4-H fair project, complete with the blue ribbon.

"My mom and I can make a card," Sally said. "And my grandma has an empty perfume bottle I bet she'll let me have since I'm her favorite."

Instead of asking Laurie what she might bring, Marie said, "What do you think, Laurie?"

Her granddaughter's lips were pursed like she was in deep concentration mode. "Sure, I guess," the nine-year-old said slowly.

"We're all set then!" The excitement Millie exuded came across perhaps a little too perky, as if she wanted everyone to remember she was still there. "Be here at six o'clock sharp on Christmas Eve. Our program is at seven, and the candlelight service is at eight."

To the two other adults in the room, it appeared Millie wanted to say more. But the clueless kids were already moving to fetch their coats and, chattering away, race out the door into the cold wind and spitting snow. Laurie, however, hung back. She also kept quiet until she and her grandmother were in the pickup while Walter turned off the church lights and locked the doors.

"Grandma?"

"Yes, sweetie?" Marie had already sensed the concern in her granddaughter's voice.

"I like the idea of making a gift, but I don't know what." The little wise woman spoke very cautiously, sounding out each line with care.

"I'm thinking I could give Jesus some of the black walnuts Grandpa and I picked. He said they cost just about as much as gold would in the grocery store."

"Do you have something more on your mind?" Marie prodded gently.

"I—"

"Brr!" Walter opened the driver's side door. "It's cold out there. Let's go home for one more hot chocolate, and then I'll take you to town, Laurie."

The ride back was on the quieter side, which both adults had to recognize. Their normally lively granddaughter was still fairly silent as they sat around the kitchen table with cups of steaming hot chocolate. After Walter placed his mug on the table and eased into his chair, Marie looked over at Laurie even though she spoke to her husband.

"Walter, Laurie has a great idea." Marie saw the girl's eyes light up when she heard her grandmother's affirming comment. "She wants to give the baby Jesus some of the black walnuts as her wise woman gift."

"And here I thought you were just in it for the candy." He grinned.

Laurie didn't pay much attention to the teasing, still set in her solemn mood. "You did say black walnuts in the grocery store cost about as much as gold."

"Yes, I did," Walter agreed. "Hey, I know. We picked all those walnuts on holy ground so your grandmother and you could make divinity. How about you two make a box as your gift to Jesus? You could label it 'Gold Nuggets from Hopkins Grove.'"

"You're silly." Laurie giggled. Yet when she turned to her grandmother, it was with pleading eyes. "Can we?"

"I'm not too hard to convince," Marie said with regal certainty. "We're making it for family and friends anyway. And you'll be the one to carry on the divinity tradition, so I suppose I can give you your own copy of the secret recipe this year."

That surprised Laurie. "I didn't know you had a secret recipe."

"I do," replied Marie.

"Does Grandpa know it?" Laurie asked.

"No." Marie shot him a mischievous look. "He's tried to find it, too, but only Betty Crocker and I know where it is."

"Who's Betty Crocker?" Laurie was beginning to think her grandmother was sounding a bit like Grandpa.

"I'll introduce her to you when we make our divinity on the twenty-third."

"I'll be ready," she assured her with growing excitement, and then squinted in thought. "Does Jesus know Betty Crocker?"

"We need to get you to town, young lady." Walter was still laughing while he said it. "Your mom and dad are probably thinking we went to Florida."

"No, they won't." Laurie rolled her eyes but took her grandfather's hand, and together they walked out to the pickup.

December twenty-third came really quickly for Laurie. School let out the twenty-second for Christmas break, and Laurie and her mother went Christmas shopping right after school. When they stopped for their traditional after-shopping supper, Laurie enthusiastically told her mother about her gift of gold for the baby Jesus, the secret recipe she was going to learn, and how she and Grandma planned to make the black walnut divinity.

It took a little while for Ann to get a word in edgewise. "Does Grandma's secret recipe just happen to be shared with Betty Crocker?"

"How did you know that?" Laurie's eyes were big.

"It seems to me," Ann said, unable to keep from smiling, "when I was about nine, she shared the same recipe with me. I think I made the divinity for the Sunday school Christmas party. Your grandpa ate the whole plate!"

They both got a laugh out of that, but it died off after Laurie's follow-up question. "Did you make more after that?"

"Funny thing," Ann said, but she didn't sound amused anymore. Instead, she sounded sad. "I don't think I ever did."

They went back to eating until Ann looked down at her watch. "Oh my word, we need to go! I have a conference call in an hour, and I still need to e-mail your father. He had to work late tonight."

So, Laurie spent the rest of the evening reading and writing a Christmas poem for her grandparents, making sure she went to bed early so she'd be well-rested for a busy day of candy making.

Just as promised, Walter drove into the driveway to pick Laurie up at eight in the morning, right on the dot.

Laurie had been watching for him, so she grabbed her jacket and ran to the back door, yelling, "Grandpa's here, Mom! I'm leaving. I'll see you later."

"Goodbye! Tell Grandpa and Grandma 'hello' for me. I'll phone after I finish writing this proposal!" Ann shouted back from her office in the den.

Outside, Laurie greeted her grandfather eagerly, expecting to hear the same enthusiasm in his voice. Instead, he was getting out of the car, looking pretty solemn.

"I need to talk to your mom a minute, sweetie. Is she in the house?"

"She's in the den." Subdued, Laurie turned to follow him back into the house.

"Ann," Walter explained, "your mother woke up with a lot of pain in her shoulder and arm. We called the doctor and I have some medicine to take home, but it seems to be an arthritic flare-up."

"Oh no!" Anne said.

Laurie didn't say anything, wondering how bad it was.

"She hasn't had trouble with her shoulder for a long time, but the doctor wants her to wear an arm sling to relax her shoulder." Walter ran a hand across his hair. "Since she won't be able to help Laurie make candy, she's going to try coaching Laurie and me. But—" His voice trailed off.

"But what?" Ann looked nervous now.

"We thought maybe you could rearrange your schedule and come over and help," he said awkwardly. "We could make a day of it. Tom could come after work, and I'll order pizza and—"

Ann interrupted. "I can't, Dad. I just can't. I need to finish this proposal and hold this conference call. It's all set up. If I don't, I'll have to cancel our family ski trip after Christmas." She didn't look at her father. "I just can't."

"It was just a thought," Walter said quietly, and then walked back down the hallway.

Laurie followed at first, but she shook her head before they could get to the door. "Just a minute, Grandpa."

She slipped back into the den just as her mother was turning back to the computer screen. "Mom?"

Hearing her daughter, Ann glanced up from the computer screen and dutifully moved her chair closer to her.

"I'd rather make Jesus' birthday present with you and Grandma than go skiing." Then she ran toward the door before her mother could say another word.

Two hours later, Walter and Laurie had the kitchen all ready for candy making.

"Let's go through our list," he suggested while they stood by the counter.

"Sure." Laurie didn't show any extreme amount of enthusiasm, but at least it was a little more than she had displayed up to that point. "Walnuts, sugar, eggs."

"Check, check, check!" Walter pretended to check off each item with his index finger. "We have it all."

"No, you don't!" Marie called out.

"What?" Both amateur bakers turned in surprise to see her slowly walk into the kitchen.

"You forgot the vanilla and syrup," she said, gingerly lowering herself into a chair and trying hard not to give in to the pain she was feeling.

"Oh." Walter looked around. "Now, let's see. The syrup is—?"

"In the right cupboard next to the coffee." Marie's tone was somewhere between scolding and amused. "You see it every morning when you take the coffee out."

"I do?" Walter sounded surprised. He looked it, too.

Glancing at her grandmother and seeing her discomfort, Laurie followed her eyes as they led a trail to the cupboard. In an instant she discovered what her grandfather was searching for. "The vanilla is right next to the coffee on the other side, Grandpa," she said.

"Well, look at that. It certainly is." He pulled out both ingredients and placed them on the table. "Now, let's try this again: sugar, syrup, vanilla, eggs, and walnuts."

Laurie nodded in agreement.

Looking from her to his wife, Walter rubbed his chin in genuine thought. "Hmm. Now, what do we do? What do we do?"

"Well, you don't say 'abracadabra,'" Marie said, trying to smile.

"I'll get the bowl and mixing spoon," Laurie volunteered.

"Good idea," Walter said. "You can beat the eggs together 'til they're scrambled."

"No, you can't!" Marie said in her outside voice, and then she lowered her volume. "You have to separate the yolks from the egg whites."

"Are you sure?" he asked.

Laurie tried very hard not to giggle. She could tell her grandmother really wanted to be stirring things up, not sitting on the sidelines painfully coaching.

Walter shook his head in bewilderment. "I can see this is going to be a long day."

It wasn't looking any shorter by the third egg he and Laurie tried to separate. It was his turn to give it a go, yet the yolk most definitely cracked into the white under his inexperienced fingers.

"Oops." Laurie pointed to the mistake. "Grandpa, it's running again."

"Shhh," he said. "Don't tell Grandma."

"You know I can hear you, Walter." Either from pity or frustration—probably more of the latter—she rose from her chair and walked over to the counter, taking off the sling in the process. "Here, let me try." Pain or no pain, she was determined nothing that looked or tasted like a failure would come from her kitchen.

"Grandma, no!" After hearing about the doctor's orders, Laurie had a definite fear of what would happen if those orders were disobeyed.

So did Walter. "Marie, sit down. We can handle it."

In the exchange, no one heard the back door open, nor did they see Ann walk into the kitchen.

"I can handle it," Marie was declaring when Ann spoke up. "What's going on here?"

"Mom!" Laurie shouted as she turned toward her mother.

"Ann!" Walter said, surprised to see his daughter. "What are you doing here?"

"Well." Ann sat down at one of the kitchen chairs while kindly patting the one beside her and looking expectantly at her mom. "I was just about ready to log my proposal in when I remembered something. Mom, do you remember when the Jamesons lived down in the valley?"

"Yes." Since her usually absent daughter was in the room, Marie didn't put up much of a fight about sitting back down.

"Their daughter, Eve, was in 4-H with me," Ann said, "and you were our leader."

"I remember the family," she said.

While they were talking, Walter was struggling with figuring out where this was all leading. Then, as if a light bulb turned on in his brain, he added, "Hey, now that you mention it, I remember them, too. Nice family. Hard workers. Never seemed to have much fun, though."

"Exactly." To her, it seemed as if he'd summed up everything, but she fortunately went on. "That's the point. They worked so hard it seemed like whatever little Eve was allowed to do, her mom and dad rarely had time to enjoy it with her. I never saw them at our music concerts. They never came to the fair to see our demonstrations or attended our Christmas programs. Eve always went with us. And Mom, you taught her everything about baking, gardening, and—"

"No." Marie tried to downplay her role. "I'm sure she learned a lot from her parents."

Ann disagreed, though. "They gave her a lot of practical things—food on the table, and clothes—but no thrills or frills. They gave her what was needed. She'd tell you that, too, but the last time I saw her—" Without warning, she started to tear up. "The last time I saw her, she told me I was blessed with a very special gift wrapped in everyday love."

Walter squinted in puzzlement. "What did she mean?"

"She meant the two of you. You were my gift." Ann wiped one eye and then the other before turning to her daughter. "And then what you said before you left, Laurie. I heard it.

"But . . ." she sniffled. "Well, it just took half an hour to settle in."

"What did you say?" Technically, Marie's question was aimed at her granddaughter, but the way she said it sounded much more like she was wondering aloud.

"I said—" Laurie looked thoughtful. "I said I'd rather be making and giving Jesus His Christmas present than go skiing." When she finished, her silence led her to glance directly at her mother.

Ann opened her arms, and her daughter went running into them. "And that's exactly what we'll do! I worked things out at the office so someone else could take on the proposal."

While Laurie was buried in her mother's embrace, it was still obvious she was beaming.

"I talked to your dad," Ann continued, "and we both agreed that a wise woman's divine present and the Christmas program are much more important than a ski trip."

327

"Well, hey!" Walter said, his voice unusually loud to cover for the tears sliding down his face. "Why waste your time going out west to ski? You can go skiing in the back pasture. It's not the Rocky Mountains, I know, but I can throw some rocks in your path if you want."

"Grandpa!" Laurie looked over her shoulder to her grandpa and laughed.

After a lovely interlude of hugs and happy tears, the foursome found their way back to the table, wrapped gently in a peaceful silence. It was Ann who spoke first, still smiling when she did.

"I see we have everything we need for divinity." She looked over at the counter, which was covered with bags of home-grown walnut meat. "You guys certainly must have cracked a lot of black walnuts."

Walter managed the semblance of a solemn expression. "The baby Jesus might be pretty hungry by the time we arrive at the manger."

"We're making the divinity as my gift—I mean, our gift—for the baby Jesus." Laurie said it as if she was telling her mother for the first time, handing her a trimmed piece of paper. "Grandma cut these from a pattern she had so we could make some small boxes for the divinity. See? We can give golden nuggets to every person there."

"Golden nuggets?" Ann asked.

Laurie grinned. "Grandpa named them."

"The three of you are very creative," Ann said, "but we've still got plenty to do now, don't we?" She stood up. "Dad, you start putting some boxes together. And Mom, start telling Laurie and I how to make these golden nuggets!"

"Yippee!" Laurie pretended to roll up her sleeves as she joined her mother at the counter.

And so they went to work, spending the hours laughing and chatting and making a gift fit for a king. It was late in the afternoon by the time the last batch of divinity was setting on the counter. Laurie handed everyone a piece to try.

"This is really good." Ann munched approvingly.

"Better than what I've made before," Marie said.

"This is better than gold." Walter reached for another piece while still chewing on his first.

"Of course it is." Laurie looked just as matter-of-fact as she sounded. "It's made with everyday love."

"Yes, it is!" Ann, Marie and Walter agreed in unison.

To Millie Samson's amazement, everyone arrived at church on time for the Christmas program. Marie, with her arm still resting in its sling, was busy helping Tony and Jenny into their places while Millie took her script and went down to the front row. There sat a chair Walter had marked "Reserved for Director"—at Millie's insistence.

There had already been one slight snag, since their narrator, Dr. Gillman, had been called away at the last minute to deliver a baby. But that problem was solved when Laurie went out into the audience to recruit her mother.

Ann didn't object one bit, only casting a smile at Tom before getting up and following Laurie to the stage and behind the curtain.

"Let's see now." Marie paused long enough to give her daughter a one-armed hug. "Clara, the angel; Kurt, shepherd number one; Edward, the innkeeper; JoAnn, shepherd number two; and our three wise women. Get in your places and be ready to go."

"When?" Kurt wanted to know. "When do we go?"

"I'll tell you," Marie assured him, and then nodded at Ann to start the show.

"Be sure to follow Mrs. Samson's instructions," Marie whispered to each actor before she prompted them out on stage. Admittedly, it was a little confusing watching Millie from her director's chair. Her placement was fine, but sometimes her hands moved faster than those of a football coach calling signals from the sidelines. Even so, for the most part, everyone seemed to know their cues and what to say until the three wise women appeared at the manger.

Janet was the first to offer her gift to Mary and Joseph. She held her 4-H picture, complete with the attached blue ribbon, up over her head, adding a quick walk around just to make sure the audience could clearly see her prize. Returning to the manger with apparent reluctance, she handed the picture to Mary to present her just-as-showy ad-libbed line.

"This is for Jesus. My mom said you should hang it up in His bedroom. Don't put it in His baby book." Satisfied with her message, Janet stepped back.

Sally stepped forward next to quietly hand Mary a dark purple bottle and a homemade card. But as she turned back to the audience, Sally looked over at Millie, who was placing her left hand to her lips and extending her right hand.

Puzzled but gamely trying to interpret the gestures, the girl decided she was supposed to add a word or two, just like the preceding wise woman had. So, she turned back and looked toward the nativity couple.

"My mom and I made the card. We want you to show it to Jesus, and He can put it in His scrapbook someday." The girl went on with no hesitation. "Mom said Grandma won the perfume at a bingo game. That's what's in the bottle. And Mom also said if it's good enough for Grandma, it's good enough for the baby Jesus."

With that said, Sally went and stood by Janet while her mother groaned in embarrassment, covering her face and shaking her head. Her father thought it was hysterical, however, as did the audience. They all hooted in delight, either not noticing or minding how flustered the admission had made their program director.

When everyone quieted down and Millie had composed herself, she very cautiously looked to the side of the stage for the next and last wise woman. Laurie, however, didn't really need a cue. The shepherds were by the manger and her two traveling companions were by one side of Mary. All she had to do was say the lines she'd written and hand over her gift. So, with her mission well in mind, she walked over to Mary's side holding her box of golden nuggets in front of her.

Even though they had practiced the play so many times by then, no one had really talked to a certain shepherd about stage etiquette. As such, when Laurie passed by Kurt, his eyes fixated on the box of nuggets. He recognized only that there was food in front of him and he was hungry.

"Hey!" He didn't sound much like a shepherd as he reached his hand out. "I didn't know Jesus got candy for His birthday. Can I have some, too?"

Laurie, even then, was standing between Kurt's outstretched hand and the still in-character Mary, who was waiting patiently to receive this last wise woman's gift. She could have just ignored the erstwhile shepherd, yet she turned toward him instead.

"I'm sure Jesus won't mind if you have some. It's okay, isn't it, Mary?"

Caught off guard a bit, Jenny recovered quickly enough. "Yes, I'm sure He wouldn't mind. I think He likes it when we share. Don't you think so, Joseph?"

331

Now it was Tony's turn to be surprised, but he was more than happy to follow Kurt's lead. Reaching into the box to help himself to one of the nuggets, he smiled. "I guess you're right, Mary. I think Jesus is very happy we're sharing His present with others."

Unable to help themselves, all the members of the audience lost it. And for a few minutes, there was nothing but laughter and applause.

When they settled down once more, Laurie unrolled her scroll to read:

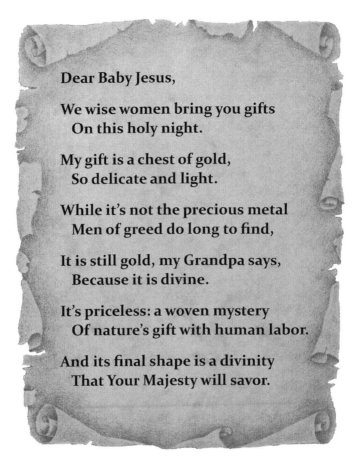

Dear Baby Jesus,

We wise women bring you gifts
    On this holy night.

My gift is a chest of gold,
    So delicate and light.

While it's not the precious metal
    Men of greed do long to find,

It is still gold, my Grandpa says,
    Because it is divine.

It's priceless: a woven mystery
    Of nature's gift with human labor.

And its final shape is a divinity
    That Your Majesty will savor.

After Laurie finished, she rolled the scroll back up, tied it with a red ribbon, and put it in the manger. She'd delivered her lovely lines so perfectly that there was a hush in the room as if no one dared to move. That was true of the adults, anyway.

Kurt, now kneeling at the manger, knew just what to say, however. Looking up at the nativity couple, he said with the perfect stage voice, "Look! The baby Jesus is smiling."

And so He was.

Later that evening, Laurie and her parents stopped by Walter and Marie's for one more hot chocolate. Around the kitchen table, they chatted about how surprisingly delightful the unexpected happenings in the play had been, coming together in such a natural and right way, despite how unplanned they were.

"I didn't know what was going to happen when Kurt stuck his hand into your box and grabbed his second piece of divinity." Tom grinned as he gave his daughter a fatherly hug.

"Well." Laurie looked very scholarly sitting there, despite the hot chocolate mustache around her mouth. "I just thought if Kurt really was a shepherd, he would probably be hungry by the time he arrived at the manger, and I don't think the baby Jesus gave it a second thought."

"I suppose Mary didn't have any peanut butter sandwiches back then," Walter added.

Ann rolled her eyes as she looked at her father with good-natured affection. However, she had her own commentary to add. "I just think we forget sometimes that while we see the night of Jesus' birth as such an extraordinary event for the people in the nativity story, it was really a very ordinary night with unusual occurrences."

Laurie appeared to puzzle through that for a moment, but she ultimately shrugged it away in favor of another thought in normal nine-year-old style. "You know, everything we did—going out to church to pick walnuts, getting out the meat, making the candy, and practicing for the play—was special because we did it together."

Marie's eyes were a little moist. "I think everything was special because we all saw everyday love happening through each other's eyes."

They all agreed over another round of delicious, heavenly black walnut divinity.

Meet the Author

M. Wayne Clark

Wayne Clark is a retired United Methodist minister. He has been a member of the Iowa conference UMC under appointment for forty-two years. Wayne has had a dual career in parish ministry and as a therapist. He has served congregations in Iowa as a pastor and as a District Superintendent and appointments beyond the local church.

Wayne has a Doctor of Ministry focusing on Pastoral Psychotherapy with special interest in the impact genetics has on couples and families. He also has certification in Pastoral Counseling from Care and Counseling, St. Louis, Missouri. Before retiring full-time, Wayne was an approved supervisor in the American Association for Marriage and Family, a Diplomate in the American Association of Pastoral Counselors, and a licensed Marriage and Family Therapist. Wayne has been published in professional journals and magazines. He has given presentations at national and regional conferences for AAMFT and AAPC, Hospice, and the United Methodist Board of Ministry.

Since retirement, Wayne has volunteered in numerous ways but particularly enjoyed his work with a local therapeutic horse riding program designed for children and adults.

Wayne wrote his first Christmas Storybook in 1977 followed by stories every year since. He folds messages for both children and adults into each story.

Wayne's wife, Susan, is a retired nurse. They have two children: Nathan and Nicole Jones. Nicole's husband, Andrew, is also an important part of their lives. Wayne and Susan live in Ankeny, Iowa, where Wayne maintains a small counseling practice and continues to write.

Order Info

Available from amazon.com
or your favorite bookstore

For autographed books
or to schedule speaking engagements, contact

M. Wayne Clark
suespruce@aol.com
515.964.5119

For bulk orders, contact
Candy Abbott
Fruitbearer Publishing, LLC
302.856.6649 • FAX 302.856.7742
info@fruitbearer.com
www.fruitbearer.com
P.O. Box 777, Georgetown, DE 19947